LEGACY

Copyright © 2021 by Nora Roberts.
Thorndike Press, a part of Gale, a Cengage Company.

LIBRARY OF CONGRESS CIP DATA ON FILE.
CATALOGUING IN PUBLICATION FOR THIS BOOK
IS AVAILABLE FROM THE LIBRARY OF CONGRESS.

ISBN-13: 978-1-4328-8858-9 (hardcover alk. paper)

Published in 2021 by arrangement with St. Martin's Publishing Group.

Printed in Mexico
Print Number: 01   Print Year: 2021

LEGACY

NORA ROBERTS

THORNDIKE PRESS
A part of Gale, a Cengage Company

For my children, and their children.
And all who come after.

■ ■ ■ ■

PART ONE:
AMBITIONS

Power to do good is the true and
lawful end of aspiring.
— Sir Francis Bacon

■ ■ ■ ■

CHAPTER ONE

Georgetown

The first time Adrian Rizzo met her father, he tried to kill her.

At seven, her world consisted primarily of movement. Most of the time she lived with her mother — and Mimi, who looked after them both — in New York. But sometimes they stayed in L.A. for a few weeks, or in Chicago or Miami.

In the summer, she got to visit with her grandparents in Maryland for at least two weeks. That, in her opinion, was the most fun because they had dogs and a big yard to play in, and a tire for a swing.

When they lived in Manhattan, she went to school, and that was fine. She got to take dance lessons, and do gymnastics, and that was way better than school.

When they traveled for her mother's work, Mimi homeschooled her because she had to be educated. Mimi made learning about the place where they stayed part of being educated. Since they were in DC for a whole month, part of school meant visiting the monuments, taking a White House tour, and going to the Smithsonian.

Sometimes she got to work with her mom, and she liked that a lot. Whenever she got to work in one of her mom's fitness videos, she had to learn a routine, like a cardio dance or yoga poses.

She liked learning; she liked dancing.

At five, she did a whole video with her mom geared toward kids and families. A yoga one because, after all, she *was* the baby in Yoga Baby, her mother's company.

It made her proud, and excited that her mother said they'd do another. Maybe when she was ten, to target that age group.

Her mom knew all about age groups and demographics and things like that. Adrian heard her talking about them with her manager and her producers.

Her mom knew plenty about fitness, too, and the mind-body connection, and nutrition, and meditation, and all sorts of things like that.

She didn't know how to cook — not like Popi and Nonna, who owned a restaurant. She didn't like to play games like Mimi — because she stayed really busy building her career.

She had a lot of meetings, and rehearsals, and planning sessions, and public appear-

'd change.
her pink shorts and flowered T-shirt, she
ck a pose. And turning on the music in
head, danced.

e loved her dance classes *and* gymnastics
n they were in New York, but now she
gined not taking a class, but leading one.
e twirled, kicked, did a handspring, the
ts. Cross-step, salsa, *leap!* Making it up as
went.

e amused herself for twenty minutes. The
innocent twenty minutes of her life.
hen someone pushed the buzzer on the
t door. And kept pushing it.

had an angry sound, and one she'd never
get.

e wasn't supposed to open the door
self, but that didn't mean she couldn't go
. So she wandered out to the living room,
n the entranceway as Mimi marched in
n the kitchen.

imi dried her hands on a bright red
ncloth as she hustled through. "For Pete's
e! Where's the fire?"

e rolled her deep brown eyes at Adrian,
ked the cloth in the waistband of her jeans.

small woman with a powerful voice, she
uted, "Hold your damn horses!"

e knew Mimi was the same age as her
ther because they'd gone to college to-
her.

What's your problem?" she snapped, then

14

ances, and interviews.

Even at seven, Adrian understood Lina
Rizzo didn't know a whole lot about being a
mom.

Still, she didn't mind if Adrian played with
her makeup — as long as she put everything
back where it belonged. And she never got
mad if they worked on a routine and Adrian
made mistakes.

Best of all on this trip, instead of flying back
to New York when her mom finished this
video and all the interviews and meetings,
they got to drive to visit her grandparents for
a long weekend.

She had plans to try to negotiate that into a
week, but for now she sat on the floor in the
doorway and watched her mother work out
another routine.

Lina had chosen this house for the month
because it had a home gym with mirrored
walls, something as essential to her as the
number of bedrooms.

She did squats and lunges, knee lifts,
burpees — Adrian knew all the names. And
Lina talked to the mirror — her viewers —
giving instructions, encouragement.

Now and then she said a bad word and
started something over again.

Adrian thought her beautiful, like a sweaty
princess, even though she didn't have her
makeup on because there weren't any people
or cameras. She had green eyes like Nonna

11

and skin that looked like she bathed in the sun — even though she didn't. Her hair — pulled back in a scrunchie now — was like the chestnuts you could buy all warm and smelling good in a bag at Christmastime.

She was tall — not as tall as Popi — and Adrian hoped she would be, too, when she grew up.

She wore tight, tiny shorts and a sports bra — but she wouldn't wear anything that showed so much for videos or appearances because Lina said it wasn't classy.

Since she'd been raised to be mind-body-health conscious, Adrian knew her mom was fit, firm, and fabulous.

Muttering to herself, Lina walked over to make some notes on what Adrian knew was the outline for the video. This one would include three segments — cardio, strength training, and yoga — each thirty minutes, with a bonus fifteen-minute express section on total body.

Lina grabbed a towel to mop off her face and spotted her daughter.

"Crap, Adrian! You gave me a jolt. I didn't know you were there. Where's Mimi?"

"She's in the kitchen. We're going to have chicken and rice and asparagus for dinner."

"Great. Why don't you go give her a hand with that? I need a shower."

"How come you're mad?"

"I'm not mad."

"You were mad when you were ta the phone with Harry. You yelled didn't tell anybody, especially some b tabloid reporter."

Lina yanked the scrunchie out of the way she did when she had a h "You shouldn't listen to private c tions."

"I didn't listen, I *heard.* Are you Harry?"

Adrian really liked her mother's He snuck her little bags of M&M's o and told funny jokes.

"No, I'm not mad at Harry. Go he Tell her I'll be down in about a half

She was, too, mad, Adrian thoug her mother walked away. Maybe not but at somebody, because she'd mad mistakes when she'd practiced and of bad words.

Her mother hardly ever made mist

Or maybe she just had a headacl said people sometimes got headach worried too much.

Adrian got up from the floor. helping with dinner was boring, she the fitness room. She stood in fro mirrors, a girl tall for her age with hair — black as her grandfather's been — escaping a green scrunchie. had too much gold in them to ra green like her mother's, but she ke turned the lock and opened the door.

From where she stood, Adrian saw Mimi's expression go from irritated — like it got when Adrian didn't pick up her room — to scared.

And everything happened so fast.

Mimi tried to close the door again, but the man pushed it open, pushed her back. He was big, so much bigger than Mimi. He had a little beard with some gray in it, and more in his hair, like silver wings on the gold, but his face was all red like he'd been running. Adrian's first shock at seeing the big man shove Mimi froze her in place.

"Where the fuck is she?"

"She's not here. You can't barge in here like this. Get out. You get out now, Jon, or I'm calling the police."

"Lying bitch." He grabbed Mimi's arm, shook her. "Where is she? She thinks she can run her mouth, ruin my *life*?"

"Get your hands off me. You're drunk."

When she tried to pull away, he slapped her. The sound reverberated like a gunshot in Adrian's head, and she leapt forward.

"Don't you hit her! You leave her alone!"

"Adrian, you go upstairs. Go upstairs right now."

But temper up, Adrian balled her fists. "He has to go away!"

"For this?" the man snarled at Adrian. "For this she ruins my goddamn life? Doesn't look

15

a thing like me. She must've been whoring around, and she's trying to pin the little bastard on me. Fuck that. Fuck her."

"Adrian, upstairs." Mimi whirled toward her, and Adrian didn't see mad — like what she felt. She saw scared. *"Now!"*

"The bitch is up there, isn't she? Liar. Here's what I do to liars." He didn't slap this time, but used his fist, once, twice, on Mimi's face.

When she crumpled, that fear dove into Adrian. Help. She had to get help.

But he caught her on the stairs, snapped her head back as he grabbed the tail of curly hair and yanked.

She screamed, screamed for her mother.

"Yeah, you call Mommy." He slapped her so the sting burned like fire in her face. "We want to talk to Mommy."

As he dragged her up the stairs, Lina ran out of the bedroom in a robe, her hair still wet from the shower.

"Adrian Rizzo, what the —"

She stopped, stood very still as she locked eyes with the man. "Let her go, Jon. Let her go so you and I can talk."

"You've done enough talking. You ruined my life, you stupid hick."

"I didn't talk to that reporter — or to anyone about you. That story didn't come from me."

"Liar!" He yanked Adrian's hair again, so

ances, and interviews.

Even at seven, Adrian understood Lina Rizzo didn't know a whole lot about being a mom.

Still, she didn't mind if Adrian played with her makeup — as long as she put everything back where it belonged. And she never got mad if they worked on a routine and Adrian made mistakes.

Best of all on this trip, instead of flying back to New York when her mom finished this video and all the interviews and meetings, they got to drive to visit her grandparents for a long weekend.

She had plans to try to negotiate that into a week, but for now she sat on the floor in the doorway and watched her mother work out another routine.

Lina had chosen this house for the month because it had a home gym with mirrored walls, something as essential to her as the number of bedrooms.

She did squats and lunges, knee lifts, burpees — Adrian knew all the names. And Lina talked to the mirror — her viewers — giving instructions, encouragement.

Now and then she said a bad word and started something over again.

Adrian thought her beautiful, like a sweaty princess, even though she didn't have her makeup on because there weren't any people or cameras. She had green eyes like Nonna

11

and skin that looked like she bathed in the sun — even though she didn't. Her hair — pulled back in a scrunchie now — was like the chestnuts you could buy all warm and smelling good in a bag at Christmastime.

She was tall — not as tall as Popi — and Adrian hoped she would be, too, when she grew up.

She wore tight, tiny shorts and a sports bra — but she wouldn't wear anything that showed so much for videos or appearances because Lina said it wasn't classy.

Since she'd been raised to be mind-body-health conscious, Adrian knew her mom was fit, firm, and fabulous.

Muttering to herself, Lina walked over to make some notes on what Adrian knew was the outline for the video. This one would include three segments — cardio, strength training, and yoga — each thirty minutes, with a bonus fifteen-minute express section on total body.

Lina grabbed a towel to mop off her face and spotted her daughter.

"Crap, Adrian! You gave me a jolt. I didn't know you were there. Where's Mimi?"

"She's in the kitchen. We're going to have chicken and rice and asparagus for dinner."

"Great. Why don't you go give her a hand with that? I need a shower."

"How come you're mad?"

"I'm not mad."

"You were mad when you were talking on the phone with Harry. You yelled how you didn't tell anybody, especially some bad-word tabloid reporter."

Lina yanked the scrunchie out of her hair the way she did when she had a headache. "You shouldn't listen to private conversations."

"I didn't listen, I *heard.* Are you mad at Harry?"

Adrian really liked her mother's publicist. He snuck her little bags of M&M's or Skittles and told funny jokes.

"No, I'm not mad at Harry. Go help Mimi. Tell her I'll be down in about a half hour."

She was, too, mad, Adrian thought when her mother walked away. Maybe not at Harry, but at somebody, because she'd made a lot of mistakes when she'd practiced and said a lot of bad words.

Her mother hardly ever made mistakes.

Or maybe she just had a headache. Mimi said people sometimes got headaches if they worried too much.

Adrian got up from the floor. But since helping with dinner was boring, she went into the fitness room. She stood in front of the mirrors, a girl tall for her age with her curly hair — black as her grandfather's had once been — escaping a green scrunchie. Her eyes had too much gold in them to rate a true green like her mother's, but she kept hoping

13

they'd change.

In her pink shorts and flowered T-shirt, she struck a pose. And turning on the music in her head, danced.

She loved her dance classes *and* gymnastics when they were in New York, but now she imagined not taking a class, but leading one.

She twirled, kicked, did a handspring, the splits. Cross-step, salsa, *leap!* Making it up as she went.

She amused herself for twenty minutes. The last innocent twenty minutes of her life.

Then someone pushed the buzzer on the front door. And kept pushing it.

It had an angry sound, and one she'd never forget.

She wasn't supposed to open the door herself, but that didn't mean she couldn't go see. So she wandered out to the living room, then the entranceway as Mimi marched in from the kitchen.

Mimi dried her hands on a bright red dishcloth as she hustled through. "For Pete's sake! Where's the fire?"

She rolled her deep brown eyes at Adrian, tucked the cloth in the waistband of her jeans.

A small woman with a powerful voice, she shouted, "Hold your damn horses!"

She knew Mimi was the same age as her mother because they'd gone to college together.

"What's your problem?" she snapped, then

turned the lock and opened the door.

From where she stood, Adrian saw Mimi's expression go from irritated — like it got when Adrian didn't pick up her room — to scared.

And everything happened so fast.

Mimi tried to close the door again, but the man pushed it open, pushed her back. He was big, so much bigger than Mimi. He had a little beard with some gray in it, and more in his hair, like silver wings on the gold, but his face was all red like he'd been running. Adrian's first shock at seeing the big man shove Mimi froze her in place.

"Where the fuck is she?"

"She's not here. You can't barge in here like this. Get out. You get out now, Jon, or I'm calling the police."

"Lying bitch." He grabbed Mimi's arm, shook her. "Where is she? She thinks she can run her mouth, ruin my *life*?"

"Get your hands off me. You're drunk."

When she tried to pull away, he slapped her. The sound reverberated like a gunshot in Adrian's head, and she leapt forward.

"Don't you hit her! You leave her alone!"

"Adrian, you go upstairs. Go upstairs right now."

But temper up, Adrian balled her fists. "He has to go away!"

"For this?" the man snarled at Adrian. "For this she ruins my goddamn life? Doesn't look

15

a thing like me. She must've been whoring around, and she's trying to pin the little bastard on me. Fuck that. Fuck her."

"Adrian, upstairs." Mimi whirled toward her, and Adrian didn't see mad — like what she felt. She saw scared. *"Now!"*

"The bitch is up there, isn't she? Liar. Here's what I do to liars." He didn't slap this time, but used his fist, once, twice, on Mimi's face.

When she crumpled, that fear dove into Adrian. Help. She had to get help.

But he caught her on the stairs, snapped her head back as he grabbed the tail of curly hair and yanked.

She screamed, screamed for her mother.

"Yeah, you call Mommy." He slapped her so the sting burned like fire in her face. "We want to talk to Mommy."

As he dragged her up the stairs, Lina ran out of the bedroom in a robe, her hair still wet from the shower.

"Adrian Rizzo, what the —"

She stopped, stood very still as she locked eyes with the man. "Let her go, Jon. Let her go so you and I can talk."

"You've done enough talking. You ruined my life, you stupid hick."

"I didn't talk to that reporter — or to anyone about you. That story didn't come from me."

"Liar!" He yanked Adrian's hair again, so

16

hard it felt like her head was on fire.

Lina took two careful steps forward. "Let her go, and we'll work it out. I can fix this."

"Too fucking late. The university suspended me this morning. My wife is mortified. My children — and I don't believe for one fucking minute this little bitch is mine — are crying. You came back here, back to *my* city, to do this."

"No, Jon. I came for work. I didn't talk to the reporter. It's been over seven years, Jon, why would I do this now? At all? You're hurting my daughter. Stop hurting my daughter."

"He hit Mimi." Adrian could smell her mother's shower and shampoo — the subtle sweetness of orange blossoms. And the stink from the man she didn't know was sweat and bourbon. "He hit her in the face, and she fell down."

"What have you . . ." Lina took her eyes off him to look over the railing that ran across the second floor. She saw Mimi, face bloody, crawling behind a sofa.

She tracked her gaze back to Jon. "You have to stop this, Jon, before someone gets hurt. Let me —"

"I'm hurt, you fucking whore!"

His voice sounded hot and red, like his face, like the fire burning in Adrian's scalp.

"I'm sorry this happened, but —"

"My family's hurt! Want to see some hurt? Let's start with your bastard."

17

He threw her. Adrian had the sensation of flying, brief and terrifying, before she hit the edge of the top step. The fire that had been in her head now burst in her wrist, her hand, flared up her arm. Then her head banged against the wood, and all she could see was her mother as the man lurched toward her.

He hit her, he hit her, but her mother hit back, and kicked. And there were terrible sounds, so terrible she wanted to cover her ears, but she couldn't move, could only sprawl on the steps and shake.

Even when her mother shouted at her to run, she couldn't.

He had his hands around her mother's throat, shaking her, and her mom hit him in the face, like he had Mimi.

There was blood, there was blood, on her mom, on the man.

They were holding each other, almost like a hug, but hard and mean. Then her mother stomped down on his foot, jerked her knee up. And when the man stumbled back, she shoved.

He hit the railing. Then he was flying.

Adrian saw him fall, arms waving. She saw him crash into the table where her mother put flowers and candles. She heard those terrible sounds. She saw the blood run out from his head, his ears, his nose.

She saw . . .

Then her mother lifted her, turned her,

18

pressed her face to her breast.

"Don't look, Adrian. It's all right now."

"It hurts."

"I know." Lina cradled Adrian's wrist. "I'm going to fix it. Mimi. Oh, Mimi."

"The police are coming." Her eye swollen, half-closed, already blackening, Mimi wobbled up the steps, then sat and put her arms around both of them. "Help's coming."

Over Adrian's head, Mimi mouthed two words. *He's dead.*

Adrian would always remember the pain, and the quiet blue eyes of the paramedic who stabilized the greenstick fracture in her wrist. He had a quiet voice, too, when he shined a little light in her eyes, when he asked her how many fingers he held up.

She'd remember the policemen, the first ones who came after the sirens stopped screaming. The ones in the dark blue uniforms.

But most of it, even as it happened, seemed blurry and distant.

They huddled in the second-floor sitting room with its view of the back courtyard and its little koi pond. Mostly the police in the uniforms talked to her mother because they took Mimi to the hospital.

Her mother told them the man's name, Jonathan Bennett, and how he taught English literature at Georgetown University. Or did, when she knew him.

Her mother said what happened, or started to.

Then a man and a woman came in. The man was really tall and wore a brown tie. His skin was a darker brown, and his teeth really white. The woman had red hair cut short, and freckles all over her face.

They had badges like on TV shows.

"Ms. Rizzo, I'm Detective Riley, and this is my partner, Detective Cannon." The woman hooked her badge back on her belt. "We know this is difficult, but we need to ask you and your daughter some questions."

Then she smiled at Adrian. "It's Adrian, right?"

When Adrian nodded, Riley looked back at Lina. "Is it all right if Adrian shows me her room, if she and I talk there while you talk to Detective Cannon?"

"Will it be quicker that way? They took my friend — my daughter's nanny — to the hospital. Broken nose, concussion. And Adrian has what the paramedic thinks is a greenstick fracture on her left wrist, and she hit her head."

"You look a little rough yourself," Cannon commented, and Lina shrugged. Then winced at the movement.

"Bruised ribs will heal, so will my face. He really focused on my face."

"We can have you taken to the hospital

now, and talk there once you've seen a doctor."

"I'd rather go when . . . you're finished downstairs."

"Understood." Riley looked back at Adrian. "Is it okay if we talk in your room, Adrian?"

"I guess so." She got up, holding her arm in its sling close to her chest. "I won't let you take my mom to jail."

"Don't be silly, Adrian."

Ignoring her mother, Adrian stared into Riley's eyes. They were green, but lighter than her mother's. "I won't let you."

"Got it. We're just going to talk, okay? Is your room up here?"

"Two doors down on the right," Lina said. "Go on, Adrian, go with Detective Riley. Then we'll go check on Mimi. Everything's going to be fine."

Adrian led the way and Riley put her smile back on as they walked into a room done in soft pinks and spring greens. A big stuffed dog lay on the bed.

"This is a pretty great room. And really tidy."

"I had to clean it up this morning, or no going to see the cherry blossoms and get ice cream sundaes." She winced, much like Lina had. "Don't tell about the sundaes. We were supposed to get frozen yogurt."

"Our secret. Is your mom really strict about what you eat?"

21

"Sometimes. Mostly." Tears sparkled into her eyes. "Is Mimi going to die like the man did?"

"She got hurt, but not real bad. And I know they're taking good care of her. How about we sit here with this guy?"

Riley sat on the side of the bed, gave the big dog a pat. "What's his name?"

"He's Barkley. Harry gave him to me for Christmas. We can't have a real dog now because we live in New York and travel too much."

"He looks like a great dog. Can you tell me and Barkley what happened?"

It poured out, a flood through a break in a dam.

"The man came to the door. He kept buzzing and buzzing, so I went out to see. I'm not supposed to open the door myself, so I waited for Mimi. She came out from the kitchen and opened the door. Then she tried to shut it again, really fast, but he pushed it open, and he pushed her. He almost knocked her down."

"Did you know him?"

"Nuh-uh, but Mimi did, because she called him Jon and told him to go away. He was mad and yelling and saying bad words. I'm not supposed to say them."

"That's okay." Riley kept petting Barkley like he was a real dog. "I get the gist."

"He wanted to see my mom, but Mimi said

she wasn't here even though she was. She was upstairs taking a shower. And he kept yelling, and he slapped her face. He hit her. You're not supposed to hit. Hitting somebody's wrong."

"It was wrong."

"I yelled at him to leave her alone because he had her arms, and he was hurting her. And he looked at me — he didn't see me before, but he looked at me, and it made me scared how he looked at me. But he was hurting Mimi, and I got mad. Mimi said to go upstairs, to me, I mean, but he was hurting her. Then he — he hit her with — with his fist."

Adrian made one with her good hand while tears began to slide down her cheeks. "And there was blood, and she fell, and I ran. I ran to try to get to Mom, but he caught me. He pulled my hair, he pulled it so hard, and he pulled me up the stairs like that, and I was yelling for Mom."

"You want to stop, honey? We can wait for you to tell me the rest."

"No. No. Mom ran out, and saw him. And she kept saying for him to let me go, but he wouldn't. He kept saying she'd ruined his life, with a lot of bad words. The really bad ones, and she kept saying she hadn't told, and she'd fix it, but to let me go. He was hurting me. And he called me bad names, and he — he, threw me."

"He threw you?"

23

"At the stairs. He threw me at the stairs, and I hit, and my wrist, it went on fire, and I hit my head, but I didn't fall down the stairs very far. Just like a couple, I guess. And my mom screamed at him, and she ran at him, and she fought with him. He hit her face, and he had his hands on her like . . ."

She mimed choking.

"I couldn't move, and he hit her face, but she hit back, she hit back hard, and she kicked him, and they kept fighting, and then . . . then he went over the railing. She pushed him to get away, to get to me. Her face had blood, and she pushed him, and he went over the railing. It was his fault."

"Okay."

"Mimi crawled up the steps while Mom got me and held me, and she said help was coming. And everybody had blood on them. Nobody ever hit me before he did. I hate he was my father."

"How do you know he was?"

"Because of what he was yelling, what he called me. I'm not stupid. And he teaches at the college where my mom went to college, and she told me she met my father in college. So." Adrian lifted her shoulders. "That's it. He hit everybody, and he smelled bad, and he tried to throw me down the stairs. He fell because he was mean."

Riley put an arm around Adrian's shoulders and thought: That sounds about right.

24

■ ■ ■

They kept Mimi in the hospital overnight. Lina bought hospital gift shop flowers — the best she could do — to take to her room. Adrian had the first X-ray of her life, and would earn the first cast of her life once the swelling went down.

Rather than try to complete Mimi's dinner plans, Lina ordered pizza.

God knew the kid deserved it. Just like she herself deserved a really, really big glass of wine.

She poured one, and while Adrian ate, broke her long-standing rule and poured a second.

She had a million calls to make, but they'd wait. Every goddamn thing would wait until she felt steadier.

They ate in the back courtyard with its shady trees and privacy fence. Or Adrian ate while Lina nibbled on a single slice between sips of wine.

Maybe it was a bit cool for outdoor dining, and more than a little late to have Adrian fill up on pizza, but a vicious day was a vicious day.

She hoped her daughter would sleep, but had to admit she was a little vague on the nighttime ritual. Mimi handled that.

Maybe a bubble bath — as long as she kept

the temporary cast dry. The thought of the cast, and how much worse it could have been, had her longing to top off her wineglass again.

But she resisted. Lina had a good handle on self-discipline.

"How come he was my father?"

Lina looked over, saw those gold-green eyes watching her.

"Because I was once young and stupid. I'm sorry. I'd say I wish I hadn't been, but then you wouldn't be here, would you? Can't fix what used to be, only what's now and coming up."

"Was he nicer when you were young and stupid?"

Lina let out a laugh, and her ribs whined pitifully. How much, she wondered, did you tell a seven-year-old?

"I thought he was."

"Did he hit you before?"

"Once. Only once, and after that I never, ever saw him again. If a man hits you once, he's probably going to hit you again, and again."

"You said before that you loved my dad, but things didn't work out, and he didn't want us, so he didn't matter anymore."

"I thought I loved him. I should've said that. I was only twenty, Adrian. He was older, and handsome and charming and smart. A young professor. I fell in love with who I thought he was. And he didn't matter be-

26

tween then and now."

"Why was he so mad today?"

"Because someone, a reporter, found out, and wrote a story. I don't know how, I don't know who told him. I didn't."

"You didn't because he didn't matter."

"That's exactly right."

How much did you tell? Lina thought again. Under the circumstances, maybe all of it.

"He was married, Adrian. He had a wife, and two children. I didn't know. That is, he lied to me, and told me he was in the middle of a divorce. I believed him."

Had she? Lina wondered. So hard to remember now.

"Maybe I just wanted to, but I believed him. He had his own little apartment near the college, so I believed he was essentially single. Later I found out I wasn't the only one he lied to. When I found out the truth, I broke things off. He didn't really care."

Not fully true, she thought. Screamed, threatened, shoved.

"Then I realized I was pregnant. Later, much later than I should have realized, I felt like I had to tell him. That's when he hit me. He wasn't drunk, like today."

He'd been drinking, she thought, but not drunk. Not like today.

"I told him I didn't want or need anything from him, that I wouldn't humiliate myself by telling anyone he was the biological father. And I left."

Lina edited out the threats, the demands she get rid of it, and all the other ugliness. No point in it.

"I finished out the term, graduated, then I went home. Popi and Nonna helped me. You know the rest, how I started doing classes and videos when I was pregnant with you — for pregnant women, then after for moms and babies."

"Yoga Baby."

"Right."

"But he was always mean. Does that mean I will be, too?"

God, she sucked at this mother thing. She did her best to think what her own mother would say.

"Do you feel mean?"

"Sometimes I get mad."

"Tell me about it." But Lina smiled. "Mean's a choice, I think, and you don't choose to be mean. He was right, too, that you don't look like him. Too much Rizzo in you."

Lina reached across the table, took Adrian's good hand. Maybe it felt too much like speaking adult to adult, but it was the best she could do.

"He doesn't matter, Adrian, unless we let him matter. So we won't let him matter."

"Are you going to have to go to jail?"

28

Lina toasted with her wineglass. "You're not going to let them, remember?" Then she saw the quick fear, and squeezed Lina's hand. "I'm joking, just joking. No, Adrian. The police could see what happened. You told the detective the truth, right?"

"I did. I promise."

"So did I. So did Mimi. You put that out of your mind. What is going to happen is because there was this story, and then this happened, there'll be more stories. I'm going to talk to Harry soon, and he'll help me deal with that."

"Can we still go to Popi and Nonna's?"

"Yes. As soon as Mimi's better, after you get your cast, after I deal with some things, we're going there."

"Can we go soon? Really soon?"

"As soon as we can. Just a few days, maybe."

"That's soon. Everything will be better there."

A long time, Lina thought, before things would be better. But she polished off her wine. "Absolutely."

CHAPTER TWO

Lina's career had its roots in her unplanned pregnancy. In a matter of months, she went from college student and part-time personal trainer/group fitness instructor to the world of exercise videos.

The green shoots took awhile to break through the ground, but determination, persistence, and a canny head for business pushed them toward bloom.

In the months before Jon Bennett had shoved through the door in Georgetown, her career blossomed, with Yoga Baby's sales — videos, DVDs, personal appearances, a book (with another planned) — generating over two million in profit.

An attractive, quick-witted woman, she made the most of segments on morning shows — then late-night appearances. She wrote articles for fitness magazines — and boosted those with photo shoots.

She was a young, attractive woman with a long, buff body and knew how to use both to her advantage.

She even snagged a couple of cameos on network series.

She liked the limelight, and wasn't ashamed of it, or her ambitions. She believed, absolutely, in her product — health, fitness, and balance — and believed, absolutely, she was the best person to promote that product.

Working hard posed no issues for Lina. She thrived on it, on the travel, the packed schedules, and the planning for more.

She had a line of fitness gear in the works, and in consult with a nutritionist and MD, had begun plans for supplements.

Then she'd shoved the man who'd inadvertently changed the direction of her life to his death.

Self-defense. It didn't take long for the police to conclude she'd acted in defense of herself, her daughter, and her friend.

And in a horrible way, the publicity boosted her sales, her name recognition, and the offers.

It didn't take her long to decide to ride that wave.

A week after the worst happened, she made the drive from Georgetown to rural Maryland with plans to make the best out of it.

She wore enormous sunglasses, as even her skill with makeup couldn't hide the bruises. Her ribs still ached, but she'd started a modified workout routine, and added extra meditation.

Mimi still got the occasional headache, but her broken nose was healing, her blackened eye fading to sick yellow.

Adrian found her cast annoying, but liked getting it signed. In two weeks, according to the doctor, she'd need another X-ray.

It could have been worse. Lina reminded herself constantly it could have been worse.

Since Harry bought Adrian a new Game Boy, she entertained herself in the back seat during the drive. Lina saw the shadows of the Maryland mountains, the pale lavender against a bold blue sky.

She'd wanted so desperately to escape from them, from the quiet, the creepingly slow pace, and into movement, crowds, people, everything out there.

And she still did.

She wasn't made for small towns and country living. God knew she'd never wanted to make meatballs or pizza sauce or run a restaurant — family legacy or not.

She'd craved the crowds, the city, and, yes, the limelight.

She considered New York home base if not fully home. Home was, and always would be, she thought, where the work and the action lived.

When she finally turned off I-70, the traffic vanished, and the road began to wind through rolling hills, green fields, and the scatter of homes and farms that spread over them.

Well, she thought, you *could* go home again, but you just couldn't stay there. At least not Lina Theresa Rizzo.

"We're almost there!" Adrian's voice came like a cheer from the back seat. "Look! Cows! Horses! I wish Popi and Nonna had horses. Or chickens. Chickens would be fun."

Adrian opened her window, stuck her face in the opening like a happy puppy. Her black curls danced and blew.

And would, Lina knew, end up in a rat's nest of knots and tangles.

Then the questions poured out.

How much longer? Can I swing on the tire? Will Nonna have lemonade? Can I play with the dogs?

Can I? Will they? How come?

Lina let Mimi field the questions. She'd have others to answer before much longer.

She turned at the red barn where she'd lost her virginity at not quite seventeen in the hayloft. Son of a dairy farmer, she recalled. Football quarterback. Matt Weaver, she thought. Handsome, built, sweet-natured but no pushover.

They'd sort of loved each other, the way you do at not quite seventeen. He'd wanted to marry her — one day — but she'd had other plans.

She'd heard he'd married someone else,

33

had a kid or two, and still worked the farm with his father.

Good for him, she mused, and meant it. But not and never for her.

She turned again, away from the little town of Traveler's Creek, where Rizzo's Italian Restaurant had stood on the pokey town square like an institution for two generations.

Her own grandparents who'd built it had finally accepted they needed a warmer climate. But hadn't they started another Rizzo's on the Outer Banks?

In the blood, they said, but somehow — thankfully — that gene had skipped hers.

She followed the creek, drove toward one of the three covered bridges that brought photographers, tourists, and weddings to the area.

Charming, Lina supposed, standing as it did on the little rise at the curve of the creek. And as always, Mimi and Adrian let out twin *Woos!* as she drove between those barn-red walls, under that peaked blue roof.

She turned again, ignoring the way Adrian bounced like a rubber ball on the back seat, and at last onto the winding lane, across the second bridge over the creek that gave the town its name, to the big house on the hill.

The dogs came running, the big yellow mutt and the little long-eared hound.

"There's Tom and Jerry! Woo! Hi, guys, hi!"

"Keep your seat belt on until I stop,

Adrian."

"Mom!" But she did as she was told, just kept bouncing. "It's Nonna and Popi!"

They came out onto the big wraparound porch, Dom and Sophia, hands linked. Sophia, chestnut curls framing her face, hit five-ten in her pink sneakers, and still her husband towered over her at six-five.

Fit and strong, both looked a decade younger than their ages as they stood in the shade of the second-story porch. How old were they now? Her mother around sixty-seven or sixty-eight, her father four years older or so, Lina thought. The high school sweethearts with nearly fifty years of marriage under their belts.

They'd weathered the loss of a son who'd lived less than forty-eight hours, three miscarriages, and the heartbreak of a medical opinion that there would be no baby for them.

Until — surprise! — with both of them in their forties, Lina Theresa came along.

Lina parked under a wide carport beside a shiny red pickup and a burly black SUV. She knew her mother's baby — the sleek turquoise convertible — had its place of honor in the detached garage.

She'd barely set the brake when Adrian jumped out. "Nonna! Popi! Hi, guys, hi!" She hugged the dogs as Tom leaned against her and Jerry wagged and licked. Then ran full out into her grandfather's open arms.

"I know you think I'm making a mistake," Lina began, "but look at her, Mimi. This is best for her right now."

"A girl needs her mother." So saying, Mimi pushed out, put on a smile, and walked to the porch.

"Jesus, I'm not sticking her in a basket and leaving her in the reeds. It's one damn summer."

Her mother walked down to the porch steps, met Lina halfway. Sophia cupped her daughter's bruised face in one hand, then, saying nothing, just enfolded her.

Nothing else in the past horrible week had come so close to breaking her.

"I can't do this, Mom. I don't want Adrian to see me cry."

"Honest tears aren't shameful."

"We've all had enough of them for a while." Deliberately she drew back. "You look good."

"I can't say the same."

Lina worked up a smile. "You should see the other guy."

Sophia let out a quick bark of laughter. "That's my Lina. Come, we'll sit on the porch, since it's so nice. You'll be hungry. We have food."

Maybe it was the Italian or maybe it was the restaurant genes. Either way, Lina's parents assumed anyone who came to their home had to be hungry.

The adults sat at the round table on the porch while Adrian played in the front yard with the dogs. They had bread and cheese, antipasto, olives. The lemonade Adrian hoped for filled a glass pitcher. Though it had barely struck noon, there was wine.

The half glass Lina allowed herself helped ease the tensions of the drive.

They didn't speak of what had happened, not as Adrian ran back to sit — briefly — on Dom's lap and show off her new Game Boy, or drank lemonade and chattered about the dogs.

Patient, Lina thought, her father. Always so patient with children, so good with them. And so handsome with his snowdrift of hair, the laugh lines crinkling around his golden-brown eyes.

She'd thought all her life how he and Sophia made the perfect couple — tall and fit, handsome, and so completely in tune with each other.

While she'd always felt just a beat out of step.

Well, she had been, hadn't she? Just a beat off with them, with this place, with the town that locals called the Creek.

So she'd found her rhythm elsewhere.

Adrian giggled when, after her grand-parents dutifully signed her cast, her grand-mother sketched the dogs and added their names.

37

"Your rooms are ready," Sophia said. "We'll get your bags upstairs so you can unpack, take a rest if you want."

"I have to go into the shop," Dom added, "but I'll be home for dinner."

"Actually, Adrian's been talking about the tire swing for days. Mimi, maybe you could walk around back with her, let her play for a bit."

"All right." Mimi rose and, though her single glance toward Lina signaled disapproval, she called cheerfully to Adrian, "Let's go swing."

"Yes! Come on, boys!"

Dom waited until Adrian ran around to the side of the house with Mimi following. "And what's this?"

"Mimi and I aren't staying. I have to get back to New York, finish the project I started in DC. It's just not possible to finish it there now, so . . . I'm hoping you'll be willing to keep Adrian."

"Lina." Sophia reached over to take her daughter's hand. "You need a few days, at least, to rest, to recover, to help Adrian feel safe again."

"I don't have time to rest and recover, and where would Adrian feel safer than here?"

"Without her mother?"

She shifted to her father. "She'll have both of you. I have to get ahead of this story. I can't let it derail my career, my business, so I

38

get ahead of it and I take the lead."

"The man might have killed you — you, Adrian, and Mimi."

"I know, Dad, believe me. I was there. She'll be happy here, she loves it here. It's all she's talked about for days. I have the medical records so she can see a doctor here for the next X-ray. The doctor in DC thinks she'll be able to have a removable splint in a week or two. It's a common injury, and minor, so —"

"Minor!"

When her father exploded, Lina held up both hands. "He tried to throw her down the stairs. I couldn't get to her in time. I couldn't stop him. If he hadn't been so stupid, stinking drunk, he'd have pulled that off, and she could have broken her neck instead of her wrist. Believe me, I'm never going to forget that."

"Dom." Sophia murmured it, patted her husband's hand. "How long do you want her to stay with us?"

"For the summer. Look, I know it's a long time, and I know it's a lot to ask."

"We'd love to have her," Sophia said simply. "You're wrong to do this. You're wrong, Lina, to leave her now. But we'll keep her safe and happy."

"I appreciate it. She's basically finished the school year, but Mimi has a few more assignments for her, and instructions for you. When the school year starts up again, this will be behind her, and me, us."

Her parents said nothing for a moment, only stared at her. Her father's golden-brown eyes, her mother's green made her think of how her daughter was so much a blend of these two people.

"Does she know you're leaving her here?" Dom demanded. "Going back to New York without her?"

"I didn't say anything because I needed to ask you first." Lina rose. "I'll go talk to her now. Mimi and I should get on the road soon." Lina paused. "I know I've disappointed you — again. But I think this is the best thing for everybody. I need time to focus, and I wouldn't be able to give her the attention she might need right now. Plus, there's no chance of some reporter getting pictures and slapping her face on a supermarket tabloid if she's here, with you."

"But you'll go after publicity," Dom reminded her.

"The sort I can control and guide, yeah. You know, Dad, a lot of men aren't like you. They aren't kind and loving, and a lot of women end up with bruises on their faces." She tapped a finger under her eye. "A lot of kids end up with an arm in a cast. You can be damn sure I'll speak about that issue when I get the chance."

She stalked away, furious because she

40

believed she was right. And frustrated because she suspected she was wrong.

An hour later, Adrian stood on the porch watching her mother and Mimi drive away.

"He hurt everybody because of me, so she doesn't want me around."

Dom folded himself down from his considerable height, laid his hands gently on her shoulders until she met his eyes.

"That's not true. None of this is your fault, and your mom's letting you stay with us because she's going to be so busy."

"She's always busy. Mimi watches me anyway."

"We all thought you'd like to spend the summer with us." Sophia ran a hand down Adrian's hair. "If you're not happy — let's say in one week — Popi and I will drive you up to New York ourselves."

"You would?"

"That's right. But for a week, we get to have our favorite granddaughter with us. We'll have our *gioia*." Our joy.

Adrian smiled a little. "I'm your only granddaughter."

"Still the favorite. And if you stay happy, your popi can teach you how to make ravioli, and I can teach you how to make tiramisu."

"But you'll have chores." Dom tapped a finger on her nose. "Feeding the dogs, helping in the garden."

41

"You know I like to do that when I come for visits. They're not like chores."

"Happy work is still work."

"Can I go to the shop and watch you toss pizza dough?"

"This visit, I'll teach you how to toss the dough. And we can start when your cast comes off. I have to go to the shop now. So you go wash your hands, and you can come with me."

"Okay!"

When she raced inside, Dom straightened. Sighed. "Children are resilient. She'll be fine."

"Yes, she will. But Lina will never get this time back. Well." Sophia patted Dom's cheek. "Don't buy her too much candy."

"I'll buy her just enough."

Raylan Wells sat at a two-top at Rizzo's doing his stupid homework. The way he looked at it, he already *had* homework because he had chores at home, so why couldn't schoolwork stay in stupid school?

At ten, Raylan often felt beleaguered and bewildered by the adult world and the rules laid down for kids.

He'd finished his math, which he found easy because math made sense. Lots of other shit just didn't. Like answering a bunch of questions about the Civil War. Sure, they lived sort of near Antietam and all that, and the battlefield was cool, but all that was like *over.*

The Union won, the Confederacy lost. Like Stan Lee said — and Stan Lee was a genius: 'Nuff said.

So Raylan answered a question, then doodled, answered another question, and day-dreamed an epic battle between Spider-Man and Doc Ock.

Since they'd hit what his mom called the lag time — after lunch, before dinner — most of the customers were high school kids coming in to play video games in the back, maybe grab a slice or a Coke.

He couldn't plug in any quarters himself until he finished his stupid homework. Mom's rule.

He glanced across the mostly empty dining room, past the counter, and to the big open kitchen where she worked.

Six months earlier, she'd done all her cooking at home in their kitchen. But that was before his father took off.

Now his mom cooked here because they needed to pay bills and stuff. She wore the big red apron with RIZZO'S across the front, and had her hair up under the goofy white hat all the cooks and kitchen prep people wore.

She said she liked working here, and he thought she told the truth about that because she looked happy when she worked at that

43

gigantic stove.

And, mostly, he could recognize when she didn't tell the truth.

Like when she told him and his sister everything was fine, but her eyes didn't say they were.

He'd been scared at first, but he'd said everything was okay. Maya had cried at first, but she'd only been seven, and a girl. But she got over it.

Mostly.

He figured he was the man of the house now, but he'd learned really fast that didn't mean he could skip his homework or stay up later on school nights.

So he answered another dumb Civil War question.

Maya had permission to go to her friend Cassie's house to do homework together. Not that she ever got very much. For him? Permission Denied.

Maybe because he and his best friend and his other two best friends had shot hoops and hung out instead of doing their homework the day before.

And the day before that.

Doc Ock had nothing on Mom Wrath, so now he had to report to Rizzo's after school instead of hanging out at Mick's, or at Nate's or Spencer's.

It wouldn't be so bad if Mick or Nate or Spence could hang out with him at Rizzo's.

But their moms also had the wrath.

When he saw Mr. Rizzo come in, Raylan perked up a little. When Mr. Rizzo went into the kitchen, he'd toss dough. Raylan's mom and some of the other cooks could toss it, too, but Mr. Rizzo could do tricks, like toss it up, spin around, catch it again behind his back.

And if they weren't too busy, he let Raylan try it, let him make his own personal pizza with any toppings he wanted — for free.

He didn't pay much attention to the kid who came in with Mr. Rizzo, because girl. But she had a cast on her arm, which made her marginally more interesting.

He made up reasons for the cast while he finished the last stupid questions on his assignment.

She'd fallen down a well, out of a tree, out of a window during a house fire.

With the questions answered — finally! — he started the last assignment.

He'd done the math first, because easy. The history junk next, because boring.

And saved the assignment of using this week's spelling words in a sentence for last, because fun.

He liked words even more than math and almost as much as drawing stuff.

1. Pedestrian. The getaway car from the
   bank robbery ran over the pedestrian

as it raced away.

2. Neighborhood. When aliens from the planet Zork invaded, the world counted on the one and only friendly neighborhood Spider-Man to protect them.
3. Harvesting. The evil scientist kidnapped bunches of people and started harvesting their organs for his crazy experiments.

He finished up the last of the ten words as his mother sat down at the two-top.

"I did all the dumb homework."

Because her shift had ended, Jan had taken off her apron and cap. She'd cut her hair short after her husband left and felt the pixie suited her. Plus, it required almost no time to fiddle with.

She thought Raylan could use a haircut himself. His once sunflower-blond hair had begun to turn toward her own dark honey tone. He was growing up, she thought as she gestured to Raylan to show her the work.

He rolled those wonderful bottle-green eyes at her — her dad's eyes — and pushed his binder across the table.

Growing up, she mused, his hair no longer baby fine and spun-sugar blond but thick, a little wavy. He'd lost the baby roundness in his face — where did the time go? — and had the fined-down, sharp edges he'd carry into adulthood.

He'd gone from cute to handsome right in front of her eyes.

She checked his work, because though she might be able to see the man he'd become one day in the boy, the boy liked to goof off.

She read the spelling sentences, sighed.

" 'Plight. The Dark Knight's plight was to fight for right with might.' "

He just grinned. "It works."

"How come somebody so damn smart spends so much time and effort avoiding homework he can get done in under an hour?"

"Because homework stinks."

"It does," she agreed. "But it's your job. You did good today."

"So can I go hang out at Mick's?"

"For somebody so good at math, you're having a hard time counting the days left in the school week. No hanging out until Saturday. And if you screw off on your assignments again —"

"No hanging out for two weeks," he finished in a tone more sorrowful than aggrieved. "But what am I going to *do* now? For *hours.*"

"Don't you worry, sweetie." She pushed the binder back to him. "I've got plenty of things for you to do."

"Chores." Now the aggrieved. "But I did all my homework."

"Aw, do you want a prize for doing what

you're supposed to do? I've got it!" With a huge smile, with dancing eyes, she clapped her hands together. "How about I kiss your whole face?" She leaned toward him. "Just kiss your whole face right here in front of everybody. Yum-yum, kiss-kiss."

He cringed, but couldn't stop the grin. "Cut it out!"

"Big, noisy face kisses wouldn't embarrass you, would they, my precious baby boy?"

"You're weird, Mom."

"I get it from you. Now let's go get your sister and go home."

He shoved his binder back into his loaded backpack.

People were starting to come for a beer or a glass of wine, or to meet friends for an early dinner.

Mr. Rizzo had put on the cap and apron now, and was doing his toss-the-dough tricks. The girl kid sat at the service bar on a stool and applauded.

" 'Bye, Mr. Rizzo!"

Mr. Rizzo caught the dough, twirled it, winked. "*Ciao*, Raylan. Take care of your mama."

"Yes, sir."

They went outside onto the covered front porch, where some people already sat at tables drinking and eating. Pots of flowers sent out fragrances that mixed with the scent of fried calamari, of spicy sauce and toasted bread.

The town had big concrete tubs of flowers spaced along the square, and some of the businesses had more pots or hanging baskets.

As they waited for the walk light at the crosswalk, Jan had to stop herself from taking her son's hand.

Ten years old, she reminded herself. He didn't want to hold his mother's hand to cross the street.

"Who was the kid with Mr. Rizzo?"

"Hmm? Oh, that's his granddaughter, Adrian. She's going to stay with them for the summer."

"How come she's got that cast on?"

"She hurt her wrist."

"How?" he asked as they crossed the street.

"She fell."

Because she felt Raylan's eyes on her as they walked down the next block, she glanced over. "What?"

"You get that look."

"What look?"

"You get that look when you don't want to tell me something bad."

She supposed she did get a look. And she supposed in a town the size of Traveler's Creek, with the Rizzos so much a part of its fabric, Raylan — with his bat ears — would hear anyway.

"Her father hurt her."

49

"Seriously?" His father had said and done a lot of mean things, but he'd never smashed up his wrist or Maya's.

"I expect you to respect Mr. and Mrs. Rizzo's privacy, Raylan. And since I'm going to take Maya over there — she and Adrian are the same age — to see if they'll make friends, I don't want you to say anything to your sister. If Adrian wants to tell her, or anyone, that's her business."

"Okay, but jeez, her dad broke her arm!"

"Wrist, but it's just as bad."

"Is he in jail?"

"No. He died."

"Holy crap." Stunned — and a little excited — he bounced on his toes. "Did she like kill him or something to defend herself?"

"No. Don't be silly. She's just a little girl who's been through an ugly ordeal. I don't want you peppering her with questions."

They reached Cassie's house, right across the street from theirs.

They got to keep their house because the Rizzos gave his mother a job after his father walked out on them and took most of the money out of the bank.

That was one of the really mean things he'd done.

Raylan had heard his mom crying when she thought he was sleeping after that — and before she got the job.

He'd never do anything, say anything to

50

hurt Mr. or Mrs. Rizzo.

But the girl kid seemed a lot more interesting now.

CHAPTER THREE

Everything about the summer changed when
Adrian met Maya. Her world opened up with
sleepovers and playdates and secrets shared.

For the first time in her life, she had a real
best friend.

She taught Maya yoga and dance steps —
and almost a handspring — and Maya taught
her how to twirl a baton and how to play
Yahtzee.

Maya had a dog named Jimbo, who could
walk on his back legs, and a cat named Miss
Priss, who liked to cuddle.

She had a brother named Raylan, but all he
wanted to do was play video games or read
comic books or run around with his friends,
so she didn't see that much of him.

But he had green eyes, greener and darker
than her mother's and her grandmother's.
Like they got a super-charge of green.

Maya said he was mostly a doody-head, but
Adrian didn't see any real evidence of it, since
he steered clear of them.

And she really liked his eyes.

Still, it made her wonder what it would have been like to have a brother or a sister. A sister would be better, *obviously,* but having somebody close to the same age in the house seemed like fun.

Maya's mom was really nice. Nonna said she was a jewel, and Popi said she was a fine cook and a hard worker. Sometimes when Mrs. Wells had her shift, Maya came over and stayed all day, and if they asked in time, some of the other girls could come, too.

After the cast came off, she had to wear a removable splint for three more weeks. But she could take it off if she wanted a bubble bath or if she got invited to swim in Maya's friend Cassie's backyard pool.

One day deep in June she went upstairs with Maya to get everything they needed for the tea party they planned to hold outside under the big shade tree.

She stopped by Raylan's open bedroom door. Always before, he'd kept it closed with a big KEEP OUT sign on it.

"We're not supposed to go in without permission," Maya told her. She had her sunny blond hair in French braids today because it was her mom's day off and she'd had time.

Maya put a hand on her hip the way she did and rolled her eyes. "As if I'd want to. It's messy and it's smelly."

53

Adrian didn't smell anything from the doorway, but messy hit the mark. He hadn't made the bed even a little. Clothes and shoes spread all over the floor along with action figures.

But the walls gripped her attention. He'd covered them with drawings.

Superheroes, battles with monsters or supervillains, spaceships, strange buildings, scary-looking forests.

"Did he draw all these?"

"Yeah, he draws all the time. He draws good, but it's always stupid stuff. He never draws anything pretty — except he did once for Mom for Mother's Day. He drew a bouquet of flowers and colored them and everything. She cried — but because she liked it."

Adrian didn't think the drawings were stupid — some were kind of scary, but not stupid. Still, she didn't say so, since Maya was her best friend.

As she poked her head in just a little farther, Raylan ran up the stairs. He froze in place a moment, eyes narrowed. Then he bounded over and into the doorway to block it.

"You're not allowed in my room."

"We didn't go in, poop-brain. Nobody wants to go in your stinky room." Maya gave an exaggerated sniff, slapped a hand on her hip.

54

"The door was open," Adrian said before Raylan could retaliate against his sister. "I didn't go in, honest. I was just looking at the drawings. They're really good drawings. I especially like the one of Iron Man. This one," she added, and posed as if in flight, with one arm out, hand fisted.

Now those furious eyes tracked to hers. Instinctively she cringed back as her wrist throbbed with phantom pain.

He saw her cover her braced wrist with her hand — and remembered about her father.

Anybody would be scared if their own father broke something on them.

So he made himself shrug like he didn't care. But maybe he was a little impressed she even knew who Iron Man was.

"It's okay. That was just practice. I can do better."

"The one of Spider-Man and Doc Ock's really cool, too."

Okay, more than a little impressed. None of Maya's other girl dopes knew Doc Ock from the Green Goblin.

"Yeah, I guess." Considering that enough conversation with a girl, he sneered at his sister. "Keep out."

So saying, he went in, shut the door.

Maya smiled her sunny smile. "See? Poop-brain." Taking Adrian's hand, she skipped down to her room to get tea party supplies.

That night before bedtime, Adrian got some

paper and a pencil to try to draw her favorite superhero, Black Widow.

Everything she drew looked like blobs connected to lines or more blobs. Sadly, she went back to her standard — a house, trees, flowers, and a big round sun.

Even that wasn't very good, none of her drawings were — even though Nonna always put one on the refrigerator.

She wasn't good at drawing. She wasn't really good at cooking and baking, even though Nonna and Popi said she learned fast.

What was she good at?

To comfort herself she did yoga — even though she had to be careful not to put too much weight on her wrist.

When she finished the nightly ritual, she brushed her teeth, then put on her pajamas.

She started to go out to tell her grandfather she was ready for bed — her grandmother had the shift at Rizzo's — when he tapped on her open door.

"Look at my girl. All clean and shiny and ready for bed. And look at this," he continued when he saw her drawing. "This has to go in our art gallery."

"It's baby drawing."

"Art's in the eye of the beholder, and I like it."

"Maya's brother, Raylan, can really draw."

"That he can. He's very talented." He glanced at her, and her sulky face. "But I've never seen him walk on his hands."

"I'm not really supposed to do that yet."

"But you will again." He kissed the top of her head, then nudged her toward the bed. "Let's get you and Barkley tucked in so we can read another chapter of *Matilda*. My girl reads better than most teenagers."

Adrian snuggled in with her stuffed dog. "Active mind, active body."

When Dom laughed and sat on the bed beside her with the book, she curled up against him.

He smelled of the grass he'd mowed before dinner.

"Do you think Mom misses me?"

"Sure she does. Doesn't she call every week to talk to you, to see how you're doing, what you're doing?"

I wish she'd call more, Adrian thought, but she doesn't ask so much what I'm doing.

"I think tomorrow I'll teach you how to make pasta, then you can teach me something."

"What?"

"One of those routines you make up." He tapped her nose. "Active mind, active body."

The idea delighted. "Okay! I can make up a new one for you."

"Not too hard. I'm new at this. For now, read me a story."

When Adrian looked back on that summer,

she realized it had been idyllic. A pause in reality, responsibility, and routine she'd never fully know again.

Long, hot, sunny days with lemonade on the porch, the cheer of dogs in the yard. The thrill of a sudden thunderstorm where the air turned silver and the trees swayed and danced. She had friends to play with, to laugh with. She had healthy, energetic, attentive grandparents who made her, for that brief moment of time, the center of their world.

She learned good kitchen skills, and some would stay with her for the rest of her life. She discovered the fun in picking fresh herbs and vegetables that grew right outside in the yard, and how her grandmother smiled when her grandfather brought in a handful of wildflowers for her.

That summer she learned what family and community really meant. She'd never forget it, and would often yearn for it.

But the days passed. A parade and fireworks on the Fourth of July. A hot humid night of colored lights and whirling sounds when the carnival came to town. Catching and releasing fireflies, watching hummingbirds, eating a cherry Popsicle on the big wraparound porch on a day so still she could hear the creek bubble.

Then everyone talked about back-to-school clothes and supplies. Her friends buzzed about what teacher they'd have and showed off new backpacks and binders.

And summer, despite the heat, the light, the long days, rushed to an end.

She tried, and failed, not to cry when her grandmother helped her pack.

"Oh now, my baby." Sophia drew her into a hug. "You're not leaving forever. You'll come back to visit."

"It's not the same."

"But it'll be special. You know you've missed your mama, and Mimi."

"But now I'm going to miss you and Popi, and Maya and Cassie and Ms. Wells. How come I always have to miss somebody?"

"It's hard, I know, because Popi and I are going to miss you."

"I wish we could live here."

She could live in this big house, with this pretty room where she could walk right out on the porch and see the dogs, the gardens, the mountains. "I wouldn't have to miss anybody if we could live here."

After a quick rub on Adrian's back, Sophia stepped away to lay a pair of jeans in the suitcase. "This isn't your mom's home, my baby."

"It *was*. She was born right here and went to school here and everything."

"But it's not her home now. Everybody has to find their own home."

"What if I want this to be mine? How come I can't have what I want?"

Sophia looked at that sweet, mutinous face and her heart cracked a little. She sounded so like her mother.

"When you're old enough, you might want this to be home. Or you might want New York, or someplace else. And you'll decide."

"Kids don't get to decide *anything*."

"That's why the people who love them do their best to make good decisions for them until they're ready to make their own. Your mama does her best, Adrian. I promise you, she does her best."

"If you said I could live here, she might say yes."

Sophia felt the crack in her heart widen. "That wouldn't be the right thing for you or your mama." She sat on the side of the bed, took Adrian's tearful face in her hands. "You need each other. Now wait," she said when Adrian shook her head. "Do you believe I always tell you the truth?"

"Yes, I guess. Yes."

"I'm telling you the truth now. You need each other. It might not feel like it right now when you're sad and you're angry, but you do."

"Don't you and Popi need me?"

"Oh boy, do we." She pulled Adrian in for a fierce hug. "*Gioia mia.* That's why you're going to write us letters, and we're going to write you back."

"Letters? I never wrote one."

"Now you will. In fact, I'm going to give you some pretty stationery to get you started. I've got some in my desk, and I'll get it. We'll pack it up for you."

"And you'll write letters just to me?"

"Just to you. And once a week, for sure, you're going to call and we'll talk."

"Promise?"

"Pinky swear." Sophia locked a finger with Adrian's and made her smile.

She didn't cry when the car drove up — a big, shiny black limo — but she clung to her grandfather's hand.

He gave hers a squeeze. "Look at that fancy car! Aren't you going to have fun riding in style. Go on now." He gave her hand another squeeze. "Go give your mom a hug."

The driver wore a suit and tie, and got out first to open the door. Her mother slid out. She had on pretty silver sandals, and Adrian saw that her toes were painted bright pink to match her shirt.

Mimi got out the other side, her face all smiles even though her eyes glistened.

Even at not quite eight, Adrian knew it was wrong to want to run to Mimi first. So she walked across the lawn to her mother. Lina bent down for the hug.

"I think you're taller." As she straightened, Lina ran a hand down Adrian's curly ponytail. And her eyebrows drew together the way they did when she didn't like something. "You

61

definitely got a lot of sun."

"I wore sunscreen. Popi and Nonna made sure."

"Good. That's good."

"Where's mine?" Mimi threw out her arms. This time Adrian did run. "Oh, I missed you!" She lifted Adrian off her feet, kissed her cheeks, hugged harder. "You got taller, and you're all golden, and you smell like sunshine."

Everybody hugged, but Lina said they couldn't stay for food and drink.

"We flew in from Chicago. It already feels like a long day, and I have an interview on the *Today* show in the morning. Thank you so much for looking after Adrian."

"She's nothing but a pleasure." Sophia took both of Adrian's hands, kissed them. "An absolute pleasure. I'm going to miss your pretty face."

"Nonna." Adrian flung her arms around her.

Dom hauled her up, gave her a swing, then a cuddle. "Be good for your mom." He kissed the side of her neck, then set her back on her feet.

She had to hug Tom and Jerry, and cry a little with her face buried in fur.

"Come on, Adrian, it's not like you're never going to see them again. It'll be summer again before you know it."

"You could come for Christmas," Sophia said.

"We'll see how it goes." She kissed her mother's cheek, then her father's. "Thank you. It took a lot of stress off knowing she was away from . . . everything. I'm sorry I can't stay longer, but I have to be in the studio by six in the morning."

She glanced back to where Mimi already had Adrian in the limo and was trying to distract her by showing her how the lights worked.

"This was good for her. Good for everybody."

"Come for Christmas." Sophia gripped her daughter's hand. "Or Thanksgiving."

"I'll try. Take care now."

She got in, closed the door.

Ignoring her mother's orders to put on her seat belt, Adrian knelt on the back seat so she could look through the rear window of the big car, see her grandparents waving goodbye as they stood in front of the big stone house with the dogs at their feet.

"Adrian, sit down now so Mimi can buckle you in." Even as she spoke and the limo slid under the covered bridge, Lina's cell phone rang. She glanced at the display. "I need to take this." She shifted down to the far side of the bench seat. "This is Lina. Hello, Meredith."

"We've got fizzy water and juice." Mimi

63

spoke brightly as she buckled Adrian's seat belt. "And some berries, and those veggie chips you like. We'll have a car picnic."

"That's okay." Adrian unzipped the little cross-body bag her grandparents had bought her and took out her Game Boy. "I'm not hungry."

New York City

From that long-ago summer, Adrian developed the habit of writing letters. She called her grandparents at least once a week, shot off the occasional email or text, but the weekly letter became a tradition.

Taking advantage of a warm and breezy September morning, she sat outside on the rooftop terrace of her mother's Upper East Side triplex to write about her first week of the school year.

She could've typed it out on her computer and mailed it, but that felt no different from email to her. It was, she thought, the act of writing that made letters personal.

She texted, and often, with Maya, and even sent an occasional handwritten card.

She no longer had a nanny — Mimi had fallen in love with Issac, gotten married, and had two kids of her own. Besides, Adrian would be seventeen in six weeks.

Mimi worked for Lina still, but as an administrative assistant, helping schedule appointments, working with Harry to line up interviews and events.

Her mother's career had skyrocketed with books and DVDs, fitness events, motivational speeches, TV appearances (she'd played herself on an episode of *Law and Order: SVU*).

The Yoga Baby brand shined sterling.

The flagship Ever Fit gym in Manhattan had franchises all over the country. Its fitness wear line, its health food line, its essential oils, candles, lotions, its branding on gym equipment had, over slightly more than a decade, turned what had been a one-woman operation into a billion-dollar national enterprise.

Yoga Baby financed camps for underprivileged kids and donated heavily to women's shelters, so Adrian couldn't claim her mother didn't give back.

But most days after school Adrian came home to an empty apartment. She'd joked with Maya that she had a closer relationship with the doorman than her mother.

Their closest contact, essentially, Adrian thought, came during the weeks they worked together on their annual mother-daughter exercise DVD.

But that was her life, and she'd already decided what to do with the rest of it when she could make her own choices.

She'd already made one of her first, and sat now in the warm breeze waiting for the hammer to drop.

It didn't take long.

She heard the glass doors behind her slide open, hit the stops with a solid thump.

"Adrian, for Christ's sake, what are you doing? You haven't begun to pack. We're leaving in an hour."

"You're leaving in an hour," Adrian corrected, and kept writing. "I don't have to pack because I'm not going."

"Don't be such a child. I've got a full schedule in L.A. tomorrow. Get packed."

Adrian set her pen down, shifted in her chair to meet her mother's eyes. "No. I'm not going. I'm not letting you haul me around the country for the next two and a half weeks. I'm not going to live in hotel rooms, do school online. I'm staying here, and I'm going to the damn private school you pushed me into after you bought this place last spring."

"You'll do exactly what I tell you. You're still a child, so —"

"You just told me not to be a child. Can't have it both ways, Mom. I'm sixteen — seventeen in just a few weeks. I've had barely three weeks in this new school where I have no friends. I'm not going to sit alone most of the day in a hotel room or a studio or some event center. I can sit alone here after school."

"You're not old enough to stay here alone."

"But I'm old enough to stay alone in some other city while you're signing your new book

66

or DVD, while you're doing interviews or events?"

"You're not alone there." Flustered, baffled, Lina dropped down to sit. "I'm a phone call or text away."

"And since Mimi's not going with you because she has two kids she doesn't want to leave for two weeks, she's a phone call away. But I'm capable of taking care of myself. If you haven't noticed, I've been doing that for a while now."

"I've made sure you've had everything you could need or want. Don't you take that tone with me, Adrian." Flustered and baffled turned to shocked and angry. "You're getting the best education anyone could want, one that'll get you into the college of your choice. You have a beautiful and safe home. I've worked, and worked hard, to provide those things for you."

Adrian gave Lina a long, steady look. "You've worked and worked hard because you're an ambitious woman with a genuine passion. I don't hold that against you. I was happy in public school. I had friends there. Now I'm going to try to be happy and make friends where you planted me. I can't do that if I'm out for two weeks."

"If you think I'm leaving a teenager alone in New York so she can have parties and screw off from school and go out at all hours, you're very mistaken."

Adrian folded her arms on the table, leaned forward. "Parties? With who? I don't drink, I don't smoke, I don't do drugs. I came close to having a boyfriend last year, but I have to start from scratch there now. Screw off from school? I've been on the honor roll since I was ten. And if I wanted to go out at all hours, I could do that when you're here. You'd never know the difference.

"Look at me." Adrian tossed up her hands. "I'm so responsible I annoy myself. I've had to be. You preach about balance, well, I'm going to take some for myself. I'm not getting pulled away from my routine again. I'm not."

"If you're determined not to go, I'll see if your grandparents can have you for a couple weeks."

"I'd love to visit them, but I'm staying here. I'm going to school here. If you don't trust me, have Mimi check on me every day. Bribe one of the doormen to report my comings and goings, I don't care. I'm going to get up in the mornings and go to school. I'm going to come home in the afternoons and do my assignments. I'm going to work out right in there, in that very nice home gym you set up. I'll fix myself something to eat or order in. I'm not after parties and sex and drinking till I drop. I'm after a normal start to the school year. That's it."

Lina pushed up, paced over to the wall, and

stared at the view of the East River. "You talk like . . . I've done my best for you, Adrian."

"I know."

Her grandmother's words on that long-ago summer came back to her. *Your mama does her best, Adrian.*

"I know," she repeated. "And you ought to trust me not to do something to embarrass you. If not, then you ought to know I'd never want to upset or disappoint Popi and Nonna. I just want to go to goddamn school."

Lina closed her eyes. She could force it — she was in charge. But at what cost? And for what benefit?

"I don't want you going out past nine, or leaving the neighborhood — unless it's to go to Mimi's in Brooklyn."

"If I wanted to go to the movies on a Friday or Saturday night, it might be ten."

"Accepted, but you'll check in with me or Mimi in that case. I don't want you letting anyone into the apartment while I'm gone — excepting Mimi and her family. Or Harry. He's going with me, but he may fly back for a day."

"I'm not looking for company. I'm looking for stability."

"One of us — me, Harry, or Mimi — will phone every night. I won't say when."

"Spot-checking me?"

"There's a difference between trusting you to be responsible and taking chances."

"Accepted."

The breeze stirred through Lina's hair, the roasted chestnut sweep of it. "I . . . I thought you enjoyed the travel."

"Some of it. Sometimes."

"If you change your mind, I'll arrange for you to go to Mimi's or your grandparents', or to fly out to meet me wherever I am."

Because she knew her mother would do any of those things, and without too much I-told-you-soing, Adrian felt something soften inside her. "Thanks, but I'm going to be fine. School's going to keep me busy, and I'm researching colleges. And I've got a project I want to start."

"What project?"

"I have to think about it some more." At sixteen, Adrian knew how to evade, and breezily. She also knew how to distract.

"Plus, I need to go buy a five-pound bag of M&M's, a couple gallons of Coke, five or six bags of potato chips. You know, basic supplies."

Lina smiled a little. "If I thought you meant that, I might knock you out and drag you with me. I have to go. The car's going to be here soon. I'm trusting you, Adrian."

"You can."

Lina bent down, kissed the top of Adrian's head. "It'll be late here by the time I land in L.A., so I won't call. I'll text."

"Okay. Have a safe trip, and a good tour."

With a nod, Lina started back inside. Something twinged inside her chest when she looked back and saw Adrian had picked up the pen again.

She continued to write as if it were any other afternoon.

As she started down the stairs to the next level, Lina took out her phone and called Mimi.

"Hey, are you on your way?"

"In a minute. Listen, Adrian's staying here."

"She's what?"

"She made a good case for it. I know it's not what you'd do, but you probably would have thought through booking a national tour on the third week of the new school year. When she's in a new school on top of it. I didn't. Hold a minute."

She used her house phone to call downstairs. "Hi, Ben, it's Lina Rizzo. If you could send someone up for my bags, please. Thanks.

"Mimi, I have to trust her. She's never given me a reason not to. And, Jesus, she's tougher than I realized, so good for her, I guess. Would you just give her a call later, see how she sounds?"

"Of course. If she wants to stay here while you're gone, we can make that work."

"Her mind's set — if it changes, I guess she'll let you know — but she's determined and that's that."

"Her mother's daughter?"

71

"Is she?" Lina stopped at a mirror, checked her hair, her face. In looks, yes, she thought. She saw a lot of herself in her daughter. But the rest . . . maybe she hadn't paid enough attention.

"Anyway, she'll be fine. Just call or text her now and then."

"No problem at all. I'll stay in touch with her, and with you. Sorry, Lina," Mimi added as the shouts blasted through the phone. "Jacob's apparently decided to murder his sister again. I have to go, but you have a safe trip. And don't worry."

"Thanks. Talk soon."

When the buzzer rang, she walked to the door.

And put everything else aside. She had some prep to do on the plane, and a full schedule ahead of her.

CHAPTER FOUR

Alone in New York, Adrian followed her morning routine. She got up with her alarm, did her morning yoga. She showered, dealt with her hair — always a chore — applied minimal makeup — she'd always had a love affair with makeup.

She dressed in the detested school uniform — navy pants, white shirt, navy blazer. Every day she donned the uniform she vowed never to voluntarily wear a navy blazer after graduation.

She put together a breakfast of mixed fruit with Greek yogurt, a slice of ten-grain toast, and juice.

Because Mimi had ingrained the habit in her, she did her dishes, made her bed.

A quick check of the weather on her phone promised mostly sunny and continued warm, so she didn't bother with a jacket.

She shrugged on her backpack and took the penthouse's private elevator down.

She couldn't complain about the five-block

walk to school, especially with the weather so fine. She used the time to go over her plan — her deviation from routine.

And the single rule laid down she fully intended to break.

When her phone rang, she checked the display. "Hi, Mimi."

"Just doing my duty."

"You can tell Mom when she asks that I was on my way to school when you checked. Of course, instead of going there, I'm going to grab a train to the Jersey Shore and soak up some rays, use my fake ID to buy a bunch of beer, and have lots of sex with strangers in a cheap motel."

"Good plan, but I think I'll leave that part out of my report. I know you're fine, honey, but checking in is the right and loving thing to do."

"I get it."

"Do you want to come here for the weekend?"

"Thanks, but I'm good. If that changes, you'll find me on your doorstep."

"If you need anything, you call me."

"I will. Talk soon."

With that done, she put her phone away.

She had a backup plan if her first didn't work. But she'd done her research, and thought Plan A had real potential.

She clipped her ID on the blazer as she walked up the short stone steps to the digni-

74

fied brownstone that served as a school for grades nine through twelve — if you were rich enough and smart enough.

She went inside, through the small security vestibule.

The quiet, the gleaming wood floor, the pristine walls contrasted with the noise and movement and slight dinge of her old school.

She missed it, all of it.

Two years, she reminded herself as she turned away from the wide entrance to the hall on the left. Two years and she could make her own choices.

She intended to preview that by making one today.

By junior year, most of the students had formed their own tribes. Making room for the new girl took time, and she hadn't had a full three weeks.

She knew those established tribes studied her, sized her up, considered. Though she'd never been shy, Adrian took her time as well.

The jocks could make sense for the next couple of years. Sports might not be so much her thing, but athleticism was. The fashionable girls could be fun, as she did love clothes. (Another reason to hate the uniform.)

The party animals didn't interest her any more than the scarily serious eggheads.

As always, the group as a whole had scatters of the snobs, the bullies — often intertwined.

The nerds were, always, anywhere, deadly to social strata.

But for her project, that's exactly where she aimed.

She made the choice during lunch period that would almost certainly doom her chances of joining the social hierarchy.

In the dining hall, Adrian carried her tray — field green salad with grilled chicken, seasonal fruit, sparkling water — past the table of jocks, away from the fashionable girls, and to the lowest of the rung, the nerd table.

She caught the lag in some of the conversational buzz, and a few snickers, as she paused by the lowly table and its three occupants.

Since she'd done her due diligence — reading back issues of the school newspaper, combing last year's yearbook — she targeted Hector Sung.

Asian, coat-hanger thin, square-framed black glasses with dark brown eyes behind them. Those eyes blinked at her now as he stopped in the act of biting into a slice of veggie pizza.

"Is it okay if I sit here?"

He said, "Um."

She just smiled and sat across from him. "I'm Adrian Rizzo."

"Okay. Hi."

The girl beside him, with skin like caramel cream and a gorgeous head of braids, rolled big, round, black eyes. "He's Hector Sung, and he's thinking nobody sits here but us. I'm Teesha Kirk."

She jerked a thumb with a thick silver ring to the boy sitting warily and red-faced beside Adrian. "The ginger is Loren Moorhead — the third. You've got about five-point-three seconds to move before you're infected by nerd germs and permanently ostracized from society."

Adrian had done her due diligence on Teesha as well, who'd have ranked with the scarily smart eggheads but for her nerd bones. She preferred Dungeons & Dragons tournaments or *Doctor Who* marathons to meetings of the National Honor Society or National Merit Scholars.

"Oh well." Adrian shrugged, added a squirt of lemon to her salad, took a delicate bite. "Guess time's up. So, nice to meet you, Hector, Teesha, Loren. Anyway, Hector, I've got a proposition for you."

He dropped the pizza onto his plate with a little splat. "A what?"

"Business proposition. I need a videographer, and since that's your interest, I thought you could help me out with a project."

His gaze darted between his two friends. "For school?"

"No. I want to do a series of seven fifteen-minute videos. One for each day of the week. I'd want voice-overs for some of them, real-time audio for others. I thought about setting up like a tripod and camera, just doing it myself. But that's not the look I want."

His gaze finally came back to hers, and she read interest in it. "What kind of videos?"

"Fitness. Yoga, cardio, strength training, and so on. To put on YouTube."

"Maybe you're messing with us."

She shifted to Loren. His hair, painfully red and cut close to his head, framed a milk-white, freckled face. He had soft blue eyes and a good fifteen pounds of extra pudge.

She thought she could help him with that if he wanted.

"Why would I? I need somebody to video my segments, and I'll pay fifty dollars for each one. That's three-fifty for seven. I guess that's negotiable, within reason."

"I could think about it. When did you want to start?"

"Saturday morning — sunrise. I want to do segments at sunrise, and at sunset. I have a big terrace, and it would work for this."

"I'd probably need assistants."

Adrian ate more salad, considered. "Seventy-five per segment. Split it however you want."

"What time's sunrise?" Loren wondered.

Before Adrian could speak — because she'd looked it up — Teesha said, "Sunrise on Saturday, six-twenty-seven a.m. Sunset, seven-twenty p.m. EDT."

"Don't ask," Loren suggested. "She just knows stuff like that."

"Great. You'd need to get there in time to set up and whatever you need to do. I've got my address, and what I've outlined, the basic scripts."

Adrian took a thumb drive out of her pocket, set it beside Hector's tray. "Look it over, think it over, let me know."

"Your mom's the Yoga Baby lady, right?"

Adrian nodded at Teesha. "That's right."

"How come you don't have her people do it? She's got her own production company."

"Because this is for me. It's mine. So, if you decide to take the job, I'll have you cleared to come up. It'll probably take the whole weekend. Maybe longer. I don't know how much postproduction time you'd need to get it done, get it up."

"I'll take a look, let you know maybe tomorrow." Hector offered her a little smile. "You know, you really are screwed around here now. I hope it's worth it for you."

"Me, too."

She got through the rest of the day by ignoring the smirks, the snide comments, and the snickers.

When she stepped back out into the air, Hector and his little tribe came after her.

"So hey, listen. I had a chance to look at some of your outline. Seems doable."

"Great."

"I'd want to see the space, though, before committing. Make sure it'll work for what you're after."

"I can show you now if you've got time. I'm only a few blocks from here."

"Now's good."

"We're all going," Teesha told her.

"Fine."

"So . . ." As he trooped along beside her, Hector shoved up his glasses. "I took a look at a couple of your mother's videos during my free period. Her production values are total, right? I've got some good equipment, but I'm not going to be able to match what she's got going in the studio."

"I don't want what she's got. I want mine."

"I looked up stuff about her, and you."

Adrian glanced back over her shoulder at Loren.

Debate team nerd, she remembered. Always picked last for any team in PE — and first to volunteer for hall monitor.

"And?"

"People are always running scams and stuff, so I wanted to take a look. Your mom seriously killed your dad."

It wasn't the first time someone had prodded her on it, but Adrian had to admit, Loren hit the most direct.

"He wasn't my dad, he was my biological father. And he was trying to kill me at the time."

"How come?"

"Because he was drunk and mean and maybe crazy. I don't know. It was the first and the last I'd seen of him. And since it was almost ten years ago, it's not relevant to any of this."

"Jesus, Loren, let it go." Teesha gave him a solid poke with her elbow. "Didn't your uncle do time for insider trading?"

"Well yeah, but that's a white-collar crime, not —"

"Said by the whitest white boy in white boy history," Teesha tossed back. "Loren's family's the WASPiest of the WASPs. Three generations of high-class, high-priced lawyers."

"So he likes to argue," Adrian said.

"You got that. You say up, Loren's going to say down and go off about it for an hour."

"Up depends on where you're standing."

Teesha poked him again. "Don't get him started."

"Well, we're standing down here, so we're going in, then up. Hi, George."

The doorman gave Adrian a big smile as he opened the door. "How was school today?"

"Same as always. This is Hector. And Teesha and Loren. They'll be visiting now and again."

"All right. You all have a real nice day."

As they crossed the fragrant lobby with its small, exclusive shops, Adrian took out her

81

key swipe. She passed the banks of elevators to one marked PRIVATE. PENTHOUSE A.

"If you decide to come Saturday, I'll give your names to security and the desk. The desk will call up, and I can release the elevator to bring you up."

"How high up are you?" Loren asked as they got on.

"Forty-eighth floor. That's the rooftop level."

"Uh-oh," Teesha murmured as Loren blanched. "He's got a thing about heights."

Since that hadn't come out in her research on him, she turned to him now with genuine sympathy.

"Sorry. You don't have to come out to the terrace."

"It's no big." He stuck his hands in his pockets. "No big. I'm cool on it. I'm cool."

The opposite thereof, Adrian thought, as he already had a little bead of sweat sliding down his right temple.

But she let it go. Nobody liked being embarrassed.

"Well, anyway, you'd take the other elevator on Saturday, and that would bring you to the main level, front door. You need a swipe for this way, then the alarm code."

Teesha wiggled her eyebrows. "Swank."

And Adrian shrugged. "My mother likes swank."

The elevator opened into Lina's home gym.

A rack of free weights ran along a mirrored wall, and racks and shelves — stability balls, yoga mats and blocks, exercise bands, jump ropes, medicine balls, and kettlebells — flanked it.

A huge flat screen dominated the wall over a long, narrow gas fireplace. In the small, open kitchen area, energy drinks filled a wine fridge. A glass-front cabinet held Yoga Baby water bottles.

A wall of glass doors opened to the expansive terrace, and the city beyond.

"No machines?" Teesha wandered the space.

"Your body's the machine, in my mother's world."

"Well, organic complexities are different from mechanical complexities."

"The Terminator had both organic and mechanical complexities," Loren pointed out.

"We're years from Skynet," Teesha pointed out. "Anyway, I get she means you use your body, your body weight, keep it in tune and all that."

Adrian waited a beat. "Right. There's a bathroom around the left of the kitchen if anybody needs it." Adrian unlocked and pulled open the glass doors. "I want to do the videos out here."

"Awesome." Hector stepped out. "Awesome. We'll want to move the furniture, have a clear space." He glanced over to the hot

83

tub humming under its cover on a platform. "And turn that off. You get some city noises, even way up here, but that'll just add to it. Shoot this way, you get the river in the background."

"And the sunrise," Adrian added. "For the sunset shoots, we go the other way. You could see the Chrysler Building, the Empire State. I'm not sure what's best for late morning or afternoon. I just want different angles."

"Yeah, yeah. I can maybe hit my dad up for some equipment, bounce the light. Maybe he'd let me use his good camera."

"Hector's dad's a cinematographer." Loren spoke from just inside the doorway, where he'd stopped. And stayed. "He's on *Blue Line* — the cop show. So, is there like anything to drink besides that health stuff? Like, you know, sodas?"

"Banned in this house — but I'll get some for Saturday. There's juice down in the main kitchen."

"I'll live without it."

"Okay, so . . ." Hector did another walk around, studying angles. "Can we do like a rehearsal, one segment, get a solid feel?"

"Oh, sure. I need to change. I can't work out in this."

"How about you do that?" Teesha said. "Me and Hector can move some of the furniture. Loren can go out and maybe buy some Cokes."

84

"There's a shop right off the lobby downstairs if you want." Adrian walked back, dug into her backpack, and took out ten dollars. "On me."

"Cool."

By the time Adrian had changed into yoga pants and a tank, Hector and Teesha had muscled two tables, two sofas, and a chair to the far side of the terrace.

She brought out a yoga mat, angled it so she faced southeast.

"I tested this out the other day, and you should be able to get me, the river, the sunrise."

"I'm gonna video with my camera, just to test it. I mean, the light'll be different and all that jazz, but we can check the timing, the angles, and I can plan better."

"Great." She glanced back as the elevator opened. Loren put her swipe on top of her backpack, then set the bag on the counter in the kitchen.

"Got Cokes, got some chips and stuff."

Adrian thought of her mother, and had to laugh. "That would be the first time either of those came into this place since we moved in."

"Man, what do you eat?"

"You mean for snacks?" Adrian smiled at Loren as he passed out Cokes. "Fruit, raw veggies, hummus, almonds, baked sweet potato fries are sometimes acceptable. It's

85

not so bad. I'm used to it."

"Your mom's way strict."

"Fitness and nutrition? That's her religion. She practices what she preaches, so it's hard to bitch too much. Anyway." She stepped to the front of her mat. "I want to do this, like I said, without the vocals, then voice-over after."

"Fifteen, right?" Teesha pulled out her phone. "I'll time it."

She'd practiced the routine countless times, tweaked it until she felt it met her goals. A gentle and, well, pretty morning salute to the sun.

She let her mind go.

Since she was used to camera and crew when she did videos with her mother, Hector and the others didn't distract her. When she ended with Savasana, she added the vocals.

"I'm going to talk this part out now, so you don't think I've just fallen asleep. The voice-over's going to instruct how to breathe, how to empty the mind, allow the body to fully let go. Relaxing from the toes, to the ankles, the shins, and up the body, how to visualize soft colors or light on inhales, expel dark and stress on the exhales."

"You've got like ninety seconds left," Teesha told her.

"That's right. I'll say to stay in Savasana as long as they like, then . . ."

She stretched out, arms overhead, before

turning on her side, knees drawn up. Smoothly, she rolled into a cross-legged position on the center of the mat.

"Meditation position," she said, putting her right palm over her left, thumbs touching. "Breathing in and out, blah blah." She crossed her arms over her midsection, bowed forward. "Thanking yourself for showing up, holding the practice in, then . . ."

She sat up again, put her palms together, bowed her head. "Namaste. That's it."

"Fifteen minutes, four seconds." Lips pursed, Teesha nodded. "That's really good."

"You're really bendy." Loren had edged out onto the terrace to sit on one of the sofas and munch chips. "I can't even touch my toes."

"Flexibility's important. The thing is, a flexible person has to go farther than an inflexible one to get any benefit." She could help him, she thought again. "Stand up, try to touch your toes."

"It's embarrassing."

"It's only embarrassing when you don't try."

He gave her a doubtful look but bent over from the waist, arms down. His fingertips didn't come within six inches of his toes.

"You're feeling the stretch."

"Shit, yeah!"

She mimicked his pose. "I get nothing, nothing until I go all the way down." She

87

stretched down, palms on the floor, nose to her knees. "We're getting the same benefit. Stand up, now inhale. No, when you inhale, you're inflating the balloon. Fill your lungs, extend the belly."

"Mine's extended twenty-four-seven." He laughed with it; so did the others. Adrian only smiled. "Just try it. Inhale, fill the balloon. Now you're going to deflate it, drawing the belly to the spine as you bend over to touch your toes."

When he tried it, she nodded. "And that's already a full inch closer. Breathing. It's all about the breath."

She glanced over, saw Hector leaning against the wall, studying his camera display.

"How does it look?"

"It's okay. I can study it and work out the angles. I can talk my dad into letting me use some stuff. You're going to need to be mic'd for the other stuff, and you need like an introduction or opening bit, right?"

"Yeah, I've been working on it. Oh, thanks." She took the Coke Teesha handed her, drank without thinking. Then stopped, closed her eyes. "Okay, that's so freaking good."

"I've got about twenty before I have to get home." Hector switched off the video. "Maybe we could go over the opening, and the transitions between each segment."

"We could storm the brain tomorrow." Loren tried another toe touch. "At lunch

88

period if you want to risk sitting with us two days in a row."

"I'll risk it."

By the time they left, and Adrian disposed of empty Coke bottles and chip bags, she realized she hadn't just found the production team for her pet project.

She'd found her tribe.

They brainstormed at lunch, rehearsed, and worked on details after school.

On Friday evening, she ordered pizza, stocked drinks. She helped her crew set up the equipment Hector scored. The light stand and barn doors and gels for evening shoots, the bounce, the umbrella for afternoons, the mic, the cables.

They managed to set up a makeshift studio with what Hector had begged or borrowed.

They ate pizza in the main level dining room with Loren's playlist of '80s hits rocking out.

With Wham! demanding to be waked up, Adrian finally had to ask. "Why the eighties?"

"Why not?"

"Because none of us were born?"

He pointed a finger. "That's a why, not a why not. It's history, dude. Music history. I'm thinking of doing one of the nineties next. You know, to analyze the societal fabric — where music plays into it — during our birth decade."

"That is totally nerd."

"Accepted." He bit into another slice. "I dig on music, man."

The Music Man," Teesha said between bites. "Robert Preston, Shirley Jones — the movie version, 1962. Preston also played the lead in the 1957 Broadway production, with Barbara Cook as Marian."

"How do you know that?" Adrian stared in wonder. "And why?"

"She reads it, she remembers it," Hector supplied.

"Hey, I should do a playlist of Broadway musical scores. Now that is total nerd."

"You get right on that, son." Hector glanced around. "This is an awesome space."

"Says the kid who lives in a mansion every other week and a penthouse not unlike this one the next." Teesha gulped some Coke.

Hector just shrugged. "Parents split, so I bounce between. Stepparents are okay, so far. And I got a little bro from the dad, little sis from the mom. They're cool."

"I used to want siblings. I had to get over it because that's never happening. What about you?" Adrian asked Teesha.

"Two older brothers, and parents stuck together like glue. The brothers are mostly okay, except when they're pains in my ass."

"Sister." Loren peeled a pepperoni off the pizza, popped it into his mouth. "She's ten. Parents separated for a few months back when, worked it out, got back together, and out popped Princess Rosalind. Kind of a brat."

"Kind of?" Teesha said with a laugh.

"Okay, a complete brat, but she's way spoiled, so it's not her fault so much. You got the only child deal," he said to Adrian. "All the attention."

"My mother's career gets that, and I get what's left. That's okay," she said quickly. "It means she's not on my back most of the time. And I'm going to have my own career. You guys are helping me start that."

"And when you're a YouTube star . . ." Teesha heaved a big, exaggerated sigh. "We'll still be the three nerds while you sit at the cool kids' table."

"Not a chance. And since it's the nerd table for me for the duration, I should be an honorary nerd."

"No honorary about it. You are a nerd," Hector told her. "You drink carrot juice and eat granola on purpose. Your mom's gone for a couple weeks, but you're working instead of running on the wild side. You're the fitness nerd."

She'd never considered herself a nerd, by any standards, but when she'd finished her bedtime yoga practice and slipped under the covers by ten, she realized the term applied.

And she really didn't mind.

CHAPTER FIVE

They started before dawn on Saturday morning. Adrian had what she called "craft services" set up with juices, bagels, fresh fruit, and since she'd learned all three of her friends went for fancy coffee, a pod coffee maker with a variety.

She'd have to store that in her room afterward, as Lina ran a strict no-caffeine household.

Pleased with the first segment — the light had been perfect — she went down to change her gear, maybe her hair before starting the next.

Teesha went with her as wardrobe assistant.

If it surprised Teesha that Adrian stripped down to the skin without a blush once the bedroom door closed, she tried to pretend otherwise.

"I was going to see if I can get my hair pinned back, but unless I spray it with concrete, it probably won't stay through fifteen of cardio dance."

Teesha pursed her lips as Adrian wiggled into sleek, snug, midcalf leggings. "Why don't you braid the sides, pin those back?"

"Braids?" Adrian pulled on a matching blue sports bra. "With this hair?"

"Hey, I got Black girl hair. You see these braids? I can do it. What product you got?"

Adrian slipped a bright pink tank over the bra. And since she'd choreographed a hip-hop-influenced routine, she'd tie a plaid hoodie around her waist and wear high-tops.

"All of them, out of desperation and despair."

"Sit down, girlfriend. I got this."

And she did. Adrian stared in the mirror, awed with the results. "I can't believe it. It's a miracle. It looks cute and, you know, funky, but contained. You're going to have to teach me."

"Can do." Teesha smiled into the mirror. "It's nice, you know, having another girl join the club. I got me some balance now. You know, Rizz, maybe you can teach me some of the yoga stuff. It looks like fun."

"It is fun. I'll teach you."

The cardio dance segment was fun, too. It took three takes before she and the others signed off with Loren working the audio, Hector the camera, and Teesha moving between both.

By the time the lunch she'd ordered in arrived, they had three segments. They fit in two more before the dinner break, and finished the day with the evening yoga at sunset.

"I didn't think we could get so much done in one day. That only leaves the total body session, the voice-overs, and the introduction." Adrian flopped down on one of the outdoor sofas. "Maybe I'll work in a ten-minute ab bonus."

"I'm going to burn a copy," Hector decided. "I want to play around a little."

"Like how?"

"Just try some stuff. No problemo if it doesn't work, we've got the master. How about we start at like ten tomorrow? We keep up this pace, it's done by one or two. Some production, editing, la-di-da, we get it up by the end of the week. If we need to reshoot anything, we can work that in, but I think we're good."

"That would be amazing."

By the time they left, ravaging through any lunch and dinner leftovers, it neared midnight. Adrian stretched out in bed and smiled into the dark.

She had friends, she had work, she had a path, and she knew just where she intended to go on it.

They rolled right into it with Adrian doing the intro first so she wouldn't get sweaty or need another change. She looked right into the camera, the city at her back.

"Hi, I'm Adrian Rizzo, and this is *About Time.*" She slid into her spiel, highlighting each segment, emphasizing the fifteen-minute length, the ability to do one, do a combination.

"You're good at this," Hector told her. "I hang with my dad sometimes when he's shooting. The actors never — hardly ever — get it in one take."

"I practiced. A lot."

"It was solid, but let's do a second take, just backup. And you could move around more. I'll follow you."

They wrapped the video by noon. They had to drag the furniture back into place before they set up in the quietest spot in the triplex: her mother's dressing room.

"Wow." Wide-eyed, Teesha wandered the ruthlessly organized room. "Your mom's got some awesome clothes. I thought my mother had the duds, but yours beats her to hell and back squared. There's like . . ." Her gaze tracked back and forth. "A hundred pairs of shoes. Twenty-six athletic shoes. Nice colors."

"It used to be when she did a video or an appearance, they'd give her the workout clothes and shoes she wears in them. They get credit on the DVD, and she gets the gear. Now she has her own line."

And so would she, Adrian thought. One day.

95

Adrian stood in the center of the room, Hector's laptop open on a shelf in front of her and cued up to the first yoga segment.

"The mic has a pop filter," Hector told her as he fixed it to the stand. "So you don't like pop your *p*'s and all that shit. Dad let me borrow it. And the headphones. Everybody's going to wear a pair and be like totally silent. You gotta fart, you hold it in.

"Loren's on sound. He starts the recording, I give you the signal, I start the video, you start talking."

"Got it."

She put on her headphones, took some slow, easy breaths. When Hector swiped a finger through the air toward her, she began.

"Morning Sun Salutation. Stand at the top of your mat."

When she finished with a Namaste, Hector waited a moment, then gave Loren the cut signal. "That was freaking perfect. Tell me you got it all, Loren, because that was freaking on!"

"Sound's good. It's really quiet in here. All inside walls. And she — you, Adrian — sounded, like, soothing."

"Then the plan worked. Can we go ahead and do the sunset one, since we're on a roll?"

"Fucking A!" Hector told her, and set it up.

At the end, Loren pulled off his headphones, shot up both thumbs. "Dudes, we got the gold."

"We need to play them back, make sure everything worked like my dad said it would. Any screwups, he said I could call him and he'd walk us through."

"He sounds nice," Adrian said.

"Yeah, he's a good one."

"Let's take it downstairs." Blowing out a breath, Adrian rolled her shoulders. "Sit down, spread out, check it out."

"And order pizza."

She looked over at Loren. "We had pizza Friday."

Rising from her seat on the floor, Teesha angled her head. "Your point?"

"Okay, I'll order up pizza."

She'd stocked Cokes, and knew she had to have any evidence of them out of the apartment before her mother's return. She worried, a little, she'd developed an attachment to them that wouldn't be so easy to break.

But as she sat slouched next to Teesha on the sofa while Hector cued up the video, she decided it was worth it. It was all worth it.

"You're sure I sound okay? Not boring?"

"Calm," Teesha said. "You got the calm down, Rizz."

"Soothing," Hector said at the same time.

"Do the cues really work? Wait! Let's find out. I'm going to get a couple mats. Teesha and Loren can do the practice."

"What? I can't do that stuff."

97

Adrian spared Loren a glance as she jogged up the stairs. "How do you know? And I'll show you how to modify. Then Hector and I can do the sunset segment."

Hector opened his mouth to protest, but she'd already jogged up to the third floor.

"I can't do that stuff," Loren repeated, his head ticktocking between his friends. "I could puke, or maybe break something."

"Don't be such a dumbass." Teesha got up when Adrian ran back down with the mats.

"This is just what we need to make sure. Test out the segments. I should've thought of it before. Let's take it out on the terrace. Fresh air, plenty of room."

"I'm game." Teesha marched over, opened the doors to the main level terrace. "Come on, Loren. Don't be a wuss."

"If I puke, it's not my fault. And I could get like vertigo from the height."

"*Vertigo,* 1958, Alfred Hitchcock classic starring Jimmy Stewart and Kim Novak." Teesha shrugged. "I saw it on TV."

Loren didn't puke, but he did groan a lot. And flushed hot pink whenever Adrian moved to him, adjusted his stance or position with hands on his hips or shoulders.

"It's working," Adrian murmured to Hector. "I can see it's working. They're both total beginners but they can follow the cues. Just need help with alignment, need practice. But that's what yoga is. It's continual practice so . . . Pizza. I'll get it."

Thrilled, Adrian grabbed the money she'd set on the table inside and danced her way to the door.

Then froze when she opened it.

"Pizza party?" Harry Reese, Lina's publicity director, held two pizza boxes.

His left eyebrow arched up the way it did when he was being sarcastic or amused, or both. As always, he looked trim and stylish in black jeans, a black leather jacket with a pale gray T-shirt, and low black boots.

"Harry. I didn't think you were back until . . ."

He angled his head. "Until it was safe?"

"No. No. And it's not a party. It's work."

"Uh-huh." He stepped inside the foyer, six feet of handsome with perfectly styled brown hair, clever brown eyes, and a face her grandmother once said had been chiseled by skilled and magic elves.

"It is! You can see for yourself." She took the pizza boxes. "My friends and coworkers." She gestured to the glass doors through which she could still see Teesha and Loren trying to do the segment, and Hector grinning at them.

She also saw, as he did, the Coke bottles, the bag of chips, the pairs of sneakers, somebody's hoodie, scattered over the living area.

"Did she send you to check up on me?"

99

"No. I came home for a couple days because Lina has this afternoon and all day tomorrow off, and I wanted to deal with some things. And I wanted to see Marsh. I ran into the pizza guy downstairs. I took care of it."

"Thanks."

Marshall Tucker and Harry had been together for three years, and though she adored them both, Adrian still cursed the timing.

"Going to introduce me to your friends?"

"Sure. Listen, Harry . . ."

"I'm not going to bust you for having friends over, unless I discover you're holding sex orgies and didn't invite me."

"As if. We're working, I swear. I had a project, and they've helped me put it together."

Maybe her stomach jittered as she crossed to the doors, but she did her best to radiate confidence as she pulled them open. "Hey, guys, let's pause it. This is Harry. He's my mother's publicity director."

Maybe they could have looked more guilty, but Harry figured they'd have needed to work on it.

"How's it going? Outdoor yoga with a pizza chaser. Sounds pretty good."

"Harry, this is Hector and Teesha and Loren. We go to school together."

So she'd made friends already, which he considered a positive — as he'd argued on her behalf when Lina decided to transfer her in her junior year.

"We've been working on a video," Adrian continued. "Hector's a videographer — his father let us borrow some equipment."

"Yeah?" Harry moved toward the laptop. "What kind of video?"

"A seven-segment fitness video. We're going to put it up on YouTube."

"For school?"

"No. No, not for school."

"Does this mean I can stop?" Loren pushed at his hair. "I'm getting sweaty."

Harry walked around the table to look at the laptop screen where Adrian, on pause, held in Warrior II with the sun rising over the river at her back.

"Wow, that's great light."

"It's the first fifteen-minute segment. The morning Sun Salutation. We were just trying it out."

"Don't let me stop you. Hector?"

Hector, who'd very carefully said nothing, shoved his glasses up his nose and nodded. "Yes, sir."

"Jesus, let's not do the 'sir' thing. How about pushing play."

"Ah, sure."

Continue to gaze over your right hand as you turn it, palm up, then raise your right arm up, looking up to your palm, lowering your left arm down the back of your left leg as you move into Reverse Warrior.

"I'm getting a Coke. Anybody want a Coke?"

Teesha gave Loren the bug eye and said, "Ssh!"

"What? I'm thirsty."

"Got enough for the whole class?" Harry asked as he continued to watch Adrian on-screen. "Wouldn't mind one myself. And the pizza smells good. A slice is the price for my silence."

"I'll get plates and stuff," Teesha volunteered.

"Thanks. Harry," Adrian added.

"Ssh." He gestured her back, watched another minute before he hit pause. He looked at Hector again.

"You shot this?"

"Yes, sir. I mean, yeah."

"How old are you?"

"Um. Seventeen."

"What are you, a freaking prodigy?"

Hector hunched his shoulders, let them fall.

"Seven segments, Ads?"

"Yeah, I thought seven to —"

"How many have you finished?"

"Seven."

"Jesus. Show me another."

"Cardio dance. It's instruction in eight-count beats, cumulative, repeating until we've got the whole deal, and we do that three times. I got the music from public domain. It's okay, we just needed the beat."

He watched the first few minutes, taking the glass of Coke from Teesha when she brought it over. "Changed your outfit and hair, smart, different angle on the city backdrop, that's good. Lighting and sound are good, too. You've got presence and talent, Adrian, but you always have."

He hit pause himself, sat back. "And you're not putting these on YouTube."

"Harry!"

"You're not putting them up when your mother has a production company."

"This is mine. We did this. It's not hers."

He took a slow sip as he studied her stubborn face. "You've got a product, she's got the means to highlight and market that product. If the rest of this is as good as what I've seen, I'm going to bat for you. If it's not, you'll make it as good, and I'll go to bat for you. What are you calling it?"

"*About Time,* and my company is New Generation. My company, when I work that out."

He smiled at her. "I'm going to help you work that out. Don't be stupid and not use what's in your lap, Ads. Your mother's agent, her well-established company, me. New Generation works, and for now that production company can be under the wide umbrella of Yoga Baby. DVDs, Adrian. The agent, the lawyers, you, and your mom will work out all the details, and the deal. You'll get money up front, you'll get a solid percentage of sales. The lion's share — I'm going to push for that, don't worry. I'm on your side here."

"You're always on my side."

"That's right." He put an arm out to draw her close to where he sat. "You know you can trust me to look out for you."

"I do trust you."

"Then listen to Daddy. Let me bring this to your mom — after I preview it all."

Considering, trying her best to weigh each side — she'd really wanted just her own, but . . . "You guys have a say, too. We did this together."

"Yeah, but it's your project," Hector reminded her.

"DVDs would be cool. Like for sale and everything. I'm just saying," Loren added when Hector stared at him. "I mean YouTube, that's cool, too, but if you look at the big picture . . ."

"Teesha?"

Teesha lifted her shoulders. "Your call, Hector's right. But we did a really good job. I mean, like seriously."

Adrian paced to the wall, stared out, paced back. "Say we did it your way. Say Mom agrees to produce and market. It's my production company on the DVD, under the umbrella, like you said. And I'm billed as executive producer and choreographer."

"That's fair."

"Hector's billed as producer and videographer. Loren as producer and sound, Teesha as producer and lighting. And they get scale for each title."

"What's scale?" When Loren murmured it, Hector waved him away.

"And five percent of the profits on the back end. Each."

"I think, realistically, your agent's going to say two percent."

"We'll negotiate. If it gets that far."

"DVDs like this sell for — it's going to be a two-disk set because of the length." Teesha, head angled, looked up at the sky. "Like $22.95."

"She's already a brand," Harry pointed out. "Two-disk set, we'll price it around $29.99."

"Okay. Figure what Adrian's invested, the cost of production and manufacturing, producing the cover and case, the vendor discount, marketing costs . . . Call it net $10.50, but that's a guess until I do some research. So that's — at the two percent — like twenty-one cents for each of us per sale, on top of the scale payment. Maybe it sells like a hundred thousand copies. That would be like twenty-one thousand dollars. Each."

"With Yoga Baby behind it, the Rizzo brand, the fresh take?" Harry studied Teesha as he spoke. "We'd project a million in sales."

She stared at him. "Two percent's good."

"Are you all prodigies?"

"We're nerds," Hector told him.

"Okay, nerds, let's eat some pizza and look at what you've got here."

When he finished, when nothing remained of the pizzas but fond memories, Harry sat back. "Okay. Okay, boys and girls. In my never humble opinion, you've got something here. Hector, can you burn me a DVD?"

"Sure. I could email you the file."

"Do both. I'm flying out Monday afternoon to hook up with Lina in Denver. I'll show it to her, give her the pitch." He rose, rolling his shoulders as he strolled around the terrace. "It's too late to get it produced, promoted, and distributed for holiday sales, but we can hit the January guilt spike in workout sales and interest."

He turned back. "Nerds, if you haven't told your parents what you've been doing, now's the time. They need to clear you to sign contracts." He dug into his pocket, pulled out his silver business card case, set a few cards on the table. "Any questions, your parents can contact me. Hector, you can send the file to the email address on the card. And be prepared. This is going to move fast."

Hector carefully labeled the disk he'd copied. "My dad knows. I mean, except all this today. And, you know, he's in the business and all." He cased the disk, handed it to Harry.

"All right then, I've got to get home. Thanks for the pizza."

"You paid for it," Adrian pointed out as she rose to walk him out.

"You're right. You're welcome." He draped an arm around her shoulders as they walked. "Does Mimi know?"

"No."

"Tell her. She'll be on your side."

"Okay, but, Harry —"

"Trust me." He kissed the top of her head. "I've got you."

Two seconds after she closed the door, cheers erupted from the terrace. Awkward dancing ensued.

They didn't know Lina Rizzo, Adrian thought. But what the hell, they had Harry in their corner.

She did a handspring.

Some thirty-six hours later and at thirty thousand feet, Lina watched two segments on Harry's laptop. She sipped sparkling water — no ice — as the plane soared toward Dallas.

"Seven of these?"

"That's right."

"She should have done six ten-minute segments to make it a clean hour."

"Two-disk set, the intro and opening and

107

three segments on the first, four segments on the second. Two clean hours. Fifteen is more of a commitment, and put two together, you've got a thirty-minute workout."

"What was that music in the cardio routine — and that outfit?"

"It's hip-hop, Lina. It's a good, fresh, energetic vibe. A fun one, and she outfitted herself to suit it."

Lina just shook her head, played the next two segments. Knowing his quarry, Harry said nothing.

"You knew nothing about this?"

"No. She wanted to do it herself. She was enterprising, creative, work-focused. She found contemporaries at school who had the skills to help her realize it. They're good kids."

"You spent, what, a couple hours with them and know that?"

"Yeah. I also spoke with their parents, but yeah, they're clearly good, smart kids. Seriously smart," he added. "She's made friends, Lina, and with them she accomplished something special."

"And now, saying nothing to me, going behind my back to do this when I'm out of town, she expects me to not only approve, but to produce."

"No, she doesn't. I do. You can look at it as her doing it behind your back or you can look at it as her wanting to do something on her own. To prove herself. And you can't look at what she did and claim she hasn't proven herself. You should be proud of her."

Lina studied her water, then took a slow sip. "I'm not saying she didn't do a decent job, but —"

"Stop there." He held up a hand. "Don't qualify it. And we both know it's a damn good job. Let me set aside my personal relationship with you, with Adrian, and talk to you as your publicity director. You help her set up her company, and you produce this two-pack DVD, you're going to help her boost her brand. And you're going to add more shine to your own."

"A bunch of teenagers as producers."

"It's the hook, Lina." He grinned, and grinned broadly. "You know a shiny gold hook as well as I do. And that story's going to sell a crap ton of DVDs. I can pitch the angles to the moon and back."

"You can pitch dirt to the moon and back."

"That's my skill," he said cheerfully. "But this? This is solid, shiny gold."

"Maybe. Maybe. I'll think about it. Watch the rest and consider it."

And he was right, she thought. She knew he was right. She just didn't want to give in too easily.

"If you hadn't gone home and dropped by . . . Which irritated the hell out of me," she added, "you taking those two days."

"I needed to keep an appointment, which I

told you before we left."

"Deserted in Denver."

He smiled as she'd meant him to. "It was important."

"And apparently a deep, dark secret."

"Not anymore." He blew out a breath. "Marshall and I have a surrogate."

"A surrogate?" She'd lifted her water glass and now set it down with a clink. "For a baby?"

"Yeah. And before you start, we agreed not to say anything until she hit twelve weeks. It's like the line. We want a family, Lina, so we have a surrogate, and Monday morning, we went with her for that twelve-week check. And we — we heard the heartbeat."

His eyes teared up. "We heard the heartbeat and . . ."

He pulled up the briefcase at his feet, opened it to take out an ultrasound. "It's our baby. Mine and Marsh's."

Lina leaned over, studied it, blinked at her own tears. "I can't see a fucking thing in there."

"Me either!" On a watery laugh, he gripped Lina's hand. "But that's my son or daughter — somewhere in there. And on or about April sixteenth, I'm going to be a father. Marsh and I are going to be daddies."

"You'll be great ones. You'll be great." She signaled the flight attendant. "We need champagne."

"I want to tell the world, but you're the first." He gave her hand a hard squeeze. "Give me a present, and produce Adrian's DVD. You won't be sorry."

"Tricky of you to get me when I'm emotional." She let out a sigh. "All right."

That didn't mean she didn't have things to say to her daughter, advice and demands she expected to be heeded. When she walked back into the apartment, tipped the bellmen for taking her bags into the master, she wanted nothing more than a long shower and the eight hours' sleep she found impossible on tour.

But first things first. She couldn't seem to help putting first things first. She unpacked, separating laundry from dry cleaning, putting away her shoes and the small selection of jewelry she allowed herself on the road.

She hung up the scarves and jackets she'd needed in the cooler cities.

She went downstairs, poured herself a sparkling water, added a slice of lemon. And decided she'd timed it very well when she heard the door open.

She walked out to see her daughter in her school uniform with a light jacket, as the weather had cooled enough, a backpack on one shoulder. And a careful expression.

"George said you were back. Welcome home."

"Thanks."

111

They crossed the room to each other, exchanged light cheek kisses.

"Let's sit down and talk about this project of yours."

"I spoke with Maddie, and since you approved, she's willing to represent me and my friends. She said the contract should be ready soon."

"I'm aware." Lina sat, gestured for Adrian to do the same. "You can thank Harry for cheerleading you through this."

"I do thank him."

"Which wouldn't have been necessary if you'd consulted with me."

"If I'd consulted with you, it would have been a collaboration. I wanted to do it myself, and I did. Or I did it with Hector, Teesha, and Loren."

"Whom I've never met, and know little to nothing about."

"What do you want to know — that you haven't already looked into?"

"We'll get to that. If you'd wanted to do a project like this, I could have provided you with some guidance, a studio, professionals."

"Your studio, your professionals. I wanted something else, and I did it. And it's good. I know it's good. Maybe it's not as slick and polished as it would have been with your studio, your professionals, but it's good.

"You started from scratch," Adrian continued before Lina could speak again. "I know

I'm not. I know I've got advantages you didn't because you built something important. I know there are people who'll say I have it all easy, breaking in, because you held the door open and boosted me up. Some of that's true, but I'll know I could do this. And I know I can build my own."

"And how? On a rooftop with borrowed equipment and schoolmates?"

"It's a start. I'm going to get into Columbia, and I'll major in exercise science, minor in business and nutrition. I sure as hell don't intend to get knocked up and —"

She broke off, shocked at herself, as Lina stiffened and sat forward.

"I'm sorry. I'm sorry, that was ugly and wrong and disrespectful. You make me feel like I have to justify everything I want or don't, everything I do or don't. But I'm sorry."

Lina set her glass down, then rose to walk to the terrace doors. She opened them to the air. "You're more like me than you realize. That's a tough break for you. The video's good — you have talent, we both know that. The concept and delivery are . . . interesting. Harry will hype the crap out of it, you'll do whatever publicity he pulls out of his hat, and I'll, naturally, endorse it. We'll see where it goes."

She turned back. "How long have you been working on this?"

"I've been working on the idea, the routines, the timing, the approach for about six months, I guess."

With a nod, Lina walked back for her glass. "Well, we'll see where it goes. I want a shower. We can order in for dinner."

"I planned to make that chickpea curry you like. I thought you'd be tired of room service and restaurant food."

"You're right about that. That would be nice."

New Generation, in association with Baby Yoga, launched *About Time* on January second. Adrian spent her winter break doing publicity, and so deeply missed spending Christmas with her grandparents she vowed never to do so again.

The sales for the first month told her she'd chosen the right path, and that she'd keep right on climbing it.

She started planning her next project.

She got her first death threat in February.

Lina studied the single sheet of white paper. The block printing, black and thick, composed a poem.

Some bring roses to the stone that marks
    the grave
As to their grief they are a slave.
But you will have no flowers and no stone,
For when I bring you death, you'll be alone.

"It came in this." With a trembling hand, Adrian held out the envelope to her mother. "It was in the post office box we got for the fan mail on the DVD. I picked it up after school. There's no name or return address."

"No, of course not."

"The postmark, it says Columbus, Ohio. Why does somebody in Columbus, Ohio, want to kill me?"

"They don't. It's just someone being ugly. I'm surprised this is the first of this type of thing you've gotten. Harry keeps a file of mine."

That shocked nearly as much as the poem.

"Threats? You have a file of threats?"

Lina reached for a towel. She'd been choreographing a new routine when Adrian burst into the gym.

"Threats, equally ugly sexual suggestions, garden-variety bitchiness." She handed the letter back to Adrian. "Put it in the envelope. We'll report it, make a copy. The police will take the original. But I can tell you, it won't go anywhere. So we put it in a file, you put it away and forget it."

"Forget somebody said I should die? Why would anybody want that?"

"Adrian." Lina tossed the towel over one shoulder, reached for her water bottle. "A lot of people are just screwed up. They're jealous, obsessed, angry, unhappy. You're young, pretty, successful. You've been on TV, you were on the covers of *Seventeen* and *Shape*."

"But . . . You never told me you'd gotten threats."

"No point in it. And no point in you worrying about this. We'll give it to Harry, and he'll take care of it."

"So you're saying death threats are just part of the rest?"

Lina hung up the towel, set the bottle aside. "I'm saying this won't be your last, and you'll get used to it. Call Harry. He knows what to do."

Adrian glanced back as she left, saw her mother facing the mirrored wall again as she restarted a series of burpees.

She'd call Harry, Adrian thought. But she'd never, never get used to it.

CHAPTER SIX

To make up for missing Christmas, Adrian spent two weeks over the summer with her grandparents. She reconnected with Maya, spent time with the aging Tom and Jerry, spent time in the garden, in the kitchen with her grandparents.

They welcomed her three New York friends for a week so they could shoot another video.

She'd carry with her, always, the memories of her grandparents sitting on the big porch watching her set up an outdoor yoga segment. Of coming downstairs in the morning to see her grandmother and Teesha chatting away over coffee in the kitchen.

Then fall brought school and the color-washed leaves. Though Harry wanted to screen her mail, she insisted on looking through it herself. She found some of the ugly, some of the obscene, but the good far outweighed it.

She didn't forget it, but she set it aside.

But the poet didn't. Thoughts of her lived in that angry and patient brain. But there was time, so much time yet. And there were others. Many others who would come before.

She, a crescendo, a culmination. But before the crescendo, one needed to begin.

From a list, a name was chosen to be the first. Adrian Rizzo would be the last, and Margaret West, the first.

It began with the stalking, the hunting, the watching, the recording. Such a thrill! Who knew there could be such a thrill in planning?

Well planned, with a simple, straightforward termination seemed best all around. Easy strolls by the quiet house, hours at the computer. Just another diner in a trendy restaurant enjoying a meal while the prey ate and laughed and drank.

See how she moves, with no idea her time is ticking, ticking away. How she samples a spoonful of dessert and rolls her eyes in pleasure and laughs with the man she'd be lucky to spread her legs for later.

Divorced and on the prowl, that was Maggie!

And when the plans fell into place, how the heart beat in the blood. All the time, the skill, the practice merging together. Cut the alarm on that quiet, now sleeping house. Pick the lock on the back door, safe in those shadows.

Another thrill, walking through the house, all but gliding up the stairs. Make the turn toward the room where the lights went out last at night.

Bedroom.

Sleeping. Sleeping so peacefully. Hard, so hard to resist the urge to wake her, show her the gun, tell her why.

Two hands to hold the gun steady. Not trembling with nerves, but excitement. Pure excitement.

The gun barely popped the first time with the silencer. The second, a bit louder and the third, louder yet. Still a fourth, just for the delight of it.

How her body had jumped. How that small sound she'd made echoed in the dark room.

How terrible, they'd say. Murdered in her own bed! Such a fine neighborhood. Such a lovely woman!

But they didn't really know the bitch, did they?

To throw the police off — idiots — steal a few things.

Souvenirs.

The thought of taking a photo of the work came too late, blocks from the quiet house.

Next time. Next time there would be photos to look back on.

Adrian released the second video in January, but since she'd insisted on learning to drive, she drove to Maryland in the car she'd bought with her profits to spend Christmas at the house on the hill.

She'd agreed to do some remotes, some phoners, but she would spend Christmas in Traveler's Creek.

Lina spent most of the month, including the holidays, in Aruba shooting.

The second poem arrived, like the first, in February, though this one carried a postmark from Memphis.

You think you're special and so elite,
But you're a fraud and incomplete.
One day you'll pay for living a lie.
That's the day I help you die.

She didn't bother to tell Lina this time — as Lina had said, what was the point? She made a copy for her own file and gave the original to Harry.

She concentrated on school, on a concept for her next video.

And tried not to obsess about admittance to Columbia after Teesha got her letter, after Loren got into Harvard and Hector into UCLA.

She had backup colleges, of course. She wasn't stupid. But she wanted Columbia. And she wanted to room with Teesha.

She wanted.

When she opened the acceptance packet

120

from Columbia, she danced on all three floors of the triplex.

She called her grandparents, texted her friends, texted Harry. Since her mother was doing an event in Las Vegas, Adrian copied the acceptance letter and put it on her mother's desk.

She said goodbye to high school with no regrets, and began what she thought of as the next leg of her path.

Adrian attacked college strategically, selecting electives she felt enhanced her goals, pumping her energies into learning and earning solid grades, and earmarking summers for video shoots and long visits to Maryland.

She had plans, lots of plans, and by her senior year at Columbia, many had fallen neatly into place. She and Teesha shared an apartment in easy walking distance to campus — paying the rent with the profits from Adrian's annual DVDs.

She'd begun working with another student, a fashion design major, on developing her own line of fitness and athletic wear.

While Teesha fell in and out of love, or at least lust, with careless ease, Adrian kept her dating life casual.

She didn't have time for love. Lust she considered not only a simpler matter, but the satisfaction and release of it a part of good health — when approached safely and without demands.

Her business relationship with her mother, while complex, boosted both their brands. Their personal relationship remained as Adrian felt it had always stood: distant but amicable.

As long as neither crossed the other.

On a blustering February evening, Adrian walked into the restaurant struggling to push aside her anxiety over what she thought of as her annual Ugly Valentine. This one, postmarked from Boulder, made the sixth. The fact that there'd been no follow-through, no escalation, didn't comfort her. Their consistency signaled someone very focused and unnaturally obsessed.

She'd nearly called off the dinner meeting with her agent and Harry, but pushed herself out the door with the latest poem weighing like lead in her purse.

Since, as always, she arrived early, she thought to have a drink at the bar to ease her nerves rather than sit alone at a table in the dining room.

The thrum of conversation and energy helped. She gave her name to the hostess, then turned into the bar with its dark wood, its old exposed brick. She started to grab a stool, then spotted a familiar face at one of the high-tops.

She'd seen Raylan a handful of times since

he'd left home for college in Savannah, and since Maya kept her updated knew he'd scored coveted internships with Marvel Comics that led to an entry-level position as an artist at its New York headquarters.

The boy with sketches all over his bedroom walls had landed what she assumed was his dream job.

And the gorgeous blonde with him had to be the artist he'd fallen for in college and now had a long-distance relationship with while she, like Adrian, completed her senior year.

She hesitated — they looked so involved with each other they might have been on some deserted beach in the moonlight. But she could hardly pretend she hadn't seen the brother of her oldest friend.

They looked like artists, she thought as she started toward their table. Raylan with that burnt honey hair waving over the collar of his shirt, the woman — Adrian couldn't pull out the name — with her sun-washed braid halfway down her back.

Raylan glanced over as she approached, and those green eyes scanned her face, first with puzzlement, then dawning recognition.

She felt a little buzz — but then his eyes always managed that.

"Well, hey, Adrian."

"Hey back, Raylan. I heard you were working in New York."

"Yeah, Lorilee Winthrop, this is Adrian Rizzo, a good pal of Maya's. Adrian, this is Lorilee, my . . ."

"Fiancée. Just today!" Even in excitement Lorilee's voice carried images of magnolias, Spanish moss, and cold sweet tea sipped on verandas. She stuck out her hand, with its pretty diamond on the third finger.

"Oh my God." Instinctively, Adrian took the offered hand, felt the warmth, the thrill. "It's beautiful. Congratulations. Wow, Raylan, congratulations. I can't believe Maya didn't text me."

"We haven't told anybody yet."

"I'm a blabbermouth. I can't help it."

"Do me a favor, don't tell Maya we told you first. You know," Raylan added. "Maybe act surprised when she tells you."

"I can do that. Consider it an engagement present."

"Do you want to sit down?" Lorilee invited. "Maya's told me a lot about you, and I met your grandparents. They're just wonderful, aren't they? Oh, I love your DVDs. And I just can't stop talking. Raylan, honey, get Adrian a chair."

"No, no, but thanks. I'm meeting people — I'm just a little early."

"You live in New York. I can't believe I'm going to move here next spring."

Raylan looked at his fiancée as if she were the only woman in this world or any. Adrian

124

felt a little sigh, a little tug inside her.

"In case you couldn't tell, Lorilee's a southern girl."

"Really? I'd never have guessed. And an artist, too, I'm told."

"I'm trying. What I really want to do is teach art. I love kids. Raylan, honey, we have to have a dozen."

He smiled at her. Adrian swore she could count the stars on the deep green sea of his eyes.

"Maybe half a dozen."

"Sounds like a negotiation." Adrian laughed, and tried to imagine the boy she'd known with half a dozen kids.

And oddly, she could.

"Raylan, your mom and Maya are going to be over the moon. They're crazy about you," she told Lorilee.

"Oh! That's so sweet of you to say."

"I speak true. Maya's told me a lot about you, too, and one thing she told me is you're too good for Raylan."

"More true," Raylan said. "As long as she doesn't believe it until a year from June when it's official, I'm gold."

"You're so silly." Lorilee leaned over the table to kiss him.

"And there's my dinner meeting. I'm so glad we ran into each other. And whatever Maya thinks, I say the two of you look perfect together. Congratulations again."

125

"It was just wonderful meeting you."

"You, too."

Adrian walked away to exchange quick hugs with her agent, with Harry. Before they settled at their table, she ordered a bottle of champagne for Raylan's.

Perfect together, she thought again, and found their happiness so infectious she didn't realize she'd forgotten about the poem in her purse.

Three days later, she received a thank-you note — with hand-painted tulips on the front — from Lorilee.

Dear Adrian,

Thank you so much for the champagne. It was incredibly thoughtful, so unexpected. We wanted to thank you in person, but didn't want to interrupt your meeting.

I'm so glad we met, and on the happiest day of my life. Jan and Maya love you so much, and I love them. That means, by connection, I love you, too. I hope you don't mind.

I'm going to keep doing your workouts, and they're going to help me look amazing on my wedding day.

Thanks again,
Lorilee (the future Mrs. Wells!)

Though Adrian didn't consider herself

sentimental, she found the card so charming, she kept it.

After she graduated in the spring, she dived straight into a new video. Though she'd hired dancers and trainers to participate in previous shoots, this time she strong-armed Teesha and Loren.

"I'm going to look like an idiot."

In his sweatpants and New Gen tee, Loren stood six feet now. He'd trimmed down, had let his fire-red hair grow enough to handle what Teesha called his "lawyer do."

"You won't," Adrian assured him. "You did fine in the rehearsals. Now you just follow my cues."

"You can't cue me to suddenly develop rhythm. I'm going to screw up that cardio dance bit. Why Latin style, Ads? With the hips and all that."

"Because it's fun." She poked him in the stomach. "And you look great. How much did you lose?"

He rolled his eyes. "Twenty-five after I put on the Freshman Ten and you started nagging my ass long-distance."

"She never gave me a chance to gain the ten. Long-distance?" Teesha rolled her eyes back at him. "That's nothing compared to rooming with."

"You look good."

Teesha wiggled her hips, fluffed at the

ebony halo she wore since she'd whacked off her braids. "I do. I surely do. I am rocking this outfit."

"What there is of it," Hector said as he walked the space again.

She wore snug black shorts, a black sports bra with candy-pink piping, and a pink New Gen hoodie tied around her waist.

"Got it, flaunting it."

"Uh-huh." Hector, sporting a goatee and a short ponytail, shoved up his wire-framed glasses. "You know there are pigeons in here."

"Adds ambiance."

Adrian had picked the old building, the roofless-in-some-spots building, for just that. She'd yet to use an actual studio or slick gym, and from the feedback, her audience enjoyed her more offbeat locations.

She only grinned when the scream of a siren echoed. "Authentic ambiance. And instead of professionals, we have two regular people."

Except for the lighting and sound crew, Hector's assistants.

But still, when it came down to it, not that far from a weekend on a rooftop that ce-mented friendships and launched her dreams.

"Okay, thirty-four-minute dance cardio's up first."

She wore candy-pink shorts with a faux black belt, pink halter-style sports bra with black piping. She let her shoulder-length hair do whatever the hell it wanted for this routine.

She took her mark, waited for Hector — who doubled as director — to give her the go. And smiled into Hector's camera.

"Hi, I'm Adrian Rizzo. Welcome to *For Your Body*. This two-disk set will take you through a fun and challenging cardio dance with Latin flavor. A thirty-minute routine focused on your core, thirty minutes of strength training with light and medium weights, a bonus round for thirty-five minutes for a full-body workout that hits every muscle. And finally, thirty-five minutes of yoga.

"We're in New York City today." She glanced up as a pigeon flew overhead. "Joined by some local wildlife. I have my friends with me. Teesha."

Teesha gave a snappy salute.

"And Loren."

Adrian laughed when Loren held his hand up in the Vulcan greeting.

"Remember, you can do any part of this video, switch it up, combine it. Do what's good for you, but do something, because it's for your body."

It worked, she could feel it. She knew it when she heard Teesha laugh, heard Loren's muttered counts.

It worked when, during the core session, Loren collapsed back on his mat and called for his mommy.

129

It worked for three long, full days and ended with pizza and wine on the floor of the apartment Adrian and Teesha shared.

"My abs are still screaming," Loren claimed.

"We woke them up."

He took a huge bite of pizza. "They want to go back to sleep. Maybe forever. Next time I'll run the camera and Hector can melt into a pool of his own sweat."

"I'm a behind-the-scenes guy." Hector took a sip of the wine he hoped to develop a taste for. "And I'm going to be behind the scenes in Northern Ireland for the next two months."

Teesha pushed straight up. "What scenes?"

"An HBO series. I'm assistant on the B-roll crew, but I'm in." He grinned a mile wide. "Hollywood, baby. Well, Northern Ireland's version."

"That's big time, dude." Loren shot out a finger. "Big time."

"It's a step toward middle time that could lead to big. You better not boot me as your videographer." Hector shot his own finger at Adrian.

"Never. Jesus, Hector Sung, this is huge! When do you leave?"

"We start next week, but I'm flying out day after tomorrow so I can do a little touristing. You guys should come over this summer."

"Yeah, like it's a subway ride to Queens." Teesha shook her head. "I'm loading in summer classes, Hec. I'm going for my MBA ASAP."

"After which she's going to be my business manager. And when Loren finishes law school and passes the bar, he'll be my lawyer. So." Adrian lifted her glass in toast. "We keep the band together."

Over the next few months, Adrian jockeyed her time with appearances, visits to her grandparents, promotions for her new sportswear line, and a new project.

A weekly fitness blog, including a short, streaming demonstration of what she called the Five-Minute Workout of the Week.

Since she could stream from almost anywhere — once Hector taught her how — she often included someone else in the demo. The owner of her local deli, a random dog walker, a cop on the beat (whom she dated satisfactorily for a few months thereafter).

One of her favorites, and one she'd watch again countless times in the years to come, starred her grandmother.

With a foot of snow outside, the fires crackling, and the big house sparkling with Christmas, Adrian set up in the kitchen.

"Just have some fun with it," she told Sophia.

"The kitchen's for cooking, for gathering, for eating."

Adrian adjusted the camera. "You cook,

131

gather, eat, you need to move." Satisfied, Adrian turned, smiled at her grandmother.

"You look terrific. Scratch that. You look hot."

Sophia flicked a hand in dismissal, then laughed and shook back her hair. "It's the outfit. Your design."

"Well, my brand. But it's who's in it that counts."

It did flatter, Adrian thought, the forest-green support tank, the cropped leggings of green, blue, and pink, with pink low-tops.

"You've seen enough of these to know how it works. Just follow my lead. You have something to say, say it. It's easy, fun, and fast."

"I already pity me."

With a laugh, Adrian slid a hand in her pocket, hit the remote. "For this week's five minutes, I'm with the amazing Sophia Rizzo, or as I know her, Nonna. We're in her kitchen where she — and my grandfather — cook like culinary angels. He's currently tossing pizza dough at their restaurant here in the Maryland mountains. So Nonna and I are taking five out of our holiday baking to move the bod and up the heart rate.

"Ready, Nonna?"

Sophia looked straight into the camera. "This isn't my idea, but she's my only grandchild, so . . ."

"High knee march, get those knees above

the waist to work the abs. That's the way, Nonna. Nobody's going to deny themselves some holiday treats. I won't, not when they're made by Dom and Sophia Rizzo, so when you indulge — in moderation — don't forget to move."

"Only for you would I do this for people to see this poor old woman."

"Hah! Poor old woman, my butt. And speaking of butts. Squats. You know how to squat, Nonna. Get that bootie back. Squeeze those glutes."

She moved on to lunges, well aware Sophia sent her mock dirty looks, then combined the movements, calling out the count, then finished with hip circles and a stretch.

"And there you have it. Take five between the shopping, the baking, the wrapping, the indulging, and if you're lucky, you'll look as fit as my incredible nonna."

Adrian wrapped an arm around Sophia's waist. "Isn't she gorgeous? How lucky am I to have this DNA?"

"She's flattering me because it's all true." Laughing, Sophia wrapped her arms around Adrian and kissed her cheek. "Let's have a cookie."

"Let's." Adrian turned her head so their cheeks pressed, smiled at the camera. "Merry Christmas and happy holidays from ours to yours. Don't forget. Stay fit and fierce and fabulous. See you next year!"

Adrian hit the remote. "You were perfect!"

"I want to see it. Play it back."

"Absolutely. But with cookies."

"And wine."

"And wine. I love you to bits and pieces, Nonna."

Erie, Pennsylvania

On a cold, cloudy night in late December, with the lightest of snows swirling like bits of lace, the poet huddled in the back seat of a shiny blue sedan.

The car alarm, the locks? A simple matter when you did your research.

It had been too long between thrills, but one had to choose carefully. The gun again, though others had felt the blade, the bat. But the gun, the way it lived in the hand when it did its work.

A favorite.

As was this prey.

Hadn't she proved herself a whore? Wasn't she even now in that cheap motel room, letting someone not her husband pound into her?

She'd better enjoy it, as it would be the last time she felt anything.

No *Happy New Year* for you, bitch.

All in black, a shadow, invisible as the whore finally opened the door. Light from the room spilled over her. She blew a kiss to the cheating fuck inside, then smiled all the way to her car.

She hit her fob for the locks — reengaged, slid behind the wheel.

Her eyes widened in the rearview mirror for just an instant, that final instant, before the bullet tore into her brain.

A second shot for good measure. And the now traditional photo.

Only a moment later, an easy stroll through the lightly spinning snow to the car parked three blocks away.

And the thought rang clear and bright.

Merry Christmas to all, and to all a good night.

In February, Adrian opened the poem. They upset her, always, but this one stole her breath, had her lowering shakily into a chair.

The old woman with her fake red hair's
   your latest trick
To preen and pose and make me sick.
Be careful who you use to get ahead,
Or, like you, they'll end up dead.

She reported it, as always, made copies, as always. But this time she contacted the police in Traveler's Creek.

Then her grandparents. Though it took a lot of doing, she finally convinced them to install an alarm system.

Seven years now, she thought while she

135

paced the apartment and avidly wished Tee-sha would get home. What kind of person wrote and sent a sick poem to someone every year for seven years?

A sick one, just like the poems, she thought. One who obviously followed her blog, her public life.

"And a coward," she murmured.

She had to remember that. A coward who wanted her upset and anxious. Though she knew she shouldn't give whoever it was the satisfaction, she couldn't rid herself of the upset or anxiety.

Walking to the window, she stared out, watched the cars stream by, the people hurrying along the sidewalks.

"Why don't you come out?" she muttered. "Wherever you are, whoever you are, come out and we'll deal face-to-face."

As she watched, a thin sleet began to fall and the light dimmed. And she knew she could do nothing but wait.

CHAPTER SEVEN

Adrian hadn't expected an invitation to Raylan's wedding, and found herself genuinely sorry she had a conflict and couldn't go.

She thought of the blustery night more than a year before when she'd run into him and his Lorilee celebrating their engagement. And she thought of the sweet note Lorilee had sent her with the hand-painted tulips.

Instead of simply marking the card with her regrets, she sat down and followed her grandmother's tradition of writing a note.

Lorilee,
I'm sure you're busy with wedding plans, but I wanted to send a note along with my regrets to let you know I wish I could come to your and Raylan's special day. I'm going to be in Chicago that weekend. I'm sorry I can't be there to wish you both the very best.
When I met you last year, it struck me just how right you looked together. No

doubt Maya will share all the lovely details of the day, and you must know how thrilled she is to be your maid of honor.

You're becoming part of a wonderful family.

Please give Raylan my congratulations, and take my best wishes for yourself — pretty sure that's the way it's done. In any case, I know the two of you will be incredibly happy together.

Enjoy every moment.

All my best,
Adrian

When she mailed the note, she had no idea she'd started a friendly correspondence that would last for years.

Brooklyn, New York
Even when chaos ruled, which was often, Raylan loved his life.

Most likely he and Lorilee would find themselves in the midst of fixing up the fixer-upper they'd bought in Brooklyn when their kids graduated from college. But despite its many issues, the two-story old brick, with its huge attic and musty basement and squeaky stairs, suited them right down the line.

Maybe they'd been crazy to buy it weeks before their first child came into the world, but they'd both wanted to bring him home

138

— to a home.

And maybe he'd spent too much of his so-called free time in the five years since testing his carpentry skills, improving his painting skills, or learning along with Lorilee how to install tile, but it worked for them.

They'd both wanted to raise their family in a house with a yard, in a neighborhood with character. And since Bradley came along just thirteen months after their I dos, they'd led with optimism and bought the old place.

Two years later, they had Mariah.

They'd agreed to take a short break on making another kid until they'd fixed up more of the house, added at least some to their nest egg. And until the graphic novel publishing company Raylan launched with two friends eased out of the red.

With Bradley in kindergarten, Mariah in preschool, Lorilee teaching art at the high school, and — finally — Triquetra Comics chugging along, they'd decided to give kid number three a go.

He came home after a day of meetings, strategy sessions, scheduling sessions — and the pleasure of working on his next graphic novel — to the familiarity of chaos.

The dog — and the dog was entirely on him, as he'd brought the puppy home the summer before — raced and barked his way around the living room, into the dining room — knocking one of the chairs aside — zipped into the kitchen, where Lorilee stirred something on the stove, then back around again.

Mariah, in one of her many princess costumes, starred wand in hand, gave chase. Meanwhile Bradley popped Nerf balls out of his shooter, aiming at either or both of the runners indiscriminately.

"You'll be sorry when Jasper chews those up," Raylan warned his son.

"But it's fun." Bradley, flaxen-haired, blue-eyed, with a lightning grin that could melt lead, ran over to grab his father's legs. "Can we go to Carney's for ice cream after dinner? Please."

"Maybe. Pick up your balls, kid. Trust me, you'll appreciate that advice one day."

Bradley clung to his legs as Raylan shuffled across the floor, greeted the now leaping Jasper, then scooped up his fairy princess.

"I'm gonna change Jasper into a rabbit."

Her *r*'s still came out as *w*'s, and just melted his heart. He kissed her nose. "Then he's going to want carrots."

His messenger bag flapped against his hip as he carried his daughter, dragged his son into the kitchen to kiss his wife.

A lanky man who'd passed six-two in high school — and added one more inch in college — he bent down to nuzzle Lorilee's cheek.

And sniffed the air. "Spaghetti night. Yay."

"With a nice salad to start."

At Raylan's feet, Bradley said, "Boo!"

Lorilee merely aimed a look down at her son.

"If certain people eat all their salad without complaining, we could enjoy the spaghetti and then take a nice walk down to Carney's for ice cream."

"Yay. Can we?" Bradley transferred from Raylan's legs to Lorilee's. "Can we, Mom?"

"Salad and pasta first." Lorilee shook her head as Bradley jumped up to do his happy dance, as Mariah wiggled down to join him. "And how was your day?"

"Good. Real good. You?"

"Most excellent. And according to my chart" — she leaned in closer to murmur in his ear — "tonight could be the night to make another of these maniacs. So even more excellent."

"Even better than ice cream." He skimmed a hand over the pale blond hair she'd cut into a short wedge to save time and trouble. He loved how it framed her face. "Meet you in the bedroom right after story time."

"I'm there." She leaned into him as she watched their kids dance. "We do really good work, Raylan."

He ran a hand down her back, over her butt, and back up again. "Looking forward to doing some more."

After dinner — and the mess and noise — after the walk and the ice cream, after the nightly ritual of story time, they tucked their kids into bed.

There were always the questions he figured the kids saved up to draw out bedtime.

Why can't I see the stars in the daytime
    when I can sometimes see the moon?
Why do you get beards and Mommy
    doesn't?
Why can't dogs talk like people?

It took awhile, just as Raylan knew it would take awhile to be sure both kids were actually asleep so making love with their mom would go unremarked and undisturbed.

"How about some wine? If this works, you'll have to give it up again. Might as well cash in now."

"I'd love some."

He headed down to get it. The walls of the second-floor hallway still needed the wallpaper stripped. They'd prioritized the kids' rooms, the kitchen, and two of the three and a half baths.

He figured another baby, if they got lucky, meant turning another of the four bedrooms into a nursery instead of doing their own bedroom. Which meant moving his studio upstairs into the attic.

Lorilee already painted up there, but they could section part of the area off for his work. They'd find a way.

He got out a bottle of wine, opened it, and started to get out glasses when the phone on the counter rang.

He saw his mother's name on the caller ID. "Hey, Mom."

His easy smile at hearing her voice turned to blank shock. "What? No. How? When? But . . ."

When he didn't come back upstairs, Lorilee went down to find him sitting at the kitchen counter, his head in his hands.

"What is it? Raylan, what's wrong?"

He lifted his head as she rushed to him. "Sophia Rizzo. An accident. She — she was with a friend, driving home from her book club. A storm, slick roads, another driver skidded into them. Her friend's in the hospital, but Sophia . . . She's dead, Lorilee. She's gone."

"Oh my God, no." Tears rolled even as Lorilee pulled Raylan to her. "Not Sophia. Oh, Raylan."

"I don't know what to do. I can't think. She was almost like my grandmother."

"Here now, here." Lorilee kissed his cheeks. Then she got the glasses, poured the wine. "Drink some of this. Your mom —"

"That's who called."

"She'll be grieving, and Dom. And Adrian and her mother, and, God, honey, the whole town. There'll be services, a memorial. We'll go. We can stay a few days if we can help."

143

"Mom said she didn't know about a funeral or memorial, but she'd call tomorrow when she knew more. She said Maya and Joe were coming over. They were going to get a sitter for Collin and come help her close up the shop and . . ."

"Oh, the restaurant. Of course. Listen, you can stay on for a week or two if you can help. I'll bring the kids back home."

"Don't know what to do yet. I need to think. We'll figure it out. I can't take it in, Lorilee. She's always been part of my life."

"I know, honey." She held him close, stroked his back. "We're going to figure out how to help." After lifting his face to hers, she kissed him. Then she sat beside him at the counter with his hand in hers. "I can take emergency leave at work. Just go in tomorrow, get things set up. Unless you want to leave tomorrow."

"I . . ." He tried to clear his head, but he still heard the tears in his mother's voice. "No, I guess we should get things organized, have the kids go on to school, wait for Mom to call back. We could both get things handled at work and head down day after tomorrow."

"That sounds right to me, too. I can start packing when I get home."

All right, a plan, he thought. He did better with a plan, with a schedule. With something outlined.

"I can take off early, just get things set up

by early afternoon."

"You need to plan on staying at least a week. You don't worry about me and the kids," she said before he could object. "We'll take the train home. It'll be an adventure for them. Your mama's going to need you. Sophia was the next thing to hers."

"How do we tell the kids?" He reached for his wine, then just stared at it. "They're so young, Lorilee, and they've never lost anyone close like this."

"I guess we tell them Nonna had to go to heaven to be an angel, and when they ask why, we have to tell them we don't know, and we're sad she's not with us." Lorilee took Raylan's wine, sipped a little. "But how she's in our hearts forever. I think we just love them, honey, like we always do."

They agreed not to tell the kids in the morning, but to get them off to school as normal so they didn't carry the questions and the sadness through the day.

Maybe he hugged them just a little tighter, just a little longer before he helped Lorilee strap them into their car seats.

"Learn something," he ordered Bradley.

"If I keep learning stuff, I'll know everything and not have to go to school. Then I can go to work with you and make comic books."

"What's the square root of nine hundred and forty-six?"

Bradley squealed out a laugh. "I don't know!"

"See. You don't know everything yet. Learn something. You, too, Princess Mo."

He turned to draw his wife in. "Thanks."

"For?"

"For being you, for being mine. For being."

"Aww, my sweet husband. I'll see you soon." She kissed him until Bradley made gagging noises. Then she laughed. "I love you."

"I love you."

She got behind the wheel, strapped in, then sent him a smile. "I'll be home by four. Sooner if you need me."

"I'll keep in touch."

He stepped back, everyone waved. He went back in the quiet house where Jasper already curled up in his first morning nap.

"Going in early today, pal, and you're going with me. Then you're going to have a little vacation at Bick's."

Raylan's friend and partner had already agreed to take the dog for however long it took. All Raylan had to do was load up Jasper's food, his bed, his treats, his toys.

Amazing, Raylan thought, just how much stuff accumulated for a half-grown Lab retriever.

He grabbed a hoodie to put on over his No One T-shirt, the character who'd helped launch Triquetra.

146

Every day was casual Friday at Triquetra.

He grabbed the messenger bag he used as a briefcase, clipped the leash on the thrilled dog. Normally, especially on a sunny spring day, he'd have walked or biked the ten blocks to the old warehouse where Triquetra had its offices, but he intended to pack up more work in case he extended his stay in Traveler's Creek.

So he opened the rear door of his aging Prius for Jasper.

Behind the wheel, he opened the windows so the air blew in and the dog could stick his head out.

On the drive he filled his head with tasks that needed doing now if he ended up working remotely for a week or two.

They could teleconference meetings and sessions. Any work he needed to see and approve could be sent via email attachment. He could certainly set up a temporary work space in his old bedroom, and meet his deadline — ten days off — for completion of the coloring of his latest No One graphic novel.

Since he was ahead of schedule there, he reminded himself, no problem. Normally he did his own lettering, but since neither of his partners did, they had artists on staff for that. He could, just this once, turn that over if he needed to.

He'd face that one when the time came.

He pulled into the little side parking lot of the square, five-story brick building with its long, tall windows, ancient loading dock, wide steel doors, and the rooftop where they had after-work parties in the summer, the occasional shouting match meeting, or smoke breaks for those who indulged.

Before he went inside, Raylan walked the dog around to the scrubby bushes and grass at the end of the lot. Let him sniff around, let him do what dogs did outside so he wouldn't screw up and do what dogs shouldn't do inside.

He got his keys, unlocked the heavy steel door, turned off the alarm system.

Hit the lights.

All five stories stood open, joined together by open steel steps and a couple of freight elevators.

They'd set up the main level as a kind of massive game room/snack area/lounge.

Two of the three partners were guys, after all. And Bick was the next best thing. A woman who got it.

Cast-off furniture — lumpy sofas, worn plaid recliners, milk crate tables — made up the lounge. They talked about replacing it now that they could actually afford it. But sentiment won out whenever it was brought up.

They had sprung for two of the biggest flat-screen TVs money could buy, several gaming systems, some classic pinball machines (that needed almost constant repair), some old video arcade games.

They'd all agreed sometimes the mind and body needed to play, to let ideas just simmer. And that one day, some of the games would be their own.

They'd seen that end fulfilled with No One, with Violet Queen and Snow Raven.

More would come. Raylan believed it because they did what they loved, and what they loved they did well. And every new hire had to hit those two marks.

Because he had the dog, he took the freight elevator rather than the stairs. Jasper leaned hard against him and shivered as the car moaned and groaned up to the fifth floor.

He'd taken the top level for his office and work space because nobody else wanted to climb that high on a regular basis.

Most of the work, the activity, the noise spread below. He didn't mind the echoes of it all; in fact, he enjoyed them. But he liked the more solitary space, and the view from the big windows.

He could see to the river, to the south skyline of Manhattan.

Since No One fought crime in the city, and his alter ego, Cameron Quincy, worked there as a computer tech, Raylan often sketched the skyline in its varying moods for inspiration.

But now he could only think someone he loved was no longer in the world. The regret he hadn't gone home in weeks, hadn't seen her, talked to her.

And now, never would.

Life got busy, sure, and he accepted that. But they had to make more time. His sister had a son not quite two, and he'd only seen him once since Christmas.

He hadn't given his mother enough time with his kids, or them with her. They'd fix that.

And Dom . . . Would he be alone now in that big house? He'd make an effort, a real effort to give back time to those who'd given him theirs.

Because time mattered, he sat at his drawing table while the dog sniffed around the space with its pair of squeaky rolling chairs, the old dorm fridge full of Coke and Gatorade, the enormous board where he pinned sketches and notes, story lines, the mirror where he tested out facial expressions. The framed photos of his family. Action figures, the potted ficus he was slowly killing.

He had the two-page spread with its completed captions on his workstation, with some of it already inked. He'd written, revised, altered, completed the story line, done the same with all the sketches.

He could do the work digitally, but he preferred by hand. Just as he preferred doing his own inking and coloring. He understood that might have to change as the company grew, but he'd hold on to the pleasure of it as long as he could.

While Jasper settled down with his chew bone and pet stuffed kitten, Raylan picked up his tools. And lost himself in the work.

One part of his brain heard the workday begin for the others, the voices that rose up the open stairs, the clanging as people climbed them. The smell of coffee and someone's burnt bagel.

But No One was in a fix, as the girl he had a crush on was currently being lured into danger by the seductive villain, Mr. Suave.

So he sat, worked, perfected, bringing the panels to life with the sunlight streaming through the windows.

His dark blond hair tumbled over his ears. Lorilee would say he needed a haircut, but she liked to play with it when they were curled in bed together. He'd forgotten to shave that morning with his mind elsewhere so the twenty-four-hour scruff covered hollow cheeks.

His eyes stayed intense, focused, though his lips began to curve as he watched his signature character take on depth.

He didn't pay much attention when he heard the rapid clang of someone running up the stairs, but Jasper whoofed and scrambled up.

He glanced over at Bick, her long, red-tipped dreads flying.

"Hey, Bick, appreciate you taking Jasper. I'm going to finish up the —"

"Raylan." Her voice cracked before she sucked in a shaky breath. "There's an active shooter at the high school. Lorilee's school."

For an instant, his mind just went numb. "What?"

"Jojo had the TV going in the lounge, and the bulletin just came on. The school's locked down. A kid got out. He's saying there were at least two, at least two shooting people. Raylan —"

He was already up, sprinting for the doorway. Jasper tried to race after him, but Bick caught him, held him. "No, you have to stay."

Raylan flew down the steps, nearly ran through Jonah, his other partner, who waited at the bottom.

"I'll drive."

Raylan didn't argue, didn't slow down. He jumped into Jonah's orange-glow Mini. "Hurry."

"She's okay." Jonah's usual calm-at-all-costs demeanor held steady as he threw the car into reverse. "She's smart. She's done the drill over and over."

Raylan barely heard the words, couldn't hear his own desperate thoughts as his heart pounded in his ears.

With the top down on the Mini, the spring

152

air flew around him. Tender green leaves unfurled on trees, early flowers danced with color and charm. He felt none of it, saw none of it.

All he could see was Lorilee's face as she smiled before she'd driven away.

"What time is it?" It shocked him when he looked at his own watch to see that three hours had passed since he'd sat down to work.

It meant Lorilee would be in class, in the classroom before the first lunch break.

In the classroom was good. He knew the drill as well as she did, as she'd taken him through the steps, cried over the need to.

Lock the classroom door, get the kids in the storage closet, keep them calm, keep them quiet.

Shelter in place, and wait for the police to come.

As the first shock wore off, he pulled out his phone. She'd have it muted during class hours, but she'd feel the vibration.

When his call went to voice mail, just her cheerful drawl, he felt something sick rise up in his throat.

"She's not answering. She doesn't answer."

"Probably left the phone on her desk. We're almost there, Raylan. Almost there."

"On her desk."

He made himself accept that, though part of the drill ensured she had the means to communicate with the outside.

He saw the barricades, the police cars, ambulances, TV crews, the frantic parents, the terrified spouses who'd come, like him.

He was out of the car before it fully stopped.

The school stood a half block away, red brick, the sun beaming off its windows, the ground around it spring green.

He could see cops, and even from the distance he saw one of the windows had shattered.

"My wife." He managed to get the words out as he gripped the NYPD barricade. "Lorilee Wells, art teacher. She's in there."

"We have to ask you to wait here, sir." The uniformed officer spoke calmly, flatly. "We have officers in the building."

"Raylan!"

He blanked for a moment when the woman hurried to him. His mind seemed to skip between a terrible clarity and sudden blanks.

"Suzanne."

He knew her, of course. They'd had dinner in her home, and she and her husband — Bill, Bill McInerny, math teacher, chess guru, rabid Yankees fan — had dined in theirs.

She wrapped around him, this woman who smelled of grass and earth and mulch. A gardener, he remembered in the next spurt of clarity. An avid gardener who lived all but next door to the school in a ranch-style house with a big back patio.

"Raylan. Raylan, God. My day off, working in the garden. The shooting." He felt every individual tremble when she began to shake. "I heard the shooting. But I didn't think, I just didn't think. You never think it could happen here, in your own backyard."

"Have you talked to Bill? Could you reach him?"

"He texted me." She drew back, rubbed tears away. "He told me he and his kids were safe, not to worry. He loved me, don't worry." She pressed her fingers to her eyes again, then dropped them. "Lorilee?"

"She didn't answer." He pulled out his phone to try again.

Gunfire erupted. It sounded like backfires and fireworks and terror. He swore the shots went straight through his heart, sharp, deadly punches. All around him people screamed, sobbed, shouted.

People clung to each other, as Suzanne now clung to him. He felt Jonah's hand gripping his shoulder like a phantom weight. There, but not there.

Because the world had just stopped. In the void, all he heard was a terrible silence.

Then he saw police escorting a line of kids out, kids with their hands held up or on top of their heads. Kids crying, and some with blood on their clothes.

He heard parents shouting names and

weeping. He saw paramedics rushing into the building.

Noise, too much noise filled the void, like a screaming roar inside his head. He couldn't fully make out the words caught in the roar.

The shooters were down.

The situation contained.

Multiple dead, multiple wounded.

"Bill!" Suzanne pulled away, weeping and laughing. "There's Bill, there's Bill."

Parents embraced children; spouses clutched spouses. Paramedics carried out stretchers, and ambulances screamed away.

He kept his focus on the doors where any second she would come out. She would come back to him.

"Mr. Wells."

He knew the girl — one of Lorilee's students. He went in once or twice a year to demonstrate and talk about how graphic novels and comics evolved from concept to completion.

She looked so pale, the skin so white against the red splotches from tears. A woman — her mother, he assumed — had an arm tight around her, and tears of her own.

He'd never know why her name came so clearly to his muddled mind. "Caroline. You're one of Lorilee's. Ms. Wells's. Where —"

"We heard the shots. We were in class and heard the shooting, and — and laughing.

156

They laughed and shot. Ms. Wells said to go into the storeroom, like in the drills. To go quick and quiet. And she went to lock the classroom door."

"Is she still in there?"

"Mr. Wells, she went to lock the door, and he fell, right there. Rob Keyler — I know him. And he was bleeding, and he fell, and she — Ms. Wells — she started to pull him inside, to help him get inside. And then he . . ."

The tears ran and ran down her face, such a young face, still soft, still fighting a little teen acne. "It was Jamie Hanson. I know him, too. It was Jamie, and he had a gun in his hand, and she — Ms. Wells — she — she — she just threw herself over Rob. I could see. We hadn't shut the door all the way, and I saw. He . . . Mr. Wells, Mr. Wells, he shot her. He shot her."

Sobbing uncontrollably, she threw herself at him. "He shot her and shot her, and he laughed and walked away. He just walked away."

He didn't hear anything else. He didn't feel anything else. Because his world ended on a soft spring day with a sky so blue it broke the heart.

CHAPTER EIGHT

They called her a hero. The boy she'd shielded with her own body spent ten days in the hospital, but he lived.

None of the students in her class sustained any physical injuries. The wounds to their hearts, souls, minds would take years to heal. If then.

Two boys, ages sixteen and seventeen, mad at the world, despising their own lives, ended the lives of six others on a pretty day in May. Five had been fellow students.

They wounded eleven more.

The lives they shattered, the children who lost parents, siblings, their innocence, the families who would grieve forever spread much deeper.

Neither boy survived the assault.

Adrian dealt with her own grief as she sat at her grandmother's desk, chose from her grandmother's stationery.

She'd sent flowers, but flowers faded. A week after the twin blows of death, she wrote to Raylan.

Dear Raylan,

There aren't words adequate enough to tell you how sorry I am. I know your mother and sister are with you now, and I hope that gives you some comfort.

I'm sorry, too, I wasn't able to come to Lorilee's memorial, as I don't feel I can leave my grandfather.

She was one of the most beautiful human beings I've ever known. I didn't know her well, and mostly through correspondence, but her joy, her kindness, her love for you and your children came through so clearly.

The world lost an angel.

It feels empty to say please let me know if there's anything, anything at all I can do. But it's meant sincerely.

To get through this shock, this grief, I tell myself Nonna and Lorilee are looking out for each other now. And for us. For you and your children and for me.

Because it's who they were.

Some people leave a legacy of goodness behind them. Your Lorilee, my nonna did exactly that.

My deepest sympathies,
Adrian

She took it, and the note her grandfather had written, went outside to where Dom sat on the front porch.

159

"Let's take a ride, Popi. I have to mail these letters, and we could go by the shop, see what's doing."

He smiled at her, but shook his head. "Not today, honey. Maybe tomorrow."

He said the same every day.

She walked over to sit a moment in the chair beside his — her grandmother's chair. And laid a hand over his.

"Jan and Maya are coming back next week. At least that's the plan right now."

"That poor boy. Those poor children. I had a lifetime with Sophia. He had a blink of an eye. Jan should stay as long as he needs."

"She knows."

He turned his hand over, patted hers. "You need to get back to your life, Adrian."

"Kicking me out?"

"Never." He gave her hand a squeeze. "But you have to live your life."

"Right now I have to run a few errands. How about I pick up a meatball sub for lunch? We can split it."

Though she'd suggested his favorite, he just gave her hand another absent pat. "Whatever you like works for me."

He said that, too, almost every day. Rising, Adrian bent over to kiss his cheek. "I won't be more than an hour."

"Take your time."

But she wouldn't. She didn't like leaving him alone more than an hour right now. He

160

seemed too fragile and listless.

As she drove into town, she considered all of her options again, and knew she had to choose.

And really, she'd known all along what choice she'd make.

She pulled into the parking lot at Rizzo's, walked from there to the post office to mail the letters, and to open a post office box. That meant a short conversation with the postmistress, who teared up when she asked after Dom.

From there, she walked back to Main Street and down to Farm Fresh for a quart of milk, a dozen eggs — and another conversation. She didn't need a full grocery run, not when people had brought, and continued to bring, so much food.

And her grandfather wasn't eating as much as he should.

She picked up some wild raspberry jelly, hoping the big breakfast she planned to make him in the morning tempted him.

And added some lavender soy candles in the hope they helped soothe her mind through her morning meditation.

She walked back to her car — another conversation at the crosswalk while she waited for the light. She put the eggs and milk in the little cooler, stowed the rest before going into the lunchtime bustle of Rizzo's.

She went in the back because she wasn't

sure how many more conversations she had in her. She smelled garlic and spices and the tang of vinegar. She wound her way to the main dining room and open kitchen into the noise of conversations, the clatter of flatware, the swack of knives on cutting boards.

Steam rose from the sauce simmering on the big range; the door to the brick oven thumped as a cook paddled another bubbling pie out.

"Hey, Adrian." Barry ladled sauce on yet another pie. Gangly, owl-eyed, and loyal, he'd worked at Rizzo's since his high school days. Four years later, he helped run the shop while Jan — now the manager — comforted her son and Dom dealt with grief. "How's it going? How's the boss?"

"He's doing okay. I'm going to try to perk him up with a meatball sub. When you get a chance."

"No problem. I know just how he likes it. Grab a seat. You want a drink, a slice?"

"No, thanks. I'll get —" She started to say water as it remained her go-to. But she thought she could use a perk herself. "I'll get a Coke. I need to use the office for a few minutes, if that's okay."

"No problem," he said again. "Tell The Dom we miss him around here."

"I will."

She poured the fountain Coke herself with plenty of ice.

162

The office consisted of a little box off the back of the house where the dishwasher worked at the huge sink, the big dough machine stood, for now, idle, and one of the line cooks grabbed more supplies out of the cooler.

Adrian waved, then closed herself inside.

She sat at the desk in the relative quiet, then just leaned back and closed her eyes for a few minutes.

She could get past the ache in her heart when she actively did something. Cleaning around the house — though there wasn't much to do there. Working out, shopping for essentials.

But whenever she stopped, even for a moment, that ache nearly took her breath.

The solution, she reminded herself, was to keep doing things.

She figured the decision she'd made would ensure just that.

Because she knew this needed a face-to-face, she took out her tablet and FaceTimed Teesha.

Teesha came on, her short braids dangling and the ridiculously adorable twenty-two-month-old Phineas on her hip.

Life changed, Adrian thought. It just couldn't stand still.

Now her longtime friend, her business manager, her wailing wall was a mom. She'd fallen in love — and stuck there — with a sexy-eyed, slow-smiling songwriter who'd romanced her with music, with flowers, with heroic patience.

"There's that boy!"

He squealed when he saw Adrian on the screen, then clapped his hands together. He said, "Rizz!" and blew her kisses.

"Hey, Phineas, hey, Phin, hey, the one I love. And I assume that's red sauce all over his face and not the blood of his victims."

"You assume correctly. This time. We just finished lunch. Talk while I hose him down. Monroe's locked in his studio working. But that's okay. He's got the evening shift. How are you, Adrian? How's Popi? I wish we could've stayed longer."

"We're getting through. But I worry about him, Teesha."

"Of course you do." Phineas objected, strongly, to having his face and hands washed. "Suck it up, kid. Almost done. You said your mom left, too."

"She had events. She stayed three days, and for her, that's a month in Traveler's Creek. I can't slam her too hard over it, because she was hurting. I know she was."

"We all miss Nonna. I'm going to set this one up with *Sesame Street,* and we can have an actual adult conversation. Hold on a minute, Rizz."

While Adrian waited, she heard Teesha telling Phineas about Elmo, and Phineas give a

164

long, rolling gut laugh.

The sound boosted Adrian's spirits. Everything would be okay.

"There. Whew. That boy loves Elmo more than I love my new laptop. And you know I love that machine."

"I know you do."

"And this is not yet an adult conversation. Help me."

"I'm so glad you're happy, Teesha. I'm so glad you have Monroe and Phineas, and they have you."

"It's working out pretty well. I think we got really lucky with the kid. We miss you though."

"Mutual. Are you two still talking about maybe moving out to the burbs, or that fantasy country house?"

"Oh, we talk about it, yeah. I mean, both of us lived our whole lives in the city, and we're good, right? But . . ." She looked over where Adrian could hear Elmo's squeaky voice and Phineas's giggle. "It would be nice to have a house and a yard, maybe some dumbass dog. Swing set, all of it. I'm becoming frigging domesticated, Adrian. I say again: Help me."

"Not when it looks so good on you. So, here's my deal, and it's got a couple of parts. Part one is, I'm going to relocate down here."

"What? Really? You're going to stay there?"

"I'm going to ask you to arrange to have my stuff packed up. The personal stuff. The

165

furniture — you can have anything you can use or want. I guess the rest can go into storage until whenever. But I don't need it here."

"This is big. This is Godzilla big. When did you decide?"

"I think when I got here, when I saw Popi. He can't live alone in this big house, Teesh, and it would kill him to leave it. He needs me here — though he'd never say it. And I don't need to be in New York to work. I'm lucky there."

"All true, all, but New York's been your base since the jump."

"For work, but this has been home — the real deal — for a long time. I can use the lower level, with some adjustments, some design, some tech for streaming my workouts, for shooting videos, for whatever I need. And if I need to come up there, I hop in the car or on the train. But I don't feel easy about doing even that right now."

"I've got it. I do. On the practical side, you'll save five figures a year in rent. You could earmark a percentage of that toward outfitting your work space there. On the creative front, you'd switch to using settings in and around Traveler's Creek rather than New York, which we could market. And on a personal front, you wouldn't worry daily about Popi because you'd be right there."

"And this is why you're not only my friend but my manager."

"What did Popi say?"

"I haven't told him yet. I'm going to once it's a done deal. What's he going to do? Toss me out?"

"You got him there."

"You and I can work remotely as long as we need to. Unless . . ." Now she put on her best persuasive voice. "There are some really nice properties down here, some really lovely houses in and around Traveler's Creek with yards for dumbass dogs and charming little boys."

"Well, holy shit, Adrian."

Then she closed her eyes as Phineas loudly echoed her. "When will I learn?" she muttered. "That's not like moving to New Rochelle with the Petries. Rob and Laura," she said at Adrian's blank look. "Never mind."

"It could be better than that." Adrian knew how to push, when to push, and when to let things simmer. "Just something to think about. And if you do think along those lines positively, I'd drop another job in your lap. Jan Wells manages Rizzo's. Nonna and Popi handled the business end of it, but that's always been mostly her. It's not that he can't deal with it, but I think he'll need help. That's not something I can do."

"Rizz, I love the man like my own. You know I'll help with that wherever I am."

"I was hoping you'd say that. I'll talk to Popi, and Jan's coming back in a day or two,

167

so I'll talk to her. But I need your scary smart head for business."

"We could come down for a couple days, sort that part out. Let me talk to Monroe, see when he could manage it."

"Thanks." Time to add just a little to the simmer, she thought. "Hey, imagine a pretty house with a pretty yard. It has an office bigger than a closet for you. An actual music room for Monroe. A playroom for Phineas — and whoever comes after him."

"Now you're trying to seduce me with square footage and a lower tax base."

"Hard as I can. Think about it, talk about it. I've got to get back to Popi, but I need to contact the landlord, give my notice."

"I'll take care of that. And I'll find a storage place down your way. You keep the furniture for now. You may end up using some here and there."

"You're right. Thanks, just thanks. Kiss your boys for me, and we'll talk again soon."

"I can do that. Rizz? This is the right move for you. Not just for Popi. It's right for you. It feels right."

"Yeah, I think so, too. Really love you."

"Me, too, you."

After shutting down her tablet, Adrian let out a sigh. Yes, everything would be okay. Some time, some work, some figuring out, but she'd make it all okay.

She took the Coke she'd forgotten to drink

168

with her out to the dining room. This time she slid onto a stool at the counter.

"Let me put that sub together for you. I wanted to make sure you got it home warm."

"You're doing a good job, Barry, helping to keep the place running during all this."

"Rizzo's is like home to me. Always has been."

"It shows. Listen, don't you have a younger sister?"

"Got three. Why do you think this is home?"

She laughed, drank some Coke while he split the long roll. "The one who's in college. Interior design, right?"

"That's Kayla. Yeah, she's heading back in about a week or so. Got her first year in the bag."

"So, this is now a Box of Confidentiality. What you say goes no farther. Is she any good?"

"Well, she sure thinks my decor in my apartment sucks wide. She's not wrong, but it's just me since I busted up with Maxie. She redid her bedroom at home a couple years ago, and it looks like a damn magazine. She made dean's list, so she's good at it. Got an eye and all that."

"Tell her to call me. I might have a job for her."

"Really?" He paddled the sub into the oven to melt the provolone over the meatballs and sauce. "In New York?"

"No, here. If she's up for it, she can give me a consult, and we'll see if we suit each other."

"Sure. She'll go nuts. She streams your workouts."

"Does she?" Adrian smiled, drank more Coke. "She just got another leg up."

When she got home, Dom was still sitting on the porch. He started to get up when she carried up the take-out bag, the cooler.

"Let me give you a hand."

"I've got it. Let's eat out here."

"Whatever you want, baby."

"Definitely out here. It's so pretty out. I'll be back in a minute."

Sometimes, she thought as she walked through the big house to the big kitchen, the right choice was also the only choice.

She split the sub, used pretty plates, cloth napkins, and poured both water and wine. To tempt him, she added a handful of his favored salt-and-vinegar chips — damn the nutrition for one day — to each plate.

She carried the tray out, arranged it all on the long porch table.

"Let's eat, Popi. Business was good when I stopped in." She just kept chattering as he got up, slowly walked to the table. "Barry's on today, and doing a good job — but he said they miss seeing you."

"Maybe I'll go in tomorrow."

He'd said the same the day before.

"That'd be great. God, I haven't had a meatball sub in . . . who knows?" She leaned over the plate, dripping sauce onto it as she took a bite. "Oh really, I bet this is illegal in some states. One day, you're going to give me the recipe for the Rizzo secret sauce."

"You know I will." He smiled; he nibbled.

"So, I FaceTimed with Teesha — and the amazing Phineas — while I was out. They send love."

"That's a precious little boy. Smart as a whip. Smarter."

"He is. I'm hoping we'll see lots more of him if I managed to talk her and Monroe into moving down here."

"Hmm? What, here?"

And there, she thought, was a chink in the curtain that had come down over his eyes.

"Mmm." She took another bite. "I know we can work remotely, no problem, but they've been talking about getting a house — burbs, maybe even country — since Phin was born. Why not here? And her amazing business brain would help with Rizzo's, too. Monroe can work anywhere." She took a sip of wine, smiled, shrugged. "Like me."

"I don't understand."

She made another sound, ate a chip. "Oh, I know why I try never to eat one of these. My system is crying for more now. Oh." She beamed that smile again. "I'm moving in. Didn't I mention that? I gave — or Teesha

171

gave — my notice at the apartment in New York. She's arranging for my stuff to be packed up and moved down here. Storage for some — she's dealing with that. I don't think I'd get through a day without her dealing with stuff."

"*Gioia,* your life's in New York."

"It's been in New York because that's where Mom lived, and where I started out. But my home's here, and has been for as long as I can remember. I'd like to have my life in my home."

His jaw squared. "Adrian, you're not upending your life for me. I won't have it."

Casually, she licked sauce off her finger. "That's too bad, because it's done. I'm doing it for you, because I love you. I'm doing it for me, because it's what I want. I love you," she repeated. "I love this big old house. I love the views, I love the trees, the gardens. I love the town, and I'm taking it. Just try to stop me."

A tear slid down his cheek. "I don't want you to —"

"Does it matter what I want?" She laid a hand over his. "Does it?"

"Of course it does. Of course."

"This is what I want."

"To live in this old place, outside of a three-stoplight town?"

She ate another chip. "Yes. That's exactly

what I want. Oh, and I'm taking over the lower level."

"I —"

"Squatter's rights. I need the space for my fitness area, my streaming. For my work. There's that nice walk out on the back so there's light, and I'll have a crew come in to deal with the tech stuff. I might hire Barry's little sister to work on the design."

"Adrian, this is a big decision. You should take time to think it all through."

"Have thought, have weighed pros and cons. Pros win. You know the Rizzos, Popi. We know what we want, then we work to get it." She toasted him with her glass. "Get used to it, Roomie."

She set it down, got up to put her arms around him as more tears fell. "You need me," she murmured. "But I need you, too. We're giving this to each other."

"We'll be all right."

"Yes, we will." She framed his face, kissed him. "She'd expect nothing less of us. Now, I need you to eat that damn sub because if you don't and I do, I'm really going to pay for it later."

"Okay. Okay. Barry knows how I like it."

"So he said."

When she sat again, he took another bite. He drank some wine, cleared his throat. "Do you really think you can talk them into moving down here with that precious little boy?"

173

Smiling, she tapped her glass to his. "I favor my odds there. That tire swing needs a new young butt."

"It surely does. I thought, at first, I just wanted to fade away. How could I stay when she was gone? So just fade away."

Tears burned and pushed at the backs of her eyes. "I know."

"You won't let me."

"No, I won't."

Nodding, he looked directly into her eyes. "Why don't you tell me what you have in mind to do to my basement? Our basement," he corrected.

Two days later she wandered the space she intended to transform. Studying it, imagining, considering, rejecting. They'd put in a wine cellar before she'd been born, and that would stay, of course. As would the utility/storage room.

She wouldn't need to touch the guest room or full-size bath.

That left her the entire family room area with its antique bar, the old brick fireplace, all mostly used when they held big parties.

More furniture to move or store, she mused, but the bar, the fireplace would make interesting backdrops.

She wanted it to look like what it was — part of a home — but at the same time efficient, focused. Picking up her tablet, she

174

started making notes she'd share with Kayla when her — hopefully — young designer came in for a consult.

A FaceTime signal interrupted, and had Adrian staring at the screen. Her mother never FaceTimed. Adrian tapped accept.

Lina came on-screen in full makeup, her chestnut hair sleeked back in a tail. Work mode, Adrian concluded.

"Hi. This is new."

"We need a conversation, and this is the best way. I just read your blog."

"Oh. I didn't know you —"

"Adrian, you can't bury yourself in that house, in that town. What are you thinking?"

"I'm thinking this is where I want to be — and need to be — and rather than burying myself, I see it as a new opportunity."

"You established yourself in New York, and your use of locations there for your DVDs, your streaming is part of your signature."

"I'm changing my signature."

Lina waved someone away without taking her eyes off the screen. "Look, it's laudable that you'd consider uprooting your life to look after your grandfather."

"Laudable."

"Yes. It's kind and loving and laudable. I'm not stupid, Adrian, and I'm not blind to the circumstances. I know he shouldn't stay in the house alone. I'd considered trying to convince him to move to New York, but re-

175

alized that would be a study in frustration for both of us. I've been interviewing live-in nurse/companions."

"Did you mention that to him?"

"No, because he'd reject the idea off the mark. But when I find someone —"

"Stop looking." Adrian sat on the arm of a couch, reminded herself there was no point in anger. Her mother generally defaulted to throwing money at a problem or inconvenience.

On the plus side, she'd tried to do something.

"He's not sick, he's grieving. He doesn't need a nurse. He needs me. And that street goes both ways. I want to be here, and not just to look after him. I want to be in our family home. Why does it matter to you?"

"I don't want to see you tap the brakes on your career when it's still accelerating. You have a gift."

"And I'm going to keep using it."

"In an old house outside of Dogpatch?"

"That's right, and on the porch, on the back patio, in the park, in the town square. I've got plenty of ideas. We have the same root in the work, Mom, but we've grown it two different ways."

"New Gen is still under the Yoga Baby umbrella."

Now Adrian lifted her eyebrows. "It is. If my relocating causes you to rethink that, we can have the lawyers work out a split."

"Don't be —" Lina broke off, then looked away from the screen for a moment as Adrian watched her struggle for composure. "I'm trying to point out that this is a business as well as a passion, a lifestyle, and that in business you have to be practical as well as innovative. And you're not the only one dealing with upheaval. She was my mother."

After another breath, Lina looked back at the screen. "She was my mother."

"I know. You're right." And she could see grief just as clearly as she herself felt it. "And I should have given you a heads-up, on a personal and a business level. I didn't think of it. I just didn't, so I'm sorry for that. Let's try this. You give me a year, and if this relocation doesn't work the way I think it will, we'll reevaluate."

"By reevaluating you mean actually consulting me, Harry, the rest of the team?"

"Yes."

"All right." She looked off-screen again. "Yes, yes, two minutes! I want you to succeed, Adrian."

"I know you do."

"I have to go. Tell Dad . . . tell him I'll call him soon."

"I will."

When she ended the call, Adrian slid down to sit on the couch. She'd made a mistake, she admitted, not telling her mother about

177

her decision. And for the life of her she couldn't be sure if that had been deliberate on some level or just an oversight.

Done now, she thought. And once she got things moving Lina, and everyone else, would see she'd made the right move at the right time.

So she'd better get busy proving it.

Northern California
Just another sunrise hiker. Blending was both a skill and personal entertainment. The canyon offered echoing silence — sometimes the cry of a hawk or an eagle.

Predators, and much admired.

She who wouldn't live to see the sun again hiked here twice a week, three times if she could manage it, but the two were like clockwork.

Her alone time, her commune-with-nature time, her keep-body-and-soul-in-tune time.

Or so she said on Twitter.

The hunting, the planning here had been pure pleasure. Travel, such an innate part of the life led, offered so many opportunities.

New scenes, new sounds. New kills.

And here, like clockwork, she came. Striding along in her hiking boots, a bright pink fielder's cap on her head with her fake blond hair pulled into a tail through the opening in the back. Sunglasses, cargo shorts.

Alone.

The fake limp, the slight wince caught her attention.

"Are you okay?"

A wave of a hand, a brave, slightly pained smile. And voice breathless, quiet. "Just twisted my ankle a little. Stupid."

Another step, a little stumble.

And didn't she reach right out to help?

The knife slid smoothly into her belly. Her mouth opened into a shocked O that might've turned into a scream, but the knife made those glorious wet sounds as it pulled out, pushed in.

When she went down, her sunglasses slid off.

Souvenirs! Sunglasses, sports watch, key fob, and of course the now traditional photo.

Her blood soaked the ground; the hawk circled and cried.

With another crossed off the list, the killer strode away. And thought of the new poem even now winging its way to Adrian.

Back to work. Traveling time!

Three days later, Adrian made the errands run again — this time with a full grocery stop, as Teesha and family were heading down. She picked up a handful of mail from the new box she'd listed on her blog, her website, and her social media, hit the florist for fresh flowers.

Dom helped her put groceries away — and

179

she considered that a good sign. They ate Greek salads while she shared the bits of gossip she'd picked up in town.

When he laughed, really laughed, tears, happy ones, rose up in her throat.

She didn't get to the mail until late in the day. And saw immediately her poet had found her.

Do you think you can hide, do you think
    you can run?
Oh no, my dear, we're not nearly done.
Over all these years you think of me.
And with your last breath, my face you'll
    see.

Postmarked from Baltimore this time, Adrian saw, and thought: Too close.

But the postmark meant nothing, she knew. They'd come from all over the country in the past decade.

But never outside of February.

So the move hadn't just rattled her mother. It had rattled her poetic stalker. Now she'd have to share it all with the local police — because she had to be sensible. And with Harry and — though she hated it — with her grandfather.

And to be safe, because she had Dom to think of, maybe they should add something to the alarm system.

She had some ideas on that.

CHAPTER NINE

The minute Teesha's car pulled up in front of the house, Adrian ran out the door. And found herself delighted Dom wasn't far behind her. She snagged Teesha in a hug, squeezed, squeezed.

"You're here! Now hand over the boy! Hi, Monroe."

"Hi yourself, pretty girl."

Tall and lean and absurdly handsome, he leaned in the back to release Phineas from the car seat.

Phineas's daddy had skin a couple of shades deeper than his mommy's, short dreads, sexy chocolate eyes, and a trim little chin beard that suited his angular face.

Adrian ran around to hug him, and get her hands on the baby as Teesha let out a sudden: "Whoa! Is that a bear?"

Adrian stole Phineas, and planted kisses all over his face to make him laugh. "It's a dog. It's our dog as of yesterday."

"Well, holy sh . . . shoeshine, it's huge."

Instinctively Teesha backed up as the big black mountain of dog ambled her way.

"She's a Newfoundland — that's what the shelter said, and the vet confirmed. She's about nine months old, so she'll get a little bigger. And she's as gentle as a baby lamb."

"I don't know any baby lambs."

The dog sat at Teesha's feet, looked up at her with soulful eyes, and held out a paw.

"She's housebroken, sits, shakes, fetches. Her breed's called nanny dogs because they're so patient and careful with kids."

As she spoke, Adrian carried the bouncing, arm-waving Phineas over to meet the dog.

"Adrian —"

"Do you think I'd get a dog that would hurt this beautiful boy? Or anyone? This is Sadie, and she's a big, fluffy mound of love."

"Sexy Sadie." Grinning, Monroe bent down, rubbed his hands over the dog, who thumped her tail and waited for more.

"Somebody found her — they think her owner just dumped her the way some very-bad-word people do when they decide they don't want a dog. They'd taken her to the shelter the day before Popi and I went in. So it was meant, wasn't it, Popi?"

"Love at first sight," he agreed.

Adrian crouched down.

"Dog, dog, dog. Bark!" Phineas tapped his hands on Sadie's head, a gesture she accepted as willingly as Monroe's rubs. Then she licked

182

the boy's face and sent him into wild laughter.

"She's smart, too. I googled the breed right there in the shelter after she stole our hearts. Smart, highly trainable, loving, gentle, patient, adores kids especially."

"I always wanted a dog."

"Sophia and I talked about another dog after we lost Tom and Jerry. I think we never did because we had to wait for Sadie."

"Well, you combined years of waiting and wanting into one big-ass reality." Finally, Teesha laid a tentative hand on the dog's head.

"Let's get you all settled inside." Dom drilled a finger in Phineas's belly. "And we'll have some wine."

"Popi." Monroe opened the cargo door. "You're speaking my language. No, sir, I got this. If you pour that wine, I'd sure be grateful."

"I'll give him a hand." After another smacking kiss, Adrian passed Phineas back to Teesha. But he just wiggled down so he could throw his arms around Sadie.

"Why don't you give Teesha a hand with our boy here," Adrian suggested. "And pass out those cookies you baked when I wasn't looking."

"Can't have a young one in a house without cookies."

She went around to the cargo doors, grabbed a couple of bags. "So . . . any chance of talking the two of you into moving down

183

this way?"

Monroe smiled at her. "Teesha's used to the city. I wanted the country life, so we compromised on looking at the suburbs. But with you here, I think we've got a shot."

"Really? Really? You'd move here?"

"I like the quiet," he said in his dreamy way. "I can hear the music in the quiet. She's going to need something with neighbors," he continued as they carried bags toward the house. "And where she can walk to shops and stuff. We gotta think of good schools, safe streets."

"I've got three houses picked out to start."

He looked down at her, shook his head. "No moss ever has a chance on you, my Rizz."

"Popi knows everybody, including the best Realtor in the area."

"We'll work on it," he told her.

Adrian knew she'd made the right choice in design consultants when Kayla came to their meeting with a tablet full of apps, a tape measure, a paint fan, and lots of ideas.

Tall and slim, her streaky blond hair in French braids, she radiated enthusiasm.

"What a great space." She'd already crouched down to rub and coo over Sadie. "So much more good, natural light than I figured — and I worried you'd have low ceilings. But this is awesome. I'm nervous. I'm trying not to sound goofy, but I'm nervous. This is my first real consult. Friends and family don't count. I don't want to mess it up."

"You're doing fine."

She straightened while Sadie politely sat nearly on Adrian's feet. "I should've said — I want to say how grateful I am you'd give me a chance. I mean, I don't even have my degree yet."

"I hadn't graduated high school when I did my first fitness video."

Kayla's pretty hazel eyes widened. "Is that really true? You kind of think it's made-up. Like an urban legend."

"Absolutely true. Three friends and I produced it, and it gave me my start. My on-my-own start. Maybe, if we click on this, it'll give you yours."

"But no pressure." Kayla hugged her tablet and laughed. "Okay, I did some research on home gyms, but you don't have any like treadmills or circuit training machines in your videos. I watched a bunch of them, too, so I know you use a lot of outdoor locations along with I guess it's studios."

"That's right. The body's the machine. Sometimes the machine needs tools."

"Like weights, stability balls, yoga mats, and all that."

"Exactly. So I'd need those creatively displayed — and I'll give you a list of what I'd use most often."

"I've got an idea of your style from watching the videos, and some interviews, but maybe you could tell me what you want here. The look. And I'm really hoping you don't want to bust out that bar or the fireplace. They're really cool, and just a little way back and bougie."

Adrian grinned at her. "We just had our first click."

An hour and several clicks later, Kayla gathered her things. And Maya came down the steps with towheaded Collin's hand firm in hers.

"Dom said to come right down. Hi, Kayla."

"Hi. Hi, Collin. I'm so sorry about Lorilee, Maya. I didn't know her very well, but she was so nice. I'm just so sorry."

"We all are. Hard times." She took a deep inhale as Collin stared at the tail-wagging Sadie with huge eyes. "Dom said to tell you he was going in to the shop for a while."

"He did? He did!" Adrian pumped her fists in the air, executed two fouetté turns. "This is the first time he's left the house." Then she pressed her hands to her face, struggled back the tears. "Sorry, Kayla."

"No, no, don't be sorry." As her own eyes filled, Kayla hugged Adrian tight. "I'm going to work up a couple of designs, and I'll text you, okay?"

"Yeah. Good. Thanks."

She left by the glass patio doors, while

Maya and Adrian watched each other with damp eyes.

"First," Maya began, "who have we got here?"

"This is Sadie, and she's as sweet and gentle as she is huge. She loves kids."

"For breakfast?"

"This morning she took the half slice of bacon Phineas offered her before we could stop him, and took it as delicately as a duchess."

"Leaving him with five fingers?"

"On each hand. Look at that face, Maya, those eyes. Look at that tail." Adrian crouched down, put an arm over Sadie's back. "Come on down."

"Don't have to go far." But when Maya did, Sadie sniffed happily at Collin. More cautious than Phineas, Collin leaned back into his mother. Then carefully patted the flat of his hand on Sadie's face.

Then smiled and said: "Da da da da. Oooooh."

"He approves. If he doesn't, it's no. His first word was a very firm no. It still tops his repertoire."

"I know he doesn't remember me, but we're going to fix that."

"I couldn't believe you were moving here." And Maya's eyes filled again. "I'm so glad you're moving here."

"Me, too. Maya, I don't want to get us both

187

going again, but I'm so sorry about Lorilee." She had to stop, had to breathe through the rise of tears. "I'm so sorry I couldn't be there at her memorial, be there for you, for your mom, for Raylan and his children."

"Same," Maya managed in a shaky voice. "Same for you and Dom with Sophia."

"How's Raylan?"

"Functioning. I'm not sure he would be except for the kids. He's going to work at home for now, or take them with him to the office when they're not in school. He's resistant to the idea of a nanny or childcare right now, and that's probably the right call. But sooner or later . . ."

Maya smiled as Collin pulled away to sit, and Sadie lay down so they hit the same level.

"He said you wrote him. It meant a lot to him. Now before we both start crying — and Collin's seen enough of that for a while — tell me what you're doing down here. It was so damn good of you to hire Kayla."

"Young, fresh eyes and enthusiasm. I think it was so damn smart. She's talking a soft neutral for the walls, and I thought she'd lead with bold, energetic colors. But she said she thinks it could be distracting for streaming and videos."

"Small interruption. The trainers and workouts you're adding to Work Out Now online? It's rocking it, Adrian."

"Did I mention how hard I had to work to

convince my mother to open up to the streaming deal and contracting other pros?"

Maya smiled. "Maybe once or twice."

" 'Why would we compete with ourselves, with DVD sales?' " Adrian rolled her eyes. "She got reluctantly on board when Teesha hit her with some numbers on member potentials, merchandising and marketing opportunities, and viewer projections."

"Speaking of Teesha, where is she? I was hoping to get Collin and Phineas together."

"They should be back soon. They're looking at houses."

"Houses?"

"I'm this close to talking them — well, her, because Monroe's already into it — into moving here."

"Here? Seriously? Well, that's a big wow."

"Let's take my big baby and your little man outside, and I'll fill you in."

Before Adrian got up, Maya reached out to grip her hand. "We're going to be able to do this all the time now. I hate the reason for it, but I really need my friend now."

"She needs you. So tell me some news."

"I actually have some." They headed outside with Sadie walking by Adrian's side. "Mrs. Fricker's going to retire."

"How'd I miss this? I was in town just the other day pumping the grapevine and never heard about it."

"She's keeping it down low. You know I've

managed Crafty Arts since college — currently part-time. She's hoping Joe and I will buy her out."

"Buy it?" Adrian stopped in her tracks. "Buy the gift store? That would be fantastic."

"Would it?" After hunching her shoulders, Maya put Collin down. He toddled a few steps before flopping down to play in the grass. "I mean, I love the place, and sure I know the business. But owning is way different from managing."

"I think you'd be great at it. When Mr. Fricker got sick a few years ago, you ran the place. You did the buying, the displays, the payroll, the works."

"And it was a lot. And before I had a baby. If we jumped into this, I'd need somebody to do things like payroll and the books — they're not my strength, or Joe's. Plus, he's got his own work."

Adrian pointed a finger up. "Is that a light bulb above my head? I happen to know an excellent business manager who may be relocating to Traveler's Creek."

"Do you think she'd do it? It would be the answer to everything. Could I afford her? Do you think she'd run the numbers and tell me if I'm crazy to even consider this?"

"I say yes to all that. But beyond all of that, the most important thing starts with do you want it?"

"That's the trouble. I do. I really do. I can

190

talk myself out of it a half dozen times a day. But I always come back to wanting it."

She glanced down at Collin while he held what seemed to be an intense conversation with a blade of grass.

"I've always loved that place. When we were in high school, I'd tell myself I was going to move to the big city like you, get some slick job where I wore fabulous clothes. Then I started working at Crafty to earn some summer money, and fell in love. Then Joe happened. Then Collin happened. And this is what I want."

"Then I'm going to tell you to let Teesha look things over, then go for it. Because the one thing people regret is not reaching for dreams. Will he let me pick him up?"

"He likes girls," Maya told him. "He's more shy around guys until he knows them better."

"I'm a girl, so . . ." She picked Collin up, gave him a swing that made him laugh. "And I heard a car pull in. It's either Teesha and fam, or Popi. Let's go see."

"I've got about twenty minutes, tops, before I have to get this one home for lunch and a nap. He gets seriously cranky otherwise."

"This face?" Adrian kissed it. "Could never be cranky."

"Come live my life for a couple days."

Sadie moved from Adrian's side, even picked up the pace when she spotted Phineas. Fully confident now, Teesha put her son down so he and the dog could have a loving reunion.

"Maya! And Collin's gotten so big. He's beautiful! Gimme."

She snatched him from Adrian, and Monroe bent down to rest his chin on Teesha's shoulder.

"Boy, you look like summer sunshine."

After a shy smile, Collin wiggled.

"Okay, okay, who can compete with another boy and a dog mountain?"

After setting him down, Teesha wrapped around Maya. Whatever she murmured had Maya holding tight.

"Thanks. And thank both of you for the flowers. They were beautiful, and appreciated. Oh, it's good to see you. All of you. Look at Phineas. He's a little man."

Sadie stretched out, in obvious bliss, as the boys crawled all over her.

"And you." Teesha pointed a finger at Adrian. "I hate you."

With a laugh, Monroe draped an arm around his wife's shoulders. "Dream house."

"I knew it." Adrian did a quick hip-shaking boogie. "I bet it's the pretty blue two-story with the covered porch, open concept, and sweet backyard — fenced — on Mountain Laurel Lane."

"I'd call you a nasty name for that, but there are children present. In my life I'd never imagined myself living on a place called

Mountain Laurel Lane."

"We put an offer in," Monroe said, grinning from ear to ear.

"Holy — you know what! Wow and freaking A, and . . ."

When words failed, Adrian did a trio of handsprings.

"Show-off. It's crazy." Teesha put her hands to the sides of her head, shook it back and forth. "I know it's crazy, but I want that house. We only looked at two. We only looked for a few hours, one day, and . . . it was ours." She reached back over her shoulder, and Monroe took her hand.

"Because it's perfect for us. We can walk into town to a restaurant, to have a drink, shop, but we've got a yard. We've got neighbors in a nice neighborhood, and it's not Stepfordland."

"He's right." Teesha sighed. "He's right, and still it's crazy. But I want that house."

"Two — no, three, counting Monroe — of my best pals going after what they want. And hey, me, too! Come back for dinner tonight, Maya. You and Joe and Collin. We'll celebrate."

"I haven't even talked to Teesha about it yet — and Joe and I need to talk some more."

"About what?" Teesha asked.

"Maya's going to buy the best shop in town, but she needs you to look at the numbers. Bring them tonight. You'll take a look, won't you, Teesh?"

"Sure."

"Great. Come at five. We'll have wine. Teesha can take a look, and Sadie and I will run herd on the kids."

"Bossy," Teesha said to Maya.

"Tell me."

"Organized, efficient, and goal-oriented. It's been a hard few weeks." Adrian slid an arm around Teesha's waist, around Maya's. "So fresh starts, new ventures, and going after what you want. That all works for me."

"We'll see if the numbers work for me and Joe — and what Teesha has to say. But I know I can speak for him when I say we'd love to come to dinner. Nobody turns down a meal at Casa Rizzo.

"Meanwhile." She bent down to lift Collin. "I've got to get this one home. We'll see you tonight. And thanks in advance, Teesha."

"Numbers, business, projections. It's who I am." After they waved Maya off, Teesha turned to Adrian. "Which shop, how long has it been in business, why are the owners selling, where's it located?"

"I'll have those answers and more when we sit on the porch with some lemonade."

Ten weeks later, Teesha lived on Mountain Laurel Lane, Maya owned a business, and Adrian stood in her new studio with Kayla.

"It's perfect. It's just exactly right. I was

194

nervous when you talked about doing a light whitewash on the fireplace, but you were right there, too. It softens the brick."

"Do you love it? I love it. I want you to love it."

"I love it. You took what I wanted — or thought I did — and made it better. Refinishing the hardwood, completely worth it. Setting the bar up as a smoothie station, adding that pottery tray of wheat-grass speaks to the nutrition angle of fitness. And it still feels homey, accessible."

The good, natural light had the refinished floors glowing, a big seagrass basket held colorful yoga mats, while an old coatrack served as visible storage for exercise bands.

She'd used floating shelves for stability balls so they looked like wall art. Instead of a standard free weight rack, Kayla had repurposed an old wine rack.

"I love the way you used some of what was here — my grandparents' things, my great-grandparents' — like that cabinet. Using it for holding towels, sweatbands, yoga blocks. And putting plants and candles on that old bench. It puts the 'home' in home gym."

"So the little sitting area over by the fireplace isn't too much?"

"Nope, and I'll use it. The colors work, too. You were right about the soft, sagey green. I thought it would be too gray and dull, but it's just soft and it makes the equipment colors pop. The green of the plants go vibrant against it. Any angle I stream from is going to work."

Absently Adrian lowered her hand to rub Sadie's head as the dog sat by her side. "It was thoughtful of you to find those family pictures, have them framed for the mantel."

"You kept saying home, and what's home without family?"

"Well, Kayla, you just nailed your first professional design job. It won't be your last."

"I'm so happy!" She bounced in her lavender running shoes. "You said it was okay if I took pictures and used them in my portfolio."

"Absolutely. And I'll write your first client review."

"Oh God!"

"And I know you head back to college soon, but if you can squeeze in another consult, my friends Teesha and Monroe could use a little help on their new house."

Eyes widened; mouth dropped open. "You're kidding."

"Not kidding. I told Teesha if you had time you'd stop by after you left here. I'll give you her address. She's right on Mountain Laurel Lane."

"I know the house. I know it. Everybody knows about them moving here. It's such a great house. I'll go right now! Oh my God!"

"Thank you, Kayla, for giving me exactly what I needed."

Adrian offered a hand, but Kayla just went in for a hug. "You're not just my first client. You're going to be my favorite client forever. Bye, Sadie!" She raced for the glass doors, then stopped, posed. "I'm an interior designer."

Laughing, she jogged away.

Adrian knew how it felt to see a dream realized. Thinking of just that, she took out her phone to text Hector, Loren, and Teesha.

Hi, gang, time to coordinate for our first production in my new home studio. Which looks freaking fantastic. I've got the theme, have the routines nearly nailed down. My schedule's open, so work out when you can fit me in, and we'll go. Teesha, Kayla's on her way to you now. And, guys? Wait until you see Teesha's new house. Not to mention my new studio. Talk soon.

She jogged up two flights of stairs, delighted the house was empty because her grandfather had gone in to work. Every day now, she thought as she went into her bedroom to change. Sometimes just for an hour, but often for most of the day.

The work, she thought, his love of it, brought him both joy and solace.

She felt the same about her own.

After donning workout gear, she went back down to her new space. She opened the glass doors so Sadie could wander out as she pleased or needed. She put on her basic keep-the-beat music, set a timer. And, facing her mirrored wall, got to work.

As she rehearsed and refined the warm-up, she had a flash of herself as a child, watching her mother rehearse. The house in Georgetown, the sleek room with mirrored walls and her mother's reflection.

How she'd yearned.

How, alone again, she'd danced in that room, imagining herself a ballerina, or a Broadway star, or what she'd become. And so good, so exceptional, her mother would watch her with the same yearning she felt.

Then the man had come, bringing fear and blood and pain.

His face — she remembered every detail of it — blurred everything else from her vision so she had to stop the timer.

"No point, no point, no point going back there."

Closing her eyes, she breathed through it. Even the media rarely dug that horrid old story up now. Old, old news. No point.

She reminded herself she rarely had moments like this, when the fear rushed back, turned her cold, then hot, then breathless.

She'd push through it. She had pushed through it.

"I'm strong," she told her reflection. "And I'm not defined by one horrible day in the whole of my life."

She started to turn the timer back on, then caught a glimpse of Sadie in the mirror, sprawled a few feet back, watching her.

Yearning, Adrian thought.

Instead of turning on the timer, she walked back to sit on the floor, nuzzle the big bear of a dog who made love noises in her throat. A sound that always made Adrian laugh.

"I'll come back to this. Let's you and me go outside and play chase the ball."

You made time for the ones you loved, she thought as she went outside, picked up the big orange ball that put a light of joy in Sadie's eyes.

If her childhood had taught her anything, it was to make time for her passion, her responsibilities. And for the ones she loved.

CHAPTER TEN

Through the summer after his wife's death, Raylan worked almost exclusively from home. And almost always at night. Sleep hadn't been his friend since Lorilee's death, so he turned nights into work time, and snatched some sleep in the early morning hours.

He napped when — if — the kids napped.

He couldn't handle the idea of a nanny, couldn't stand to bring yet another drastic change into his children's lives. And he couldn't bear the idea of leaving them with someone else.

And since for the first few weeks Bradley often woke up crying in the middle of the night, sleep became more luxury than priority.

He'd never forget the help, the comfort, the attention his mother and sister had provided, but they couldn't stay forever.

He had responsibilities, first to his kids, then to his work. And the work not only provided for his family, but kept his company solvent and employees who counted on him paying their bills.

For snatches of time, he could lose himself in the work, or in the needs of his kids. The laundry, the grocery runs, the food prep, the attention, the trips to the park. The everything that added up to trying to give them a sense of security, a sense of normal.

He'd always wondered how single parents managed.

He found out a lot of the managing involved desperation and exhaustion — and a complete lack of self-anything-at-all.

He lost weight — a pound here, a pound there, until he went from lean to gaunt. He barely recognized himself whenever he caught a glimpse in the mirror.

But he didn't have time to do anything about it.

In the fall, he went into the office after he took the kids to school, before he picked them up again.

He worked out a routine that included hiring a weekly housekeeper to handle the cleaning chores he and Lorilee had always managed to deal with.

At Christmas, when he simply wanted to close himself in the dark and grieve all over again, he forced himself to put up a tree, to string lights.

And broke down, thankfully alone, when he started to hang the stockings and unpacked

Lorilee's. The grief simply rolled through him, a dark, terrible wave that dropped him to the floor.

How could he do this? How could anyone get through this?

As he clutched the stocking, Jasper padded over to him, crawled into his lap, and laid his head on Raylan's shoulder.

He pulled the dog in, held on and held on until the worst passed.

He would do it, and he would get through it. Because his kids slept upstairs, and they needed him.

But instead of having Christmas morning at home, then driving to his mother's for the holiday dinner and Boxing Day, they had their little family Christmas the morning of Christmas Eve, then made the drive down.

Santa brought the presents and filled the stocking early, he told the kids, because he knew they were going to Nana's. Because Santa knew everything.

New traditions, he told himself. He had to make them so the old ones didn't break him into pieces he'd never put together again.

So he got through the summer, the fall and winter, and on the anniversary of Lorilee's death, he sat alone in the dark, his kids asleep, and dreamed of her.

She slid onto his lap as she'd often done in their quiet, alone times. He smelled her, that soft floral fragrance she'd used. It filled him like breath.

"You're doing fine, honey."

"I don't want to do fine. I want you."

"I know. But I'm here. I'm in the kids. I'm in here." She laid a hand on his heart. "You just have to keep going. I know today's hard, but you'll get through it to tomorrow."

"I want to go back. I want to stop you from going to work that day."

"Can't." She nuzzled at his throat. "And if I hadn't gone, that boy would be dead. Don't say you don't care, because that's not true. Who knows who he'll grow up to be, what wonderful things he might do?"

"He came to see me," Raylan murmured. "With his parents. I didn't want to talk to them."

"But you did."

"They wanted me to know . . . they just wanted me to know how sorry, how grateful. I didn't want to care."

"But you did."

"They got permission to plant a tree on the school grounds. A dwarf cherry — the ornamental — that you can see from your classroom window. They wanted me to know they'd never forget you."

"We can't know what other good and kind things he might do with his life. And if I hadn't been there, maybe whoever took my class wouldn't have gotten the other kids to

203

safety. We can't know, honey, we just can't know."

"We can't know what you'd have done with yours. What we'd have done with ours."

"Oh, Raylan, I did what I had to do with mine, and I guess what I was meant to do. You know that. Now you're doing what you need to do. Remember how we talked the night before it happened, about how to tell the kids about Sophia?"

"We were going to tell them she had to become an angel, and she'd be looking out for them, for others who needed it."

"It seemed the right thing because they're so young. But you can think of me that way, too. Because I'm always with you, Raylan, honey. Looking out for you and our babies."

"Adrian wrote me. She said you were an angel."

"Well, there you go, right?" She kissed him, so soft, so sweet. "I love you, Raylan. And you have to let the grief go now. It's not the same as letting me go, the memories, the love. Let the grief go now, and turn it into something else. For me, for our babies."

"I don't know if I can."

"I know you can. I know you will."

She kissed him again, and then he sat alone in the dark.

He got up, turned on the lights in his office. Though it was nearly midnight, he sat at his workstation.

He began to sketch her, his Lorilee. First her face — so many expressions. Happy, sad, angry, amused, seductive, surprised.

Then her body, full front, profile, turned away. He filled pages of drawing paper before he added wings.

He drew her with them folded, spread, with her flying with them, spinning with them. Fighting with them.

At first he drew her in a long white dress, and immediately knew he'd gone wrong.

White wings, yes, large, beautiful, and somehow ferocious. But her outfit should be bolder, stronger, fiercer than angelic white.

He tried again, sketching her in a snug one-piece, slim boots, considered a halo, rejected it as too clichéd. He brought the long sleeves into a point on the backs of the hands, dipped a V on the front of the boots.

Simple, strong, and when he reached for his colored pencils, he chose blue. Like her eyes.

She'd died saving others, he thought, but before her time. A mistake in the order of things. So . . . she'd been given a hundred years to live as human, but only if she contin-ued to fight for others, to save them, to work for right, for the innocent.

Lee, she'd be Lee Marley — part of her first name, a combo of their kids' names — in human form, in her alter ego. An artist.

And when she spread her wings, when she

was called to protect, she became True Angel.

He pinned the sketch to his board.

Before his kids waked in the morning, he had the outline of her origin story.

He'd done what she asked, he thought. He'd let a little of the grief go, and made it into something else.

He got the kids dressed, hunted up the sparkly pink sneakers his daughter had to wear to preschool and couldn't find. Since that ate up time, he made Eggos for breakfast — got some cheers for that.

Bundling them and his night's work in the car, he did the drop-offs and headed into the office. And for the first time in a year, with real purpose, real excitement.

He snagged Jonah first.

"Jesus, Raylan, you look like hell. Like hell on uppers."

"All-nighter. I need a meeting with you and Bick."

"She just went up. Look, I need to round up Crystal for the lettering on —"

"After." To save time, he dragged Jonah to the freight elevator.

"I know yesterday was rough on you, but did you seriously do a bunch of drugs?"

"Coffee, too much coffee."

While the elevator started its moaning grind, Raylan texted Bick.

My office, right now!

"You hardly ever drink coffee."

"I did last night. I've got something." He patted his bag. "I need you guys to see it, give me your honest take."

"Okay, sure. But no more coffee for you. We've got a partners' meeting this afternoon anyway. Why don't you catch a nap, and we'll —"

"No. Now."

He clamped a hand on Jonah's arm again, pulled him to his office. Opening his bag, he took out sketches, started pinning them up. Ignoring the half-finished work on his desk, he added the outlines, chapter by chapter, of the origin story.

"She's beautiful." Jonah spoke quietly. "It's Lorilee, and she's beautiful."

Raylan shook his head. "She's Lee Marley in human form. She's True Angel, guardian of the innocent."

"Where's the fucking fire?" Bick demanded as she came in. "I've got . . . Oh." She stopped, studied the sketches. "Those are fantastic, my man."

"I need you to look these over, I need you to listen to the story line. Then I need you to tell me if it's a go. Not because you feel sorry for me. Not because you loved her, too. But because it's right. No, it has to be better than right if we go with this. If you see flaws, I want to know. If it doesn't work, I need to know. It's her face. It's her heart. So I need to know."

Jonah had already moved to the board, already started scanning the outlines. "You already know it works. You already know it's more than right. An homage to her, sure, but . . ."

He broke off as his voice shook. "Take over," he mumbled to Bick.

"I'm reading."

"I can tell you where it's going," Raylan began. "I've already fleshed out the outline in my head."

Bick just wagged a finger at him. "Quiet. Move her from Brooklyn. Put her in SoHo. Give her a loft in SoHo. She works in the gallery downstairs to afford it."

"Okay." Raylan nodded as he thought it through. "Okay, and that keeps her in Manhattan. That's better."

"You've got her saving this woman in a store robbery. Could it be a kid? Like a ten-year-old boy? Street kid. It's more poignant."

"Could be better. I can work with it."

"I'll tell you what. Having her code in the ambulance, them trying to bring her back while her spirit goes to what you call the In-Between? That could be magic. How they've just called it when she's sent back, breathes. Yeah, could be magic."

She turned to him. "How hard is that going to be for you, to write and illustrate all that? Bringing her back?"

"It's going to be solace." It already was. "It's going to be making something positive out of losing her. But only if I can make it matter."

"It's going to matter. Jonah?"

He'd pulled himself together, smiled now. "Here's to True Angel. Long may she fly."

They launched True Angel on the second anniversary of Lorilee's death. Raylan pitted her against Grievous, the half-demon who infected human hosts until their ordinary resentments and frustrations turned to crazed violence.

The work kept Raylan busy, involved, and the reader reception to his Angel boosted his spirits, and his company.

But by summer, and the end of another school year, he accepted he needed to make a change. For his kids, for himself, for the quality of his work.

He took a long overdue vacation, a beach week with just the kids.

With even the thought of work left behind, he tossed the rules on bedtime, on breakfast so the world turned on sandcastles and sunscreen slathering, hot-dog grilling and clambakes. He woke to the sound of ocean waves and kids bouncing on his bed.

At night if he hadn't succumbed to a sun-and-sea-day coma like his kids, he sat on the little deck, watched the stars shower over the dark sea.

When he dreamed of her, she wore a long white dress covered with purple flowers. He remembered the dress, one of the last he'd finally made himself pack up for donation.

She stood at the deck rail with the ocean breeze streaming through her hair and the moonlight bathing her.

"We always loved coming here. We talked about buying a cottage or bungalow one day." She smiled as she looked over. "We never got around to it."

"Too many things we never got around to."

"Oh, we got to the important ones. They're sleeping inside right now, all curled up and sun-kissed, with Jasper on guard."

"He loves the beach as much as they do. I could buy a place now. True Angel's kicking serious butt. I could look on Cape May, it's closer to home, but . . ."

"It's hard, even for a good daddy, to do everything."

"I worry I let some of it slide. Baking two dozen cupcakes — gluten-free — for Bradley's class, making sure Mariah has the right color hair ribbon to match her outfit — that kid is fierce for fashion. How did you do it?"

"Honey, I had you, so if I couldn't get to the cupcakes, you picked them up at the bakery. If I couldn't find the hair ribbon, you found the hair clip with the flower on it that did the job."

She sat beside him, a comfort, picked up

210

the glass of wine he'd barely touched. "There's no shame in needing help, Raylan."

"It's not that. Every time I start down the road of looking for a nanny, it just feels wrong. For them. For us. I don't know why, but it feels wrong."

"Yes, you do know why." She patted his leg as she sipped his wine. "Just like you know what you should do, need to do, and, in your heart, want to do."

"And that feels like leaving you, turning away from everything we had, that we built, that we wanted."

"Oh, Raylan, honey, I left you. I didn't want to, I didn't mean to, but I left you. Now you have to do what's right for our babies, for yourself." After setting down the wine, she kissed his cheek. "I count on you for that."

Then she rose, spread her white wings, and flew into the night.

When he got back to Brooklyn, he made the painfully precise arrangements to set up a playdate for both kids, then made the much simpler ones for a partners' meeting.

This meant using the third-floor conference room and ordering in Chinese for lunch.

Jonah, clean-shaven after his winter beard experiment, scooped up sweet and sour chicken. "Marta just got me the sales reports on Angel, and Snow Raven — preorders for Queen's July issue. I'll shoot them out to both of you, and put them up in here so we can eat real hearty. 'Cause we are kicking it, pals."

"Good to know." Deftly, Bick manipulated chopsticks in her noodles. "Because I peed on a stick this morning. Pats and I are going to have another mouth to feed next spring."

"Holy crap." Jonah pointed at her while Raylan sprang up to round the table and hug her. "You're knocked up?"

"That's affirmative. Keeping it down low for now, and we're going into the clinic for the official test, but you guys should know."

"How you doing?" Raylan asked her. "How're you feeling?"

"Five by five right now. May it continue. And really happy. Stupid, crazy happy. Look, I don't want to tell anybody else until I go to the doc's, get the all clear, make sure everything's baking right. That means keep it zipped, Jonah."

He looked offended. "I can keep it zipped."

"Usually we have to weld it shut, but this is important. Zipped until I give you the green."

"How come you're not ragging on Raylan?"

"Because he doesn't blab."

"Blab!" Jonah huffed. "I do, too."

Bick laughed, punched his shoulder. "A wise man knows himself."

"This is great news, Bick. I'm happy for you and Pats."

"I'm happy for us, too, Raylan. Now, you

212

called the meeting. Is this to tell us how you spent your summer vacation?"

"I can sum that up pretty easy. Pretty damn perfect. The kids loved it. I have to confess, Bradley continues his Dark Knight obsession."

"You have to do something about that kid," Jonah told him.

"An icon's an icon, but I had to make the difficult decision to help him re-create Wayne Manor out of sand."

"What? What about Snow Raven's Aerie! It's cooler!"

"He's only seven, Jonah." Nearly eight, Raylan realized with a jolt. "Give him time. Now, before we see the numbers, and deal with any other business, I need to ask you both — as partners, not friends — if me working from home puts any hitches in the company, in production, in creativity, and in the division of responsibilities."

"You were working from home when you came up with *True Angel,*" Bick reminded him. "That's the opposite of hitches."

"And we're already set up for you to work remotely over the rest of summer, or the bulk of it," Jonah put in. "We've got the tech, Ray-Man. Yeah, it's great when we can all be in the same building and brainstorm, or make decisions, or argue about decisions. But we're doing all that, when we need to, by videoconference."

"How would you both feel if it wasn't just over the summer, or school vacations, or kid-home-sick days?"

Bick sat back. "Is something wrong with the kids?"

"No. But I feel I have to do better for them. I'm not enough. They need more. They need family and a steadier routine than I can give them on my own. I put it off, for me, and I can't keep doing that. I decided to move back home, back to Traveler's Creek."

"From Brooklyn to Boondocks?" Jonah said, obviously shocked.

"I came from Boondocks to Brooklyn. Their grandmother's there, and they don't see enough of each other. Their aunt and uncle, their cousin. Family. And I know they're all busy, but they'd be there. And so would we. I wouldn't have to send Mom a video of Mo's dance recital or Bradley's Little League game. She could be there. I know, if I needed, they could sit and do homework in Rizzo's, like I did."

"This feels sudden, but it's not," Bick said.

No, Raylan thought, not sudden at all.

"I've been thinking about it for a while, but putting it off because selling that house we bought together, fixed up together, brought the kids home to when they were born, that felt like a betrayal."

"It's not," Jonah murmured. "It's not."

"Appreciate that. I can take the train up or

214

drive up, maybe once a month, or whatever works. And I wouldn't worry about the kids because they'd be with my mom or my sister. If it doesn't work, if it affects the company, I'll step out. You can buy me out and —"

"Shut the fuck up." Bick stabbed a finger at him.

"Ditto. This is our baby, womb to tomb. It's the three of us," Jonah said, "or it's none of us. You're the one who said let's make our own fucking comics."

"I was sort of drunk at the time."

"Well, we made our own fucking comics even after we sobered up. Maybe you're going to move to Shit's Creek, but we've got three paddles."

"Jeez, Jonah." Bick patted a hand on her heart. "You're a frigging poet. How do the kids feel about it? You wouldn't have told us if you hadn't talked to them first."

"They're for it. It surprised me how fast they got on board. They have friends here, school, the house. But they're excited about it. Mo wants a house with a princess tower. I'm afraid Brad's pulling for a Wayne Manor."

"Jesus." Jonah only shook his head over his chicken. "The kid's killing me."

"We'll live with Mom at first — at least I'm going to dump that on her — because it'll take awhile to find a place down there, and that's after the time it takes to deal with the house here, get it ready to sell, put it on the market."

"Don't." Bick immediately slapped a hand to her mouth, eyes wide over it.

"I can't keep two houses. The numbers aren't that good."

"No, I mean . . . How would you feel if we bought it? Pats and me. Oh my God, I just said that."

"Say it again?"

"It's crazy, right? But we were talking after I peed on the stick, and after we jumped around, we both said how we should buy a house. Stay close to her work and mine, but have a house, a yard, kid-friendly neighborhood. Holy shit, what if we bought your house? Is that terrible? Would it be bad for you if people you knew lived in it? Would it —"

His heart just opened wide, and all the good poured into it.

"I can't think of anything that feels better. Not strangers. Family."

"Really? Oh man, oh boy, I need to talk to her. I mean, she loves your house, but I can't just say deal."

"It's meant." Jonah ate more chicken. "I got the tingle in the bones. You know I don't get the bone tingles unless it's meant."

"I'm going to go call her. You're sure about this?"

"Yes. I'm sure. In fact, I think I feel a slight bone tingle myself."

"That's my deal, man. You can't steal a man's tingle."

"I'm going to call her right now." Bick sprang up, then dropped down again. "No, put up the numbers first. I need to see the numbers before I go and buy a house."

Jonah chugged some Mountain Dew and grinned as he swiveled to his computer. "Let me preface this reveal by saying we can all afford to buy a house."

Because the day begged for it, Adrian recorded her blog workout on the patio, opting for a quick, effective yoga session, and ending sitting cross-legged on her mat, an arm around Sadie, who'd wandered over to join her.

"Don't forget, flexibility is one of the essential legs on the fitness stool. Make time for it, make time for you. Until next time, Sadie and I say enjoy today."

She clicked off the remote, nuzzled her dog. "And that's a wrap for this week."

"You looked good, too."

She turned her head, spotted Dom. "Hey, I didn't know you were back. You should've come into it. You know people love seeing you on the blog."

"I'll leave those Down Dogs to you and Sadie."

"Tai chi next week then. You're good at it."

"Maybe. How about we sit in the shade, if

you're not busy, and enjoy some of this summer day?"

"Not busy. Sit, and I'll go get us some lemonade."

"Wouldn't mind that a bit."

"Five minutes. Stay with Popi, Sadie."

When Dom sat at the little patio table, Sadie went to him, laid her big head on his thigh.

As he stroked the dog, Dom looked out over the garden, one alive with summer. Tomatoes ripening, roses thriving, the big rosemary bush tossing scent into the air.

He could hear the hum of bees, the song of birds.

He hated knowing he couldn't do as much work in the garden as he used to, but knew Adrian liked picking up the slack.

"She picks up a lot of slack, Sadie."

He watched her as she came down from the kitchen with a tray. The pitcher and glasses of ice, the little bowl of berries, the plates for fruit and cheese.

A lot of slack, he thought again.

"How are things at Rizzo's?"

"A little slow this afternoon. People want to be out and about on a pretty day like this. But I've got news."

"Gossip?" Adrian wiggled her shoulders as she poured the lemonade, made the ice crackle. "I love gossip."

"More news than gossip, I'm afraid, but

218

good news. Jan told me Raylan and his kids are moving back to the Creek."

"Really?" Adrian popped a raspberry into her mouth. "She must be thrilled."

"Thrilled doesn't cover it."

"What about his work, his company?"

"He'll work from here, go up to Brooklyn when he needs to. They'll stay with her until he finds a house. I'd say she'd be happy if that took forever."

He sipped some lemonade. "Just like your grandmother's."

"I watched her make it enough times. Which is something you still won't allow with your sauce."

He smiled. "One day."

"I've heard that before." She tossed Sadie a blueberry, amusing everyone when the dog snatched it out of the air.

"There is something I wanted to talk to you about."

"Oh?"

"About the house, the business. I made the changes in my will long ago —"

"Oh, Popi."

He cut her off with a shake of his head. "A man — or woman — who doesn't put affairs in order is selfish and shortsighted. I like to think I'm neither."

"You're not."

"It occurred to me I'd never discussed it with you, and what I've done may be more burden than gift. Leaving you the house and the business."

"Oh, Popi."

"It's not only that your mother doesn't need either, but she wouldn't want them. This isn't her home, and hasn't been for a long time. She's never had any real interest in the business. She has her own. But then, so do you. I want you to be honest with me because these are responsibilities, ones that don't end. You may want to move back to New York, you may not want to think about owning another business."

"I'm not moving anywhere. This is home. You know that. And Rizzo's isn't just a business, not to you, not to me. Not to the town either."

He'd expected just that, but still his heart lightened.

"All right then. I know I can trust you with both. As for what's inside the house, I'd ask you to let your mother have whatever she wants. Some of her mother's jewelry. Sophia wasn't one for the fancy, but there are sentimental pieces. And the furniture, the things. Lina should have what means something to her."

"No question. I promise you."

"You're a good girl. A treasure to me, always, but in these last two years . . . I wouldn't have made it without you. Or you." He rubbed Sadie's head again. "My big girl."

"We love you, Popi. And having this?" She spread her arms. "Having you? You gave me roots. It's made all the difference for me."

"Seeing what you've grown from those roots makes me proud." He let out a sigh. "Now that's done, and we do just what you said on your recording. Enjoy today."

Part Two: Changes

All things change;
nothing perishes.

— Ovid

CHAPTER ELEVEN

It wasn't as simple as loading up the car and heading south. It wasn't, Raylan discovered, even as basic as packing. First you had to cull and purge and decide and organize. And guide a couple of kids into doing the same with all their stuff.

How and when had they accumulated so much stuff?

Then he had to deal with the baby stuff he and Lorilee had tucked away in anticipation of one or two more babies.

It didn't hurt his heart as much as it might have, as he could offer it all — the crib, the bouncer, the changing table, the swing, the slings, the whole lot — to Bick.

Whatever didn't work for her and Pats, he'd donate.

And because he could admit that other than his own office, he'd left most of the furniture choices to his wife, and because he didn't know what he'd need or want in the next house, he offered some of that as well.

Even so, it took time to sort through and pack up eight years, and all the memories that went with a bedside lamp or a set of pots, the birthday and Christmas gifts, even the living room rug — slightly chewed on one corner by the puppy Jasper had been.

He rented the storage unit, hired the movers, canceled what needed canceling, transferred what needed transferring, and kept himself insanely busy for three weeks.

At dawn on moving day, he wandered the nearly empty house, listening to the echoes of the life he'd had. Laughter, plenty of it, but tears, too. The wail of a teething baby at two a.m., the couch naps. Stubbed toes, spilled milk, morning coffee, tangled Christmas tree lights, first steps.

Hopes and dreams.

How did he say goodbye to all of that?

Hands in the pockets of the sweat shorts he'd pulled on, he rounded back into the living room. And spotted Bradley sitting on the steps.

His boy had a sleep crease in his left cheek, bright hair tousled, big blue eyes still heavy. And watching him.

"Hey, pal."

"Don't be sad."

Raylan crossed over to the steps, sat beside his son, draped an arm over his shoulders. In his Batman pj's — what could you do? — Bradley still smelled like a forest.

"I'm not so sad."

"I said goodbye to my friends and to my team, and to Mrs. Howley across the street. When I woke up, I said goodbye to my room."

Raylan hugged him closer, kissed the top of his head. "Am I doing the right thing, kid?"

"Mo's excited, but she's just a baby whatever she says. I love Nana, and Aunt Maya and Uncle Joe, and Collin's kind of funny. I like Nana's house and going to the pizza place where she works. And Ollie who lives next door to Nana's okay. But it's going to be different because it's not just a visit."

"Yeah, it's going to be different."

"When we get our own house, will she go with us?"

Raylan didn't have to ask who. "She's in you and Mo as much as I am. Where you go, she goes."

Bradley leaned his head against his father. "Then it's okay. But when we get our new house, it can't be pink, right? No matter what she says."

Raylan understood this "she" referred to Mariah. "No pink house. That's a pact between men. How about a manly breakfast of Pop-Tarts before we get dressed, get Mariah moving? We can get this adventure started."

"Pop-Tarts! Can we stop at the place that has the McDonald's and get Happy Meals for lunch?"

"I'll put it on our travel agenda."

The agenda included the ceremonial passing of the keys to Bick and Pats, a send-off by Jonah that included two sacks of travel snacks, games, comics that would have kept a busload of kids happy for a five-hour drive, horn honking, waving — and a pit stop less than thirty minutes out when Mariah had to pee.

That delicate dance — Raylan hovering outside the women's bathroom and feeling like a pervert — would be repeated at the lunch stop, which nobody actually needed with the sacks of snacks, and fifteen minutes shy of target when both kids had to pee.

And, naturally, every pit stop required putting the leash on Jasper and walking him so he could pee.

They arrived in Traveler's Creek with empty bladders and gummy worm sugar highs.

Jan rushed out of the tidy house she'd lived in for more than thirty years with her braid bouncing at her back and her eyes shining with happy tears.

"You're here! Welcome home! I need hugs. I need them bad!"

A little zoned from what had turned into a five-and-a-half-hour drive, a little buzzed on sugar himself, Raylan peeled himself out of the car. Already unstrapping Mariah, Jan turned to give him a huge hug.

Jasper leaped out to race in circles around

the front yard like a dog who'd suffered captivity for weeks.

"I've got a cold beer waiting for you," she murmured. "I bet you earned it."

"I did, and I'll take it. Mom. Thanks."

"Stop."

The kids talked nonstop, so his mother had the appropriate noises on tap — amazement, disbelief, delight — as she herded them into the house.

"Your rooms are all ready. With surprises."

"What surprises?" Mariah demanded. "What?"

"Go and see."

Shouting, shrieking, they shot up the stairs with Jasper barking and running behind them.

"I got a 'Merican Girl doll! Nana!"

"A remote-control Batmobile! It's so cool!"

"Batmobile. You're not helping my cause." Raylan just put his arms around his mother, laid his cheek on her head. "Mom."

"Oh, my boy, my baby. It's going to be fine. It's all going to be fine." She turned, kept her arm around his waist as she led him back to the kitchen. "Let's get you that beer. Now, if you're up for it, Maya and her crew are coming over for a family cookout, but that'll keep if you're not."

"No, that would be great."

She got out his beer, opened it. Once she'd handed it to him, she brushed at his hair.

"You're tired. You need a trim and a shave and a good night's sleep."

"It's been a crazy couple of weeks."

"You're here now. When you catch your breath, drink your beer, we'll get your stuff inside so you can settle. Raylan, I wish you'd take the bedroom."

"I'm not taking your bed, that's a firm negative. I'll be fine on the pullout in the den."

"With your big feet hanging over the bottom?" She leaned back against her snowy white kitchen counter. "If I had my selfish way, I'd have that basement finished off, and talk you into living here until the kids graduated college. But being a sensible woman, I know you need your own place."

"If the kids have their way, it'll be a hybrid of a pink castle and Wayne Manor."

"I don't know if I can help you there, but there's a house I think you're going to want to look at."

"Really?"

"I got the inside word — or Dom did. Two-story, four-bedroom, home office on the first floor, quarter-acre lot. Just renovated. Somebody bought it to flip and is just about ready to list it."

"Just about?"

"Inside word," she repeated. "It's on Mountain Laurel Lane."

"No kidding. Spencer used to live on

230

Mountain Laurel Lane."

"His parents still do, a few doors down. It's next door to Adrian Rizzo's friends, Teesha and Monroe and their little boy. They're nice people, they'd be good neighbors."

He smiled at her over his beer. "Sounds like it's settled."

"You're going to want to look at more than one, I expect, but I'm betting this one checks some boxes. Dom told the owner he had somebody who'd want to take a look right off, and got me the name and number for you to call."

"Then I will. How's Dom?"

"He's good. Slowing down some, but he's good. Having his granddaughter with him's made a difference. Like having you and the kids here makes one for me."

The kids ran in to throw their arms around Jan's legs, babbling their thank-yous.

She smiled over at Raylan. "All the difference there is."

They hauled luggage in, toys in, his equipment and tools. Since it obviously pleased her, he let her help Mariah put her things into Maya's old room, Bradley into his while Raylan did what he could to make his nest in the first-floor den.

He squeezed in a work space, put the rest of his things in the hall closet his mother had already cleaned out for him. The main level had a tiny bathroom with a tiny corner

231

shower, and that would do fine. For a while.

Mountain Laurel Lane, he thought, and stretched out on the couch in the den for just a minute. He'd run that street, those sidewalks and yards as a kid. So maybe.

He woke groggy, disoriented, stiff as a board. And with his sister standing in the doorway with two glasses of wine and a smile.

"You saved me from waking you."

He sat up, rubbed the back of his aching neck. "Jesus Christ, how did I forget how uncomfortable this pullout is?"

"Stretch it out, soldier. Dinner's in an hour, the kids — yours and mine — are outside with the dog. Joe's arguing with Mom over control of the grill."

"What're we having?" He stood, rolled his shoulders, tried to stretch out his back.

"In honor of your homecoming, it's steak, baked potatoes, grilled corn and vegetables, tomatoes and mozzarella, and cherry pie."

"That's a damn good deal." He smiled. "Hi."

"Hi." She went in for a hug, handed him a glass. "Let's take a walk around, front to back. Get your blood moving again and catch up a little before we hit the crowd."

"I didn't mean to drop off like that, dump the kids on Mom."

"She's in heaven, so are the kids. Good job, Raylan."

"I hope so." They went out the front, and

he paused to scan the neighborhood where he'd grown up. Some changes, sure, but not many, and the same easy feel to it. "It feels good. I wasn't sure it would. How's business?"

"It's good, too. I love it, and I wasn't sure I would. Aren't we the lucky ones?"

"Mom's done a good job."

They walked around hydrangea bushes, pregnant with fat pink blossoms.

"I hear you might put down stakes on Mountain Laurel Lane."

"I haven't even seen the house yet. Or any."

"It's a pretty house, at least from the outside. Paul Wicker — he was in your class."

"Biker dude, rough customer."

"This is his older brother, Mark. A contractor. He bought the house to flip. Paul, not so much a rough customer now, works for him. Anyway, I can tell you about your closest neighbors."

They ducked under the branches of a red maple as they walked around to the side of the house. "They're terrific. Monroe's a songwriter, Teesha's Adrian Rizzo's business manager. Their kid, Phineas, is Collin's best pal, so I know them really well."

"Maybe I'll call former rough customer Paul's contractor brother tomorrow."

She tapped her glass to his before she drank. "Why not now?"

He heard his kids playing in the backyard

where he'd once battled supervillains, shot hoops, mowed grass.

Maybe a phone call could give him the next step on giving them their own.

"I can do that."

New Orleans, Louisiana

The alley steamed, a pot of gumbo on the simmer, even past two in the morning. The dumpster stank from the day's baking. But she always left the bar last, always by the alley door.

Stupid, just stupid, for an educated woman with a degree in business management, another in hospitality. But she thought because she kept herself buff, because she carried a Taser — and an illegal knife — she could handle what came.

She wouldn't handle this, or anything else after tonight.

Another slut — twice divorced — with an ego so big she'd named her bar after herself. Stella's. Stella Clancy, who'd already poured her last shot.

Now it was just wait, sweating under the disposable black coveralls, for her to come out the door, lock up before her half-a-block walk to her apartment.

She'd never get there. She'd die in the stink of the alley like she deserved.

Near to three, she came out, her whore-dyed red hair cut short to show off the tattoo

234

on the back of her neck.

The pipe struck there first.

She went down like a tree, a toughly built woman in a skinny-strapped top and shorts that barely covered her crotch.

Whore.

She never made a sound.

Blood flew as the pipe struck the back of her skull. It struck again and again, shattering bones after she'd stopped breathing.

Too much fun! Yes, too much fun.

Pull back, get control. Job's done.

Take her watch, the ugly, gaudy ring, the cheap purse.

Smile, bitch. Take the photo.

Bag up the souvenirs, strip off the bloodied coveralls. Bag them with the pipe.

Into the Mississippi with that bag.

Then hunt up a bar, have a drink. Maybe try the Hurricane like a real tourist before it was on the road again.

The dog woke him early. Raylan calculated the pullout aged him about thirty years as he creakily crawled out of it. He dragged on gym shorts, led the prancing Jasper into the kitchen, grabbed a Coke out of the fridge before he opened the back door.

Jasper shot out like a rocket. And in the hazy morning heat, Raylan leaned on the doorjamb while Jasper sniffed around the yard to decide where to complete his morning necessities.

A considerate and oddly poop-shy dog, Jasper wandered out to the back fence and behind a butterfly bush. Used to the routine, Raylan waited in the quiet, so different from the morning bustle of Brooklyn.

He'd done the right thing. If he'd had any lingering doubts about the move, they'd dissolved the evening before around the old — newly painted bright blue — picnic table where his kids feasted and chattered like cocaine-fueled magpies, and Joe with his John Lennon glasses and Orioles fielder's cap bounced Collin on his knee — despite the boy's sauce-smeared hands and face.

With his sister holding a heartfelt discussion on fashion with Mariah. And his mom looking as if he'd given her the world.

He fed the dog, started coffee so his mother wouldn't have to, then worked out the worst of the creaks in the shower.

He reminded himself to shave and, studying himself, considered the abject terror of risking a haircut with an unfamiliar barber.

He could put that one off awhile longer.

By the time he'd dressed, Jan was at the kitchen counter drinking coffee with Jasper sprawled at her feet.

"A treat to wake up to coffee."

He walked around the counter, hugged her from behind. "Kids still asleep?"

236

"We wore them out. You want some breakfast?"

"I ate enough last night to hold me for a couple of days."

"You could use a few more pounds, Slim."

Probably, he thought. He'd gained back some of what he'd lost in the first year after Lorilee's death, but he wasn't back to fighting weight.

"With your cooking, if I don't watch it, it'll be more than a few. Maybe you could post your work schedule like you used to. We can rotate cooking nights. I'm a lot better at putting a meal together than I used to be."

"You couldn't've gotten much worse."

"Ouch."

"Egg Bread Blobs. Grilled Cheese Flambé."

"Early experimental work."

"Since the kids are obviously healthy and well-fed, I'll take you at your word you've moved into a later period."

"I'll surprise you." He kissed the top of her head. "I'm going to have to wake up the slugs, get them moving if we're going to make that appointment to see the house."

"Let them sleep awhile. They can go into work with me."

"You want to take them into work?"

"I took you and Maya when I had to. You know the drill."

He sat beside her a minute. "Help do the setups, make sure the closing crew didn't

237

skimp on cleaning the tables and chairs, and earn quarters for the video machines."

"Do the work, get the pay."

"Are you sure?"

"I'd love it, and you should take a look without them. If it strikes a chord, you can come by and pick them up to go see it, get their reaction."

"You're a sensible woman, Jan Marie."

"I'm all that." She got up to top off her coffee, squeeze a little of her creamer into it. "And who knows better what it's like to be a single parent with two kids and a full-time job? The Rizzos gave me more help than I can ever repay."

"I know it."

"Then the neighbors, the community. You've got that now, and me, Maya and Joe. We can rotate more than cooking dinner, and we will. Meanwhile, you've got more than finding a house to deal with. You've got to settle on a pediatrician, a dentist, get them registered for school, find a vet. Get a haircut."

He shot his fingers through his hair. "I'm not going there yet. I need to work up to that one. The rest I was going to start on today."

"I can tell you there's a dentist in town now. I've been using him for the last year or so, and I'm happy with him. He's got offices right across from the fire department, so there's even off-street parking."

238

"Sold." Now he ran his tongue over his teeth. "I guess."

"As for the haircut, there's always Bill's."

"They scalp you there." He poked at her. "You know they scalp you there. You never made me go there."

"Because I loved you and your goldy locks."

He rolled his eyes at her. "Then you'll love the man bun when I grow into it."

She laughed, shook her head. "I'm going up, getting dressed. I'll get the kids going, get some breakfast in them."

He'd forgotten what it was like to have someone else do something that basic. "If you're sure, I'll take Jasper with me. We'll both get a walk in. I'll see more of the neighborhood if I walk over instead of drive."

"You do that. I should tell you there's another house, already on the market. It's down the other side of town, closer to the school, so that might suit you better. It's got a smaller yard, but it's got one. It hasn't been remodeled, so it's likely going for less. Sturdy, redbrick place, decent front porch, on School-house Drive."

"Good to know."

"Take your time," she said as she rose. "We'll see you at the shop when you get there."

He took his time, rounding up the dog, the leash. Digging up the pooper-scooper and bag, sticking them in his pocket. He found his sunglasses, considered his Mets cap then, thinking of Orioles-land, left it behind.

Jasper's head swiveled, right-left, right-left, in the dog's fascination with the new surroundings. Since he didn't have to hurry, Raylan tolerated the many pauses for avid sniffing, the occasional leg lift to dribble out some pee to show his manliness.

He stopped at the corner a block off Main where a woman in a straw hat snipped off the dead blooms on an enormous climbing rose. She wore pink knee-length shorts that showed skinny, ghost-white legs spiderwebbed with purple veins.

Mrs. Pinsky, he remembered. He'd mown her lawn every week for three summers. Between mowing jobs and his part-time work at Rizzo's, he'd saved enough to buy his first shitpile of a car.

He'd thought Mrs. Pinsky a thousand years old when he was fifteen. And here she was, still deadheading roses.

"Hey, Mrs. Pinsky!"

She looked over, narrowing her eyes behind her glasses, putting a hand to her ear — and hearing aid. "What?"

"It's Raylan Wells, Mrs. Pinsky. Jan Wells's son."

"You're Jan's boy?" She put a hand on her hip. "You come to visit your ma?"

"I'm moving back to the Creek."

"Is that so? Moved away to some godforsaken place, didn't you?"

"Yes, ma'am."

"Your ma's a fine woman."

"The best there is."

"It's good you know that. You used to mow my grass. You looking for work?"

"Ah, no, ma'am. I've got a job."

"Can't get anybody to cut my damn grass who doesn't want my right leg and left foot."

She'd watched him like a hawk, he recalled, but had always paid him fair. And usually added a couple of cookies and a glass of something cold as a tip.

"I'll mow it for you," he heard himself say, right before he wanted to kick himself in the ass.

She eyed him sternly. "How much?"

"No charge."

"A body does a job, a body gets paid for it."

"I might buy a house around on Mountain Laurel Lane. If I do, we'd be neighbors. Neighbors do for neighbors."

That got a smile. "Your ma raised you right. Mower's around back in the shed."

"Yes, ma'am. I have to go look at that house right now. I've got an appointment there. I'll take care of it on the way back if that's okay."

"That'll do. Thank you kindly."

He walked on, warning himself not to volunteer if he happened to spot someone else he remembered.

Now he had to carve out time every week to mow her lawn, and he'd already committed himself — to himself — to take over that chore for his mom.

He had to buy a house, move into it, and cut that lawn.

"Why didn't you tell me to shut up?" he asked the dog. "Before I ended up back in the mowing business?"

He reached the next corner and Mountain Laurel Lane, and stopped dead.

It wasn't the house — obviously not the one he'd come to see, as a woman with a visible baby bump stood in the open front door.

It wasn't the woman in the door that stopped him, but the one with her back to him.

She had a cloud of midnight hair curling like corkscrews past her shoulders. She stood, long and lean in snug leggings — blue with gold snaking up them like flames. A blue top — tank? — snug, that showed off long, tanned arms. Blue shoes, with flames on the sides.

He couldn't see her face — didn't need to, not yet.

Cobalt Flame, he thought, demi-demon. Caught in Grievous's web, tormented by him. Her battle with his Angel would be freaking epic. And in the end, they'd become allies.

The story line just spewed out of him —

lava from a volcano.

Because that's where she'd become, that's where she'd gained her powers.

The inspiration, back still to him, took a step down from the porch. And a mountain of black fur walked from the far corner of the porch to join her.

At his feet, Jasper made a sound. Not a growl, not a warning bark, but if possible, a canine gasp. Then he trembled. As Raylan looked down, started to soothe him, Jasper leaped forward.

The lurch had Raylan stumbling forward. "Hey!"

The shout, the onslaught of man and dog, had the woman turning.

She tipped down sunglasses, laughed. "Raylan? Raylan Wells!"

Adrian Rizzo, he thought as he fought to control his dog. Yeah, the face would work. She'd always been a looker. "Adrian, hi, sorry. I don't know what's gotten into him. He doesn't bite."

Jasper flopped down at the base of the porch, then began to crawl up toward the black mountain.

"Neither does she." Angling her head, Adrian watched Jasper prostrate himself at Sadie's feet. "What's he doing?"

"I don't know."

"I think he's proposing." The other woman stepped out on the porch. She had long braids tied back at her nape and a boy of about four with one arm around her leg and a plastic hammer in his hand.

Sadie put one massive paw on Jasper's head, sent Adrian a sidelong glance.

"I think she's telling him to get a grip. They haven't even been introduced. This is Sadie."

"Jasper. Knock it off. You're humiliating yourself."

"I'm pretty sure I see stars in his eyes. Welcome home, Raylan."

"Thanks. Sorry to interrupt."

"You're not. I was out for a quick run and stopped by. This is Teesha Kirk and Phineas Grant. Teesha, Phineas, Raylan Wells."

"It's nice to meet you." Teesha offered him a smile. "I know Maya and Jan are happy you're back."

"So are we. I'm actually about to look at the house next door."

"Oh, it's a beauty!" Teesha looked over as Phineas sat and began to bang invisible nails.

The boy said, emphatically, "I have to get this work done."

"I've had a lot of peeks," Teesha continued. "Mark does really good work. You've got a couple of kids, don't you?"

"Yeah, seven and five. Well, nearly eight and six."

"It'd be great to have kids next door."

Phineas stopped banging. He said: "Gotta poop," and marched into the house.

"Sorry, gotta poop." Teesha rushed in after him.

"Well, since there's that." Laughing, Adrian came down the steps. "I've got to get home, but my grandfather would really love to see you, and your kids, and your love-addled dog."

"He's never done anything like this. But she's very impressive."

"Sexy Sadie. Teesha's right about the house — I've been through it, too. It's a good one. And as neighbors go?" She gestured toward Teesha's house, where he heard music — a piano — flowing out. "They're the best."

"So Maya told me. You look good, Adrian. I mean, it's good to see you."

"The same." She bent down, gave Jasper a stroke before she clipped a leash on the dog mountain. "I'm sure we'll meet again, Jasper. Love can't be denied. Let's go, Sadie!"

Sadie simply stepped over the dazzled Jasper, gathered herself, then matched her pace to Adrian's long, ground-eating stride.

"Impressive." He looked back at his now-forlorn dog. "She may be too much woman for you, pal, but the heart has its own agenda. Let's go see a house."

CHAPTER TWELVE

After the house tour, after some very strange high school reminiscing with the former rough customer, after talking to his contractor brother as they and a couple of others finished what they called punch-out work, Raylan needed to think.

He made arrangements to come back in an hour or so with his kids, something Mark Wicker approved of.

He stopped by Mrs. Pinsky's and used her ancient excuse for a lawn mower to trim her grass. He had to admit, the lawn had seemed worlds bigger when he'd been fifteen, so it didn't take long.

Still, he worked up a sweat, gratefully took the tall glass of iced tea she'd sweetened enough to make his teeth sting.

She told him he was a good boy, had done a fair job, and again complimented his mother for his good manners.

He walked the dog home, let Jasper's lovelorn heart brood in the backyard while he jumped into the car and drove the short distance to Rizzo's.

The early lunch crowd spread out at the tables and booths while his mother worked at the stove and Dom tossed dough.

He looked thinner, older than when Raylan had seen him briefly over the Christmas holidays, but he hadn't lost his knack in the dough-tossing department.

Mariah, with a coloring book and crayons at her counter seat, watched him in absolute delight.

"Do another, Popi! Do another!"

As he spread the dough in a perfect circle on the board, he winked at her. "I have to get this one going first. People want their pies."

"Will you make me one? Nana said we can have pizza when Bradley finishes his game in the back."

"I'll make you a very special one, just your size, and fit for a princess."

She gasped, much as Jasper had at his first sight of Sadie, then spotted her father. "Daddy! Did you hear? Mr. Rizzo's gonna make me a princess pizza."

"Amazing. How are you, Dom?"

"Can't complain, so won't. Welcome home."

"Thanks. I wonder if you could hold the princess pizza for just a bit. Mo, I want to go get Bradley and take you guys to see this house. We'll do that, then we'll all come back for pizza."

"But I get the special princess pizza."

"Absolutely. I saw your granddaughter for a minute, and the mastodon she calls a dog."

"She mentioned it." Dom added peppers, mushrooms, black olives to the pie. "It's a good, solid house with good, solid neighbors. I'm glad you're taking a look."

"What did you think?" Jan demanded.

"What Dom said, but I want the kids to see it. And here comes the gaming machine." He could see by the look on Bradley's face, the gaming machine hadn't taken top score.

"I need to earn more quarters."

"We'll get to that. We're going to go see this house right now."

"But we're going to have pizza. Nana said."

"We'll come back and have pizza, but the man who owns the house is waiting on us."

"I could starve."

Before Raylan could speak, Dom picked up a handful of pepperoni, a handful of cheese, filled a little takeaway bowl. "This'll hold you. When you get back, I'll make you a special pizza."

A boy of specifics, Bradley eyed him. "What kind of special?"

"I'm getting a princess one."

"Can I have a Batman one?"

"Go with your father, be a good boy, and Batman it will be."

"Cool! Thanks, Popi. Can we go right now

248

so we can get back?"

"Yeah, we're going."

"Don't worry about that." Jan brushed him aside as Raylan started to deal with the crayons.

"We did all the work," Mariah told him when he hauled her up. "So I got a coloring book and Bradley got quarters. Popi said we're good workers."

"Glad to hear it."

He got them out to the car, into the car seats.

"Where's Jasper?" Bradley devoured pepperoni like candy.

"He's at Nana's. He's already seen the house."

"Are we going to live there?" Mariah wanted to know.

"We have to look at it."

"I like living at Nana's house."

Try it sleeping on a pullout, he thought, and showering in a closet. "It's close to Nana's."

"How close?"

He met his son's suspicious eyes in the rearview. "You'll see. There's Nana's house," he said as they passed it. He made the left turn off Main, drove on, drove by Mrs. Pinsky's freshly cut lawn, made the right turn on Mountain Laurel Lane.

Then the left into the driveway.

"This close."

"It doesn't look anything like our old house."

Bradley's words hit straight to the heart, especially as Raylan had thought exactly the same.

"No, it doesn't."

No lovely and faded brick, but horizontal siding freshly painted a smoky gray with the contrast of dark blue shutters and sharp white trim.

A quiet street — which mattered — and a short, green front yard leading to the wide sidewalk. Sidewalks mattered.

He'd watched enough HGTV to know the foundation bushes, the tree Mark had identified as a showy pink dogwood added curb appeal.

The front door had long side lights, and the convenient side door — the one facing the neighbor he'd met — opened into a mudroom/laundry room.

That would matter.

It checked all the boxes, he thought as he unloaded the kids. He knew that. Just as he knew from his own rehabbing experience, the quality of the work inside and out got high marks.

But.

It didn't look anything like their home in Brooklyn.

As he studied it with his kids beside him, the neighbor hailed him.

She came out, crossed over, her little boy marching behind her. "I have the keys. Mark said they'd nearly finished, so he sent the crew to another job. He just needed to get them going, pick something up, and he'd be back. But he didn't want you to have to wait if you got here ahead of him."

"Thanks. This is Ms. Kirk."

Bradley's eyes widened. "Like Captain James Tiberius?"

"Exactly like that. I always figured I could be his great-times-about-four-grandmother."

Eyes widened even more. "Really?"

"I like to think so. This is Phineas." She patted her belly. "This is yet-to-be-determined. If you decide to live here, we'll be your neighbors."

"Can I touch the baby?"

Teesha looked down at Mariah. "This one? Sure."

Very gently, Mariah laid a hand on the baby bump. "My teacher had a baby in her, too. It was big. She said it was going to come out in the summertime."

"This one has to get bigger before he comes out in November."

Phineas, more interested in his own kind, offered Bradley a look at his plastic dinosaur. "This is a T. rex. They'd have eaten people except they got extinct before people. They ate other dinosaurs though. He's my favorite."

"That's cool. I like velociraptors because they hunt in packs."

"I got them, too! They probably evolved from birds. You wanna see?"

"Maybe sometime, but we've got to look at the house."

"They bang and saw in there. I've got a hammer and a saw, too."

"He will never shut up," Teesha warned them, and reached down for her son's hand. "Say see you later, Phin."

"Okay, see you later."

"Mark said just to leave the keys inside on the kitchen island if he misses you," she called as she walked back to her house. "He's got another set."

"Thanks. Well, gang, let's go inside."

"I like the lady with the baby in her belly. She has pretty hair."

"Yeah, she does." He opted to go in the front, like a guest, as that's what they were at this point.

The floors gleamed, he couldn't deny it, and the gleam carried straight through from the front to the back, to the kitchen, to the wide patio doors that led to a very nice backyard.

"It looks really big," Bradley decided.

"Well, it's open and it's empty."

"It has a fireplace. We had a fireplace." Mariah walked over to it. "So Santa knows where to come in."

But not brick. Tiled in a subtle white-on-white pattern. Gas, not wood-burning. A sleek mantel, not a chunky one.

"It echoes!" Bradley shouted his own name to amuse himself.

But no memories in those echoes.

His son raced back, and Mariah followed. Not for the kitchen — white cabinets, stainless appliances, a stone-gray countertop, a deep farm sink — but for the view out those wide doors.

"Man, the backyard's big! Jasper would like that."

"No swings?" The shock reverberated in Mariah's voice. "How come?"

"Nobody lives here yet, dummy." Bradley poked her. "Dad will get us swings and stuff."

"You're the dummy." She poked him back. "What's this room?"

She ran back to double-glass-paned doors off what would be the dining area. "Is it our playroom?"

"There's a bonus room — like a playroom area — upstairs."

Behind the doors would be, he had to admit, the perfect home office. Good light, a view of the yard, room for everything he needed.

"I wanna see. Can we go up?"

"We're here to see. Bedrooms are up there, too."

He hung back a minute as the kids raced

253

back to clatter up the stairs.

Powder room under those stairs, family room/lounge area off the kitchen, the mudroom/laundry room off the other end of the kitchen. New furnace, and a good storage area in the fully waterproofed, ready-to-finish basement.

A good house, he reminded himself, with a price well within his means.

He went up where the echoes carried the rushing feet, the voices of his children.

Eyes shining, Mariah raced to meet him. "Which would be my room, Daddy? Can I pick?"

"Well, it's set up with what they call a Jack and Jill bath. This room." With her hand clutching his, he led her into one of the four bedrooms. "And that bathroom opens to this room and the one on the other side. They're about the same size, so —"

"I can't share a bathroom like that with a boy! They smell!"

Her horrified face made Raylan want to gobble her up like a pink parfait.

"There's another bedroom across the hall, but this one's bigger so —"

He broke off as she ran off to see for herself.

"It has a bathroom for its ownself! Look, look! No boys allowed to use it! My own bathtub and everything! Can I have this room, please?"

Bradley raced back. "The playroom is huge!

And I got dibs on the bedroom with a fire-place and the big bathroom."

"No dibs there. That's the master. You have to pay all the bills to get the master."

"I can't pay bills."

"Which means you get one of these two rooms if we buy the house. With a pretty big bathroom of your own, since Mo's looking at the room over there."

Bradley wandered through, lips pursed, head nodding. "Okay, I guess. I want the one back there, 'cause it's more away from her."

Grinning, he turned, then the grin faded when he looked at his father. "You don't like the house?"

"What? No — I mean, sure I like it."

"Your face says you don't."

Mariah danced back in. "Can we paint my tub pink? What's a matter?"

"Dad doesn't like the house."

"Why not? It's nice. It smells good."

They wanted it, he realized. They wanted this house, this fresh start. He just had to make it a home. To let go — all the way — and make a home.

"You, weak-minded beings as you are, have been taken in by my great restraint," Raylan told them. "I wanted you to have your say in it, and not to use the vast power of my superior mind to influence your puny little brains."

"Dad." The stress fell away as Bradley let

out a snort. "Come on!"

"Can we have it?" Mariah hugged his legs with her face turned up to his. "Can we paint the tub pink in my very own bathroom?"

"Yes, and no. You can get a pink shower curtain, pink towels, but no tub painting."

"But Bradley can't ever, ever poop in my bathroom."

"I've got my own bathroom — bigger than yours — and you can't poop there."

They assailed each other with poop insults. Raylan decided they'd already started making a home.

With the deal struck, the paperwork and legal work underway, Raylan began counting down the days of pullouts and working in a corner, or the kitchen counter.

He had to start back-to-school shopping soon, which seemed impossible. But he was determined to put that nightmare off until the last possible moment.

What he did have, despite his current working conditions, was a solid new story line with a fascinating new character who would serve first as foe, always as foil, and eventually as friend to his Angel.

He could thank, and did, his mother and sister for helping keep the kids busy and entertained through the summer. And for keeping the kids overnight while he traveled up to his headquarters to round out that

256

story, that character, with his partners.

He'd spent his single night in Jonah's hot mess of a bachelor pad because he couldn't bring himself, not yet, to stay with Bick and Pats in his old house.

But before he could go ahead with doing the real work on creating the novel, he had to clear it with the inspiration.

If she gave him a thumbs-down, he'd change up the physical appearance, but he didn't want to. Everything worked. He had some hope because he remembered the girl who'd recognized Iron Man from the sketch on his bedroom wall.

Since he'd put it off long enough, and since the kids were hanging with Maya and Collin for the afternoon, he took his sketch pad, and the dog, to drive to the big house on the hill.

He'd always loved the house, the way it sat so sturdy and timeless with that wraparound porch, the wonderful old growth of trees at its back and side. Its gables adding just a touch of mystery.

"Jesus, Jasper, I'm an idiot. I can use it. Just goth it up some, and it's Flame's hideout. Darken the stone, bring the trees in closer, add a tower. Yeah, this would work."

Sketching it in his head, he walked to the front door, used the big bronze knocker. He changed it from a star to a gargoyle. A snarling one.

When no one answered, he did as his sister

had advised and walked around the house, adding details to his sketch as he circled to the lower-level patio doors.

Since they stood open, he started to knock on the jamb, then just stood, hand lifted. He actually felt his mouth drop open and couldn't seem to close it again.

She stood in the center of the room, facing a mirrored wall. She wore black, tiny shorts, a sports bra that crisscrossed with thin straps in the back. Her hair she'd pulled up and away into a topknot that spilled curls.

And, standing on one bare foot, she lifted her left leg until it pointed at the ceiling and she stood in a single vertical line.

It shouldn't have been anatomically possible.

Then she lowered the leg only to draw it up behind her, and, still balanced, grabbed her toe, flowed out the other arm as she leaned forward, and as she drew the leg up to a fluid arch.

By the time a few blood cells returned to his brain and he realized he'd entered Peeping Tom territory, he started to step back.

But she turned her head, just an inch, and saw him.

Rather than scream and call for her monster dog, she smiled, used her forward hand to gesture him in.

He eased through the opening a little.

"Sorry. I was just . . . I didn't want to interrupt."

"Nearly done. I just needed a good stretch."

"Do you —" He broke off as Jasper caught a scent, shoved through the door, and raced to his love, who'd sprawled in front of the fireplace.

"Jasper, damn it. Sorry."

"No problem."

Especially since Jasper simply collapsed in front of Sadie, who ignored him.

"Just have to do the other side. Were you looking for Popi?"

"Um, no, actually." He couldn't look away. "How do you do that? How does anyone do that? Why don't you have joints?"

"I have them. They're well-oiled. Flexibility is essential to fitness."

"That's not flexible. Even Gumby can't do that."

"Ballet, DNA, gymnastics, practice. How's your flexibility?"

"Not like that. But I'm from the planet Earth, which, obviously, you aren't. Which brings me to —"

"Touch your toes."

"What?"

"Can you touch your toes without bending your knees? Let's see."

He felt ridiculous, but still guilty from watching her, so he touched his toes.

"Good. There's potential. Do you work out?"

"Well . . ."

"Aha," she said as she put both feet on the floor.

"Two kids, work, buying a house, dealing with a dog, sleeping on a pullout."

"Busy." She smiled when she said it. "Aren't we all? Everyone's thrilled you bought the house on Mountain Laurel Lane. Once you're settled in, I'll work out some routines for you. Thirty minutes a day. Do you have weights?"

"No, I —"

"You'll get some. You need a little building up."

Annoyed, he gave her one long stare. "Okay."

"That's not an insult. It's a professional observation. Cardio, core, strength-and-resistance training, flexibility. Everybody needs them. You have beautiful children."

Annoyance eased back a little. "I do, thanks."

"They're a blend of you and Lorilee, who I liked very much. It's clear, from the few times I've seen them, you're a pretty terrific father."

"They make it easier than I let on. For survival purposes."

"Part of your job is to stay healthy for them."

He had to laugh a little. "I think that's play-

260

ing dirty."

"It really is, but also true. Anyway, I'll work up some basic routines for you. Now, what can I do for you at the moment?"

"Do you do that to everybody? Give them the health and fitness pitch?"

"Not everybody, because not everybody's ready to hear it. Maya's one of my best friends. I love Jan. They worry about you, and you know that so I'm not telling any secrets here."

"No, you're not."

He had to move away from that, so started to look around her studio. "You've got a serious but not intimidating place here. I'd have thought . . . look at that."

Adrian glanced over to see Jasper curled up against Sadie, his eyes closed.

"I think that's a blissful smile on his face. She's giving him a chance. You, too," she said to Raylan. "If she didn't approve of you, she'd be standing right here, watching you."

"May that continue. I have to ask your permission for something."

"Oh. Should we sit down for that?"

"Maybe."

"Go ahead." She gestured toward the sofa before going to fill two New Gen water bottles. She handed one to Raylan as she sat beside him. "This is now yours. It'll be useful for keeping hydrated when you work out."

"Right. So anyway. I've been working on a

new novel, with a new character."

"I loved the debut of *True Angel.*"

She threw him off — again. "You read it?"

"Sure I did. Not only are you my good friend's brother, but I like graphic novels."

And that could — should — work in his favor. "This character will be a foil for Angel — first an enemy, then an ally. She's a demi-demon."

"Like Grievous."

"Initially bound to him, forced to work for him. She's solitary, tormented, in a struggle against her darker impulses, and to round it up, Angel will eventually help free her. She passes as a human, lives alone. She writes horror stories — or turns her experience and history over her five hundred–plus years into books."

"Can't wait to read it, but I don't understand why you'd need my permission."

"Okay, well." He opened his sketchbook, offered it. "That's her."

"That's me! That's me wearing Hot Stuff."

"Yeah, you looked pretty hot."

That earned him another amused glance. "Thanks, but I meant that's the name of the design, because of the flames."

"Right, yeah, well . . . You were wearing it when I came to look at the house for the first time. You had your back to me, and I just had this character jump into my head. Cobalt Flame."

Fascinated, she looked up from the sketch. "Is that how it works?"

"Sometimes. Not usually. Hardly ever."

"Are there more drawings?" Even as she asked, Adrian turned the page. "Oh my God, she's riding a dragon! A dragon!"

"Yeah. Dragon fire. Fire's her thing. The dragon's Vesta — Roman goddess of fire."

"A girl dragon. Even better. I look good. Strong. Fierce." She kept turning pages. "Oooh, mean and violent. Oh, oh, tormented! I love it!"

"Really? You're okay with this?"

"Are you kidding me? I'm a freaking half-demon superhero. Well, villain, then hero. Either one works. And I ride a dragon. She's got a spear."

"If I keep that, it'll shoot flames."

"A flame-throwing spear. It just gets better. Where does she live?"

"Here. I mean a big old house like this, except spookier, darker, but I just figured this house would be the base for it."

"Now Popi's going to flip. His house immortalized, and the home and hideout of a demi-demon."

"So he'll be okay with it?"

"Okay with it? He's got the sketch you did of him tossing pizza dough framed in his office."

"He does?"

"He admires your talent. Why wouldn't he?"

It struck him, as she continued to look through his sketches, how much that meant to him.

"She could have a secret room, even if she doesn't need one. And a tower, maybe turrets. Oh, like you need me to tell you what works. What's her alter-ego name?"

"Adrianna Dark, and I already decided on the tower."

"Perfect! Raylan, I'm so freaking flattered."

"That's a relief, because I'm ready to start work on it, and I didn't want to change her look."

"And now you can't, or you'd crush my fragile ego."

"I don't think it's very fragile, but I'm not changing her look."

"Can I see it sometime? In progress, I mean. Or are you temperamental about your art?"

"In Brooklyn I worked in a converted warehouse. Everybody saw everything. I have to go," he said as he checked the time. "I have to pick up the kids from Maya's."

When he took the sketchbook and rose, Adrian got to her feet with him. "Come back, will you, when Popi's here? Bring the kids. He misses having kids around the house."

"I'll do that. Let's go, Jasper."

Jasper opened his eyes, turned his head away.

"Let's go, Romeo, or next time I come, I leave you behind."

Adrian said, "Sadie," and the big dog got up, walked over. With Jasper right behind her. "Why don't we walk you out?"

"It would save me dragging him."

It didn't save him from having to pick Jasper up bodily to get him into the car, where Jasper howled like the grievously wounded.

"Girls don't like whiners, pal. Suck it up." He gave a wave, drove away.

He glanced in the rearview, saw Adrian in her very tiny black outfit, a hand on the enormous dog. And felt a low tug he hadn't felt in a very long time.

Recognizing lust, he ignored it.

Not ready for that, he told himself. And not with one of his sister's oldest friends if he ever got ready for that again.

CHAPTER THIRTEEN

A new poem arrived on a sizzling August day with a sky the color of old plaster. This one carried a postmark from Wichita.

She read it, the third of the year, in her car in the grocery store parking lot.

> When you are a rage in my mind, a fury in
> my heart,
> Why have I tarried so long and kept us
> apart?
> So delicious I find the wait, your blood to
> spill.
> I alone choose the time to kill.

It twisted her; it always did. She sat another minute, waiting for some calm, listening to a weary voice outside the car tell a whiny one they'd get ice cream later.

She followed her own protocol, slid the poem into the envelope, the envelope into her purse. She'd make copies when she got home, send them, as usual, to the police, the federal agent, to Harry.

Nothing would come of it, of course. Nothing ever did.

And now the number had increased again. From one for so many years, to two, and now three.

She knew the FBI would keep the file, just as she knew they largely dismissed any real risk. Vaguely threatening poems, a few lines, and never any overt or actual threat or action.

An obsession, yes, but a cowardly one that inflicted mental and emotional distress, and no attempt at physical harm.

She knew what they thought, the agents, the cops. She was a public figure, had chosen to be. That choice came with a price.

She knew what her mother would say — had said. File it, forget it.

Adrian got a cart, wheeled it into the overly chilled air of the supermarket. She called up the shopping list app on her phone, got started.

And reminded herself to give a hat tip to gratitude because her grandfather hadn't insisted on coming with her. When he did, the process took twice as long.

Food, after all, was his passion. And people came in a close second.

So he'd talk to everyone, examine every peach with great care, see some vegetable that would inspire another dish, which equaled adding more to the list to fulfill that.

When they hit the weekly farmer's market, it turned, inevitably, into a marathon of food studying, food discussions, and socializing.

As she gathered produce — with care, but not intensity — she had to smile a little. It took much longer to shop with him, but he was always entertaining.

She checked items off her list in dairy, moved on.

By the time she got to the cereal aisle — her grandfather did love his Wheaties — she was on a roll. And heard the aggrieved male voice.

"Come on, man, we agreed on Cheerios."

"But these are magically delicious."

She saw Bradley clutching a cereal box while his sister executed a very fine pirouette across the aisle, and Raylan looked like a man under siege.

"Magic and delicious are both good," Bradley insisted. "Don't you want us to have good cereal?"

"Will he stick or will he cave?" Adrian wondered as she rolled up to him. "Hello, adorables."

"We had a deal." Obviously hoping for backup, he appealed to Adrian. "The deal was Cheerios."

"We could mix the magically delicious with the Cheerios. You say we're supposed to compromise." Bradley turned to Adrian. "He always says we're supposed to compromise."

"You're a very bright light, aren't you?" She reached around for Dom's Wheaties.

"You got whole bunches of stuff. You must eat a lot!"

Raylan smiled thinly. "Bright light, you say?"

"I do, and I do have bunches of stuff because we're going to have a houseful of people for a few days."

"We had a houseful of people because I had my birthday. I'm eight now. I had a Batman cake."

"I've always thought the Dark Knight's magically delicious."

That got a grin, before Mariah claimed her turn.

"I'm going to be six next month and I'm having a ballerina cake. Or a princess cake. I have to decide."

"Why not both? A ballerina princess?"

Her eyes, green like her father's, lit up. "I want that. Daddy, I want a ballerina princess cake."

"So noted."

"I like your sandals."

Adrian smiled. "Thanks. I like yours, too, and I love your pedicure. Such a pretty pink."

"Daddy painted my toes. You have a French manicure pedi. It looks really good with your skin tone."

"Thank you very much. She's going to be six?" Adrian asked Raylan.

269

"Chronologically. In fashion years? About thirty-five. I heard you've got a crew coming in to do a new DVD."

"And a lot of the crew are friends — who'll be houseguests and eat whole bunches of stuff. My grandfather's already in heaven."

She saw Bradley, quietly, gently, ease the magically delicious cereal box into the cart. Remembering how Mimi had once snuck her cookies, she smiled. "How's everybody liking the new house?"

"I have pink towels in my bathroom. Bradley has red, and we have a playset in the backyard, but we are not getting a pool, so we can forget that. Do you think I'm old enough to wear lipstick?"

"You mean you're not?" Adrian said, even crouched down a little for a closer look. "I would have sworn you were, because your lips are so pretty and perfect and pink."

"Really?"

"Oh my, yes. You're so lucky to have that wonderful natural color in them."

"Impressive," Raylan murmured as she straightened.

"I've got to get moving. Nice to see you. Give my best, and Sadie's, to Jasper."

"Come by sometime," Raylan heard himself say. "Jasper pines for her."

"And you can see my room. I have new curtains and everything."

"I'd like that. See you later."

As she rolled away, as Raylan watched her, he said, "I saw the move with the cereal, Bradley. But in the spirit of compromise, we'll go with it."

"How did you see?"

"Because . . ." Raylan turned around, drew a Darth Vader breath. "Bradley, I am your father."

At home, Adrian put the groceries away, let Sadie out, made the copies of the poem. Since Harry and his family would arrive the next afternoon, she'd just hand him his copy.

She considered going down to her studio to rehearse, then went upstairs instead to check, unnecessarily, on the bedrooms.

She'd run into town for fresh flowers in the morning, but for now everything looked just right. The room Harry and Marshall would share, the ones for their two kids, Hector's room — solo, as his live-in lady of the past year and a half couldn't make the trip this time. And Loren's.

She checked the bathrooms — equally unnecessary, but it gave her something to do, something to help keep her mind off the damn poems.

Like her grandfather, she looked forward to having the house full of people. Nothing could take her mind off worry easier than friends and work.

Or a good, sweaty workout, she thought,

and started to turn into her own room to change when she heard the front door open.

She went to the top of the step. "Popi. You're back early."

"They've got everything under control. And I wanted to talk to you about a couple things."

"I got the ribs, I got the chicken," she began as she started down. "Everything you wanted for the summer trifle."

"Not that." When she reached him, he held out his car keys. "I'm turning these in. I nearly went through the stop sign on Woodbine, and it's not the first time."

"Popi." She took the keys, then wrapped him in a hug. "I know this is hard. I'll be your chauffeur. Anytime, anywhere. I promise."

"I've got more than half a dozen people willing to haul my ancient butt around. You can be one of them. Starting now."

She tipped her head back. "Where do you want to go?"

"Something I want to show you, talk to you about."

"Mystery!"

"Where's our girl?"

"She's out back."

"Let's get her, take her for a ride."

They took Adrian's car, since Dom's for the last several years had been a compact pickup she knew he loved. Because she knew he didn't like the AC, she opened windows. Sadie happily stuck her head out the one in the back.

"Go on into town, turn right on Main."

"Gotcha. I ran into Raylan and his kids at the grocery."

"Those are good kids."

"They are." She entertained him with cereal wars and makeup debates on the drive in.

"Monroe brought that pistol of a boy of his in for pizza right before I left. Said they were having a man day — and giving Teesha a break. You want to turn left at the light. And right there." He gestured. "Pull up right over there."

"The old schoolhouse."

"Old elementary, so old I went there. They still used the paddle back in those days."

"Ouch."

With a grin, he nudged up his glasses. "So I said more times than I care to remember."

The old, scarred brick with its loose mortar formed a squat square. What had once been a playground had become pitted asphalt and weeds blocked off by an old chain-link fence.

A few of the windows, broken over time by weather or a well-aimed rock, sported plywood boards. Gutters, what was left of them, sprouted more weeds.

"Tried a few things with it over the years," Dom said. "It was an antiques shop for a while, but that just turned into a dusty old

273

flea market. I recall it being a repair shop once — lawn mowers and the like. Nothing stuck."

"It's pretty easy to see why. It's a mess."

"Been let go, that's why. Man who owns it had big dreams, sly ways, and not enough money for either. He was going to open it as a bar. Now he's just getting fined for a safety hazard, and there's talk of condemning it."

"Well —"

"Can't have that, Adrian." That jaw set solid as Dom shook his head. "Can't have it. That building's a hundred years old. It has history. It needs to have purpose again."

She understood sentiment, she understood history. But.

"You want to buy it?"

"I want your say-so in this because I'd be pulling from your inheritance."

"Popi, don't be silly."

"And not only that, when I join your grandmother, this would be your responsibility."

"What would? What are you thinking?"

"Let's have a look. I've got the keys."

"Of course you do," she muttered. She intended to leave Sadie in the car, but Dom was already opening the door.

"Come on, girl. We're going to explore."

"Is it safe? It doesn't really look safe."

"Safe enough for a look-see." In his khaki shorts and navy golf shirt, he led the way across the sidewalk, up crumbling concrete steps to the double front doors.

"You've got to use your imagination," he told her as he fished out the keys.

"I bet."

It smelled. Her first impression was it smelled, of spiderwebs, dust, muck, disuse, and the mice and — potentially — rats who'd used it as a toilet.

But Dom's face shined.

"You feel that?"

"I might feel something crawling up my leg."

He put an arm around her shoulders. "Kids, all those memories of kids, walking through here. Now there's not much left of the original woodwork, and that's a damn shame. But the asshole who owns it gutted the place right out without a thought for that. Foundation's still sound," he continued as he walked on. "Roof's not, but we'd raise that, add a second story."

"Would we?"

She saw ancient plaster walls, yellow with age, a chipped vinyl floor where someone had tried to pull it up.

Dom pointed down. "There's hardwood under there, and I'm betting it can be sanded down and polished again. Needs all new plumbing, and the electric brought up to code from the old knob and tube. Need to clean up the exterior brick, repoint. Outside,

275

you've got to clear up, clean up, new asphalt, and it needs a handicapped accessible ramp."

He turned to her, to see what she thought, but all she saw was a big, ugly, smelly space with broken and dingy windows. "I had Mark Wicker — he's a damn good contractor — take a look. He figures it'll take most of a year, and about a million."

"Dollars? A million dollars? Popi, I think you need to lie down. I think I do, too."

"Maybe, but hear me out first. The selling price is — or was — way over the moon. I countered, he came back. I walked away because he needs to sell, and he's living in some greedy dream world. He came more down to earth today, so I said I'd talk to my partner and let him know."

"I'm your partner?"

"You're my everything."

Damn it. He wanted it, whatever it was, so much.

"Let's go outside, because I don't want to think what we're breathing in right now. And you can tell me what you want to do for a million — God, that takes my breath away — a million dollars."

He walked out with her, locked up again. Then, taking her hand, walked around to the sagging fence.

"Skinned my knees there, more than once. Played tag and ball and keep-away."

She leaned against him.

"Not so many people in town back then, not so many kids. And a lot of them living out on farms. It's different now. The town's grown. It's a good town. You know what it doesn't have, Adrian?"

"What?"

"A place for those kids. Somewhere to go after school, during the summer. A place they can play ball, or Ping-Pong, their video games, maybe even study or just hang out in a safe place. A lot of working parents, a lot of latchkey kids. That's how it is."

"You want to build a youth center."

"Maybe we'd have some classes. Like learning music or art. Activities, some structure." He smiled down at her. "Healthy snacks."

"Now you're pandering."

"Just a little. After-school care, some exercise classes."

"More pandering," she said, but put her arm around his waist.

"Sophia and I talked about this place more than once. But we didn't have a way to get our hands on it, until now. It may be out of reach still, but —"

"Nothing's out of reach if you keep trying for it. It's a little terrifying, I'm not going to lie. But if I squint, and toss away all my common sense, I can almost see it."

And he wanted it. Nothing else mattered.

She stepped back, held out a hand. "Let's go for it, partner."

He took her hand, squeezed it. "*Gioia mia. You make me proud.*"

There was little Dom loved more than cooking for a crowd, unless it was having the sound and motion of kids in his house.

With Adrian's friends, he got both.

He marinated pounds of fat pork ribs in a tangy sauce he made himself, roasted summer vegetables from his own garden, made a cold pasta, colorful as a carnival with fat olives, grape tomatoes, and thin strips of zucchini. Baked focaccia bread.

He polished it off with a cake filled with rich cream and strawberries.

The groans of the well-fed, the chatter of children, the sheer mess generated by a complicated meal perfectly prepared brought him profound joy.

He loved seeing Adrian with friends she'd made in high school. And seeing Harry, who'd almost been a father to his girl, with the family he'd made.

Generations at the table made a family, made a home.

Over cappuccino and cake, he appealed to Hunter, Harry's oldest. "Tell me what you want, especially, in a youth center."

"Swimming pool." Hunter, with his dark gypsy eyes, shoveled in cake. "The dads say . . ." He held his thumb up, then turned it down.

"Horseback riding and a stable." Hunter's younger sister, Cybill, dug out more cream filling.

"And how about you, Phineas?"

"A planetarium."

Dom nodded soberly, then looked at Adrian. "We're going to need a bigger building."

"I'll say. How about games? Table games, video games, a basketball court. Arts and crafts, music lessons — I'm looking at you there, Monroe."

Hunter wagged his fork at him. "Can you play the guitar?"

"I can. You like the guitar?"

"Yeah, so if I get one for Christmas, can you show me stuff when we visit?"

"Sure. Maybe you can come by my house tomorrow for a while, and I'll show you some stuff."

"For real? Cool!"

"Your Harry dad has to work here tomorrow." Phineas eyed Harry as he might an experiment. "So your Marshall dad can bring you. You can come, too," he said graciously to Cybill. "I'm getting a telescope for Christmas."

"Are you?" Monroe asked over his cappuccino.

"Yeah, because I'm going to be an astronomer/astronaut and discover life on another planet. 'Cause it's there."

"He doesn't get that from me," Monroe told his wife. "He just doesn't."

"Well, mathematically and logically, he's right. It's there."

Now Monroe wagged his fork at Teesha. "See? Dom, Adrian, this was an incredible meal. I'm volunteering the rest of us for KP."

"I'll sign up for that. In fact, if I don't move, I may root to this chair." Hector, with his horn-rims and stubby ponytail, rose. "I always think Sylvie and I are halfway decent cooks until I have a meal here. We don't come close."

"Sorry she couldn't make it." Loren levered himself up to help gather plates. He'd tamed his fiery hair into a brush cut and — to Adrian's mind — managed to look like a lawyer even in jeans and a T-shirt.

"So's she, but she's pretty busy packing up, since we're moving to New York."

Despite the baby bump, Teesha came straight up out of her chair. "What?"

"Yeah, I thought I'd save that one." He grinned, shrugged. "She got a great offer, so I put out some feelers of my own. It's back to New York, which makes my dad pretty happy. Especially since I asked Sylvie to marry me."

Loren punched him in the arm. "And you don't tell us?"

"Telling you. I figured I'd catch a ride with

you to look at a couple places, fly back from there."

"Road trip!"

Adrian rose to hug him. "This is great news. We need to break out the champagne."

"Dishes first, for sure."

Harry waited until they'd finished the dishes and while his kids ran off the cake with Marshall supervising.

He grabbed Adrian's hand. "How about we take a walk?"

"Sure. I was just going to go down and check on the setup for tomorrow."

"Hector's got that." He tugged her toward the front of the house.

"Is something wrong? Is everything all right with you, with Mom?"

"I'm fine, she's fine. She'll head back to New York in a couple of days. And she'll want to talk to you about another mother/daughter production. Probably over the winter."

"It'll have to be here. I don't want to leave Popi. Plus, she should come see him."

He stepped out with her onto the front porch. "Hell of a view. Even this confirmed urbanite can appreciate it. Dom's revved about this youth center project."

"Boy, is he. We'll jump into that once this production's underway. We signed the contract — after Teesha pushed the seller down another twelve thousand."

"She's a wonder."

281

"She is." She studied him as they walked. Slim and trim and handsome as ever. Maybe more so with the hint of silver threading through his hair.

"What's this really about, Harry?"

"It's about me wondering why you haven't told Dom, and the others, about the latest poem."

"Who says I haven't?"

"I do, Ads, because I know you. We'll walk and appreciate the last of this long summer day while you tell me why."

"I didn't see the point, Harry, and I still don't. Especially with Popi. It's like you said, he's revved right now. Why would I tell him something upsetting he can't do a thing about? He's ninety-four, Harry."

"And the others?"

She hissed out one long impatient breath. "I'm lucky to see Hector and Loren in person twice a year, and what could they do about it? Teesha's pregnant, so again, why? It's been going on for years."

"It's escalating. You and I know that."

"And I dutifully file the reports. Yes, it's escalating, and that worries me. It's upsetting and nerve-racking — which must be what this person wants. But there haven't been any strange phone calls, no vandalism or attempted break-ins. Nothing more personal than nasty poetry."

"Already three this year. I know you've got

an alarm system, and you've got an enormous dog, but you're still pretty isolated here, Adrian. I think it may be time for you to consider personal protection."

Truly stunned, she stopped short. "You want me to get a gun?"

Equally stunned, he stopped short right along with her. "No! God, no. Too much to go way, way wrong there. But you could get a bodyguard."

She laughed. "Come on, Harry."

"I'm serious. Lina has security at her events, and she hasn't had this kind of continual threat. It's common sense."

"I'm not doing outside events," she reminded him, "because, as I said, Popi's ninety-four. And since I made that decision, I've learned how much I like working from home, how much I can get done, how many people I can reach."

"Understood, but security here — human security, experienced security — would add another layer."

"And skew my privacy, and Popi's. The police are like five minutes away. Whoever's doing this has had years to do something more threatening or violent. It's emotional stalking."

"And stalkers often act on their obsession."

He sure as hell wasn't making her feel any better, she thought.

Then again, he didn't want to.

"I'm not dismissing any of that. I can't. But if we consider worst-case — someone tries to hurt me — I'm strong, I'm agile, I'm fast. I'm not helpless, Harry."

"You never have been."

"I hate that you're so worried, but the fact you are just cements my decision not to say anything to Popi. I'll take a self-defense course."

Harry rolled his eyes. "Where?"

"Online. You can learn anything online if you're committed. I'll commit. It's another layer."

"All right, okay. I knew this wouldn't fly, but I had to give it a shot."

"I love you for it, but then, I love you anyway. I'll research the classes, pick one next week. And, being the goal-oriented competitor I am, I'll graduate at the top of the class."

"Wouldn't surprise me."

"And you know what? When I learn enough, it might make a good video for the blog, or even a segment."

"And there," he said as they walked back toward the house, "is where you take after Lina."

Though it irritated her, she shrugged. "Maybe. A little."

"She's a self-made woman, Adrian, and so are you. One of the reasons is when either of you see an obstacle, you figure out the way not to shove it away so much as work it to your advantage."

"Sometimes I wonder if that's what I was. An obstacle."

"No." He put an arm around her shoulders. "You were never that to her, believe me. You were a choice."

Maybe, she thought again. But she'd never figured out why her mother had made that choice.

CHAPTER FOURTEEN

She actually sent him a personalized fitness video. Raylan found it short, surprising, and not-so-sweet.

He supposed he should feel . . . what, exactly, that she'd taken the time to put together a month-long regimen? Seven days a week — really? — for four weeks.

Warm-ups and cooldowns required. Every damn day.

He watched the first segment on his laptop, standing in his kitchen while the frozen chicken fingers and Tater Tots baked (he'd had a long day; plus, he'd steam some broccoli to make up for it) and the kids ran around the backyard with the dog — maniacs all.

Cardio, day one. She demonstrated a high knee jog in place, instructed him to do that for thirty seconds before moving straight into jumping jacks, front lunges, back lunges, squats, burpees, and so on. Then she, without even breathing hard, told him to repeat all that twice before a thirty-second water break, then moving on to football shuffles, standing mountain climbers, and other tortures. For a thirty-minute sweat fest.

Repeat once a week, where she assured him he'd progress to forty-second intervals by the end of the fourth.

He also had the option — highly recommended — to add in the ten-minute core routine every day.

"Sure, why not? I've got nothing but time."

He let it play while he got out the broccoli, and she moved into strength training, day two. Amazing to him, he thought as he chopped, how soothing her voice sounded while she pushed the innocent into biceps curls, hammer curls with shoulder presses, chest flys, rows, something called skull crushers.

Maybe he found it fascinating to watch her muscles work — and he'd use that for his art — but he didn't have any dumbbells.

He'd been busy.

Day three equaled core, and that just looked painful.

Despite the soothing voice, the fascinating muscles, he shut her off.

He put the broccoli on to steam, got out plates. Belatedly remembered the laundry he'd tossed in that morning before they'd left for the last of the marathon back-to-school shopping.

He made the transfer from washer to dryer and wondered why he hadn't just ordered pizza. Then remembered he'd done just that the night before after that leg of the marathon.

But the kids had their new shoes and fall clothes, their new backpacks and lunch sacks, their binders and folders and new pencils with their pristine erasers.

Their every-damn-thing and more.

And with the enthusiasm of new, of fresh starts, they helped him organize everything. So now those backpacks, sans the lunch sacks he'd fill in the morning, hung on the hooks in the mudroom.

Just in time, he thought, as the big yellow bus would arrive at 7:20 a.m. for the first day of school.

Was he a crap father for harboring relief and joy over that moment? No, he was not, he assured himself. He was realistic. The idea of hours of empty house, of quiet without interruptions?

Bliss. Single-tear-sliding-down-the-face bliss.

He checked on dinner, judged it about five minutes out, so went to the door to call the kids.

Then just stood, watching them.

Mariah used her dance moves against Bradley's ninja warrior while Jasper raced around with a yellow tennis ball in his mouth.

288

Grass stains streaked the seat of Mariah's petal-pink shorts. The laces of Bradley's old Converse Chucks fell loose again, and showed gray with grime.

He loved them so much it hurt.

He opened the door to the smothering heat and humidity that had both his kids glossy with sweat.

He started to call them in, like the civilized, then went with impulse.

He got the backyard hose, turned the spray on full, and soaked them.

They squealed, danced, ran away and back again.

"Dad!" Mariah screeched it as she tried to outrun the stream, but her face, like Bradley's shined with delight.

"Down with all backyard invaders. My powerful hose defeats you!"

"Never!" Bradley charged, made exaggerated swimming motions as the stream hit him in the gut.

Appreciating the creativity, and when Mariah joined him in the attack, the teamwork, Raylan let them take him down.

The hose plopped in the grass with Jasper happily lapping up the spurting water as he wrestled with his kids.

As soaked as they, he flopped on his back, a child caught in each arm. Because he'd left the back door open, he heard the oven timer beep.

"Dinner's ready."

In the morning, he took pictures of them with their shiny faces, new shoes, and backpacks. And he watched that yellow school bus swallow them up, felt a twinge in his heart.

It didn't last, but he felt it before he turned to the dog. "It's just you and me, pal. How about you do the breakfast dishes while I get to work? No? It doesn't work that way?"

He dealt with the kitchen, listened to the quiet. Yeah, some bliss there, but he thought about them both. The new kids in school. They'd made local friends over the summer, but still, they'd be the new kids.

When they got home, they'd be full of stories — and loaded with forms for him to fill out. So he'd better take advantage of the quiet while it lasted.

In his office, he sat at his drawing board while behind him Jasper sneakily crawled up on what Raylan thought of as his thinking couch.

He'd finished his script, edited it, fiddled, polished. It could and likely would change here and there along the way, but he felt it hit solid.

He'd gotten a good start on his rough panels, and now studied the full spread — two pages — on his board. He had his thought and dialogue bubbles in place, any additional text lettered in. Now, taking up a blue pencil, he filled in more details on the characters, the background. With other colors he highlighted certain details, added shadowing and light.

Now and then he checked the sketches pinned to his board for profiles, facial features, body types.

His villain had a slim build, almost slight, and an artistic, romantic, poetic face with gilded hair waving to his shoulders.

All a thin coating over monstrous evil.

Raylan gave his eyes a slight slant — nearly fairylike. They'd be crystalline blue, until he fed. Then the bloodred of the demon would rise.

Satisfied, he moved to the next spread, the next panels, consulting his script, his template for his layout. By the time he'd measured and marked the panels, Jasper slid off the couch, wagged to go out.

Raylan let him out, then got a Coke for himself.

He started, as always, with the bubbles. No point drawing something they'd cover. More text than dialogue on this spread, he thought, as Adrianna wandered her house, struggling to resist Grievous's call, then the full-page panel of her surrendering to it to become Cobalt Flame, spear in her hand, grief in her eyes.

Yeah, he had to admit it. She was hot.

As his blues took shape, he built her house, again referring to sketches, to his previous panels for details.

The tower, with her in its long window, looking out at the night. Lonely, he thought. Conflicted. Haunted. Tormented.

Who didn't love a hero who hit those marks?

Strong cheekbones — not diamond sharp like her master, but strong and defined. He'd have to experiment with his paints to get the right shade of golden, greeny brown. But for now, shape, expression, composition.

He'd just begun the long panel, her transformation, when he heard Jasper howling like the damned and demented.

Dropping everything, he raced to the back door. When he didn't see Jasper, his heart tripped, but the howls came again.

Following them, he saw his dog, front paws planted on the top of the fence, tail wagging madly, head thrown back in a fresh howl.

He hadn't heard the car pull up, but he saw it now with Adrian pulling a gym bag and what looked suspiciously like a yoga bag out of her car while Sadie sat patiently.

She swung the strap of each bag on a shoulder before she spotted Raylan.

"Sorry about the noise. I can let her back with him for a couple minutes if that's okay."

"Yeah, do that. Jasper, you're an embarrassment to your sex. And you know he's . . ." He made snipping motions.

"Love isn't always about sex, sex isn't always about love." So saying, Adrian walked to the gate. "Go on, Sadie, give the guy a break. I brought you some stuff."

Thinking of the personalized torture video, Raylan eyed her warily as she came through the gate with Sadie. "You brought me some stuff?"

"There's more in the car, but I need help with that."

Jasper raced around Sadie, rolled in the grass, jumped in the air. And Adrian smiled as she handed Raylan the black yoga bag. "How's the first day of school going around here?"

"Okay so far, but now I'm starting to worry about it."

She passed him the gym bag, and it proved heavier than it looked.

"Yoga mat, blocks and straps, exercise bands, wrist and ankle weights."

"Oh. You shouldn't have."

"What are friends for? You got the instructional video?"

"Yeah. Yeah, but things . . ."

She smiled her thousand-watt smile. "Busy, busy."

She positively beamed amused understanding. He didn't trust it for a minute.

"Why don't we take these in, then we can

get the free weights out of the car. I can help you take them downstairs — assuming that's the best area for you. Then I'll get out of your way so you can go back to busy."

What, he asked himself, was happening?

"Free weights? You brought me free weights?"

"And a complimentary membership month so you can stream Work Out Now dot com when you're ready." She slid right by him into the kitchen.

Smooth as a snake in the grass.

"Oh, Raylan, this looks really nice. It looks happy. Organized and happy," she added. "The schedule calendar, the board with kid art and snapshots."

She turned to him. "Can I be a pain in the ass and —"

"You've already qualified."

She just laughed, shook back all that hair. "I can't deny it. But you said I could come by sometime and see your work. If you've got anything done on the new character."

"Yeah, it's moving along." Trapped, he set the bags on the kitchen island. "My office is around here." He led the way, around the island and through the open glass-paneled doors.

She stopped in the doorway. "Oh, this is wonderful! All the drawings. And it's such good light — I guess that matters. And so organized, again, with all the pencils and the

294

brushes and an actual drawing board. I guess I thought you did it all on a computer."

"Some do. Sometimes I do. But I like old-school."

"This is old-school?" She stepped to the board and the spread on it. "The house, I love it. It looks like ours with a shot of *Beetlejuice.*"

That not only made him grin, it hit straight to the heart of pride. "Yeah, I guess it does."

"And she looks so . . . so sad, so alone. It makes her sympathetic, so even if — when — she does terrible things, the reader will feel for her. And this, you're drawing her big, full body, in movement."

"Her transition, yeah."

"You studied anatomy?"

"Well, yeah, in college. You've got to know how things connect to make them come alive on the page. Musculature, spine, rib cage."

"There's common ground. You can't teach fitness, not safely, not well, unless you know how things connect, react. So, I love your setup here, and your happy home, and one day I'd also love you to explain this whole process to me. But you're working, and I have to get back. Let's get those weights inside."

"How do you know I didn't already buy weights?"

"I asked Jan."

"Betrayed by my own mother."

It took half an hour, after which Raylan

deemed he'd thoroughly worked out for the day. By the time he'd carted in the last set — thirty-five freaking pounds each — she'd put together the two-tiered rack, and had it filled but for the last two slots.

His ready-to-finish basement now looked a little terrifying.

"You really need a bench."

"Stop."

"You'll see." She waved a hand. "It's good it's already got hardwood flooring, and the light's not bad at all. The space is more than adequate."

She stood on long, long legs in black running shorts with bright blue piping. To match, he assumed, the bright blue tank that showed off long, toned arms.

The running shoes matched, too. That same blue with the discreet NG — New Generation — logo in black.

Mariah, he thought, would approve.

"You won't like it much at first," Adrian said as she wandered that space. "But by the end of the second week, you'll see benefits. You'll sleep better, feel better. And by the third week, it'll be a habit. You'll come down here to work out just like you take a shower, brush your teeth. Just part of your day."

"So you say."

"Yes, I do. Just remember, if something hurts, back off. If it's uncomfortable, push through. But pain means stop."

"It already hurts."

"Man up, Wells." She poked a finger in his chest, then turned to go up the stairs.

He paid attention because he needed that back view for the art.

"Oh, do you have a blender?"

He was a little afraid to answer. "Yes."

"Great. There's a sample of our superfood smoothie in the bag, and some suggestions for other homemade health drinks."

"Get out of my house."

"I'm going, and I'm taking your dog's girlfriend with me."

When she stepped out, she saw Sadie lying on the grass with Jasper's many offerings in front of her. Sticks, two balls, a half-chewed rawhide bone, a ragged tug rope, and a stuffed kitten.

"God, that's so damn sweet. She's going to cave," Adrian predicted. "How can she resist all that love? You know, you could drop him off with me sometime. Let them hang together while you work."

"You work, too."

"Yeah, but big yard, big house, and Popi would love it."

"All right, sure."

"Great. Come on, Sadie. Tell the kids I said hi."

"I will."

She rubbed the now dejected Jasper as she started for the gate.

"I'm going to say thanks for the stuff, but I don't actually mean it."

She tossed all that hair again. "You will."

To avoid any more howling, Raylan bribed Jasper with a Milk-Bone. He got him back into the house, stood there, shaking his head.

"I get you having all this for that big, beautiful girl. But it doesn't feel right, not really, for me to have this — this thing starting up with the tall, gorgeous fitness queen. And I don't know what the hell to do with it."

Since he didn't, he ate a leftover chicken finger for lunch, then went back to work.

Summer beat hot fists against oncoming fall straight through September. Backyard pools stayed open, gardens burgeoned, and air conditioners continued to hum. Floaters brought their tubes and rafts and kayaks to Traveler's Creek to cool off on lazy rides under the shade of arching trees that stayed stubbornly green.

In October, like a fingersnap, summer sizzled out. Fall blew in on brisk breezes, painting the trees with vivid, striking colors that drew the hikers and bikers and sent the Canadian geese honking their way north.

Adrian pulled into Rizzo's parking lot on what she considered a perfect fall day with madly colored trees against a wildly blue sky. The crisp autumn breeze sent some of those bright leaves tumbling and scuttling and swirling like miniature gymnasts.

After she and Dom got out of either side, she opened the back to clip the leash on Sadie.

"Don't work too hard, Popi."

"You either. Barry's going to drive me home before dinnertime. How about I bring home some manicotti?"

"Who'd say no to that?" She kissed his cheek, and loitered an extra minute until he'd gone in the back door.

It would be his first full day back at the shop after a late summer cold had laid him low for a few days. Probably, she thought as she walked Sadie toward the post office, because he — they, she corrected — had run around so much meeting with the architect, the engineer, the contractor, the town planner.

Worth it, now that he was back to a hundred percent, she thought, and if all went as planned, work would begin on the youth center.

She started to tie Sadie's leash to the bike rack outside the post office when she heard the desperate howl.

"Uh-oh, sounds like your boyfriend's around. Just let me get the mail, and we'll go give him a quick thrill."

Sadie sat, always obedient, but she cast her pretty eyes toward the howls. And Adrian saw longing in them.

She had, as predicted, caved.

"Five minutes," Adrian promised, and stepped into the lobby.

She saw Raylan, with a huge box on the counter, talking to the postmistress. She gave him the once-over, nodded. Trim, slim, but no longer too thin. He looked, to her critical eye, well on the way to being fit in his jeans and hoodie.

Summer, as she'd noted before, had combed sun-kissed fingers through his hair.

She felt a little of Sadie's longing, pushed it back, then poked her head in the door. "Hi, Ms. Grimes. Hey, Raylan, I heard Jasper singing the song of love when I leashed Sadie outside."

"I better get out there before he eats his way through the car door."

"If you've got any time, we could walk them down to the park, along the creek." Where she'd planned to take a run with Sadie anyway.

"Sure. We could do that. Thanks, Ms. Grimes."

"Oh, not to worry. We'll get this up to New York for you. And don't you look pretty today, Adrian."

"Thanks. I'm trying out our new style of running tights."

"My granddaughter loves your brand. She wears them every day for training. Cross-country," she told Raylan. "Varsity. We're going to take States again this year. Mark my word."

"What size is she?" Adrian asked.

"Slim as a wand, long of leg — like you. She wears a size two. I couldn't get my left leg in a two, even at her age."

"Favorite color?"

"She's fond of purple."

"I'm going to bring her in a pair in the new brand, see how she likes them."

"Oh, now, Adrian, you don't have to do that."

"Good running for her, good marketing for me."

"She'll be just thrilled."

"I want her honest opinion. I'm just getting the mail from my box."

"You have a good day now, both of you. And those sweet dogs."

Raylan stepped out as Adrian pulled her post office box key out of one of her snug side pockets.

"Does that make green your favorite color?"

"Yes, how did you . . . the tights. We're calling this color Forest Shadows, pants and hoodie, the top Loden Explosion." She sent him a bland smile as she put the key in the lock. "We also make men's running tights."

"No. Never. Death will come first."

She opened the box, started to reach in for the stack of mail. He saw her hand stop, ball

301

into a fist. He saw her face change. Amusement dropped away into apprehension. And, he thought, fear before she grabbed the mail, stuffed it in the bag she wore cross-body.

"Well, good to see you. I've got to get going."

He closed a hand over her arm before she could bolt. "What's wrong? What's in there?"

"It's nothing. I should —"

"Tell me what's shaken you up," he finished, and steered her outside. "Hey, Sadie."

Before Adrian could do so herself, he untied her leash from the rack.

"None of my business, you're thinking." Sadie tugged him, as politely as possible, toward the pitiful whines coming from the lowered window of his car. "You'd be right. Then again, it was none of somebody's business who hauled a ton of dumbbells over to my house."

Jasper began to bark now — a thrilled bark as they approached the car. Inside, he bounced like a dog on springs.

Raylan handed the leash back to Adrian and went around to the passenger side to get the spare leash out of the glove compartment.

He found his arms full of desperate dog before Jasper broke free to rush to his heart's desire.

The dogs greeted each other as if both had been off to war on separate continents. When Raylan finally managed to clip the leash on

Jasper's collar, he straightened, shoved a hand through his now thoroughly disordered hair.

"We'll give the dogs their lovers' walk, and you'll tell me."

"And people say I'm pushy."

"You are."

"You're no slouch," she tossed back, but fell into step with him as the dogs gave her little choice.

"Not when it matters."

By tacit agreement, they took the side street rather than Main, and he gave her time to settle. She needed to; he could see that. He knew faces, expressions, body language. It played into his work.

And the usually confident, straightforward Adrian Rizzo was shaken, scared, and silent.

He waited until they'd walked by houses, the backside of businesses, to the pretty green park where the creek wound its way under the first stone bridge.

"You got something in the mail," he prompted.

"Yes."

"From?"

"I don't know, which is part of the problem."

They took the walking path along the creek, here where it ran slow and easy. Beyond the park, she knew, it widened, began to dip and rise. Beyond the town where the foothills rolled on, rougher, higher, where cliffs speared out and up, the water quickened its pace.

Deeper into those hills, the white water rushed. It could swell in the spring rains, in the sudden, flashing summer storms, and spill over its banks to flood.

Often, too often, in Adrian's opinion, what looked innocent, harmless, could turn deadly.

"I need to ask you to keep what I tell you confidential."

"Okay."

"I know you'll keep your word. For one reason, I've run into you about three times since Maya told you she was pregnant. I know she told you and your mom before she told me just a few days ago. But you never mentioned it."

"She said not to, yet."

"Exactly. I don't want to upset my grandfather. Teesha's in the last weeks of her pregnancy and doesn't need the added stress. Nothing they can do anyway but worry."

"What was in the PO Box, Adrian?"

"I'll show you." With the leash looped around her wrist, she dug into the bag, found the envelope.

"You haven't opened it."

"But I know what it is, because I've been getting them since I was seventeen, that same careful printing, no return address. The postmark on this . . . Detroit. They're rarely from the same place twice. I don't suppose you have a penknife."

"Of course I have a penknife. Who doesn't have a penknife?"

"Me, and I like to open them carefully."

He dug in his pocket, handed her a small folding knife.

Despite all, she had to smile. "It's a Spider-Man penknife."

"I won it at the carnival when I was a kid. It works fine."

"You don't lose things," she murmured, and carefully slit the top of the envelope.

They stopped by the next stone bridge to make room for some runners. And letting the dogs sprawl on the grass, Adrian took out the single sheet of paper. Raylan read over her shoulder.

Another season, another reason you
should die.
As the autumn winds blow, on one thing
you can rely.
Wherever you go, wherever you run, I will
follow,
And when at last we meet, your pleas for
mercy will ring hollow.

"Okay, Jesus, sick fuck. You need to go to the cops."

"I have, since I got the first one. I was seventeen, my first solo DVD had come out the month before. The first came in Febru-

305

ary. They always came in February, like some twisted Valentine's Day card."

Carefully, she slid it back into the envelope, and the envelope into her bag. "There's a routine — a kind of protocol. I make copies. The original goes to the FBI. I have an agent assigned — the third who's taken this over since it started. I make a copy for the detective in New York. It started there, and it's still an open case. I make a copy for the police here, one for Harry, one for myself."

"So no prints, no DNA on the back of the stamp, no leads because there's been no follow-up."

"That's right."

"It isn't February."

"They came once a year, until I moved here. The first blog I did with the Traveler's Creek address, two years ago in May, I got one shortly after. The next year, I got one in February, one in July. And this is the fourth this year."

"He's escalating."

"That's what they say. But it's still just poems, four-line poems, every time."

"Stalking's stalking." Raylan looked out over the park, all the pretty trees and paths. "Emotional abuse is emotional abuse. Someone who travels, that's the most logical."

"That ranks high on the list," she said, and realized she felt steadier for talking to him. "Cheap, standard envelope, basic white paper, black — always black — ink. A ball-point pen, that's the analysis. Always printed, no cursive, no computer or typewriter."

"Writing with a pen, by hand, is more personal. It's more intimate."

She frowned at him. "So I'm told by the criminal psychologist who weighed in. Why do you think so?"

He shrugged. "I mostly write the scripts on the computer, but I do the drawing, the lettering, the inking, the coloring by hand because —"

"It's more personal."

"And you've got no one you can think of who'd have this kind of grudge, this obsession? You'd have been asked that by every cop who ever interviewed you about it. You'd have thought about it a hundred times. So you don't."

Yeah, she thought, she felt steadier talking it through with him.

"I barely knew anyone when this started. I was in a new school, had just hooked up with Teesha and Hector and Loren."

"But people knew you, from the videos you made with your mother, then the one you made yourself. So it doesn't have to be someone you know, some guy you dumped, some wannabe boyfriend."

"I didn't have boyfriends when this started anyway."

"That's too bad. Still, it's unlikely if you

had some guy you tossed over when you were seventeen, he'd carry a torch so hot he'd keep this up all these years."

He glanced back at her. "Not that you're not torch worthy."

"Thanks for that. It doesn't feel that kind of personal. Not the 'I loved you, but you rejected me' sort of way."

"They don't know you any more than you know them."

Now she frowned at him. She'd thought the same, but couldn't pinpoint the reason she believed it.

"Why do you say that?"

"Someone who does this?" He tapped a finger on the bag she carried. "It seems to me they'd want you obsessing as much as they are. That's the purpose. They want — probably more need — to stick in your mind, screw up your life. But they don't. You're too tough for that."

"I don't feel all that tough right now."

Because it came as natural as breathing to offer comfort or support, he put an arm around her for a quick side hug.

"It messes you up in the moment — and you'd be an idiot if you didn't react. You're not an idiot. But you'll follow your protocol, and you'll shake it off, and get on with your life and your work. I don't think he knows that, so he's not around here where he could see you do just that."

"I hope to hell not."

"Not. There's not enough rage in the poem, not enough frustration. He thinks he's clever, insidious. He's smart enough to cover his tracks and to put a few lines and beats on a page, but he's not especially clever. And he's no student of human nature. If he was, he'd know by watching your videos — and I bet he has them all — you're a force."

"I'm a force."

Absently, he stroked a hand down her hair. "You know you are because you're a student of human nature. It's why you're good at what you do."

As she stood fascinated, he scanned the park, and idly rubbed her back.

A gesture of comfort, of support.

"It's why you moved back here after your grandmother died. My mom told me she didn't think Dom would have lived another six months if you hadn't. You knew that. You're going to bring in those legging things — and probably the whole outfit deal — to Ms. Grimes because you know what that'll mean to a young athlete, to her grandmother. Hell, you brought me those damn weights because you knew I wouldn't bother."

"But are you using them?" Brows lifted, she reached over to squeeze his biceps. They lifted higher in genuine surprise. "Yeah, you are."

"Well, they keep sitting there." He looked

309

at her, into her eyes — that wonderful, unusual shade he needed to color. "He doesn't know you. He doesn't even know the Adrian Rizzo, not really, who's on the DVDs."

"I don't know if that makes me feel better or worse. Better," she realized immediately. "I don't want that son of a bitch to know me. Or bitch, because it could be a woman. Either way. You made me feel better, and I appreciate it. I'd have gone home, worried at it for a lot longer than this."

"Making you feel better doesn't mean you shouldn't be careful."

"I am. I have the big dog who goes everywhere with me. I make sure the doors are locked and the alarm's set every night. And I've been taking self-defense, and tae kwon do online for nearly two months."

"Really. You got moves?"

"Oh, I've got moves. What are you doing for dinner?" He blinked, made her laugh. "That wasn't that kind of move! Come to dinner, bring the kids, Jasper. Popi's bringing manicotti, and I'll tell him to bring enough for company. He'd just love it. Do your kids like manicotti?"

"It involves pasta, sauce, cheese. So it goes without saying."

"Come to dinner."

"We could do that. The kids would love it, too."

"Is six too late?"

"Six works fine."

"Great. Come on, Sadie. I really do have to get back," Adrian said, as her dog lifted her head from where it rested beside Jasper's. "I'm supposed to be writing a blog. You're supposed to be working."

"We'll get to it."

He didn't have to call to Jasper, as Jasper trotted right alongside Sadie like a dog who'd had his every wish fulfilled.

"If I bring a sketch pad tonight, could you do a couple moves? Flame kicks ass, so I could use her prototype demonstrating same."

"I'm more warding off than kicking ass at this point. But I can give you a sample."

He wasn't convinced she couldn't kick ass already, but decided if not, she would before much longer.

CHAPTER FIFTEEN

Dom enjoyed dinner with Raylan's family so much, Adrian initiated a weekly dinner party with rotating guests. She kept the number small, the hour on the early side. Whatever her grandfather believed, she knew he tired more quickly than he once had.

Since most of his contemporary friends had passed or relocated to warmer climes, the guest lists skewed toward the younger side. That only seemed to energize him all the more.

So once a week, they planned out a menu, cooked, entertained as October swept into November with fires in the hearths and hearty stews.

With the fires and candles lit, with music — Dom's favorite old standards mix — playing low, Dom and Phineas carried on a serious conversation about Oscar the Grouch.

"I say thank God not only for this fabulous meal," Teesha murmured, "but for Dom's inexhaustible patience. What four-year-old

312

wants to discuss anger management for a Muppet?"

"Last week he was obsessed with molecules," Monroe reminded her. "I'll take psychoanalyzing Muppets."

"Your mom's coming down, right?" Adrian gestured with her wine. "To help with TBD? She'll at least pretend to talk about Muppets."

"Yeah." Teesha stuck with water as she rubbed the mound of her belly. "Except, Monroe's mother's decided to come, too."

"The Battle of the Grannies." Shaking his head, Monroe spooned up more beef stew — Northern Italian style. "It's going to be epic."

"My mother planned to come down Monday, since I'm due in a week, to take care of Phineas while we're busy bringing this one into the world."

"We had my mother heading down when I texted her Teesha's in labor. But she heard her competition would already be here, so she called to tell us she's coming Monday, too."

"Then my mother hears that, and decides she's coming this weekend."

"Now they're both coming this weekend."

"Pray for us," Teesha finished. "One hitch in the plans." She continued to rub her belly. "TBD's decided to come tonight. Or by morning anyway."

Monroe and Adrian spoke as one. "What?"

313

"No panic, early labor. Still six minutes apart."

Phineas looked down the table at his mother. "Daddy needs to time them. That's his job. You have to call the midwife lady when they get to five minutes apart."

"I know the drill, little man." But Teesha smiled at him. "Don't text your mom or mine yet," she said immediately to Monroe. "We're all fine here."

"Babe, it's going to take them some time to get here."

Phineas folded his arms — his rebel stance. His dark eyes gleamed defiance. His little jaw set. "I don't wanna stay home with Gram or Nanny. I want to go to the birthing center. It's my baby, too."

"We talked about this, Phin. Your mom's got a lot of work to do, and I need to help her."

"If I could make a suggestion?"

Teesha nodded at Dom. "Suggest away. Start the clock, Monroe. I'm just going to get up and walk with this one."

Adrian popped right up with her.

"Why don't we — Adrian and I — bring Phineas to the birthing center? They must have a waiting room."

"They do."

"We could get whatever Phineas needs from your house, take him there. Wait together."

"It could be hours — bound to be."

"I took ten hours and thirty-five minutes to come out," Phineas said proudly. "I already had hair, too."

"It would be an honor," Dom told Teesha. "And a pleasure."

"Easing off . . . and done."

"Twenty-eight seconds long. We'll see how close the next one is. I could put off the texts," Monroe considered. "I mean, we wouldn't want to get them both down here on a false alarm."

Teesha met his eyes, smiled. "Of course not. We wouldn't want that. We'll just wait to be sure."

"And I can go and wait with Popi and Adrian because babies need to bond with their family." Phineas gave Dom a sober look. "I read it in a book."

"We can start that way — thank you. But if it gets very, very late, and everybody's very, very tired, you can't complain if Popi and Adrian bring you home to sleep."

"Can I sleep here?"

"You bet." Adrian slipped an arm around what was left of Teesha's waist as they walked.

Eight hours later, with the grandmothers making it in the nick, Adrian walked out to the waiting room, where Phineas curled in Dom's lap.

They both slept so sweetly, she took out her phone to memorialize it before she went

315

to them, gently touched Dom's shoulder.

"Popi." She stroked his arm while his eyes opened, stared blankly, gradually cleared.

"How's Teesha?"

"She's terrific. She's amazing."

Phineas's eyes popped open. "Is my baby here yet?"

"You have a baby brother, and he's perfect. He's waiting to meet you."

"Come on, Popi! He's waiting."

"I'm not sure I should —"

"Teesha asked for you," Adrian told him. "If you're not too tired."

"Too tired to meet the new baby? I don't think so."

In the birthing room, the two grandmothers forged a teary truce. Monroe straightened from kissing the bundle Teesha held.

"Come on, my little man. Come meet your brother." He gave Phineas a boost so he could sit on the bed.

"He's wearing a hat. Does he have hair like I did?"

"Yes, just like you."

"Can I hold him? I have to take my pajama top off 'cause we're supposed to skin with him."

Tears ran down Teesha's cheeks as she nodded. "That's right. Help him, Daddy."

As teary grandmothers moved in to take pictures, Teesha laid the baby carefully in Phineas's arms.

"He's looking at me! I'm the big brother, and I already know lots of things. So I'll teach you."

"We need to pick his name," Monroe began and shot a warning look at his mother before she could blurt out her choice. "Do you remember the three we decided we'd pick from if you had a brother?"

Phineas nodded. "But he's not the other two. He's Thaddeus. You're Thaddeus, and I'm going to help take care of you."

Monroe reached for Teesha's hand as his eyes filled. "That settles that."

Christmas came easier for Raylan. The new house, new routine, family right there. He made another lightning trip to Brooklyn, and found that came easier, too.

His kids thrived here, he couldn't question it, so that brought relief, and the assurance he'd made the right choices.

Maybe he felt a pang at Mariah's holiday ballet recital. But his family was there, watching with him as she danced in her spangly pink tutu.

And though he half hated to admit it, those daily basement workouts did the job.

He slept better, he felt better.

Damn it.

For socializing he had the occasional beer with Joe, dinner at the Rizzos' with the kids, reconnecting with his old friends when they breezed into town.

The hard turn his life had taken pushed him in a different direction. He could be happy he'd followed it to Traveler's Creek.

On New Year's Eve, with the kids passed out on the sofa, the dog snoring under the coffee table, Raylan lifted his beer in toast.

"Another year, Lorilee. I miss you. But we're okay here. I wouldn't mind if you came to visit again. It's been awhile. But I'm here whenever you're ready."

At the same time, a short distance away, Adrian sipped a solitary glass of wine as the ball dropped. With the icy sleet falling outside, she'd made excuses not to go out to any of the parties. She didn't want her grandfather out and about in that weather, so used her own apprehension of her driving skills to convince him to stay home.

Since he'd faded before eleven, she knew she'd made the right call.

Maybe she'd have enjoyed the company, but this suited her, too. Fire crackling, the sleet snapping against the windows, wine in hand.

In any case, they'd gone to and hosted plenty of parties over the holidays. Her mother had come in the weekend before Christmas, and stayed four days — a record.

To be fair, Lina had spent a lot of time with

Dom, had even toured the in-progress youth center. If Lina preferred a tropical holiday to the cold winds of the foothills, her choice.

They'd barely discussed another joint project, as both agreed to nail down details early in the New Year.

Since Adrian already had her own ideas, a specific vision for it, she felt keeping it out of the holiday bustle was the smart decision.

When the crowd in Times Square cheered, she toasted them. Sipping her wine, she rubbed her foot on Sadie's broad back.

"A pretty good year gone by. Let's have an even better one starting now."

When she switched off the TV and rose, Sadie rose as well to follow Adrian through the quiet house as she checked locks, turned off lights. Even as she stood a moment looking out the window.

"It's gone to snow, Sadie. We like that better. We'll bundle ourselves up tomorrow and take a walk in it. Can you see all the lights? Lots of people still up, celebrating. Happy New Year, Traveler's Creek.

"I know we're alone tonight, and maybe it's a little lonely. But we're part of something. We can be glad about that. Let's go to bed."

Her phone signaled a text as she started up. Puzzled, she pulled it out of her pocket.

Happy New Year, Adrian. Tell Popi the same. Mom

"Well, that's a first."

Touched, amused, Adrian texted back.

I will. Happy New Year to you, too. Enjoy the Aruba sunshine. Adrian

"A different start to this year, Sadie. We'll take that as a good, positive sign."

The New Year barreled in on brutally cold winds. Even when they stilled, the air crackled with icy temperatures that struck down to the bone. Though she didn't believe the legend, when Punxsutawney Phil spied his shadow, Adrian considered hibernation.

Too much to do for that, she reminded herself.

Over and above her work, she had meetings and questions to ask and answer on the progress of the youth center. And thank God they'd gotten closed in before the freeze hit.

She had a dog and a grandfather to tend to, more details to work out on her vision for the project with her mother.

And a ninety-fifth birthday party to plan.

She had a month to finalize those plans, and the fervent hope that by mid-March the weather would gentle up.

As she dressed — warm suede pants, insulated shirt under a cashmere sweater, thick-soled boots lined with shearling — she ticked off her errands and her route.

Youth center check first, then the drive to Rizzo's to park before she braved the elements to walk to the town florist — to go over the flowers for the party. Walk from there over to the bakery to discuss the cake and other desserts, trudge to the post office — and that brought dread as her February poem was due — then finish at Rizzo's to nail down the party menu with Jan.

A solid two hours, by her calculations, if not closer to three. But then she'd come home to the warm.

She went downstairs to find Dom in the kitchen brewing tea.

"You bundle up, my baby girl."

"You can bank on it. I'll take pictures at the site so you can see the progress."

"I'll look forward to them a lot more than I would going out in this. My old bones would crack and shatter. Instead, I'm going to spend my day off sitting by the fire in the library, drinking spiced tea, and reading the Stephen King novel you picked up for me last week."

"Alone in the house on a cold winter day reading a scary book? Are you sure you don't want me to leave Sadie with you?"

He laughed. "I ain't 'fraid of no books."

"Braver than me. Let me carry that in for you."

"Adrian."

"I'm carrying it in for you, and the plate of cookies you were going to put on this tray."

He nudged up his glasses. "Caught me."

"I know my man. Go on, settle in. I'll bring this."

She got the cookies, added some apple slices, peeled a Cutie from the fruit bowl, then carried the tray through the house to the library, where the fire already simmered.

She set the tray on the table beside his chair, poured the first cup of tea before tucking a throw over his lap.

"You spoil me. We should get packing and catch that plane."

"Where are we going?"

"Sorrento. Sophia loved Sorrento. We were just talking about it."

She brushed at his hair. He'd often mentioned talking to his wife over the winter. "I'd love to go to Sorrento with you."

"We'll find you a nice Italian boy. One who's handsome, kind, and rich and deserves you." He tugged her down for a kiss. "And we'll dance at your wedding."

"In that case, I'll start packing as soon as I get back."

"What would I do without you?"

"That one's mutual. Enjoy your scary book, and I'll be home soon."

"Look out for our precious girl, Sadie," he called out as they started out of the room.

She bundled up — insulated vest, coat, scarf, wool cap, gloves. And that first blast still felt like the Arctic.

And the world was a snowscape as she drove toward town. Narrow paths shoveled, snowpeople frozen in place with shocked smiles — or so they looked to her.

In town, the few people out on the street resembled quick-moving lumps, heads down, shoulders hunched. Snow from the last plowing glittered in frozen piles against curbs, and the mountains glimmered frosted white.

She drove straight through to pull up at the construction site.

The old stone would wait for spring to be repointed, repaired. But the new second story stood under the roof, its blue-boarded walls waiting for that seemingly distant spring for the board and batten siding they'd chosen — after endless deliberation. And the windows — all new — looked wide and wonderful.

She turned off the car, hunching her own shoulders as she and Sadie hurried to the new double doors.

Inside, the temperature rose to a blissful sixty. What had been a rubble of disaster now stood open, clean — if she didn't count tarps, sawdust, ladders, tools. Everything echoed with the sounds of work — banging nail guns, buzzing saws.

She noted the two main-level restrooms had been framed out, and dutifully took pictures. Then switched to video, knowing her grandfather would enjoy hearing the sound effects — especially when someone on the second floor let out a stream of inventive curses.

With Sadie, she went up the temporary stairs to the second floor, thrilled to see more areas framed in.

"Hey there, Adrian." Mark Wicker stepped back from the power saw. "Hey there, Sadie. There's that big girl. There's that big beauty."

A big man himself, Mark leaned over to rub and ruffle the wagging dog. "Where's the boss today?"

"In front of the fire, I'm glad to say. It's too damn cold out there. I'm taking pictures back to him." She waggled her phone. "He's going to be thrilled. There's so much progress since we were in last week, Mark."

"Coming along." Satisfaction on his face, he hooked his thumbs in his tool belt. "It's something seeing this old place come back. Dom sure has the vision. We got the plumber and electrician coming in this afternoon, get that roughed in. Inspector gives us the go there, we're cooking."

"You really are. I've never done any sort of project like this, but it sure looks and sounds, even smells, like good work."

"We don't do any other kind."

She believed it, and when she got back in her car with her phone loaded with pictures and videos, she couldn't wait to show her grandfather. She added a mental note to drop by in a few days to take more of plumbing and electrical.

"I couldn't really see it, Sadie, even when we had the drawings done. Popi could, but I couldn't. I sure can now."

Energized, she spent nearly an hour at the florist. Maybe the long cold winter played in, but she wanted to fill the house with flowers for his party.

She shivered her way to the bakery, then tried to keep her mood up as she entered the post office.

"Maybe he caught pneumonia, or frostbite, and we'll skip this year."

But there it was, mixed in with pink and yellow and creamy white envelopes, that single cheap white with the block printing.

She wouldn't read it yet, not yet. She wouldn't let it spoil the party mood she'd worked up.

Instead, she stuffed it in her bag with the others, and crossed the street to Rizzo's.

Huddling with Jan in the tiny office perked her back up again.

"I love the idea of having the big buffet in the dining room, and these stations spread around, great room, main living room, the library. I'm thinking three bars. One nonalcoholic, one wine and beer, one mixed drinks. Then a coffee station."

"You know we can get servers, bartenders from right here."

"Nope. Nobody from Rizzo's works that night. It's their party, too. Teesha's helping me line all that up."

"How's that baby?"

"Fat and happy, and Phineas is still in love with him. Maya's getting closer. She looks great."

"Fat and happy," Jan repeated. "Collin's a little dubious about having a baby sister. Phineas got a brother, and he insists Maya needs to change the baby to a boy."

"Seems reasonable."

"It reminds me of Raylan. He just didn't get why he had to have a sister. But then he was in love until she started getting into his things. There were times, I tell you, I thought they'd be enemies for life. Then, like a switch flipped, they were friends."

She pulled off her cheaters, let them dangle by the chain around her neck. "Sometimes I miss the wars, those little angry faces. But I see them, now and again, in Bradley and Mariah."

"Your kids make great kids."

"Yes, they do. So, are we final here, or are you going to let Dom put his oar in?"

"No oar for him. I've waited to tell him about the party until we finalized, so I'll tell him when I get home. He'll pretend it's all too much trouble, and he'll love every minute of it. I've got to get going. I've been longer than I planned. Thanks for this, Jan."

"I can honestly say it's nothing but a pleasure. I owe a lot of the life I lead to Dom, and Sophia. Ninety-five? It's a milestone. I can't wait to celebrate with him."

"He's planning on coming in tomorrow, so expect him to try to squeeze the menu out of you."

As they rose, Jan mimed zipping her lips.

A good productive day, she thought as she drove home again. A solid morning of things done. If her grandfather hadn't put anything together for lunch — and she suspected he'd fallen asleep over his book — she'd throw something together for both of them.

Then tell him all about his birthday party.

"It's what we call *fait accompli,* Sadie."

When she parked, she reached for the mail bag, remembered.

"Not thinking about it yet. No, no, no. Screw that asshole, right?"

She and Sadie went in the house. She tapped the alarm pad, hung up her outdoor gear. "I'm back!" She put the mailbag on the table by the staircase to deal with later, and kept going to the library.

"As I suspected," she murmured when she saw Dom, book in his lap, head bowed over it, with his glasses down his nose and his eyes closed.

She started to back out. She'd make him some lunch, then . . .

But Sadie went to him, laid her head in his lap, and began to whine.

"Ssh! Let's let him sleep." Hurrying over,

327

she made to tug the dog away, and her hand brushed Dom's.

"You're cold. You're too cold." When she started to pull the throw up, his arm fell limply off the arm of the chair.

Just dangled.

"You wake up now," she demanded. "No, no, no, no. Popi, wake up." She took his face in her hands to lift it — cold, so cold. "Please, please, wake up. Please, don't leave me. Don't leave me alone."

But he had, she knew he had, and everything in her began to shake.

When the big bronze knocker banged against the front door, she jolted, ran. "Stay with him," she ordered Sadie. "Stay with him."

She ran to the door — someone would help — wrenched it open.

Raylan's greeting smile flashed away. He stepped in, gripped her shoulders. "What is it? What's wrong?"

"Popi. It's Popi. The library."

She sprinted back, dropped to her knees by the chair.

"I can't wake him up. He won't wake up."

Though he could see Dom was gone, Raylan touched two fingers to his pulse, felt nothing but cool skin.

"He has to wake up. Can you wake him up? Please, wake him up."

Saying nothing, Raylan lifted her, pulled

her in. When she clutched around him, dissolved in wailing sobs, he just held her.

When she spoke, her voice jumped and hitched. "I left him. I shouldn't have left him. I was out too long. I should have —"

"Stop now." He understood blind, tearing grief, so kept everything gentle, his voice, his hands. "He's sitting in front of the fire, at home, with a book, with his wife's photo as his bookmark. He's got a tray of tea, and cookies, and fruit I bet you brought him. He's got a throw tucked around him. I bet you did that, too."

"But —"

"Adrian." He drew her back a little. "He slipped away, quietly, looking at his wife's picture. He lived a long, beautiful, generous life, and fate gave him a loving end to it."

"I don't know what to do." She pressed her face to his shoulder. "I don't know what to do."

"It's all right. I'm going to help you. Let's go out here."

"I don't want to leave him alone."

"But he's not alone. He's with Sophia."

CHAPTER SIXTEEN

Instead of a birthday party, Adrian planned a memorial. Instead of struggling against the grief, she used it to allow herself to make decisions based not on practicalities or logic, but on pure emotion.

At every turn, she asked herself what Dom would have wanted, what would have mattered to him.

And her heart knew the answers.

In the end, she held an open memorial in the town park on what would have been his ninety-fifth birthday.

The creek rushed under the arching stone bridges, quickened by snowmelt. Sun streamed through the bare branches of trees, glinted on patches of snow that tried to hide in shadows.

Monroe and two of his musical friends formed a trio in the bandstand to play sweet and soft while people gathered.

Despite the brisk March winds, hundreds came and dozens took a turn at the podium to share a memory or a moment.

In the end, she took her place there, looked out on the sea of faces.

"I want to thank all of you for coming, for being a part of paying tribute to a truly beautiful life. I know many of you have traveled a long way to be here, and that shows, so clearly, how many lives Dom Rizzo touched.

"Traveler's Creek wasn't just a town to my grandfather any more than Rizzo's was just a place of business. Both were his community, his home, his heart. He and his beloved Sophia dedicated themselves to community, home, and heart. Today proves what fine work they did."

She had to pause a moment as she saw Jan turn into Raylan, bury her face against his shoulder.

"He was my heart," she continued, "my anchor, my wings. And while I'll miss him, I draw comfort from knowing how many loved him, and I draw solace knowing he's with the love of his life. I draw strength knowing he expects me to continue what he and my grandmother worked for and what they built. I'll be grateful every day for the legacy they've passed to me.

"He lived well, and he lived full, and he lived here. And what he began lives on. Thank you."

When she stepped away, Hector was there,

right there, to take her hand and steady her.

Friends, dozens and dozens, came to the house. Flowers filled it — those sent in sympathy. Food spread over the tables, and there Jan had overruled her. It was prepared and served by the staff of Rizzo's.

It brought its own comfort, the crowds of people, some laughter now as well as tears. Monroe put on music in the background, the old standards her grandfather had been partial to.

It helped to see all those generations of people whose lives he'd touched in some way.

Her mother came to her, put a hand on her arm. "You did a wonderful job, Adrian. On everything."

"You helped."

Lina shook her head. "It was your vision for him, and I couldn't always see it. It seemed too much, too open. But you were right. Down to the blowup of the picture of him tossing dough."

"Was there anywhere he was happier than in the front kitchen tossing dough?"

"He had a lot of happy places. That ranked high."

She broke off as Raylan came up with his children. Each child held a white rosebud.

"We're sorry about Popi. He was your granddad. He was always really nice." Bradley held out the flower for Adrian. "He said he'd hire me to make pizza when I got old enough."

"Thank you so much." She bent down for a hug. "And when you're old enough, you're hired."

"Daddy said he's in heaven now with Nonna and our mom." Mariah looked up at Lina, held the flower out. "You can have this one because he was your daddy."

It took Lina a moment to speak before she took the flower. "Thank you. It's very kind of you. If you'll excuse me, I'll get a vase."

"How are you doing?" Raylan asked Adrian.

"Better. Today really . . ." She looked around, so many people, the voices, the connections. "Yes, better. I'd like to talk to you — another time, a quieter place."

"Sure. If you need anything in the meantime —"

"I know I can count on you. You've proven that already." She leaned in, kissed his cheek. She started to say something more, but someone called her away.

The crowd gradually thinned, and quiet began to settle again. Monroe took Phineas and the baby home, and Hector's Sylvie went along to help him. Maya, more than a little tired in the last stage of her pregnancy, gave Adrian a last hard hug before she left with her family.

For a short time, Adrian sat in the great room with Teesha, Hector, and Loren.

"I don't know anybody who got a better

333

send-off." Hector reached over, squeezed Adrian's hand. "You did him proud."

"I don't know anybody," Loren added, "anybody who's a regular person, who'd have so many people want to come and say adios. But . . . are you sure you're going to be okay in this big house?"

"Yes. It's not just a big house. It's home."

"I know, but . . . I thought Harry and Marshall would stay a couple more days."

"They've got kids in school," Adrian reminded him. "And my mother's here, for now."

"Is she staying?"

Adrian glanced at Teesha, shrugged. "I honestly don't know. She hasn't said."

"Are you still looking to do the production at the beginning of May?" Hector wondered.

"I'd like to. I have to . . . I have to talk to her, finalize things. I've let that, and a lot of things, go these past couple weeks."

"Give yourself a break."

"I am, Teesh. I absolutely am. But getting back to work, that's what Rizzos do. And that'll help me. Like it helped me to have all of you here."

"We loved him, too. And you." Loren scooted over to kiss her. "You know, Ads, these two are spoken for. How about if we don't find the ones worthy of us, we pledge to marry each other. Let's give it till we're forty."

"I can work with that."

"Which tells me Rizz is exhausted, and her brain's already gone to sleep." Teesha rose. "I'm taking these two home with me. And you, get some rest."

Adrian stroked Sadie's head. "I will. Maybe take a little walk with my friend here first."

Part of her wanted them to stay, to all stay the way they'd once bunked together in the big house. She wanted to put off the moment of alone, and the quiet, and the knowledge she'd wake in the morning without all the planning, all the details that had kept her so occupied since her grandfather's death.

But people had lives to get back to, and so — however hard it was to imagine — did she.

She walked through the kitchen — offering thanks to Jan and the crew — grabbed a jacket from the mudroom.

When she rounded the house with Sadie, she found her mother on the back patio, sitting with a glass of wine in the light of a scatter of candles.

And felt instantly guilty, as she'd forgotten about Lina.

"It's too chilly to sit out here."

"I wanted the air, and the quiet, but you're right. I heard the cars. Did your friends leave?"

"Yes."

"I hope they didn't feel they couldn't stay here because of me."

"No, of course not. It just seemed with everything, staying with Teesha and Monroe made more sense."

"Harry would have stayed longer if he could. And Mimi."

"I know. We couldn't put this off forever. Getting back to . . . things," Adrian finished.

"No, we can't. I know you're probably tired, but I'd like to talk to you. Inside. You're right about the cold."

"All right. I'm going to do one last circuit with Sadie."

"I'll be in the kitchen."

"What do you suppose that's about?" Adrian blew out the candles, began to walk. "I hope she's not upset because he left me the house, the business. I really don't want to deal with hard feelings tonight."

But she finished the circuit, rounded back through the mudroom.

Her mother sat in the breakfast nook. Two glasses of wine, a plate of cheese and fruit.

She looked exhausted, Adrian realized. In the bright kitchen light, the fatigue showed clearly.

"You've had a long day, too. We can talk in the morning."

"I've been putting this off. I didn't want to bring it up until we'd had the memorial. Until we'd . . . gotten here."

So Adrian sat. "If this is about the house, about Rizzo's —"

"What? Oh God, no." Lina nearly laughed. "He knew I wouldn't want either, wouldn't know what the hell to do with either. Traveler's Creek just isn't my home, Adrian. It's where I come from, and that's different. He left me that painting his grandmother did of the sunflower field because I always liked it. It's not a very good painting, but it speaks to me. He left me his father's pocket watch because my nonno let me play with it when I was a child. He left me things like that, things he knew would mean something to me.

"I loved him, Adrian."

"Of course you did."

"No, no." Lina shook her head, picked up her wine. "I loved them both, but we lived in different worlds. I chose a different one. They never tried to hold me back."

She took a deep breath. "When my mother died, it was so abrupt, so immediate. I was so angry. It wasn't supposed to happen like that, just a slick road on a dark night. But this, somehow, it's different. I saw when I was here over the holidays. He looked older, he moved slower. I could see the time he wouldn't be there, and it scared me. He was always invulnerable. It was forever. There would always be time to make up for not being here enough."

When her voice broke, she stopped, drank some wine. "I was coming for his birthday, and making plans to stay maybe a week. Then to start visiting every couple of months, a day or two. Just to make up some of that time. And then . . . you called, and there was no more time."

"He was proud of you. They both were proud of everything you've accomplished."

"I know that, too. I always felt trapped here, closed in." She looked around. "This big old house on the hill, the little town down below. It wasn't for me. I need the crowds, the movement. This isn't about that."

Pausing, Lina pressed her fingers to her eyes.

"Justifications are crap." She dropped her hands to the table. "So is procrastination, which I'm doing now. I've been a lousy mother."

"You . . . what?"

"You don't think I know how inadequate I've been in that area? I wanted what I wanted, and I pushed for it — whatever it took, whatever it left behind. I left a lot of things behind. The bare fact is, I'm not good with kids."

"Okay." At a loss, Adrian lifted her hands. "I never went without anything."

Lina let out a short laugh. "That's a poor bar to scale. You didn't because Mimi and Harry filled the gaps. And more because your grandparents gave you a home. I've lost my parents," Lina said slowly. "I've lost them both. And it's made me face what a bad one

338

I've been."

"You gave me discipline and drive, made me understand the value of working toward my own passion. I wouldn't have New Gen without you plowing the road."

"You started down that road on your own, with the friends who've just left. You didn't come to me, because why would you? I saw it then, knew it then, but, well, you know, busy. I'm sorry."

It surprised Adrian to feel it, so she said it. "I think you're being too hard on yourself."

"No, I'm not. You know I'm not, but you feel a little sorry for me right now. I'm going to exploit that and ask for you to give me a chance to do better. You're a grown woman, I get that, and I've lost the time between. But I'd like to try to do better as a parent. As a mother.

"I love you. It's hard for me to show it. But that doesn't mean I don't feel it."

In her life Adrian couldn't remember Lina asking her for anything. Regimenting her, directing her, disagreeing with her. But never asking her for anything.

"Would you answer a question for me?"

With something between a smirk and a smile, Lina tipped her glass back and forth. "I've had more wine tonight than I generally have in a week, so now would be the time to ask me a question."

Adrian took her time, drank some wine

herself. "Why did you have me? You had a choice."

"Oh, that one." Lina drew in, let out a long breath. "I'm not going to lie to you, not going to say I didn't consider that choice. I was young, not quite through college. I'd discovered the man I thought I loved and loved me was not only sleeping with other women but had a wife he was not divorcing."

"It was horrible for you."

After a moment's hesitation, Lina leaned forward. "There's one of the big differences between us. You see that, understand that. You don't need anything more to empathize. My empathy level is well below yours. Skipped a generation."

She leaned back. "It was horrible. Mimi helped so much. She always has. I knew she'd stand by me whatever choice I made, so less horrible. I felt I needed to tell Jon. I'd stopped seeing him, of course. I already told you about that, but I felt an obligation to tell him. I went to his office at the college, and . . . it didn't go well."

Brows drawn, eyes hot, Lina stared down at the table. "He kept a bottle in his desk, and he'd obviously used it before I got there. That should've warned me off. But I was there to get this done."

She looked up. "He called me a liar, then a whore, accused me of trying to ruin his life, of trying to trap him, and so on. I told him I

340

didn't want anything from him, had no intention of telling anyone, but that didn't work. He demanded I get rid of it, deal with it, or he'd make me sorry. I was angry enough to tell him I'd decide what to do with my own body, and he had no say in it.

"He came at me. So fast, shoved me against the wall. I remember things falling off the shelves he was so violent. And he hit me, twice, with his fists."

She pressed a hand to her stomach.

"Hit the beginnings of you, all the while shouting he'd decide. He'd get rid of it right now. I'd seen what he was, Adrian, when I broke things off with him, but then I saw what came into the house in Georgetown all those years later. I saw a killing violence. I'm not sure what might have happened, but the door opened. It was the student I knew he was currently sleeping with. He rounded on her, shouting for her to get the hell out, and I managed to pull away, get away."

She lifted her glass again. "That made my choice. Maybe it was arbitrary or out of spite, but I kept thinking he'd attacked us. Us. So I chose us. I should have gone to the police, and that I regret, but I just wanted to get away from him. And when I came home, when I sat in this kitchen with Mom and Dad and told them, told them all of it, they were there for me. For us."

"You must have been so frightened."

"Not after I came home, not after I went to work. I actually enjoyed pregnancy. It was a challenge, and I had a goal. That's how I operate, after all."

"It's how Rizzos operate," Adrian corrected.

"To a point, sure." Lina shook her head again. "In any case, Yoga Baby sprang from that, from us. But it didn't take me long, after you were born, to realize I'm not very maternal, not particularly good with babies, with children. I could make sure you were healthy, safe, secure, but to do that I needed to build my career and business. That's how I saw it. And Mimi was there to do the rest. And your grandparents, then Harry. Freed me up to do what I wanted."

She looked down at the table again. "I did what I wanted," she murmured. "And you were healthy, well-groomed, well-mannered. You had a good education, travel, talent — oh, you had such talent. And didn't I make sure you had others to fill those gaps? There'd be plenty of time, later, for whatever. I didn't have that time to coddle and cuddle, or the inclination."

She lifted her hands. "So I lost all of that time."

Before Lina could drop her hands again, Adrian reached out, gripped one.

"Do you know one of my most vivid memories, one of my deepest and strongest memories of you? Of my mother?"

"I'm afraid to ask."

"He hurt Mimi. I was so shocked and scared, and I ran for you, ran, screaming for you. And he caught me, he hurt me. He was hurting me. You came out, and you were so calm, so strong."

"I wasn't. I wasn't."

"You were. You tried to talk him into letting me go. You kept talking, trying to get him to let me go. That was your focus. I was your focus.

"And when he threw me, when he tried to throw me down the stairs, it hurt. It was this white-hot pain, but I saw you. I saw you through it, the rage on your face, the fury, the way you leaped at him. For me. To save me. He hit you, he hurt you, but you didn't stop. You were bleeding, but you didn't stop. He would have killed you, killed all of us, but you wouldn't let him. And when he fell, you ran to me. To me. You held me, with blood and tears on your face."

Adrian reached out again, taking her mother's other hand so they linked across the table. "I know you loved me. In the day-to-day routine of things, you're crap at showing it."

Lina's surprised laugh ended on a half sob. "I really am."

"But when it's the hard stuff, the ugly stuff, you're right there. I've always known it. And

I didn't know or understand then that by leaving me here for that summer, you took all the heat, all the fallout, all the ugliness, and left me where I could just be."

"That was most of it, I'll take credit for that being most of it. But there was calculation, too. I needed to use what had happened to boost, and not let what had happened take down what I'd started."

"You have had a lot of wine tonight."

"I'm so sorry, Adrian. I wish I could say I'll be better, do better. I want to try, and that's the goal. I'm hoping this isn't the first goal I set I miss making. You have too much of them in you not to give me a chance. I'm using that, too."

Adrian released her mother's hand to pick up her glass. "Keep drinking," she said, and made Lina laugh again.

"Okay, I'm going to lay it out. I enjoy my life. I'm proud of what I've built, and I think — I know — I've changed some lives for the better with my work. I like the spotlight. I like the financial advantages, the travel, all of it. I like the freedom, which is one of the reasons I've never married. But at the end of the day, I know I'm smart enough, organized enough, clever enough to have made more time for you, for my parents. I'll never get that time back with them.

"Meanwhile . . ." She lifted her glass in turn. "You're better than I ever was. You're more approachable, more personable, more balanced in that way. You've got a good head for business — I beat you there, but you've got a good head for it — and you surround yourself with talented people, people you like, who like you. More balance. And you've got more natural talent than I did. I'm going to take credit again for giving you the foundation, but you've built your own on it. And I respect that."

Lina sipped, studied her daughter. "I thought you were wasting yourself coming back here. I was wrong. It only helped you expand that talent and appeal. It would have smothered me, but it just opened you."

She sipped again, looked around the room. "What are you going to do in this big, old house?"

"Live, to start. Work. Figure it out as I go."

"I'd like to stay a few more days if you're okay with that."

"I'd like that, too. I'll take you for a tour of the youth center in progress. You might have some ideas."

"Would you take them?"

"Might." Adrian smiled. "If they work for me. And I'd like you to come back in May — first week of May." She calculated. "Possibly the second week of May for the joint project. I've got most of the arrangements in place."

"We haven't even . . . What arrangements?

345

I'd assumed we'd do the production in New York."

"I've got a different angle." Lina Rizzo, Adrian thought, wasn't the only one who knew how to exploit the moment. "Traveler's Creek High School gym. We'll have students, teachers — I've cleared all that. Double-disk set."

"In a high school gym — more a small town high school? With kids?"

"Graduating seniors with parental and medical approval. Six of those, six teachers. We put them through the paces. Thirty- to thirty-five-minute routines — cardio, strength training, mat work, yoga, and a combo of all. We provide wardrobe — maybe Yoga Baby for the teachers, New Gen for the students."

"A competition?"

"Ahh, friendly."

"Fitness 101."

Adrian frowned. "Damn it, that's better than my working title."

"Which is?"

"Never mind. We use the town where I live and you grew up — and give it some nice play. We use the school where you graduated, adds some sweet nostalgia."

"Let's not mention the year I graduated."

A woman-to-woman smile now. "As if."

"You were going to do this with or without me."

"Yes. But if you don't like it, I'll do the

346

project you want with you at some point. I just think this would generate a lot of interest, and a lot of sales."

"I want to see the routines."

"I haven't perfected all of them."

"Good. I have some ideas of my own. If we come together on those, we have a deal."

Lina held out a hand to shake. Then squeezed Adrian's. "I'm going to do better."

"You already are."

Adrian had a full sack of sympathy mail to go through. She wanted to try to answer as many as possible, as quickly as possible. Some had sent condolences to the house, others to the restaurant.

She took an early run with Sadie to give her mother use of her gym. With a breakfast smoothie, she sat down at the kitchen counter to begin to sort. Many she could just put in a memorial box, as she'd already spoken in person to the sender. But others had come in from all over, all those people whose lives her grandfather had touched in some way.

Once she opened all, sorted all, she'd try to compose notes.

A man in Chicago sent sympathies, and mentioned that Dom had given him his first job. A woman in Memphis wrote that she'd gotten engaged in Rizzo's, and Dom had personally brought a bottle of sparkling wine to the table.

347

Others spoke of having a birthday party at Rizzo's, or coming there with their sports team after a win or a loss.

It went on and on, touching her heart each time.

Then her heart stopped when she came to the familiar block printing.

Not the usual envelope, she realized, which explained how she'd missed it before. A thicker, larger white one, with a Philadelphia postmark.

When she carefully slit it open, she found a card, a black-and-white photo of a cat, eyes wide, fur frazzled.

HAVING A BAD DAY?

REMEMBER SOMEBODY'S
ALWAYS GOT IT WORSE!

She opened it, read the poem.

Your popi's dead, too bad for you.
You cried lots of tears, but don't be blue.
You'll see him again, and it'll be swell,
When I send you down to join him in hell.

"That's the fucking limit." Enraged, she started to tear the card to pieces. She stopped, shut her eyes, pulled out some control. "You're not going to use him, not going to use him this way."

She pushed up to pace because she could feel herself shaking. Too angry to think, and she had to think.

She yanked open the fridge, pulled out a Coke. She'd taken the first glug when Lina walked in.

"Really? We're going to attempt some delayed bonding, and you . . . What's going on?"

Adrian just pointed at the card.

Lina read it, sat. "If you're not drinking this smoothie, I will."

"Help yourself."

"I want to tell you it's more bullshit, but I don't feel that way either. Anyone who's followed your blog, read any of your interviews knows how close you and Popi were, so this is calculated cruelty."

"I know it. I know it's designed to make me feel exactly what I feel now."

"No, Adrian, it was designed to make you sad, to enhance your grief and frighten you. What it's done is piss you off. He doesn't — or she doesn't — know you."

She stopped, looked back at Lina. "That's what Raylan said."

"You've told Raylan Wells?"

"It was one of those things. He saw me take one out of the PO Box when he was in there, and he saw my reaction. So I told him."

"Good. The more people who know who care about you, the better. Now, what do you

349

want to do?"

It threw Adrian off for a moment that her mother, who kept personal business locked-down private, approved of opening her tight circle.

"I don't know."

"I'd like to hire an investigator. The police, even the FBI aren't as invested as someone would be who's being paid to invest in this specific thing. They don't have the time."

"I don't know what a private investigator could do."

"We'll find out. Maybe nothing, but we'll find out. Let me do this for you. Let me find the right person, have them start looking into it. I should have done it years ago, but I felt — always have — this sort of thing is just a nasty side effect of being in the public eye."

"So does everyone else."

"Well, I think I, and everyone else, have been wrong. Let's try it."

"Okay." Adrian nodded. "Okay. It's more than just doing nothing and waiting for the next one to come."

Or, she thought, waiting for the poet to come. How much longer would writing a few lines suffice?

CHAPTER SEVENTEEN

Raylan sat in his car outside the house in Brooklyn. It looked the same — of course it looked the same — but it wasn't the same.

Nearly a year had passed since he'd driven away from his life there. Nothing was really the same.

But his friend, his partner, had brought another life into that house. Time to go in, he told himself. Time to deal.

He gathered the flowers, the enormous rainbow-colored stuffed dragon, and carried them to the front door.

Weird, of course it felt weird to knock at the door of what had once been his. But moments later he smiled, and meant it, as Pats opened that door.

She stood, a tall, strong-shouldered woman with a messy cap of brown hair and lively blue eyes. Immediately, she threw her arms out, dragged him into a cheerful bear hug.

"You're here! Oh, it's good to see you, Raylan."

"Congratulations, Mom."

"I can't get over it. I could stare at her all day. She's so beautiful. Come in, come in and meet our Callie Rose. A dragon! A rainbow dragon! I love it!"

"Gee, did you want one, too? Flowers for the moms, dragon for the baby. It'll watch over her."

"A guardian dragon. Only you."

She took the flowers, and his hand. She held it, strong and tight, while he took the moment to absorb.

New paint, some new furniture mixed with what they'd taken from him. A baby monitor, a frilly baby swing, a Pack 'n Play with bassinet, a box of Pampers, a Diaper Genie.

The air smelled of flowers — he hadn't been the only one to bring them — and new baby. Soft, creamy life.

New life, he thought again. Not his. And he found himself all right with that.

"Okay, pal?"

"Yes." He turned his head and kissed her cheek. "Just fine."

"Come on back. Want a Coke?"

"Oh yeah. It looks good in here, Pats. I mean it. It looks happy, and that makes it just fine."

"We love the house. It has more than good bones. It has a good spirit. Bick just took Callie up to change her. Yes, we are those mothers, as it turns out. We wanted to put her in one of her ridiculously adorable dresses when you met her. How're the kids, and everybody else?"

"Great. Excited to have a sleepover with Nana — 'When are you leaving, Dad?' Maya's on her last couple laps before we get another new baby. You guys really did the home birth thing?"

"We did, and I'm not ashamed to admit I was scared shitless." She poured the Coke over ice. "But it went really smooth. Bick is a warrior. I get teary, sorry."

"Don't be."

"She just powered through it, and Sherri, our midwife, was awesome. And there she was, the most beautiful creature in the world, yelling, waving her fists like *What the fuck is all this about?*"

She poured a second glass, and they tapped them. "And here they come."

Bick walked down the steps holding the bundle in a fussy pink dress with a matching hair wrap.

"I feel like we should have lights," Bick said, "music, maybe a marching band. Let me introduce you to the newest wonder of the world, Callie Rose."

She had that look newborns did, as if she'd just swum up from some mysterious world, big, almond-shaped eyes dominating a face the color of gold dust over chocolate. A perfectly carved pixie mouth and a button of a nose.

"Okay, she's gorgeous. Good work, Bick."

"Best I ever did. Want to hold her?"

"Damn right."

He put the Coke aside to take the baby. And his heart melted. "I'll always have candy, whatever your moms say. You can count on it."

Callie stared at him, looked as though she might be interested. Then immediately spit up on his shirt.

"That takes me back."

"Sorry, sorry." Laughing, Bick whipped the burp cloth from her shoulder.

"We're fine. We're all fine here."

"We can wash your shirt," Pats told him. "We pretty much have laundry going around the clock now."

"It's fine," he said again. "And you look terrific. And not just for somebody who gave birth a week ago."

"We're sleeping in snatches, my nipples are still in shock, and we've discovered a seven-pound human poops a half ton a day. It's the best time of our lives. You brought us a dragon!"

"I brought Callie a dragon, and don't forget it."

He sat with her as Bick eased down, put up her feet.

She'd cut her hair into a Halle Berry sort

of pixie and, to his eyes, looked nearly as adorable as her daughter.

"How's your mom doing?" she asked him.

"She's okay. It's hard. Dom was a father to her. Having the kids today, tonight, it's good all around."

"Just one night?"

"Yeah, I'll head back tomorrow. Mo's got her spring dance recital this weekend. Maya's coming to the finish line. I'm going by HQ later." He stroked a finger down the baby's cheek as he spoke. "Drop off some more work, catch up with everybody."

"You know *Cobalt Flame: Turn of the Demon*'s killer, right? Thanks, babe," she said as Pats brought her a glass of orange juice.

"Her evolving relationship with Angel adds the edge, and emotion. Plus, you know, battles. It's all gotten me thinking more about the team forming we've talked about before."

"Our superhero club."

"Yeah, not just the crossovers we've done. *The Front Guard*."

"*The Front Guard*." Considering, Bick circled her foot. "Warlike. Sort of political. I like it. We'd need a story line that builds to it, bringing the characters we want as that core together. And we'd need the infrastructure. Where's the HQ, what does it look like? You're going to want a big, big bad to incentivize them to build that team, and keep it."

"Yeah, I've been thinking about it. I've got

355

some notes, a few early sketches. I figured I'd go over them with Jonah, then we could teleconference."

"Bick, baby? Why don't you go into the office with Raylan?" Pats held up her hand before Bick objected. "You know you want to. We've got plenty of milk in the freezer. You nursed her an hour ago, so you're good there. Get out for a couple hours."

"Really? You're sure?"

"For a chance to have her all to myself? Yeah, I'm sure. Raylan can drive you there and back, it's still too far for you to walk round trip. But we can take a nice stroll when you get back. Get Callie out in the fresh air. You go."

"Two hours. That would be good. Two hours," she repeated, and looked at her daughter. "I haven't been away from her for two minutes. I'm not sure I should . . . No, I'm not going to be that mom. Am I? No."

She breathed out. "Okay, let's go to the madhouse and talk The Front Guard."

He ended up staying two nights — thrilling his kids and his mother — as the brainstorming revved up. One of those evenings he spent eating pizza from the same takeout place he and Lorilee had used at their old dining room table while he and his partners hammered out plotlines or rejected them.

"Look, I like the visual of the big-ass cavern HQ." Jonah took another bite of pizza, one loaded with meat. "The stalactites, stalagmites, the passages. But it clicks too close to the demi-demon members."

"I hate when he's got a point." Bick picked up one of the sketches scattered over the table. "Because I love this giant, self-illuminating stone table."

"Remote's the important thing. No One's still got the military gunning for him."

"We could use a cave anyway," Jonah speculated. "But not deep underground. Maybe carved into a mountain. The Andes?"

They batted that back and forth, with Jonah eating with one hand, sketching with the other. The baby woke with a squall.

"That's the hungry one," Bick said before Pats could rise. "I've got her. What about the Himalayas? It's mysterious."

She lifted Callie out of the bassinet, sat again to ease her shirt open and nurse.

"I don't know why you're pushing them into caves and caverns." Pats shrugged. "I mean, it's dark. And they're always fighting dark forces. You could give them an island, some remote tropical island. Sunshine and beaches."

For a full ten seconds, no one spoke.

"Sorry. You're the experts."

"No." Raylan shook his head. "We're all sitting here thinking: Why the hell didn't we come up with that? The Front Guard Island."

"Far off the shipping lanes," Jonah continued. "Lush and untouched. Could No One make an island disappear — not show on satellite imagery, on flyovers?"

"I can work with that."

"It rose out of the sea, back in the far mists of time." Bick beamed at Pats. "I really love you right now. I want a waterfall."

"And a volcano," Raylan said. "We have to have a volcano. HQ should be glass. Clear. Like it's not there."

"Holy shit, I'm loving that — and you, too, Pats," Jonah said as he started a new sketch.

A good, productive trip, Raylan thought as he drove under the covered bridge to Traveler's Creek. With Flame's debut novel going into full production, the bones of The Front Guard set, and his next No One adventure underway, work rolled right along.

Personally, he now knew he'd fully, finally accepted that the house in Brooklyn belonged to his friends, and could even celebrate the life they built there.

He'd have dinner at his mother's — as she'd already informed him — hear all about their Nana-cation. Once he got the kids home, bathed, in bed, he'd go right back to work.

The ideas just popped and sizzled in his head.

Then he saw Adrian, moving at a steady run with her big dog across the road. The snug pants, the color of wild violets, stopped midcalf — he could actually see the cut of those leg muscles. The tank, fluid, opened in the back, flowing out while her hair, a mass of curls, did the same.

He felt that tug, that twist and pull. He didn't feel as guilty this time, but winced with embarrassment as he nearly drove right past his mother's house.

He made the abrupt turn into the driveway, and when he got out of the car, saw Adrian and the dog turn the corner toward home.

She intended to run home, then found herself detouring. She wasn't quite ready for the quiet of home, so turned toward Teesha's.

She noted Raylan's car still wasn't in the drive. The Creek grapevine had it he'd gone to New York for a day or two. She hadn't seen him since her grandfather's memorial.

So much going on.

She started toward Teesha's door, then heard the shouts and laughter from the backyard, made another detour.

Phineas and Collin made good use of the backyard playset, both of them with flushed cheeks and bright hoodies, scrambling up the steps to hit the slide.

She opened the gate, unleashed Sadie.

The dog bounded straight to the kids, who bounded right back.

"Hi, Sadie. Hi!"

They all but fell on the dog.

"Hi, Adrian. Hi!"

"Hi, yourselves. What a nice Sunday, right? You guys want to play with Sadie awhile?"

"Mama says Sadie's my surrogate dog — that means substitute — until Thaddeus is at least one year old. And then maybe we can get a puppy. That's two hundred and eighteen more days."

Only Phineas, she thought.

"Sadie loves being your surrogate dog. How's your mom, Collin?"

"She's having a girl. They don't have a penis."

"I've heard that. You'll be a good big brother, like Phin is."

"I guess. But he got a boy with a penis."

"Well, I didn't get to have either and be a big sister, so you're both lucky. I'm going to go say hi to your mom, Phin."

"She said for us to play outside because she was going to feed the baby and put him down for a nap. She feeds him milk out of her breasts. Boys can't do that."

"This has been an education."

She went to the kitchen door, peeked in. Teesha, sitting at the counter, waved her in.

"I'm sitting down for the first time in too many hours to count. Baby's asleep, boys are playing outside, Monroe's making music."

"So I hear."

"And we're ordering in for dinner because I said so. Help yourself to whatever."

"Got my whatever." She tapped her water bottle. "You look tired."

"Teething. How quickly we forget. Your mom get off all right?"

"She did, just a couple of hours ago. It's been . . . interesting."

"Is the — should I call it a truce — holding? I mean I know she was in DC for a few days, but this is the longest I've known her to stay around here."

"A new record. I wouldn't call it a truce." Adrian sat. "More like a new direction. And it is holding. She means it, she's trying. And I wanted to tell you she's agreed to the production. We've been making those tweaks, but we've got a go on it. I'll email you everything if you want to start the ball rolling."

"It needs to if you're determined to do this by the second week in May."

"I want it before graduation, so yeah."

"I'll get on it. You look tired, too."

"Maybe a little. I met with the job boss this morning, with the inspector. I'm bringing Kayla in for design work, so we've been going over ideas in emails and texts. I know you and Jan have Rizzo's in order, but I still need to keep involved. He'd expect that."

"And let's add what you're leaving out. Did you meet with the PI?"

Adrian unhooked her water bottle, took a long drink. "Yeah, and she seems solid and smart. She actually thinks she may be able to trace this last card. It's got a publisher. It's not like the others."

"And that's another worry. He's broken pattern again."

"He wanted to kick me when I was down, so he did. But the PI — Rachael McNee — said that was a mistake. Before, no chance of tracing. Now there is. Maybe she's right. Anyway, my mother wants to do this, and I want to let her."

She looked out the big glass doors, smiled. "Sadie's in heaven."

"So are those boys. I love that Phin has a best pal. Big brains really need pals, and they can just be little assholes together."

"Collin remains disappointed his new sibling won't have a penis."

"He mentions it often."

"I'm sorry I'm going to miss seeing Phin's penis-bearing sibling, but I should get going."

"You could stay, get in on the takeout."

"I would, but I need to rechoreograph a couple of things."

"You gonna be all right, alone?"

"Yeah, the house is home. And I've got Sadie."

"If you change your mind, just come back. And don't worry about the rest. I'll get the setup started, nail down the dates."

Adrian rose. "So, Raylan's not back yet?"

"Maya said he was due for family dinner tonight." Teesha leaned back in her stool. "Why don't you make a move there?"

"What?" She literally jerked back. "Raylan? No. That's just . . . weird."

"Why? He's seriously cute, he's definitely not an ax-murdering rapist drug addict psycho. He's single."

"I'm friends with his sister, I'm now his mother's employer. I knew his wife. I really liked his wife. He still wears his wedding ring. And, on top of all that, it's been awhile since I made any moves. I'm pretty sure I'm rusty."

"You dated that guy a couple of times last fall."

"Wayne? Twice, and he made the move, I just went with it. And nothing clicked. You need that click."

She paused, sighed. Then puffed out a breath. "I miss sex, I won't lie, but not enough to make moves on a friend, or go on clickless dates."

She rehooked her water bottle. "Maybe you could lend me Monroe, just for a couple hours."

"He is good at it. But no. Find your own man."

"Maybe later. Kiss that baby for me. I'm taking myself and Phin's surrogate dog home."

Teesha laughed. "He told you that one? I had to come up with it, as he started giving me statistics on canine pets for children. I'm not going to housebreak a puppy with a not-quite five-year-old and a teething baby."

"No shame in that. I'll send you the finalized agenda and itinerary."

Teesha got up to walk to the door, then called out, "You know, Monroe and I were friends first."

"For what?" Adrian called back. "Five minutes?"

"Eight. We made it to eight minutes. Think about it."

Adrian merely waved, hooked Sadie up to the leash, then ran off.

At the end of the following week, with April struggling to bloom in the quick breaks between chilly rain and cold nights, Rachael McNee sat with Adrian in the living room.

Rachael, a sturdily built woman in her forties, drank her coffee black and wore a navy turtleneck with a stone-gray suit.

The former cop, with her short, straight hair the same color as the suit, looked more like a kindly librarian than a PI with her own agency.

Which might have been why Adrian felt comfortable with her.

"I didn't expect you to report back so soon."

"I've got a written report for you, but I thought you'd like to hear the progress face-to-face."

"I didn't expect any progress this quickly either."

"You've dealt with this a long time," Rachael said, sympathy apparent, "without any. But up to now, your stalker's used cheap white bond, cheap white envelopes, and easily obtainable American flag postage. He's smart enough not to lick the seal of the envelope. He block prints by hand, so the printing can't be traced to any particular computer software, typewriter."

"And writing the poems by hand's more personal."

Rachael quirked up an eyebrow, nodded. "Yes. Always the same kind of ink — inexpensive ballpoint pen ink. I believe he uses the same brand of pen. He's a creature of habit. This time, he broke the habit."

"You were able to trace the card?"

"I was. So will the FBI agent assigned to your case, when she's able to get to it. Right now, you're my only client — your mother made that requirement clear."

"She has that way."

"She does. What I'm saying is I could pursue this new communication right away. And exploit his mistake. He could have chosen a widely distributed card published by a large publisher. Instead, he went cheap and narrow."

"Narrow?"

"Cat Club Cards. That's a one-woman operation in Silver Spring, Maryland, and one that only started publishing and marketing the cards February eighteenth of this year. It's a shoestring operation, Ms. Rizzo."

"Adrian."

"Adrian. She works out of her home, taking photographs of her cats — she has six. Her husband helps now and then, she tells me."

"She sold him the card?"

"No. She doesn't sell out of her home — or didn't until she got a website up, started selling online. But she only got that going last week. Her sister manages a card and stationery store in Georgetown, and stocked a supply of the cards. On February eighteenth. And Mrs. Linney — the cat card lady — talked her cards into three other venues over the next two weeks. One in downtown Silver Spring, a place she regularly shops, shelved the cards on the twenty-third. And two pop-up shops — one in Bethesda, Maryland, one in Northwest DC — shelved them on March second."

"So the card he sent me had to be from one of those shops."

"Yes. And that narrows the area. The cards were sold individually or in a boxed set of eight — variety pack. Her sister took six variety packs and twenty-four individuals, including the one you received. She sold two packs, and ten individuals — including the Having a Bad Day card — up to the time yours was postmarked. Among all the other venues, we have sales of eight packs and six of the version in question."

"He lives in that area."

"Or was traveling through. None of these venues have security feeds that go back as far as we need. Some of the transactions were by credit card, some were cash. In the interviews with managers, salesclerks, no one can recall anyone who struck them as off, who was memorable."

Rachael set aside her coffee, put on a pair of red cheaters to consult her notes. "The time line. The last poem sent the habitual way had a postmark dated February tenth, from Topeka, Kansas. You state you picked up the mail from your PO Box on February thirteenth, saw the envelope, but didn't, at that time, open it."

She looked up then, with more sympathy. "This was the same day your grandfather died."

"Yes."

"His obit, and an article on him, his wife, your family, ran in area papers on February seventeenth, and was linked on the Traveler's Creek web page on that date."

"Yes." Adrian sat back. "And the next day the card went on sale in Georgetown. A few days later in Silver Spring, and a few days later in the pop-ups."

"Correct. The card was postmarked March sixteenth, ten days before the memorial, which was mentioned in the papers, on the town's website. This card, rather than being mailed to your PO Box, was mailed to your restaurant, and you opened it the day after the memorial."

When Adrian rose, Sadie lifted her head, watching to see if she was needed. She kept watching as Adrian paced. "They ran the story in the paper in Kitty Hawk, too. My great-grandparents opened a Rizzo's there when they moved — that was before I was born. My grandparents sold it when my grandfather's parents died. They couldn't run both. He could have read about my grandfather's death in a lot of places."

"He could have, yes. My thought is he scans your local papers, checks for any mention of you or your family. He can, essentially, watch you from a distance. He can access your blog, stream your workouts, buy your DVDs. He'll have them all, Adrian. He'll watch often."

She had to fight off a shudder. "The law enforcement consensus is it's not a sexual obsession."

"I'd agree. He may be asexual. He may, actually, be a straight woman, but there's never any hint of sexual obsession in the poems. He wields power and control over you in a different way. The consistency and brevity of the poems, the threat to cause you harm. He enjoys disrupting your life too much to end it."

"So far?"

Rachael just spread her hands. "The escalation's not a good sign. And while he's never acted on any of these oblique threats — may never act on them — you could consider personal security. I could make some recommendations."

"I have Sadie, and a security system. I've been taking online courses. Self-defense, martial arts. I can't think about bodyguards. For how long? This could easily go on another ten or twelve years. That's part of the torture, isn't it? Not knowing if it'll ever stop. And, God, wondering what to do when and if it does. What that would mean."

She sat again. "I want to thank you for the work you did. It's the most real detail I've gotten since this started."

"Oh, I'm not done. I have a few lines to tug on yet. Your mother wants thorough, Adrian. I'm very good at thorough."

Rachael took a large manila envelope out of her briefcase. "A copy of my written report. I've sent one to your mother. If you have any questions, if there's another poem, please contact me."

"I will. Could I ask why you left the police department?"

"After two kids, my husband and I talked about it. It's a dangerous job. Investigating's not like what you see on TV or in the movies. It's research, legwork, reports. And," she said as she rose, "I wanted my own. I wanted to call my own shots."

"I get that."

Rachael held out her hand. "Be sensible. Stay safe. I'll be in touch."

Adrian took the cup and saucer into the kitchen, washed them out. She had work she could do — there was always some work she could do.

But if she stayed in the house, she'd read the report, go over everything she'd already been told. Worry it like a bad tooth.

"The sun's shining for a change, Sadie. How about I change, and we go out for a little run?"

Sadie knew "out"; she knew "run," and hurried to the mudroom, where her leash hung. Gave a single, affirmative bark.

"Give me five to get into running clothes, and we're in business."

CHAPTER EIGHTEEN

When she visited the job site the following week, she marveled at the walls — now dry-walled, mudded, sanded.

She turned to Kayla, home on spring break. "Wow, right?"

"It's so tight. This place." In her distressed jeans and college hoodie, Kayla turned in a circle. "We used to say it was haunted."

"Might've been. But if there were any ghosts, I'd say they're happier now. And I want to say how much I appreciate you spending your spring break in a construction zone."

"I couldn't believe you wanted me to help design the new youth center. We'd've died for something like this when I was in high school. I'm so sorry about your grandfather, Adrian. He meant a lot to everybody. And I'm really honored to be a part of this."

"Well, good, because I need help." She put an arm around Kayla's waist. "I think I'm a decisive woman, and I have a decent eye, reasonably good taste. But I look around here? And I can't even begin."

"Okay, you said you wanted welcoming, happy, but easy to maintain. Nothing fussy, but nothing boring — and you want to respect the history of the building."

"And you can work with that?"

"I've got samples and design boards in my car. Can I bring them in?"

"Boards, really? Well, yeah. I'll help you."

Before she could, Mark called her from the top of the new staircase. "Hey, Adrian, can you come up and look at this? Hey, Kayla. How's the college girl?"

"I'm great, Mr. Wicker. How are Charlie and Rich?"

"Growing like weeds. Kayla used to babysit my kids."

Always a connection in Traveler's Creek, Adrian thought. "I'll be right up. Kayla's got some things in her car we need to bring in."

"Oh, I can get them."

"Hey, Derrick, go down and help Kayla bring in her stuff, will you?"

"You got it." The gangly, sharp-elbowed Derrick jogged down the stairs in his work boots. "Howzit going, Kayla?"

Adrian headed up, assessed the idea for a change — a smart one — in a storage closet.

When she got back down, Kayla had samples on a piece of plywood spread over sawhorses, and three boards with design elements grouped together.

"And I need another wow."

"You need choices. All the pictures and videos you sent me really helped. I thought you'd want your colors and tones to flow through. Stick with one family? But I think you need to have zones — defined, but with that flow. You need a little old-time mixed in for the historic aspect, so I was looking at this flooring for the restrooms, the food areas."

"It looks like brick."

"But it's an easy-to-clean, nonslip tile. Or you could go with the neutral vinyl, maybe face a wall in the brick pattern. For the cabinetry, you could go with color — for the happy — but with flat front, easy-to-clean doors. Go rustic with the hardware."

"I'm already loving the dark green for the cabinets. I'm partial to green."

"I remember. You match them with white counters — this is manmade, and you don't have to seal it, it won't hold stains. You could do a rounded edge. Looks pretty and it's safer with kids. Maybe with the antiqued bronze pulls."

Adrian studied as Kayla rearranged samples into groups.

"Keep talking."

Before they finished, Adrian settled on most of the materials, separated out a few samples to take home and look over again.

Mark came down to study some of the choices. "I like what I'm seeing. Look at you." He poked Kayla's arm. "Professional."

Mark's brother, the former rough customer, wandered over to do the same. "Green cabinetry. Snappy." He winked at Kayla, then turned a thousand-watt grin on Adrian. "Didn't know you were coming by tonight. I'd've worn my good hat."

Paul, she remembered, and smiled back at him. "I thought that was your good hat."

"This old thing?"

"Paul, how about you help the ladies take all this out to their cars."

"Glad to do it. It sure is a pleasure helping bring this old place back to life." He swaggered a bit as he hauled out the boards. "Sure am looking forward to some real spring weather if it ever gets here. I see you out running with your dog now and then. You two make a picture."

"Sadie loves her runs. Me, too." She opened the door so Sadie could jump in. "Just the top board in this car, Paul, thanks."

"Mason's going to start cleaning and repointing the brick next week, if rain holds off." He leaned against her car for a minute. "You'll see a real difference once he does. And once we get the siding on the second floor."

He rubbed his chin. "Give us a couple good weeks, and she'll shine out here."

"I'm looking forward to it. Thanks again."

"Anytime at all. I was going to stop in Rizzo's tonight for a beer and a couple slices. I'd be happy to buy you the same anytime you want to talk the work over."

"Thanks. If not, I'll see you here in a few days."

He tapped the bill of his cap. "You take care now." And swaggered back into the building.

"He was totally flirting on you."

"Yeah, I got that."

"He's really cute, and built. Barry used to date his sister. Paul's okay. He used to be kind of wild — Barry says — but he's okay."

"Yeah, well . . ." Adrian made a noncommittal sound.

"No sparkage?"

"I guess not. He is built. Something to think about. I'm going to make a final decision on the rest tonight. Or tomorrow. I know we have to talk about furnishings before your break's over."

"I've got some ideas."

"I count on it. See you soon."

No sparkage, Adrian thought as she drove away. No click. Then again, she hadn't given it much of a chance. She could always try that casual beer at Rizzo's, and just . . . see.

"Just can't seem to work up the energy for it, Sadie. Maybe after this production's finished, and the center project's done. Something to think about."

She detoured to Teesha's, hoping to show her the selections she'd yet to decide on.

No family car in the drive, which meant said family had gone off somewhere to do some family thing.

But she saw Raylan's car in his, pulled in behind it.

She'd yet to find the time or opportunity to talk to him since the memorial. Interrupting his workday, she thought as she let Sadie out again. But she could keep it short.

Bounding ahead, Sadie started her happy, full-body wag.

"I haven't brought you to see your boyfriend for a while. My fault."

Adrian knocked, then patted Sadie's head. "You ought to play it down a little, you know, make him work for it before you —"

Raylan, his phone at his ear, opened the door. The dogs, one on either side of the doorway, charged each other to end in a rolling, delirious pile of love over the living room floor.

"Or not," Adrian murmured.

Raylan signaled her in.

He had on gray sweatpants, a No One–themed sweatshirt, obviously hadn't shaved in a day or two, and looked, she thought, strangely adorable.

"Yeah, it's my dog's girlfriend. Yeah, my dog has a girlfriend." Raylan sidestepped to avoid the canine trip-pile. "Funny. No, that'll be great, seriously. My mom'll watch them, and we'll make a night of it. Yeah, way too long. Sure, see you in a couple weeks."

He clicked off, stuck the phone in his pocket. "Hi."

"Hi. Sorry to interrupt."

"No worries." He glanced at the dogs busy licking each other's faces. "We've kept the lovers apart."

"Clearly, we have to do better there."

"How about I put them in the backyard, give them more privacy?"

"Sure, but I don't want to keep you. You're probably working."

"I'll get back to it. Let's go, lovebirds."

He led the way out and through the back door, where the dogs bulleted to race around the lawn.

"Want a drink? Coke, water, juice box?"

"I'm good, thanks."

The kitchen looked like family, she thought. The calendar on the fridge with the month's schedule, the corkboard where he'd pinned kid art, some business cards, the almost-depleted bowl of fruit on the counter.

"I haven't seen you since the memorial," she began, "and there were a couple of things I wanted to talk to you about."

"How are you doing?"

"Okay. Okay, really. When Nonna died, I'd only actually visited. Extended visits a lot of times, but visits. I missed her, but I was more worried for him. Then I lived here. More than two years. Some mornings I get up, start thinking if it's my turn to drive him to work, or expect to smell his morning coffee when I go down to the kitchen. Then I remember."

"I still expect to see him behind the counter at Rizzo's half the time. He was an elemental part of a lot of lives."

"He was that. I wanted to tell you . . . I know I thanked you for all the help you gave me, for being there, right there. But I wanted you to know how much what you said meant. You said he'd lived a long, beautiful, generous life. And the fates had let him slip out of it lovingly. It helped, in that awful moment, to hear that. But more, I play those words back when I need them, and they get me through. Everything else, making those calls for me, holding my hand when I called my mother, all that mattered. But the words, they're forever."

"And now I've run out of them."

"I couldn't think then, but I have since. Why were you there? Right at the moment we needed you to be?"

"I'd stopped by to show you a mock-up of the Flame novel."

"It's done?"

"Yeah. And it was, basically. I put a mock-up together, and since I based her look on you, I brought it by."

"Do you still have it?"

"Sure."

"Can I see it now?"

"Sure," he said again. "It's in my office."

She went with him, and as he went around his workstation to open a file drawer, she scanned the sketches on his wall, his board.

"You're working on another No One story. And!" She moved closer. "Pitting him against Divina the Sorceress. I love it. They have that crackle of sexual tension even as they try to destroy each other. This is different."

She shifted over, tapping another sketch. "Like a glass fortress? Not glass," she corrected. "Some sort of transparent, impenetrable material, right? Very, very cool. Is it an island? It looks like an island. Yes, an island. With a volcano! Who doesn't love a volcano?"

She turned to where he stood watching her, completely bemused. "It's an HQ, right? Gotta be the good guys, because transparent. Tell me you're finally forming a heroes team. You're doing your Avengers, your Justice League."

"Front Guard. The Front Guard."

"The Front Guard." She said it softly, with some reverence. "That's perfect. Forging their strengths, aligning their missions, coalescing their powers to become allies against evil."

"We might actually want to use that."

"There'll be friction, have to have it. And

379

Violet Queen and Snow Raven have tangled before in *Queen's Gambit*."

"Holy shit." Dazzled, Raylan could only stare.

"But Snow Raven and No One teamed up well in *No Quarter,* and the follow-up, *All In.* Will Cobalt Flame be a member? Will they trust her enough?"

"We figure True Angel will sponsor her, and after some debate, she'll get a probationary membership. You really do read them."

"I like the struggle — the emotional one — and the battles. Good against evil, the loneliness of living a dual life, risking all. And I like what Uncle Ben told Peter. 'With great power comes great responsibility.' "

She spotted the book in his hand. "Is that it?"

He handed it to her, had to grin when she bounced on her toes.

"Oh my God, this is so utterly cool."

"It's just a mock-up, cheaper paper and binding."

"It's amazing. It's wonderful." Carefully, she paged through. "She looks so lonely and tormented when she's alone, then she's vivid, just magnificent riding her dragon. And look at the contrast between her and Angel. It's more than physical."

She looked up. "I'm totally fangirling, Raylan, but your art is just amazing."

"Hey, would you like to live in my office

and repeat that hourly?"

"Those of us who are good at what we do, and work at it, know we're good at what we do. So we keep working at it." On a sigh, she held the book back out to him. "Thanks for letting me see."

"You can keep it."

"I can . . ." She punched his arm. "Really?"

"Yes." Gingerly, he rubbed his arm. "You're very strong."

"Hot damn! Sign it, sign it, sign it."

"I will if you don't punch me again."

"Since I've complimented your art — sincerely," she said as he chose a red marker, "there's another thing I wanted to talk to you about. The youth center's on schedule, and we're looking to have it fully opened by September. Part of what we hope to offer is various demonstrations and hands-on lessons. Crafting, sports, music — Monroe's our go-to there — dance, art. I'm hoping to draft you to give some time when you can to demonstrate, teach art and illustration."

"I can do that."

"Well, that was easy."

"My partners and I did that sort of thing now and then for local schools and fairs, career days. It's fun — and we found one of our summer interns that way last year."

"Then you're definitely hired. We plan to pay with great appreciation and hearty handshakes."

381

"That meets my usual fee in this area."

"Thanks, Raylan." She took the book back, actually hugged it. "And thanks for this. Last thing, and I'll get out of your way. I'm going to start the Rizzo dinner tradition again. The house needs people in it. How about you and the kids test my solo culinary skills on Friday?"

"That sounds . . . Forgot. My mom's got them Friday. They negotiated a movie marathon sleepover. I am not invited."

"Oh, well. Just you then? Unless you want to bask in the quiet and alone, which Teesha tells me is better than champagne and caviar."

"I don't get the caviar thing," he mused. "I'm Tom Hanks in *Big* on the caviar. Anyway, ah, sure. A free meal I don't have to cook?"

"Great. You'll be my first victim. That is, my first guest. I'll hold the caviar. Seven work?"

"Yeah, that'll work."

"See you then. I'm going to go out for Sadie, and we'll just go around to the car. Do you want Jasper in or out?"

"He has to stay out until he finishes sulking. He sulks after Sadie goes home."

"Be sure to bring him Friday."

He stayed where he was while she let herself out the back. Let herself out, he reminded himself, the way a friend would.

Friends.

They hadn't made a date. She'd invited him and his kids, and his dog, to dinner. Just because the kids couldn't make it didn't equal date.

And the sad part? He wasn't sure he remembered how to date anymore anyway.

So good thing it wasn't.

And since it wasn't, he called himself a moron as he pulled up at the big house on Friday night. He'd actually obsessed about what to wear, which was just embarrassing.

He'd settled on jeans — always safe — then because he caught himself debating whether to go tucked or untucked on his shirt, switched to a light spring sweater.

He'd picked up a good bottle of wine, because that's what you did, but stopped himself from stopping by the florist for flowers.

Too much.

Now, with Jasper all but flinging himself against the door in the back seat, he took one last moment.

"She's not interested that way, never has been, so knock it off. And you wouldn't know how to handle it if she was, so knock it off."

He opened the door, let Jasper plunge out, then streak to the front door. Raylan followed more slowly, as he answered the phone ringing in his pocket. It was Jonah FaceTiming him.

"Jonah."

"Hey, man, got a minute? I wanted to run this angle by you."

"Ah, actually, let me get back to you. I'm about to have dinner."

"Oh, sure. I don't hear the kids. I always hear the kids when you're about to have dinner."

"They're at my mother's."

"Oh, cool. Well, eat while I run this by you. I think it adds a new punch, but we'd have some dominoes to deal with."

"I'm not home. I'm having dinner with a friend."

"Dinner with a friend? What friend? Wait a minute. You shaved. You've got a date."

"No. No date."

"Hey, that's Jasper. Why's he whining like that? Hold on! You've got a date with Flame! The one with the dog Jasper's hot on. Holy shit!"

"It's not a date. Shut up."

"It's the smoking-hot workout queen, right? Is she there yet? Are you cooking? No, you said you weren't home, but you've got the dog. Her place! She's cooking. Ooh la la."

"Remind me next time I see you to kick you in the balls."

"Sure, sure. Hey, text me later. I want to hear all about —"

Raylan hung up. It occurred to him the conversation he'd just had could have been replicated by a couple of hormonal teenage boys.

For some reason, that settled him down.

He let the big knocker bang against the door.

She wore jeans — so good decision — and a pale yellow shirt over a skinny white tank. She'd bundled that fabulous hair back and up.

"Right on time," she said as Jasper made a beeline for Sadie. "Perfect choice." She took the wine. "This is going to go well with tonight's menu. Let's go back and have some now."

She had music on. Dom had always had music on, too, low, just a murmur in the background.

And the thing that struck him as the same? The scents.

"Whatever the menu is, it smells amazing."

"It does, so I'm hoping it tastes that way. Popi left me his secret red sauce recipe in his will. A sealed envelope." She grinned at him as she handily uncorked the wine. "I mean sealed as in with sealing wax. I'm to memorize the recipe, then once again put it into a sealed envelope and in a safe place. I'm to pass it on to my children when and if they've earned it."

She got out wineglasses. "I know your mother has it — that was his level of trust there."

"Deserved. She's never revealed it, and she never made Rizzo's sauce at home."

"Tonight, I did. We're having lasagna, which I've never made solo. If it's not as good as it smells? Lie."

She poured the wine. "Thanks for coming," she added. "This is a real test-drive for me. Cooking on my own, having someone else eat it, figuring out how to open up this part of life again."

He took the wine she offered, tapped the glass to hers. "Here's to successful test-drives."

"*Salute.* Why don't you sit down? We can have the antipasto here before we take the main course in the dining room."

"A serious meal."

"An Italian meal." She got out the long, narrow platter, transferred some of the pepperoncini, cherry tomatoes, chickpeas, olives, and the rest — marinated in her grandmother's signature vinaigrette — to small plates.

"The start and finish? I'm confident, as Nonna taught me. You must cook some, with two kids around."

"We can't live on Rizzo's takeout, much as they'd like to. The grill and the wok are standbys, but I can actually roast a pretty good chicken. Plus, you didn't grow up with my mother and not learn to cook."

"I figured that."

"If I'm pressed . . . I'd say don't judge me, but being you, you will. I bust out the chicken fingers and Tater Tots."

"Mimi would make those now and then when my mother was out of town. Our secret. And I don't judge." She ate some provolone. "I educate. My mother judges, but she's trying to ease up on that."

"Is that so?"

"We're . . . you could say taking a test-drive. Popi's death really hit her hard. So she's reevaluated. Even before that. She sent me a text on New Year's Eve, just after midnight, to wish me a happy New Year. She'd never done that before. And she's going along, without much pushback, on the high school theme for our new DVD."

"I've been hearing about that. Lots of buzz around the Creek."

"I'm pretty buzzed myself. I love the idea of the two-generation theme. Two and a half," she corrected, "as I'm a long way out of high school."

"Are you using athletes? This is terrific, by the way."

"Thanks. We've got a cheerleader, a football linebacker, a gym teacher, the football coach, so the athletes are represented. We also have science geeks, math nerds, thespians, a student who got a full ride to Virginia Tech."

She smiled over her wine. "It's diverse in every way. Sex, age, race, in shape, not-so-much in shape. Putting together a good program that spans that's been a challenge."

"Bet you loved it."

"Bet I did. My mother's coming back in a few weeks so we can have rehearsals, make sure it all works, time it out with the full cast. Then the crew comes in, we set up, and we shoot over a weekend, two long days, with an after-school backup for a third, if needed.

"Ready for the big test?"

"If I have to smell it without eating it much longer, it could get ugly."

"Fingers crossed. Why don't you put the dogs out back, light the candles on the table? I'll get the rest."

Easier than he'd thought, he admitted when he let the dogs out. She was, always had been, easy to talk to, to be around. And if you couldn't relax in that house, you had issues.

She brought out the lasagna, soft, fat breadsticks — a Rizzo's staple — and a dish of roasted cherry tomatoes in oil and herbs.

"I'm going to plate it if that's okay with you."

"Don't be stingy."

"May you not regret that."

She plated generous squares of lasagna with the sides while Raylan topped off the wine.

She sat, took up the first forkful. "Here goes."

They sampled the first bite together. Adrian's smile spread slowly before she added an eyebrow wiggle.

"The Rizzo legacy lives on," Raylan said as he took another bite.

"Whew. I'm never going to be the passionate and consistent cook my grandparents were, but it feels good knowing I haven't let them down. Now that my performance anxiety's over, I should tell you I read your book. Twice."

"I'm too busy eating to have my own performance anxiety."

"Good, because you'd waste it, and now you can save it for a more appropriate time. I admit to personal distraction on the first read. Seeing myself on the page, in the story. That was weird and wonderful. The second read, it wasn't me, it was her, but I still felt her struggle. She's so tormented. Her attraction and repulsion for Grievous. Her admiration and her envy of True Angel."

Picking up her wine, she gestured with it before she sipped.

"And even though I'd read it, and I knew, that moment in the underground under the nightclub, under Styx, where Angel's wounded, defenseless, and Grievous is pushing Flame to finish Angel off, to light the spark that will destroy the city, it's a heart-thumper. Kill True Angel, deliver her soul to Grievous, and she'll be free of him. Damned to the dark, but she understands the dark.

"So when she turns her power, her fire on

Grievous, to save Angel, to save people who fear and loathe her, it's thrilling."

"I'm starting to wonder how my ego survived without you."

"I'm not shining you on. It could've gone the other way, because Flame's a little bit crazy. She runs on emotion, and Angel's everything she's convinced herself she can't be, so envies, darkly."

She speared up a tomato. "Destroying True Angel would've given her everything she thought she wanted — thought she deserved."

"Cutting herself off from the human part of herself, finally and completely."

"And instead, she chose the human. Do your kids get a kick out of what Daddy does?"

"Mostly it's just what I do, and Bradley continues his obsession with Batman."

Amused, Adrian sipped some wine. "I'm sure it's a phase."

"When we dyed eggs for Easter, he drew a Batman cowl on one. Pretty good cowl. I live with it, and cover for him when I can with my partner Jonah, who takes it personally."

"Do you miss it?" she wondered. "Being right there with the people you work with?"

"Some of it, yeah. There's a vibe, an energy, and you lose some of that with teleconferencing. I probably get more uninterrupted work done this way, but you gotta miss the daily bull sessions. Do you? Miss New York?"

"I thought I would, but I really don't. Most

of my work I do alone anyway. Now having Teesha and Monroe right here, that's huge for me, but work-wise, mine's not collaborative like yours, at least not until it's heading into the final stages."

"Monroe." Raylan dipped the last of a breadstick in the little dish of oil. "I had no idea when we moved in next door that he'd written about ten percent of the songs on my playlist."

"He's an understated guy."

"Yeah, he's that. Sometimes he sits out in the yard, plays the guitar or the keyboard. Or the sax. I asked him once why he didn't perform his own songs."

"He said: I like the quiet."

"Exactly. Adrian, this was an amazing meal. Seriously amazing."

"Not done yet. We have zabaglione. I'm confident going there because my nonna taught me her secret years ago. I'll just clear. Cappuccino?"

"Sure. I'll give you a hand."

They both rose, gathered dishes.

"Oh, I saw Maya today," Adrian began as they carried dishes to the kitchen. "She'd just gotten back from her weekly checkup, and all's well there."

"I heard that. Mom's going a little crazy about having a girl. Joe's happy about it. Collin, not so much, and has confided to me he thinks they're making a big mistake because girls are dopey."

"And your response?"

"I expressed some sympathy to establish a foundation of trust. Then crossed the streams in many universes to point out nondopey girls. Pink Power Ranger, Wonder Woman, Princess Leia, Storm, Violet Queen, his mother, his nana. I didn't mention his cousin because right now Mariah epitomizes his definition of dopey."

"Wise."

She turned toward the cappuccino machine as he stepped up to set down dishes. And bumped straight into him.

She looked up. Green eyes. Why did he have to have green eyes? She leaned in, to him, to that yearning.

And catching herself, jerked back.

"I'm sorry. God! Raylan, I'm so sorry. That was just —"

He closed a hand lightly around her arm to hold her in place. "Do you have to be?"

CHAPTER NINETEEN

She couldn't line up her thoughts. She couldn't find a coherent one to start the line.

"It's just that I didn't mean to . . . I didn't set this up to — set you up to . . . Oh well."

"Let's see if we're both sorry, or not."

It would change things, big moments changed things. So he took his time drawing her in, took more drawing her up just a little before he closed the rest of the distance, closed his mouth over hers.

Slow, soft, sweet. Just a taste, a test either could pull away from without damaging a long, important friendship.

Drawn to the slow, the soft, the sweet, she again leaned in.

Like a key turned in a lock. She felt the click that had eluded her for so long, and let herself sink into the kiss, into the moment.

It changed things. She laid a hand on his cheek, then slid her fingers up and through his hair, and changed things.

Did he deepen the kiss or did she? She

didn't know, only knew everything inside her wanted more.

He eased back, his eyes still on hers. "Sorry?"

"No. No, not even a little."

"Me either."

This time she linked her arms around his neck, and the hum in her body sounded in her throat as he gripped her hips.

"The smart thing," she managed before she kissed him again. "The smart thing would be to give this a few days."

"Would it though?" He brought his hands up her sides, down again. "Would it really?"

"Or we could just go upstairs now, save time."

"Time management's underrated. I vote for that."

She took his hand, took a breath. They walked out of the kitchen together.

"I wasn't expecting the evening to end this way," she began.

"Another me either. But I've thought about it."

She paused at the base of the stairs. "Really?"

"Let's keep moving. Less risk you'll change your mind."

The flutter low in her belly moved up to her chest. "Not gonna happen."

"Here's the thing. I haven't been with anyone since Lorilee, so I'm rusty."

"I've been in a long dry spell myself. We'll refresh each other's memory."

She turned into her bedroom where, as always, she'd left the pretty lamp by the window on low.

Then she turned into him.

She wanted that warmth, that jumpy, nervous thrill.

"I remember this part." He murmured against her mouth as his hands began to glide.

When he started pulling the pins from her hair, she instinctively reached up. "Oh, it's going to be —"

"Amazing. There's so much of it." Combing his fingers through it, he circled her toward the bed. "It's all coming back to me now."

In one smooth move that tripped her heart, he scooped her up, back, and had them on the bed.

"Nice one. High score."

"Thanks." He took a moment, studying her face, watching the light and shadows play over it. He'd drawn it countless times, knew every angle of it. And still . . . "Who'd have thought we'd end up here?"

And when he brought his mouth to hers, the time for thinking ended.

He'd closed off needs, so long, and rediscovered the wonder of having them spread and heat through him. Wanting again, being wanted felt miraculous, and gloriously normal. She reached for him. He didn't know if he'd ever be able to explain what it meant to have someone reach for him again.

What it meant to have a woman stir those needs awake, and offer to meet them.

He drew her overshirt off her shoulders, let his hands run over those tough muscles, and the contrast of balletically long arms and satin-smooth skin.

When he peeled her tank up and off, she arched to help him. Then he skimmed his hands over her breasts, lightly, lightly, before he simply laid his head there with her heart drumming under him.

She felt so . . . prized. His hands against her skin, nearly reverent, his lips lingering as if the taste of her was vital as breath. She wondered how it could be they fit so well together, so effortlessly together after all the years of knowing, then taking paths away, taking paths back again.

His mouth brought fresh thrills, nearly forgotten thrills that made her body shimmer and her heart swoon. His hands stoked heat, little fires in the blood.

More of him, all she knew was she wanted more.

She tugged his sweater off, then with humming approval ran her hands over his chest, around his shoulders. When their eyes met in the shadows, she smiled.

"Don't look so smug."

"You did the work," she pointed out. "I just gave you an outline."

"Some days I hated you, and cursed your name. Inventively."

"Which means we both did a good job."

His eyes, she thought, brushing fingers over his cheek. She'd always been half in love with his eyes.

"Raylan," she murmured, and drew his mouth back to hers.

He felt the shift, a turn into urgency. The way her body vibrated under his, the way her hands gripped and stroked and kneaded. And still he struggled to spin it out, slow the pace.

Magic wasn't meant to be consumed in a gulp.

While they undressed each other, he stopped the rush with a long, sumptuous kiss. When she pressed against him, offering, opening, demanding, he used his hands — and she so hot, so wet, so soft — to give her that first, gasping release.

When her body, a wonder of female strength, went weak, he felt like a god.

So he took his due, tasting her skin, nipping at pulses that thrummed and drummed, letting his hands roam everywhere, take everything until he could no longer breathe through the wanting.

And when he slipped inside her, slow, slow, slow, it was like the last key in a lock. For a moment, he lowered his forehead to hers, try-

397

ing to center himself again.

But she framed his face with her hands, looked in his eyes so he lost himself in hers.

In her.

He let himself go, taking now, riding now while she moved with him, while she wrapped around him. When he crossed that peak, finally, finally, he buried his face in her hair to breathe her in.

She lay quiet a long time, winded and dazed as if she'd run a marathon in desert heat and crossed the finish line into a moonlit oasis. And now she sank into the warm, quiet pool where her body might have wept with gratitude had it the energy.

Then, with a sigh, she ran a hand down his back.

"We definitely remembered."

"I'm trying to figure out whether to say thank you, or wow. So, wow, thanks."

He rolled so they lay hip to hip. She smiled to herself because she could swear she could all but hear the wheels turning in his head.

"Couple of things," he said. "I want to say I'm not really a one-and-done sort of guy."

Her smile widened. "Really?"

"No, I . . . ." He heard himself, let out a quick laugh. "I don't mean like this now. Although . . . I mean one night and done. I'm going to want to see you again."

Now she rolled so she could look down at him. "I'm good with that, and with the although."

"That's excellent news. We should probably go out, like a date."

"Dating's overrated."

Those fascinating green eyes narrowed. "Now you're trying to vamp me."

"Now, that's a term you don't hear every day, and I'm not. Although . . ."

She lowered her head for a casual kiss.

"Anyway, sure, catching a movie, grabbing a meal, and all those traditional social concepts are fine. It's the obligatory we need to go out somewhere on Saturday night that's overrated. If two very busy people want a night out, that's all good. If two very busy people want to stay in and have lots of sex, that's all good."

"You don't even have to try to vamp. I think it's a natural talent."

"Which I will now be compelled to hone to perfection. You said a couple of things."

"Yeah, I guess I did. The other occurred to me after we proved our memories are plenty sharp. I'd said who'd have thought we'd end up here, but after, it struck me that maybe, to be honest, I'd noticed you in something approaching that kind of way a couple of times."

"Is that so?" She tossed her hair out of her eyes and propped herself up on his chest. "Be more precise, and spare no detail."

"Not much detail, just . . . . The first summer you stayed in the Creek and you and Maya got tight. That was just noticing, not approaching. You were Maya's friend, so beneath notice. Until you talked about my sketches. You knew Iron Man, and Spider-Man. So you immediately became more interesting. For a minute, then I had to ignore you because, as Collin can attest, girls are dopey."

"Now I'll confess that I was so impressed I tried to draw after that." She frowned a moment, thinking back. "What did I try drawing . . . oh yeah, Black Widow. I wanted to be Black Widow, so I tried drawing her. And was very frustrated I couldn't."

He twirled some of her hair around his finger. "Natasha or Yelena?"

"Natasha."

"I could teach you to draw."

"I sincerely doubt it." She kissed him again. "And the noticing that approached?"

"The summer after my first year of college. I remember because I was working part-time at Rizzo's, and you came in with Maya and some other girls. I guess you were about fifteen maybe. And you looked good. You looked really good. So I had this moment of hmmm. Before I snapped that back, reminding myself you were Mr. Rizzo's granddaughter, and Maya's pal, and basically a kid, and I was a college man."

"It was the summer before that for me."

"For you what?"

"Noticing you with approaching. You were out mowing the lawn at your mom's, and you had your shirt off. You were all sweaty and skinny —"

"I wasn't skinny."

"You were always skinny — now you're lean and lanky — but you were skinny, and your hair was sweaty, too, and sort of curling, and all sun-streaked like a surfer's. I got all fluttery inside. Especially since I knew you had green eyes even though you were wearing sunglasses. I have a weakness for green eyes."

"Filing that one."

"Anyway, I had to remind myself that I was pledged, heart and soul, to Daniel Radcliffe."

"Harry Potter?" He took her shoulders to lift them both a little. "You dated Harry Potter?"

"No, I never met him, but I desperately wanted to because he would no doubt fall in love with me and we'd live happily ever after. And I apparently have a thing for nerds."

"Also filed."

"In addition, Peter Parker is on my list, and I'd be a love slave in a hot minute for Tom Holland."

"The things you learn while naked."

"True." She gave his left biceps a squeeze. "How much are you curling now?"

"Don't start."

"It's ingrained. I need to design a new

program for you."

"I joined you and your mother's online deal. I have all the damn programs."

"Well, good for you."

"It's probably seeing you most days in those tight little outfits that got me here."

"Unknowing vamping." She cocked her eyebrows. "Most days?"

"I switch around. I've started lifting with Hugo the Hammer. He's terrifying."

"Sweetest guy in the world."

"Next thing you'll tell me is that other guy — what's his name — with the diamond-cut six-pack and man bun is a pussycat."

"You must mean Vince Harris, and no, he's as mean as a snake and a diva on top of it. But he's good at what he does. Try Margo Mayfield's *Give Me Twenty* sometime. She'll take you to the mat, in a good way."

She kissed his pecs. "And all that talk about working out's made me hungry. How about dessert?"

"Okay." He rolled over on top of her.

"Not the dessert I meant." Laughing, she wrapped him in. "Although."

He stayed, which surprised them both, and delighted the dogs, who slept together in Sadie's bed.

It surprised Adrian, too, when Raylan rolled out of bed when she did.

"I'll let the dogs out," she told him. "You

can catch some more sleep."

"I'm up. Habit. Kids." He reached for his pants. "At their age weekends mean nothing to their body clocks."

"What time are you picking them up?"

"We said around ten."

"Great, plenty of time. We'll work out, then we'll have breakfast."

"I don't have any gym gear."

She grabbed his shirt, threw it on. "I can fix you up. Come on, Sadie, Jasper."

"Wait. No." He experienced deep and sincere panic. "I'm not wearing any of those skinny pants things."

"I can fix you up," she called back and kept going. "Spare toothbrush in the bathroom closet."

"Jesus, why can't we just have sex again?" he muttered. "That's a workout."

But he went into her bathroom, found the toothbrush. And caught a look at himself in the mirror. He looked like a man who'd had sex. A lot of really good sex.

His mother would know. Just like she'd known the first time he'd had sex — with Ella Sinclair in his junior year of high school.

She'd only asked him if he'd used protection, he remembered — which, duh — but it had been mortifying.

He'd better get that look off his face, or she'd spot it. And that was just weird.

By the time he came out, Adrian had pulled

403

on one of her outfits — little snug black shorts, a sports bra thing with black-and-white checks.

While they looked exceptional on her, he wasn't going to wear snug black shorts.

Ever.

"How about I sign in blood I'll work out when I get home?"

Saying nothing, she held up a pair of what he considered normal gym shorts — baggy, more or less knee length — and a New Gen T-shirt.

"You're about the same size as Popi was. I haven't gone through all his things yet. I keep meaning to."

No way out now, he thought.

"Those'll work. I can help you with that if you want. I know it's hard."

"It is. Thanks, but let me see if I can get going on it this weekend. I keep telling myself I should move into the master. There's a good feeling in there, and the terrace, and the views. I'm going to get started on that."

He pulled on the shorts, adjusted the drawstring. Not that he was skinny, he reminded himself. Lanky. He'd take lanky.

Resigned, he walked down with her.

"Did you lift yesterday? Upper body work?"

"No."

"Good, neither did I. Today's the day."

When they reached her studio, she set her hands on her hips. "Do you want a program,

404

or personal training?"

"You're going to kill me. I can already feel it."

"Personal training it is."

She picked up a remote, turned on some music, smiled.

"Let's warm up."

He knew she excelled at training — he'd streamed her workouts for months now — but it took on a different aspect when she focused one-on-one.

She adjusted his stance, and in her cheerful but intense way, pushed him more — he could admit — than he pushed himself.

When he reached for his habitual twenty-pound weights, she shook her head. And handed him twenty-fives.

"Challenge yourself. If you start to lose your form, you go lighter. Now, it's squat, hammer curl, squat, shoulder press." She demonstrated. "Your whole body's engaged. Got it?"

"Yeah, yeah."

She talked him through it; her energy never seemed to flag.

Squeeze, breathe, chest up, butt back.

When he broke a sweat, he didn't want to give her the satisfaction of saying it felt good.

Almost righteous.

Especially when she whipped him through cardio, then through a vicious ten-minute core session.

"Great! Good. Now for the reward. A little yoga to stretch and cool down."

Yoga always made him feel awkward and clumsy, but she adjusted him again — shoulders, hips — nudged him into holding poses longer than he'd have done on his own.

"You've got good flexibility, Raylan."

Maybe, but since she currently had her legs pretty much straight out from her hips — which shouldn't have been possible — and her upper body flat on the floor, he didn't think his split-legged forward fold was anything to write home about.

They ended facing each other, sitting cross-legged on their mats. "Namaste. Nice work. Let's just do a few shoulder rolls — you worked those shoulders — with a two-minute cooldown."

He moved fast, had her on her back on her mat.

"Don't wanna cool down."

He was a little late picking up the kids. And he saw by his mother's raised eyebrows and quick grin he hadn't managed to wipe the man-who's-had-sex look off his face.

Two weeks later his sister gave birth to Quinn Marie Abbott. Collin took a long hard look at the baby cradled in his mother's arms. Then he shrugged, ducked his head to hide the smile that crept over it. He declared: "Maybe she's not so bad."

Adrian came in with pink flowers just as a teary Jan offered the baby to Raylan. Moving closer for a peek, she heard him whisper: "Candy. Count on me for it."

And seeing how he stroked one of his long fingers down that sweet, downy cheek, she worried she'd fallen a little bit in love.

Kentucky

Spring road trips. What could be finer? Sweet breezes, flowers blooming. Horses in pastures chowing down on that bluegrass.

Lots to see, lots to do.

Boost a crappy little Honda pickup in Indiana — *Go Hoosiers!* — switch the plates, and cruise on down to Louisville. That's Loo-a-ville for the local yokels.

Derby was coming up soon and there'd be madness in the air.

Smelled good. Madness always did.

And in those pretty, tree-lined burbs outside the city, the target lived. The whore passing as a devoted mother of two, dedicated nurse, and faithful wife.

A life of lies, about to end.

Watching her for a handful of days — an easy pleasure.

Ending her — sweet and simple.

The idea of beating her to death had to be adjusted once the best opportunity presented. Not enough time, not enough privacy.

Too bad, as that method offered such a

deep, dark, and personal thrill.

But with the stolen truck parked in the lot of a twenty-four-seven supermarket a half mile away, walking into the employee lot of the hospital at one a.m. proved uneventful.

A short wait, really, and she came trudging along in her rubber-soled shoes.

Then it was just a matter of springing out — *Boo!* — slicing her throat. Boy, the blood just flew!

Splat, splat, glug, glug.

Grab her keys, her purse, roll her under the next car.

She had a nice, late-model Subaru. Since nobody would find her, probably for a couple hours — at least — and since switching the plates wouldn't take long, it was perfect for the next leg of that spring road trip.

Turn up the music, roll down the windows. Pop a pill to keep body and soul together on the drive. The Subaru would take them a hundred miles away, or more, before anybody so much as missed her.

Having friends as houseguests always delighted Adrian. She'd have Hector and Loren for a full week — and her mother, who didn't really qualify as a guest in the technical sense.

Add Harry, and Mimi, and it was like a mini reunion.

Hector's fiancée would take the train down for the weekend as would Harry's husband once they finished juggling their kids' sched-ules.

Even with the rest of the crew for the production staying at a local inn, she'd have a houseful.

And that suited her. While she rated her culinary skills above average — in the blood, after all — she arranged for Rizzo's to provide the welcoming meal — and the craft services for the shoot.

The week before their arrival, she tackled her grandparents' bedroom. She found it wasn't as wrenching as she'd expected. She caught herself smiling as she came across one of Dom's favorite sweaters, or the ancient, battered slippers he'd refused to give up.

His hairbrush. He'd been vain — justifiably so, she thought — about his full head of hair. She set it aside as a keepsake, and left his favored green cardigan in the closet. She could, when she needed, wrap herself in it.

He'd kept a bottle of her grandmother's perfume, so she set it aside, along with his aftershave. Little things, little memories, little comforts.

She boxed, tubbed, separated out pieces she thought someone might especially want, then carried everything out to her car before she hauled out cleaning supplies.

The cleaning crew would deal with the rest of the house, but she needed to do this herself, to show respect, affection, gratitude

409

to the two people who'd spent so many nights there.

She opened the porch doors to the spring air, and Sadie wandered out to curl up in the sunlight.

She'd put this off, she mused as she scrubbed, polished, vacuumed, telling herself the room was too big for just her. But the truth was she loved it, had always loved the big, generous space, the coffered ceiling with its creamy squares against bright white, the gleam of the hardwood floors, even the restful and soft blue gray on the walls.

Feeling sentimental, she put the bottles of scent — his and hers — on the mantel over the fireplace, added a trio of her grandmother's copper candlestands.

She changed the linens on the big bed with its high and thick turned posts, spread on her white duvet, added a mountain of pillows, a throw at the foot.

She took her time making it her own — her pretty bottles and baskets on the open shelves in the en suite, fresh fluffy towels, more candles. Her clothes in the dressing room area, along with a yoga mat, Sadie's bed in the sitting area.

Eventually she might hire Kayla to take a look, think about changing color schemes, just changing things up. But for now, as she looked around, she saw just enough memories blending with just enough her, just enough new to feel comfortable.

So she walked out to the porch, where she could look out over the hills and trees, the gardens, the turns of the creek and the more distant mountains.

They'd given her this, and so she'd treasure it, and tend it.

Then she sat on the porch floor, hugged her dog. "We're doing all right, aren't we, Sadie? We're going to be just fine."

In the morning, she gave the house over to the cleaners and finished planting the flowers she'd chosen in pots for the porches, the patio.

She'd already tried her hand — solo — with vegetables and herbs in the back, as her grandparents always had. She had her fingers crossed on that.

But now the house was ready — or soon would be — for company, and she still had energy to burn.

She went inside to wash up, changed into leggings and a support tank, and got the leash.

"Let's go for a run."

She started out at a light jog, warm up the muscles, enjoy the movement, and the way spring spread its wings with wild dogwoods and redbuds, the pretty beds freshly mulched, the smell of grass newly mowed.

But the thought of the day — the date —

weighed on her. She knew it must weigh on Raylan.

She made the turn toward his house, and when she passed Teesha's, heard Monroe's music — piano, quick and bright — through windows thrown open to the air.

And heard the mower as Raylan paced with it over his front lawn.

Not as skinny as her memory of the boy, she thought. Solid muscles in those arms now — as she had good reason to know. Still no hat on that sun-washed hair.

And this time, unlike that long-ago time — he saw her. He stopped, switched off the mower. And a moment later, Jasper sent up a plaintive howl from the backyard.

"I'll just let her back there for a minute, okay?"

"You'd better before the neighbors call the cops."

She let Sadie through the gate for the canine lovers' reunion.

When she walked back, Raylan sat on his porch steps, guzzling straight from a bottle of Gatorade. She sat beside him, unclipped her water bottle.

"Saturday chore on a Monday?"

"Couldn't concentrate on the work, so figured time for physical."

"Me, too. Yesterday and today. Hard couple of days for both of us."

"Yeah." He laid a hand over hers. Joined

412

understanding. "Three years for you yesterday, for me today. I got this bush. A mountain laurel? I'm going to plant it with the kids after school."

"That sounds like exactly the right thing. Funny, I planted flowers today, in these wonderful Italian pots Nonna loved. And yesterday . . ." She let out a long breath. "I moved into the master. And that felt right."

"Time helps," he said when she turned her hand under his to link fingers. "Lorilee loved visiting the Creek, but it wasn't home for her. She had such a crap childhood, foster homes, in and out, never really having a home of her own."

"She told me a little about that. In the letters she wrote," Adrian explained when he looked over.

"She never talked much about that, not to most people."

"Writing letters, real letters, is different. There's this odd intimacy. She told me she never felt she had a real home, until you bought the house in Brooklyn."

"She fell in love. Forever home, she called it."

Adrian let the silence hang a moment. "But you'll plant the mountain laurel for her, here in the Creek, and that matters."

"Feels like it." He shifted, to look at her. "And you're going to have a house full of people later, and a busy week."

413

"I'm ready for it. Most of the gang should be here by about three, and we'll go do a run-through at the school. Back home for dinner and discussion."

"Yeah, Monroe and I are doing the he-men with kids grilling burgers while that goes on."

"We can make room for all of you."

"Thanks, but school night." He took another swig of Gatorade. "Being the adult, I have to say that, even mean it, which often blows. With luck, the short people will be in bed before you guys finish the main course."

"We'll plan a dinner on a non-school night. Or a Sunday dinner — more special — and we can eat early enough to meet school night rules." At his long look, she shrugged. "What? I like your kids. I like kids."

"I know it. People think you can fake that, liking kids in general or specific kids. You can't."

"We could plan it a week from Sunday, if that works. This weekend —"

"Gym class," he finished.

"How about we have our Friday night, then a Sunday dinner with the kids?"

"I believe that aligns with our social calendar."

Friday nights with Adrian had become a habit. Sharing a meal, sharing her bed.

"Don't cook for Friday. I'll pick up dinner."

"I'll take it. I've got to get back."

When she rose, he rose with her, still holding her hand. And taking the other, leaned in to kiss her.

"Thanks for coming by, helping make a hard couple of days a little easier."

"For me, too." She gave his hands a squeeze, then walked around to the gate to call Sadie.

As he went back to the lawn mower, he heard Jasper's pitiful whine, and Adrian's laughing promise to bring his girlfriend back soon.

He watched her set off in a smooth run, hair flying, legs flashing. He thought of the mountain laurel he'd plant with his kids, of the memories that would root in that, the life that would bloom from it.

And he thought, as Monroe's bright music danced in the air, of the memories and the life yet to come.

CHAPTER TWENTY

The cab — a rare sighting around Traveler's Creek — pulled up to the house. The unfamiliar sight had Sadie giving one warning woof.

"It's okay." Adrian put a hand on Sadie's head as she looked out the window. "Oh, it's more than okay! It's Mimi! Happy," Adrian added and had Sadie wagging her tail.

She raced out to wrap Mimi in a hug. "You're here! In a cab! Oh, it's so good you're here. My Mimi."

"Minor change of plans." Mimi kissed both her cheeks. She took the rolling overnight bag from the driver, thanked him.

"Is that all you have? For a week. Oh, tell me you're staying for the week."

"I am. Your mom and Harry have my suitcase, as they're driving and I decided to take the train because they took an interview in DC. They'll be here within the hour, but I didn't want to leave that early, or make the detour."

"Come in, come inside. I'm going to get you a glass of wine."

"It's not even four!"

"Travel days don't count. Just leave your bag by the steps, we'll worry about it later. Happy," Adrian said again, and had Sadie wagging and leaning on Mimi's legs.

"Is she bigger?" Mimi asked, accepting the paw Sadie offered. "I swear she's bigger."

"Maybe a little. Oh, you look so good," Adrian said as she pulled her through the house to the kitchen.

"I slept on the train. I did not work. I read a book until I fell asleep, and it was great."

She did look good, Adrian thought, relaxed in her jeans and bold red shirt, her hair a marvelous wedge of curls.

"Sit, take it easy."

"I've been sitting, my baby. My butt knows it."

"Then we'll take this wine, walk outside. How's Issac, how are the kids?"

"Everyone's good. And so is this wine. Natalie landed a summer internship. In Rome."

"What? When? Wow!"

"It just came yesterday. She's out of her mind happy. God, I'm going to miss her, but —" Laughing, Mimi lifted her glass high. "It's so wonderful for her."

"It's amazing. She'll be amazing."

"My son, the pre-med student, and now my girl, summering in Rome to work in international finance. I don't know what either of them are talking about half the time now, but I'm so proud of both of them."

"It doesn't show a bit."

Mimi wrapped an arm around Adrian's waist, tugged her in for a side hug. "My kids, all three of them, keep growing up. Look what you've done with this garden. You've got gorgeous flowers going, tomatoes?"

"Tomatoes, peppers, cucumbers, carrots, squash, zucchini, herbs, and more herbs."

After pushing up her sunglasses, Mimi scanned the rows. "It's practically a farm."

"City girl, this is a backyard vegetable garden."

"Same thing to me. You did this, just you?"

"And so far, so good. I wanted to try. Nonna and Popi planted every year. I'm going to try to hold up that tradition. It's relaxing, and I've got plenty of time when I'm not actively working."

"Which is almost always."

"Half a day generally when I'm not pre, post, or in production."

With considerable pride, she studied the young plants.

"I've got a rhythm going, and I like it. I cut out the travel when I moved here for Popi, and it didn't take me long to realize I liked not being on the road. I can appreciate what Monroe says when people wonder why he writes exclusively and doesn't perform. I like

418

the quiet, too."

"You never liked the travel, not really."

"No," Adrian admitted, "not really."

"Lina thrives on it. And before she gets here I'm going to ask you for an honest answer. I know her perspective, but I want yours. And it's between us. How are things between you and your mother?"

"I hope her perspective is they're better, because they are. We understand each other better, and she does better with adults. You were the mom of my childhood."

"Aw, sweetie. She loved you always, Adrian."

"I get that more now, too." Adrian picked up the ball Sadie dropped at her feet, threw it high and long. "The fact she agreed, without much adjustment, to this production, using the high school? That's a big give for her, and I appreciate it."

"She's nervous about it."

"What?" Adrian started to laugh, then saw Mimi's face. "Seriously? Lina Rizzo, nervous?"

"Yes, Lina Rizzo, nervous, about going back to her high school, and the fact that two of the teachers know her from back then. One of them she even dated a couple times."

"You're kidding. How did I not know this?"

"I guess she didn't mention it. Nothing serious, she tells me, because she ended up going with this football farmer guy."

"A football farmer? Mom?"

"Farm boy who played football. That, apparently, was serious while it lasted."

Fascinating, Adrian thought. The things you learned when mother figures finally considered you an adult.

Just fascinating.

"She never talks about back then with me."

"Do you talk to her about the boys, the men you've dated?"

"Absolutely not." She threw the ball again.

"You said 'happy' to Sadie. You look happy, Adrian."

"I am. I've got my work, my home. I planted a garden. I have great friends, an amazing dog. That's happy."

"And I don't want to spoil that, but have you heard from the investigator?"

"She's following a lead in Pittsburgh. Or was a few days ago. It doesn't spoil it. I feel like putting it in her hands took it out of mine."

Sadie ran back, woofed again.

"She hears a car. Must be Harry and Mom — though I expect everybody soon. And here we are drinking wine before four."

With a laugh, Mimi draped an arm around her waist. "We'd better get more glasses."

On Friday evening, Adrian stood in the high school gym with her mother, her friends, the crew. Hector and his assistant huddled over cameras — the placement of the stationary, the potential movements of the two portables. The lighting director worked with his gaffers and grips to set up light stands, run cables, decide on gels and filters.

"It's a good space," Adrian said to her mother.

"I suppose it is."

"Memories?"

Lina shrugged. "I didn't play basketball or have much interest in it."

"But I'm told they held their dances here, too."

"Yeah." A ghost of a smile flitted over Lina's face. "With live bands. Very old-time. Let's go over wardrobe."

"Girls' locker room for us."

When they went back, Lina looked around. "At least they updated — some — in the last decades. And it doesn't smell like sweat, wet, and Love's Baby Soft. Popular eighties perfume," she said at Adrian's blank look.

"Which you didn't use."

"No, I didn't. How would you know?"

"Because you were never going to be one of the crowd. You stood out, made sure of it. That's not a dig."

"I don't take it as one."

"Yours." Adrian gestured to the rack Wardrobe had already set up. "Mine. Like we discussed, we'll coordinate or complement colors in each segment. They'll set up the cast's wardrobe — girls in here, boys in the other locker room. Females in leggings or capris. We've got everyone's sizes."

She wagged her hand as her mother looked over the choices.

"Boys, gym shorts or sweatpants — 'boys' and 'girls' include teachers. Girls, sports bras and a choice of tank or tee; boys, tank or tee. The tanks, tees will have either the Yoga Baby or New Gen logo. I thought we could mix that up. We have socks, athletic shoes, sweatbands, water bottles, samples of our Energy Up drink. Logo'd. The cast can keep what they use, and we'll do the hoodie with cast member's last name in addition. Harry's idea."

"He's always thinking. Intro and cardio first," Lina considered, "so why don't we go with the red? Scarlet tank, black leggings with the blaze up the side for me."

"I'll tag the red bra, black tank, and the red-and-black capris." When she had, she glanced over. "Strength training next."

"You choose."

Changes, Adrian thought as she considered her choices. Changes could happen, and little tears in relationships could mend.

Very bright and very early on Saturday morning, Adrian sat in the bleachers, going through the script one last time while Teesha sat beside her talking to Monroe on her phone.

"Yeah, it looks like we'll get started pretty close to on time. Adrian and her mom already wrapped up the main intro. If you bring them in, say, in an hour, I'll nurse Thad during the break, and Phin can ask the crew his ten million questions. You're a stand-up guy, Monroe. I'll see you in about an hour."

She pocketed the phone. "So, your mother's half flirting with that teacher dude."

Surprised, Adrian looked up to see her mother across the gym with a man with gray-streaked brown hair, horn-rimmed glasses. Both of them were in wardrobe, and did appear to be half flirting.

"That's the guy she dated a couple of times in high school."

"Okay. Why are you whispering?"

"I don't know. I've never seen her even half flirt before. It's really strange."

"Maybe she'll grab a little touch while she's in town."

"Eeww. Really? And he's married, with kids — grandkids, too. He told me."

"Probably why it's only half a flirt. A nostalgia flirt. On the other hand, Loren is all the way flirting with that pretty hot teacher."

Adrian shifted her gaze to under the far basketball hoop, where Loren definitely flirted with the ponytailed blonde.

"She's not married, no kids. Allyson — or Ally. Twenty-seven, biology teacher who works out five days a week and loves yoga."

"You've got them all memorized?"

"I don't have your mind for data — or odd trivia — but names and faces? An essential part of the production."

She saw a production assistant herding out the boys and the rest of the male teachers. The noise level rose immediately.

"You're right. We're going to get started on time." She gave Teesha's leg a pat, handed her the script.

She started down the bleachers as the girls came out, and headed to Hector while he checked the tripod camera again.

"Ready for this?" she asked him.

"You got it." He looked in the camera as assistants lined up the cast on their marks for the segment. "Looks good."

She studied the monitor. "And just what I was after. We'll give them a little pep talk, some reminders, then we can intro the segment and dive right in."

She caught her mother's eye, and they walked to the center of the gym.

"Your idea," Lina whispered. "You take it."

"All right. Okay, everybody!" Adrian held up her hands until the voices, the giggles, the nervous barks of laughter died away. "Lina and I want to thank you, again, for being part of this. We're going to work you hard over the next couple of days." She grinned over the groans. "And you're going to have fun with it. Or else. First reminder —"

"When you say left, you mean right," one of the boys called out.

"That's correct. The camera reverses. If you mess it up, just keep going. If you need to slow it down, even stop, do that — but don't be lazy! Mandy's the modifier in the first segment, so you can always follow her and modify. The water bottles are labeled with your names. Use your own bottle."

She looked to her mother to finish up.

"Hector and Charlene will roam around with the cameras. If you want to look into the camera, that's fine, but keep moving! Adrian and I will also move around now and then, adjust your form, push you a little harder, or suggest you ease back. We'll take a one-minute — that's one minute — water break at the halfway point. After the cooldown, we break so you can towel off, change, and regroup. Any questions?"

When those died down, Adrian and Lina took their marks, faced the camera. "Remember to breathe, everybody," Adrian said, and waited for Hector's signal.

"This is *Fitness 101,* cardio," Lina began. "Get ready to work it and sweat it."

"And these are students and teachers from my mother's alma mater, Traveler's Creek High. They're motivated." She glanced back.

"Are you motivated?"

She got *Yeahs!*, but put her hand to her ear. "I can't hear you. Are you motivated?"

This time, they roared. She turned back to the camera.

"Then let's warm it up."

Forty minutes later, Lina grabbed her water bottle. "That was good."

"It really was. I want to see the playback, but —"

"It was damn good. Listen, I worried the kids might start goofing off, or sniping at each other, snickering at the ones you chose — kids and teachers — who are a little out of shape."

"Only one segment in, but I don't think they will."

"Neither do I now. And if it stays smooth enough, with the two-hour break for lunch and recovery after the next segment, we may be right on schedule. One thing."

"Okay."

"The kid Kevin? I don't want to give him too much attention. You can see it embarrasses him, but you might see if he'd be interested in having you work with him some, one-on-one. Part of the embarrassment is from being a little overweight and out of shape. And it's brave of him to be part of this."

"You've always done that," Adrian murmured.

426

Instantly, Lina stiffened. "What?"

"Zoned in on someone who needs some help, and wants it but can't ask. I've always admired that about you. It's what makes you so good at what you do."

"I . . . Well, thank you."

"I've already talked to him about just that, because apparently I am my mother's daughter. I've designed a program for him he can do at home, on his own — his parents are supportive. And he'll come by my studio once a week so I can evaluate."

"With nutrition included."

"Of course. He started on it about a week ago. I can already see some improvement. Why don't I keep you updated on him?"

"I'd like that." Lina didn't reach out, it wasn't her way, but she asked, "We're better?"

"Yes, Mom." Because it was her way, Adrian leaned in to kiss Lina's cheek. "We're better."

Sunday evening, after a full, sweaty, productive two days, Adrian sat on her yoga mat, legs crossed, hands resting palms up on her knees. "Put your hands together in prayer, bow forward to embrace the practice you've just completed. And Namaste."

She smiled. "Congratulations, everyone. You've just graduated *Fitness 101*. And you aced it."

The cast began to scramble up, exchange

427

high fives, even hugs.

"Thank you for joining us," Lina said into the camera. "Remember. Keep well, keep striving." She put her arm around Adrian. "Every day is a new chance. I'm Lina Rizzo."

"I'm Adrian Rizzo. Come back and work out with us, anytime."

They went around, more high fives, more hugs.

"That's a wrap!" Hector called out. "Nice work, everybody."

By the time they broke down the set, gathered up equipment, extra wardrobe, dusk whispered down.

Lina stopped short when somebody called her name as they stepped outside.

Adrian saw a man half in shadows — and her heart thumped.

Her right hand balled into a fist; she rolled up on her toes.

He only stepped forward, a cap in his hand, a half smile on his face. Slightly familiar, she thought, laying a hand on her mother's arm, in case.

In case.

But her mother let out a gasping laugh. "Matt? Matt Weaver! Well, just . . . Jesus. Matthew."

And stepping to him put her arms around him in a hug.

Adrian saw him close his eyes a moment, and breathe out.

"Adrian, this is an old friend of mine. Matt, this is my daughter, Adrian."

"Nice to meet you. You sure look a lot like your ma. How'd we get to have grown kids, Lina?"

"God knows."

"I want to say, right off, I'm sure sorry about Mr. Rizzo. I was at the memorial, but there were so many people, and I didn't want to bother you."

"You never did like crowds."

"That hasn't changed. So, ah, my cousin's boy, Cliff, he was in there with y'all."

"Cliff, sure, the football player. Like you."

"Those were the days." When he flashed a grin, a little dimple popped at the right corner of his mouth.

"I don't want to hold you up. I just wondered if maybe you'd like to get a bite to eat, and catch up some."

"Oh, well, we're having a wrap party at the restaurant."

He nodded, running the cap in circles in his hands. "Sometime then. Some other time."

"Actually, the cast and crew are taking the back, probably spill out a bit. But I can get us a table. I've got pull with the owner."

Adrian smiled. "I'll make sure of it."

"I'll meet you there, Adrian. Is it still a pickup, Matt?"

"I brought the car, as I recollect you didn't

much care for riding in a truck."

Adrian considered as she walked to her own car. Square-jawed, straw-colored hair going white at the temples, clean-shaven, shy, kind eyes. That flash of grin and dimple.

Interesting.

Additional interesting came at the end of the evening when Adrian went to settle up.

"I'm moving them out, Jan. Sorry, I know we're right on top of closing."

"No problem for me. We like big, happy, hungry groups in here."

"We sure were all of that." She glanced around, saw only a couple tables still occupied in the main dining room. "I don't see my mother and her friend."

"Oh, right. They left about a half hour ago. She asked me to tell you she was going over to have a look at Matt's farm." Jan handed Adrian the credit card and receipt. "If I were you, I wouldn't wait up."

"Thanks, I . . . What?"

With something close to a snicker, Jan leaned over the counter. "When you work as long in a restaurant as I have, you know how to read people. Body language, expressions, tones, gestures, all of that. What I saw is — I'll call it two people moving toward a romantic finale. Old flames, honey."

"Yeah, but . . ."

"I've known Matt for a long time. He's a good man. I'll add they both looked happy

430

and had lots to talk about."

"Well, that's . . . something. I'm not sure what. I'll move the stragglers along. Most of them are headed to my place anyway."

She decided not to mention it, even to Harry and Mimi. Just too strange.

When they got home and Harry commented that it looked as if Lina had gone to bed, Adrian let out a strangled laugh and said, "Guess so."

In the morning, she rose early, got in a shortened workout while the house slept on. In the kitchen she made frittatas for the farewell breakfast, slid them in the oven with her fingers mentally crossed.

She checked the coffee maker to be sure it had water, added fresh beans, then made a smoothie for herself.

She sat at the counter with her smoothie and her tablet to check viewer email. When she heard the front door open and close, she figured one of her houseguests had gone out for some morning air.

But looking up, she saw her mother walking back toward the kitchen.

She'd assumed Lina had come home late, hadn't anticipated an overnight. After a moment's consideration, she went with instinct.

"I'm sure you know you're grounded."

"Funny."

When Lina reached for a mug, programmed

431

the fancy machine for coffee, Adrian's eyebrows shot up.

"Coffee? You?"

"Occasionally. It's about moderation and good choices, not deprivation."

"I wish you'd said that to a girl who loved Cokes."

Lina glanced back. "So do I."

"I didn't mean it like that. Forget that. And I'm having a Coke."

She got up, pulled one out of the fridge. "So, so, so. You and Matt Weaver."

"Nothing serious. Neither of us are looking for that." With the mug of black coffee, Lina sat at the counter with Adrian.

"So no real buzz."

"Oh, plenty of it." Lina brushed at her smooth swing of hair. "Then and now. It was nice to see him again, to catch up on the past, God, three decades. He and his younger son work the farm. His oldest went to law school and practices in the next county. His daughter's an RN and lives a handful of miles away. He's been divorced for about a dozen years, and has five grandchildren."

She sipped her coffee. "But now, as then, he's rooted to his farm, and I'm rooted to my career. There was always something between us, and now I realize there always will be. But we want very different things for our lives. We had nostalgia sex, and it was lovely."

Then she smiled. "And we agreed when I'm

432

in town, as long as both of us remain unencumbered — which both of us appear to want — we'll have more nostalgia sex."

"Booty calls. My mother."

"I haven't gone thirty years without sex, Adrian. I simply know how to be selective and discreet. Something smells wonderful."

"I'm making frittatas."

"Frittatas." Lina studied Adrian over her coffee. "The Rizzo gene seems to have planted in you."

"I'm trying to nurture it along, which reminds me. I'm wondering if we should do a cookbook. Healthy — but tasty — recipes. Rizzo and Rizzo, *Cook Yourself Fit.* Or something."

"We could see. We both know I'm no cook, but . . . Let me think about it, then we'll talk about it more the next time I'm in town. But right now, I'm taking my coffee up, changing. Do they still call it the walk of shame?"

"Mostly as a joke, between friends."

"I'll just avoid that altogether."

Amused, Adrian pulled her tablet back over. She saw a new email from the investigator on her personal account.

Adrian,
I'm back in DC, and would like to schedule a meeting with you this week, if possible. I will, of course, have a written report, but would like to speak to you

personally.

Please let me know what day and time would work best, and I'll schedule accordingly.

Best,
Rachael

Adrian checked her calendar, noted times she had appointments at the job site, with Teesha for business, with her young trainee for evaluation.

She responded, listing those dates and times as problematic, but opening the rest of the week.

She could shift her own work around to suit. The beauty of being self-employed, she thought.

Then she put the tablet away, put it out of her mind. Farewell breakfasts weren't the time for dark thoughts.

■ ■ ■ ■

PART THREE:
LEGACIES

The future is purchased by the present.
— Samuel Johnson

■ ■ ■ ■

CHAPTER TWENTY-ONE

Adrian read the next poem midweek, hours before Rachael was due to arrive. The poet had reverted back to the single sheet, the simple white envelope.

Postmark, Omaha.

She read it sitting on the front porch with Sadie at her feet, watching her.

"I'm all right. Don't worry."

Summer's coming at last, your last.
My time of waiting is in the past.
Yours, mine, ours again to meet,
And with your death, my life completes.

"I'm all right," she said again. "But whoever's doing this isn't anywhere in the wide universe of all right. Yours, mine, ours. What kind of bullshit is that?"

She shoved up to pace the porch while a hummingbird zipped like a flying jewel to the feeder she'd hung on a tree branch.

"And that last line, what does that mean? He kills me, he reaches a goal, or is it like murder-suicide? Kill me, end his own?

"Why am I trying to figure out the crazy?" She pressed her fingers to her eyes. "Somebody's got to figure it out."

She dropped her hands, looked out at the slope of the hills, green and lush, the trees, leafed out, the towering rhododendron in the side yard lush with fat pink blooms.

"He's right about one thing. Summer's definitely coming. And you know what? I'm sick of waiting, too."

Maybe it was impulse, maybe it was reckless, but she didn't care. At that moment, she just didn't care.

She went in and upstairs to change into workout gear. She did her makeup — carefully. After some debate, she raked some product through her hair and styled it in a high, half-up ponytail.

"Casual sexy, right, Sadie? Who says you shouldn't look your best when you throw down the gauntlet? Let's go make a fucking statement."

The dog went with her down to the studio, settled herself by the fireplace while Adrian set up for a recording.

She'd put it on her blog. He damn well followed her blog. Then she'd put it on all her social media for good measure.

"Let's see how you like it, asshole."

She hit record, beamed a smile.

"Hey, everyone. I'm Adrian Rizzo, and I

thought we'd do a little bonus round this week. Just some quick energy and stress relief when you need it. It's going to be a challenging one. But I want to send this one out, especially, to the poet — you know who you are!

"It's easy to put things off, but what does it get you? Nothing and nowhere, right? You're unhappy, stressed-out, putting off taking real action to get what you really want. You can blame someone else, you can blame the world, but what it comes down to is what's in you."

She tapped a fist lightly on her heart.

"When you feel that bad, feel that sad, feel that mad, get up and move. Now, this one's not for beginners, but this poet's been following me a long time, so this bonus is for the more experienced. Three rounds of three, thirty seconds each. We're going to do split lunges, with squats."

She stepped back to demonstrate.

"Right, left, squat. And we're going to do them fast. Remember your form — safety and performance."

She lowered into a lunge again. "Knee over ankle, weight front-loaded, get that back knee close to the floor. Then switch. Keep that landing soft. Then squat. Then drop down for pike up, spider leg — right — up again for split jacks. We do it all again, second round, left leg on the spider, then a third time, alternating legs."

She demonstrated each, tossed back her ponytail.

"This takes endurance, strength, reaching for your guts. Can you make it? Nine minutes. Eyes on the prize. Timer's set, and here we go."

She hit the speed, keeping her eyes on the camera as she called out the moves.

"If you hit your max, stop, regroup. Get your mind right, and pick it up again. No shame in hitting your limit, the shame is never really trying. Keep your chest up, head up. Lower on those squats, butt back! Drop it! Pike up, spider leg, pike up, spider leg. Move it! I'm told summer's coming, so let's get that bod in shape. Yours, mine, ours. We're ready to do this! Now jack it up!"

She couldn't stop, wouldn't stop. She'd made her damn point, finally.

"Round two. If you lose your form, take a break, then get back in. I'm challenging you to get to it."

Her heart pounded as much from satisfaction as exertion. Sweat slicked her skin, but she kept tracking her eyes back to the camera as she pushed through the third round.

To the one who watched.

"And there's nine minutes. Cool it down, stretch it out. Congratulations to anyone who gave that a shot. Now bring up your favorite cooldown, bring down that heart rate, stretch out those hard-worked muscles. And remember . . .

"My life is mine to live strong. If you think you can stop me, you're wrong. I'll push away the doubt and fear because my own destiny I steer."

And she laughed. "Ah, a little lame, but it shows everybody's a poet. Until next time, this is Adrian Rizzo. Stay fit. Stay fierce."

She watched it through once, then put it on her blog under Bonus Round Challenge, added it to her social media.

"I bet this is going to piss you off. Good."

She hydrated, stretched.

"Let's go outside, Sadie, and leave the phone here. Because when Teesha sees this — she'll probably be the first of many — she's going to be very angry. Let's just go out and check the tomatoes."

It took Teesha less than twenty minutes to storm the gates.

She marched around to the back, where Adrian threw the ball for an ecstatic Sadie.

"Not answering your phone is the equivalent of putting your fingers in your ears and going: La la la."

"Maybe, yeah, but I wanted a little cool-off time. You're fast."

"I want you to take it off — everything. You know I can, I have authorization, but —"

"You know it's my choice. Leaving it up is my choice."

441

"It's the wrong choice."

"Is it? Is sucking it up for all these years the right one? Letting other people deal with it when it's aimed at me? That's the right choice?"

"Police, Rizz; FBI, now a private investigator. Professionals. So yeah, that's the smart choice."

"And even with all of that, I got another one today."

"I figured." Teesha scrubbed her hands over her face. "And I'm sorry. You know I'm sorry, but how is challenging him going to help, at all?"

"Because he's a coward, and a bully, and it's long past time I let him know I know."

"What did this one say?"

Adrian closed her eyes, brought it back into her head, recited the words.

"Freaking psycho!" Hands on her hips, Teesha turned two circles. "What time is the PI due?"

"Four, maybe four-thirty."

"Okay, you come home with me, hang there until. He could be a mile away, Adrian."

"Or he could be in damn Omaha. And this is exactly why I had to do something. I can't keep going like this. He's accomplished at least some of what he wanted. He screws with my head. I dread the stupid mail. And yeah, yeah, a suggestion was to close the PO Box, but the conclusion was also he'd just find

442

another way."

"But he might make a mistake the other way."

"Might, maybe. And they'd still have my name on them, so they'd end up at the post office anyway. No return address. It's not an answer. I don't know if this is either, but I feel better. I feel like I did something to flick back at him."

Hissing, Teesha pulled out her phone when it signaled. "It's Harry. Hi, Harry. Yes — wait — yes, I know. I'm standing here with her right now. Uh-huh."

Teesha held out the phone. "It's for you."

"Damn it."

She let him rage at her.

"No, I'm not taking it down, and what's the point if it's already got over two hundred views? One of them's probably him — her — let's just say them. I'm not sorry I did it because, damn it, I needed to hit back. No, wait."

She drew a breath. "I'm saying this to both you and Teesha. I'm sorry it upsets you, worries you. I'm sorry it's going to upset and worry my mother and everyone else. But . . . the card he sent after Popi died, it tore at me. This one just snapped what was left. I'm done, Harry. I'm done. I'm giving the phone back to Teesha now."

Once she did, she walked over, picked up the ball, threw it again. A few minutes later,

Teesha wrapped arms around her from behind.

"We love you, Adrian."

"I know, that's why I'm sorry this worries you. I know, I do, it wasn't the safe, sensible thing to do. But, Teesha, I needed to hit back, finally. I needed to at least feel like I'd taken some control."

"I get that. I get you — we've been friends too long for me not to get you."

"Same goes, so I really am sorry I've added more worry. Just remember I've done all the other sensibles. Cops, FBI, investigator, security system, self-defense classes, big dog."

Sadie dropped the ball at Adrian's feet, looked up adoringly.

"Yeah, she's ferocious. Okay." Teesha gave Adrian a last squeeze, then stepped back. "When it comes down to it, I don't know if I could've held out as long as you have. And when you hit back, you hit hard. That asshole's going to need first, second, and third aid for the burn you gave him.

"And I've got to go. I'll see you tomorrow when I torture you with the budget for furnishing the youth center."

"The Rizzo Family Youth Center."

"Okay then. You've decided on the name."

"I've gone around and around. Do I name it after my grandparents, after Popi — since it's his vision? But he shared that vision with Nonna. Still, they wouldn't have been here,

444

had the means to have the vision, without his parents. I wouldn't be here able to bring that vision into reality without all of that, including my mother. So family, and you can add the plaque to the budget."

"We'll talk about that." Teesha looked down at the ever-patient Sadie. "Learn to growl at least."

Adrian picked up the ball again as Teesha left. "Growling's not your style, is it, baby?"

She threw the ball again, and again while she worked out how to tell Rachael what she'd done.

"Lectures, Sadie. I think I'm in for another lecture. Why are lectures worse than a solid smack in the face?"

When Rachael texted she was running a little behind, Adrian told her not to worry. She settled down on the front porch with her tablet, doing searches on plaques. Sizes, materials, shapes, fonts.

She didn't want a big, flashy statement, but something more subtle, dignified, suiting the building.

She wanted what her grandparents would have wanted.

She took another text after she'd narrowed her favorites down to three.

Adrian, delayed by traffic. ETA now six. Can reschedule if that's too late.

Adrian glanced at the time, noted the investigator had already passed the halfway point.

It's not too late for me. No particular plans this evening.

"Right, Sadie? Just you and me hanging out."

Great, Rachael texted back, see you in about thirty.

It was closer to forty when Adrian saw the car coming up the hill. But she'd spent the time well, deciding on the plaque, setting out a cheese tray and a carafe of wine.

Sadie waited until Rachael got out of the car, waited until she'd recognized the visitor before she thumped her tail.

"I'm so sorry," Rachael began, but Adrian waved that away.

"Don't be. I got everything done I wanted to get done. And I'm about to have a glass of wine. I know you have a long drive back, but unless you'd rather something else, I'd say you've earned one."

Rachael looked at the carafe, let out a sigh. "I'd love one. Thanks. Two fender benders," she said as she sat. "One breakdown, and traffic stopped dead."

She took the wine Adrian offered, sat back a moment. She wore amber-tinted sunglasses and a light blue blazer over a white tee.

"You've got a little paradise going here."

"I'm doing my best to maintain it. I'm trying my hand, on my own this year, with a veg garden in the back, and I'm crazy happy I've got some tomatoes and peppers coming. And terrified I'll kill them."

"Epsom salts, diluted with water."

"Yes!" Surprised, Adrian laughed. "My grandmother swore by that. You garden?"

"City dweller, so pots and planters. Nothing like a tomato right off the vine. So —"

"Before we start, I need to tell you, and show you. I got another poem this morning." She took the folder she'd put on the chair beside her on the table. "Postmarked Omaha. I copied the note and the envelope."

Rachael switched to her reading glasses, read the poem.

"More direct than usual, setting a time frame."

"Summer, and that's coming right up. I need to tell you, I reacted."

Rachael peered over the cheaters. "In what way?"

Adrian simply opened her tablet, cued up the video and, turning it to face Rachael, hit play.

Rachael sipped her wine, watched without comment until the video ended.

"You posted this today."

"Yes, and on my social media outlets. I've scanned the comments a few times, and nothing out of the ordinary so far."

Rachael nodded, then let her glasses dangle by her chain as she looked directly at Adrian.

"You're a smart woman, and knew issuing a direct challenge like this could spark an escalation, even a confrontation. That's why you did it."

"Yes."

"I'm not here to issue orders, and can only offer my best advice. I'll say I wish you'd waited until we'd had this meeting."

"I've waited since I was seventeen. Instead of easing off, it's gotten worse."

"That's true. Since you didn't wait, we'll assess on what is. If this video does trigger him into making a threat in the comments on social media, we can track his IP address. Which you knew."

"Yes. I'm sure he knows that, too, but he could rage post. People do. Even people who aren't sick and obsessed."

"Correct, so we'll monitor closely. I can consult with the agent in charge of your case, nudge her to do the same."

"I'd appreciate it."

"Meanwhile, I have a report." She reached into her bag. "Some progress, and some theories."

"You went to Pittsburgh."

"I did. The reporter who broke the story about your parentage relocated there several years ago. He works for a gossip online site."

"You don't think he's behind this?"

"No, and he's been interviewed since you've started receiving the poems. The attack in Georgetown, Jonathan Bennett's death generated a lot of media attention. Prior to that, your mother, and by connection you, generated some, primarily positive, but some negative, of course. Nothing's ever all."

"And some people criticized her for being unmarried, alluded she was promiscuous — which is a tame term for some of it — because she wouldn't name the father." Adrian closed her tablet, set it aside. "I didn't know any of that at the time. After the story broke, after Georgetown, some of those went after her a lot harder. Ugly stuff in some corners. I didn't know that either because she brought me here, had me stay here until that had died down or away."

Calm and steady now, Adrian drank some wine. "She shielded me, in her way, and pushed back, pushed harder in her career. Nothing was going to stop her. I resented that once. Now I can admire it."

"Stories cropped up again, from time to time. This particular reporter, Dennis Browne, tried reviving it, as it had given him a temporary career boost."

"I know, but those were easier to ignore. She's such a force, and she just refused to discuss it in interviews. Or really at all. When

Lina Rizzo locks a door, it's all but impossible to break it down."

"I agree with you, which is why I went to Pittsburgh. She'd locked the door on your biological father, but someone breached it. How and why? I don't like questions without answers. Is it old, settled business, or is it not? I wanted to find out."

"And did you? Find out?"

"It's a lot of years to protect a source, especially when that source has not only dried up but is no longer viable. And I can take angles the police can't. He's twice divorced, with three child support payments. His income is, we'll say, severely diminished. And he likes his bourbon."

Understanding, Adrian smiled a little. "You bribed him."

"I did, with your mother's permission, as she's paying the freight. A thousand dollars — I had permission to go to five, but he was a cheap date — the thousand opened him up. The bottle of Maker's Mark made him positively loquacious."

Since it was there, Rachael spread a little cheese on a paper-thin cracker. "God, this is good. What is it?"

"Rustico with red pepper."

"Amazing. So after the money and a couple shots of bourbon, I got the whole story. His source was Catherine Bennett."

"I . . . I don't understand."

"His wife knew about Bennett's predilection for attractive young coeds. She'd looked the other way, preserving their lifestyle, her family, their standing in the university, the community. But she learned about you. He'd fathered a child, and that, it seems, shook her foundation. From what I can piece together, rather than confronting him, risking divorce, she began to self-medicate — or upped her self-medication. She popped Valium, Xanax, and other drugs to get through it, but there you were, you and your mother. Yoga Baby on the cusp — maybe just over it — of becoming a household brand. She could tolerate the affairs, but not the in-your-face reminder he'd fathered a child outside of the world she'd so carefully maintained."

"She broke the story," Adrian mused. "He blamed my mother, me — never himself — but it was his wife who ruined him."

"She would be the victim, as she saw it. And he'd pay for humiliating her. Your mother would pay. You'd pay. An angry impulse or calculated, I can't tell you for certain. But she went to Browne. She had names, dates, she gave him names of other women — and he followed up with them, got the pattern. At the time, Bennett was having an affair with another student. A twenty-year-old. Maybe that broke Catherine, I can't say. But you and your mother were her targets, and the headline. A college professor diddling students — not enough to rattle anyone really, other than those involved. The same professor fathering a child outside his marriage with a woman who'd launched her career with that child? His ticket, Browne thought, to the big time."

"So rather than leaving him, she decided to destroy us, and him."

"Hell hath no fury, especially when that fury's simmered more than a decade. But you and your mother weren't destroyed. You survived, you thrived. And Jonathan Bennett? Not just destroyed, dead. Dead after attacking a child, two women and a child, his own biological child. So instead of being a stoic, heartbroken victim, she was the wife of a serial philanderer, a vicious, violent drunk, a child abuser. And that light shined back on her, harsh."

"You think she's behind this? She's sending the poems?"

"No, because she died, suicide by pills, nearly fourteen years ago. But you have two half siblings."

"Oh my God." She had to stand, to walk, to hug her arms tight.

"Nikki, age thirty-seven; Jonathan Junior, age thirty-four. Do you need a break?"

"No. No. Keep going."

"I haven't been able to interview either of them as yet. Junior's off the grid, and has been for about ten years, when he took his inheritance — considerable, as his mother's parents were wealthy — and basically vanished. I'm working on that. Nikki is a consultant. She travels to clients to devise business plans, revise current ones, streamline expenses, maximize profits. She's worked for Ardaro Consultants for fifteen years. She's in high demand."

"She travels."

"Often and country wide."

"Omaha. The last one was Omaha."

"She's scheduled for San Diego, Sante Fe, and Billings on this trip, due to return to her home in Georgetown late next week. I intend to have a chat with her. She has no criminal record, she's never married, has no children. She lives, apparently alone, in the house where she and her brother grew up. The house her mother's money bought. She's described as quiet, hardworking, pleasant. She has no close friends I could find, nor any enemies."

"Keeps to herself. Isn't that what they always say?"

"They often do. The brother has a few minor bumps. Drunk and disorderly, DUIs, a couple of assaults, which were dropped. No marriages, no children. He listed the Georgetown house as his residence until ten — nearly eleven years ago. He's described as unfriendly, unsociable. He's had a series of jobs, nothing stuck for more than a year, usually less. He did have some friends, and one, a recovering alcoholic, told me that back in the day, he always talked about building a cabin in the woods, maybe by a river or lake, and telling the world to get fucked. He may have done just that. I'm working on it."

Adrian sat again. "I have to say I don't think of the Bennetts as half siblings."

"You're entitled."

"There's a chance, and to me minor, biological connection, and nothing else. You think one of them — and you lean toward the daughter because of her travel — has this grudge against me. Like their mother did."

"She may very well have helped instill it."

"Yes, I can see that. And their father died, disgraced, died because my mother protected me, herself, Mimi. So we can be blamed for that. Their mother died, and I guess we could be blamed for that, too. She died not long before the poems started coming."

"Possibly a psychic break, that final loss. Coupled with the release of your own DVD. But the timing certainly plays into my theory. While I strongly believe one or both of them is responsible for this, I need to conduct more interviews. Because I believe this is more than poems. I was delayed leaving DC because I went to interview another of Bennett's affairs. She lives in Foggy Bottom. She had the affair, from the time line, about a year before he started one with your mother. She was

454

very forthcoming, and during the course of the interview I asked if she's received any threats, any anonymous poems. If she'd had anything happen to make her feel threatened, and so on.

"No letters, no phone calls," Rachael said, taking another cracker. "But she'd moved several years ago because of a break-in and a tragedy. Shortly after her divorce, she'd gone away — impulse with a new boyfriend — for a long weekend, and had her sister stay in her house. Just house-sitting, but mostly to give her sister a change of scene, as she'd recently been downsized out of her job. Someone broke into the house. The sister was shot, multiple times, as she slept. Several items were taken, valuables, in what appeared to be a botched burglary."

"You don't think that."

"No. I made that trip to Foggy Bottom because I'd had a conversation with the mother of another woman whose name was on Catherine's list — the names she gave to the reporter."

Absently, Rachael spread cheese on another cracker. "Let me add in that it's going to take awhile to locate everyone on the list. Marriages, divorces, moving to different locations. In this case, the mother lived in Bethesda, so was easy to reach.

"She knew her daughter had been involved with an older man while in college. A married man. A fling, nothing more. I spoke with the mother, as the woman herself was stabbed to death a few years ago while taking her usual morning hike. Attacked on a trail in Northern California, where she lived with her husband and two sons."

Very carefully Adrian picked up the bottle of wine, added more to her glass. "They both had affairs with Jon Bennett."

"Their names were on the list given to the reporter. So whether they did or not, Catherine believed they did. Police wouldn't have that list, or any reason to connect a shooting death during a break-in in DC with a stabbing death in California. The only link is that the owner of the house where the first victim was shot was a woman, like the second victim, who went to Georgetown University. At different times. I wanted to get this information to you as soon as possible. I'll start checking the other names on the list right away."

Adrian took a slow sip of wine. "My mother's name is on that list."

"I've contacted her, and she'll take precautions. I can't tell you there's no risk to her, but it's more probable they — let's use 'they' for simplicity — have focused on you. It certainly may be they intend to deal with her at some later point, but the poems come to you, and have all along. They resent you for your very existence. The fact that you were born took something away from them, diminished their standing. And it makes you responsible for their father's death, for their mother's eventual suicide. If using this theory, you read over the poems, that blame and resentment is clearly there."

"Yes," Adrian agreed. "Yes, it is."

"More? You're successful in your field, enjoy some celebrity in that field. You've paid no price for the insult of your birth. Add to that, you're a young, very attractive woman with considerable financial security, and an admirable family legacy. Their legacy is adultery, abuse, suicide, public humiliation."

"Hurting me won't change that, but I can follow your theory. What now? Will you take all this to the FBI, the police?"

"I will, but I'd like to contact the other women, if possible, first. Or as many as I can locate. And I want to talk to Nikki Bennett. If I can solidify the theory, law enforcement will be a lot more inclined to bring her in for questioning, to find her brother. And if they can tie one or both of them to these murders, to charge them."

"Okay. Okay," Adrian said again, with a decisive nod. "Because I think you're right. It makes a terrible kind of sense. You've already found out more in weeks than the rest have in years."

"I'd really like to take full credit, but I came at this late in the day and with fresh eyes.

Also without a stack of case files on my desk. I could focus on this, just this. And I got lucky with the timing. Dennis Browne was ready to spill. Once he had, it presented solid angles to work with."

"Don't care." Adrian gestured with her glass. "All I know is that for the first time I have a reason for all of this, and I can actually believe it's going to end. Those women, those two women." She shut her eyes. "There may be more."

"Yes, there may be more."

"How many on the list?"

Rachael took a moment and her last swallow of wine. "Thirty-four in the fourteen-year period before his death. That she documented. He averaged better than two a year."

"Thirty-four? That strikes me as more sex-addict behavior than straight dog. And it had to eat at her, his wife. It had to, no matter how hard she tried to normalize it. Children know when things are wrong inside the home. They feel it."

"I agree. Are psychopaths born or made? A lot of theories on that. In this case I'm inclined to go with both. I'm going to head back home unless there's something more you need from me."

"No. No, but you've given me a lot to process."

"There are more specific details in the written report. If you have any questions, contact me. Meanwhile, look out for yourself."

"I will. I hope your drive home is smoother than the drive here," Adrian added as they rose.

"It almost has to be. Thanks for the wine — and that cheese."

"Wait, let me wrap it up for you."

"You don't have —"

But Adrian had already dashed inside. She dashed back out, covered the cheese in clear wrap, put in crackers, the olives she'd seen Rachael nibble on in a little lidded tub, added a small bottle of S.Pellegrino.

"My mother's paying you. But this is from me."

"I'll take it, thanks. I'll be in touch, Adrian."

She watched Rachael drive away, then lowered a hand to Sadie's head.

"I feel sick inside. Sick. I haven't given his children a single thought in . . . I don't know if I ever really gave them one." Because her legs felt wrong, just wrong, she sat, lowered to wrap her arms around Sadie, to hold the comfort. "The idea they may have given me all this thought, all this twisted thought, it makes me sick inside."

She stayed like that until she felt steadier. Then sat awhile longer, just thinking it all through.

She had to read the report, no getting around it. And since she couldn't handle even the idea of eating, she'd make herself a smoothie — then make herself drink it.

After that . . .

When Sadie went on alert, Adrian's stomach clenched, but even as she pushed up, she recognized Raylan's car. And everything calmed.

She even managed to put on a smile when he got out of the car. When Sadie and Jasper raced toward each other. "Did you escape from the kids?"

"Briefly. I can't stay. Monroe's giving Bradley a guitar lesson, and Mariah's deigned to play with Phin. But I can't stay."

"If you're here to lecture me about my reckless behavior, I may need another glass of wine, and I've already had one and a half."

"I'm not." He came up on the porch, smelling of grass and spring.

"You've been mowing."

"Yeah, a little sweaty, but." He cupped her face in his hands, kissed her. Gently, she thought, as he might kiss someone with a mild illness. "Teesha gave me the lowdown."

"She's still pissed at me."

He wagged a hand back and forth. "I get she unloaded on you, and Harry, too. Anyway, I watched the video for myself. One day you're going to have to tell me how you do that plank to jump-in-the-air thing without breaking something important. And okay, reckless impulse maybe, but . . . brilliant."

"What?"

460

"You wanted to kick him in the nuts, and you hit the target, and never broke character. Just a short bonus workout — if you're strong enough, tough enough. You needed to take a punch, so you did. I'm behind you on that."

"You're behind me on that."

"Do I wish you hadn't done it?" He shoved his fingers through his hair — also a little sweaty. "That you hadn't gotten another poem? That you'd never gotten the first one? Sure I do. But we can all rub a lamp, and it doesn't pop the genie out. We deal with what is."

She stared at him, and started to cry.

"Come on now." He drew her in. "You've had a crappy day."

"Really crappy. You came over. You came over and said just what I needed." And she could let herself go a little, let the tears come, because he had.

"You had company," he murmured. "Two wineglasses, two little plates."

"Rachael McNee. The PI."

"And did that add more crap to the day?"

"Oh boy, did it."

"Let me ask Teesha if they can wrangle the kids for another half hour. And you can tell me about it."

She pressed her face harder into his shoulder. "Oh yes, please."

461

Chapter Twenty-Two

She went in first to slap some water on her face, then got them both a glass of lemonade. A better choice than wine at the moment, she thought.

Then she sat and told him everything.

"First, it sounds like your mom found an ace in the PI."

"Yeah, she did. She stays so calm, and . . . It feels as if how I feel matters. Facts matter more, but she's not just ignoring how I feel. And that helps."

"It always does. Next, I don't have to tell you that if her theory pans out, the motivation is pure bullshit. I don't have to tell you because you're not an idiot or the type who likes to play martyr."

"So . . . more of what I need to hear. I do know it, Raylan, but it helps, again, it helps to hear it said out loud. I separated myself a long, long time ago from the biological factor of my paternity. He is and was nothing to me, and aside from basic DNA, I don't

462

believe he's in me. At all. That would've been harder to manage without my grandparents, and, looking back, my mother. Without Mimi and Harry, Teesha, Hector, and Loren. Without Maya and your mom. Without all of it," she said, gesturing at the town in the distance.

"Because I could do that, because I had all this, I never thought of his children, his wife, any of it."

"Because they're not a part of your life." He said it simply — and that helped, too. "Why would they be? If one or both of them had contacted you, tried — for whatever reason — to make a connection, it might be different. But they didn't. Or maybe they did, but not in an Oprah kind of way."

"Definitely not. Raylan, if one of them, or both of them — those two women."

He put a hand over hers. "Those two women didn't know. They weren't on alert. For whatever reason, they want you to be. But here's the thing."

He brought her hand to his lips in a gesture she'd have found heart-meltingly romantic under other circumstances.

"They're murderers," she finished. "They're crazy, obsessed, violent killers, and they want to finish what their father started when he tried to throw me down the stairs."

He kissed her hands again, those green eyes steady on hers. "But they won't finish anything. Your ace of a PI is going to put together enough to get them arrested. But in the meantime, you could take a trip, go somewhere else — quiet, private, secure — until she does."

"Where? A cabin in the mountains, a house on some beach, a flat in Paris or whatever? Raylan, I'd be alone. Really alone. What always happens to the woman in jeopardy when she takes herself off to hide from the bad guy in some remote, supposedly secure and secret location?"

"That's fiction."

"Which is often rooted in reality. Bad guy finds woman, and she's on her own. They'll have to come at me here, if they come. Here where cops are five minutes away, and stalwart friends and lovers less than that. Where I know every corner of this house.

"I'm not alone here, and feel safer here than I would anywhere else. And I believe Rachael's going to do exactly what she said she'd do. Get enough to have them arrested."

"You can't expect me to feel good about you alone here."

"I don't, but the alternatives are worse."

"Maybe. And the maybe stops me from arguing with you. How about this? As soon as school's out we'll all go somewhere."

"We will?"

He smiled, and the smile was a challenge. "Don't tell me you're afraid of taking a summer vacation with a couple of kids and two dogs?"

"I fear nothing. I haven't taken an actual vacation in a long time."

"Then you're due. I vote beach, and so will the kids, which makes your vote moot. I'll see what I can come up with. I've gotta get back."

"School night."

"Yeah, it is." But he drew her to her feet, and this time didn't kiss her as if she were vaguely ill. "Lock the doors, okay? Then go around again to make sure you locked the doors, and set the alarm. Then text me before you go to bed."

"All right. You made me feel better than the kale smoothie I'm making myself for dinner."

"Jesus God, I hope so." He kissed her again, quick, then headed down the steps. "I'm never drinking one of those. Let's go, Jasper."

"They're surprisingly tasty."

"That's a terrible, horrible lie." He had to boost the reluctant Jasper into the car. "Unworthy of you."

"An acquired taste, maybe."

He shook his head. "Just for that, I'm eating a bag of Cheetos after the kids are in bed. Text me."

She would, she thought as she walked over to gather the dishes from the porch table.

She'd lock up, check, set the alarm.

And she'd sleep easier, she knew, because

465

he'd come to her and said what she'd needed to hear.

She filled the rest of her week — enough it threatened to overflow. Besides her own work, which included a view of Hector's first edit of *Fitness 101,* she had a long FaceTime conversation with her mother.

That included the expected lecture, some debate — and give-and-take — on the editing.

She began the serious shopping for lighting, plumbing fixtures, paint, gaming systems for the center. Even with Kayla's considerable help, she took a private vow to never, ever do an extensive rehab again in her lifetime.

It kept her mind fully occupied with normal until Rachael contacted her on Friday afternoon.

She'd located three more women. One had apparently died of natural causes after a long battle with cancer. One had been found, beaten, robbed, in an alley in New Orleans where she managed a bar. The other had been shot in the back of the head in her car after leaving the motel room where she'd left the man she'd had an extra-marital affair with.

The police in Erie, Pennsylvania, had looked long and hard at the husband, but his alibi had held strong.

Four now, she thought, at least four.

She glanced at the time. Raylan would be there soon, and that was good. He'd fill her head, and let her empty out what she'd just learned.

She didn't know what he intended to pick up for dinner, but whatever it might be, they could eat on the porch, in the air. Since it had rained all morning, everything smelled fresh and clean.

She'd decide what dishes to use when she saw what they'd be eating. Same with wine.

With little to do, she changed — a dress, simple, springy, fun, and feminine. She scooped her hair back into a low tail at her nape and let curls escape.

Leaving her feet bare, she did a quick turn in the mirror, and deemed it pretty perfect for a casual — hopefully romantic — alfresco dinner at home.

She heard Sadie's woof before she heard the car, but walked out to the second-story porch to see Raylan driving up.

And he saw her. Hell of a picture, he thought, the woman in the flowing dress at the rail of the high porch with the huge dog at her side and flowers spilling out of pots around her.

She'd be his all evening, all night. It seemed incredible to know it.

"What's for dinner?"

"Come on down and find out."

She hurried down, as she'd — following

orders — locked the doors. When she opened the front door, Jasper darted in so he and Sadie could begin their joyful and energetic reunion.

"Do you think they'll ever just go like: *Hey, good to see you?*" Adrian wondered.

"No."

"I'll follow their lead." She threw her arms around Raylan, kissed him until his eyes all but rolled back.

"Dogs are definitely my best friend. You look amazing."

"I decided to celebrate the return of the sun by putting on a dress. I hardly ever. And that doesn't look like a carry-out bag."

"Because it isn't. I'm going to fire up the grill and cook you a steak."

"A steak?"

"Anybody who drinks kale smoothies needs the occasional shot of red meat."

"Do you know how much iron's in kale?"

"No, and I don't much care." He set the bag on the counter, pulled out the steaks, then two enormous potatoes. "And what's a steak without a potato football?"

"Each one of those is a meal for a family of four." She picked one up, tested the weight. "But I could do something interesting with these."

As if in defense, he grabbed the second one. "Does it involve kale?"

"It does not. It involves butter, herbs,

468

spices, and the grill."

"Then you're on potato duty." He took out a bag of salad mix. "There will be no judgment here."

"I'll reserve judgment if we can punch up your bag o' salad with a few items I have on hand."

"So it will be done. I've got experience in that area. You can trust me." He handed her the second potato. "I'm going to leave these in your capable hands and start the grill."

When he came back in, she stood at the counter wrapping the potatoes in foil.

"Your yard's rocking it. We planted some stuff. The flowers are looking good, and the vegetables are okay. But they're not rocking it like yours."

"Do you compost?"

"I keep meaning to."

"Stop meaning to and do." She emphasized with two firm taps to his chest. "Help save the planet, make it, use it, and your garden can also rock it." She handed him the potatoes. "You should put these on, as they may take a week or two given their size. I'm going to open a nice bottle of red. Then we can sit on the back porch, look at my rocking garden. I have a progress report from Rachael. I'd like to tell you about it so we can shut it off and not talk or think about it for the rest of the evening."

"Okay." He leaned forward, kissed her

forehead. "We're going to make it all right."

That, she thought, was the daddy in him. The comfort, reassurance. She didn't think she had daddy issues — her grandfather had filled that role in every way. And she'd had Harry.

But she found that aspect of Raylan very appealing.

He came back in, put the steaks and the salad mix in her fridge, picked up the open bottle of wine. "Let's go sit."

She brought out a little bowl of olives, a little bowl of almonds. If the daddy gene was part of him, the feed the soul was part of her.

She took a breath as he poured the wine. "You're right about the yard. I always enjoyed helping with the gardening, being out here with my grandparents, even as a kid. Now that I'm doing it alone, I still enjoy it."

"I used to bitch and moan about the weeding and the work. Now, once the novelty wears off, I'll be the one listening to Bradley and Mariah bitch and moan."

"And one day they'll remember gardening with you, and plant their own."

"I like to think so." He shifted in his chair, looked in her eyes. "Tell me."

"Rachael found three more women on the list. Dead. One is pretty clearly natural causes. She lost a battle with bone cancer. But the other two."

"Not natural."

470

Adrian shook her head. "Not natural. A woman beaten to death in the alley behind the bar she owned in New Orleans. Whoever killed her took her watch, her purse."

"To make it look like a theft, like a mugging."

"Yeah. The other was out in Erie, Pennsylvania. She was in her car, parked. Shot in the back of the head by someone in the back seat. That was the determination. She'd been in a motel with someone not her husband."

"They looked at the husband?"

She nodded, thinking they sat talking of murder while the grill smoked, while butterflies danced around her flowers and the dogs raced around the yard.

"Business trip, out of town, solid alibi. They looked to see if he'd hired someone to do it. The determination there, after a lot of looking? He didn't even know about the affair. Anyway, the two killings were years apart, a few thousand miles apart, with different methods. There wasn't any reason to connect them."

"Until now. So that's four out of — what was it? — thirty-four. Eight-point-five percent."

She let out a half laugh. "You're one of Teesha's breed. A math-o-phile."

"Math is truth. That's serial killer territory. Isn't three the dividing line?"

"I don't know. But Rachael thinks it's likely

471

she'll find more. Oh Christ." She shuddered once, drank some wine. "The oldest murder she's found was over twelve years ago — within a year after my first poem."

"So he went from three years to two. That's what she's found. Odds are he didn't back off for five years. I'm sorry." He took her hand. "That sounds cold, but —"

"No, no, that's exactly what I want right now. Straight, logical, no bullshit. Nikki Bennett is on the road, driving back from her last job, so Rachael has to wait to speak with her. A few days anyway, as Nikki tends to drop by other jobs, check progress, give a booster shot or whatever. It's part of her system. Meanwhile, Rachael's going through the list."

"I hate when people try to tell me how to do my job, but shouldn't she take this to the FBI or the local cops?"

"She's going to. She thinks a week to put enough together to take to them, to make a solid case they'll pursue. She's made the con- nection — all of them were on Catherine's list — but they lived, worked in different areas, didn't know each other, were killed by different methods. None of them, as far as the investigations concluded, had received any threats. No poems."

"She needs to convince them. I get it. She's convinced me."

Picking up the bottle, she topped off his

472

glass, then hers. Smoking grills, butterflies, dogs, wine. Some normal to balance out the awful.

"What she didn't say, and you're not, is they didn't get any poems because they weren't the real focus. They aren't the reason their father was exposed, why he's dead, why their mother killed herself. Maybe they're a horrible kind of practice, or a way of releasing stress so the final act's prolonged."

He said nothing for a moment, just took her hand in his. "I know you don't feel any connection to them, and why would you? But I think whoever's writing those poems feels one to you. You're blood, you're a sibling. You matter more. They wanted or needed your attention, your awareness of them."

"But I didn't know who sent the poems."

"That's for the big reveal. Writing, especially about good against evil — and the spaces between — you have to dig into motivations, actions, reactions. Why would this character make this choice at this time? Yeah, they're just comic books, but —"

"Don't say 'just.' You write strong stories with multidimensional, complex characters."

"Well, thanks for that. It doesn't make me Freud or Jung or whoever, but it does, or should, make you think about not only what makes a hero, but what makes a villain. What are they after, what do they need? Here, it's pretty clear from where I'm sitting, the woman's to blame. Women."

She frowned, lifted her wine as she considered. "Women as a species?"

"I think, yeah. Take the woman at the motel. They wait in her car, kill her. But they don't go after the guy she was cheating with. Where was he?"

"Rachael's report says he was still in the room when it happened. His statement said he took a shower, got dressed, and came out to see her car still there. He walked over, saw her. He called it in. They looked at him, too."

"So the killer could have, if he'd wanted, gone to the room, knocked, then shot the guy. If it was about cheating, why wouldn't he? But it's about women, they're to blame. Not the father for cheating, over and over, but the women he cheated with."

"Homicidal misogyny. You think it's the son."

"Not necessarily. Plenty of women hate women."

"True," Adrian admitted. "Sad but true."

"And she's the one with a job requiring travel so she can toss a poem in the mail at various locations. Either one, or both. But I think your PI is well on her way to putting it all together, and this is going to be behind you."

She sat quietly, sipped her wine, watched the grill smoke.

"Here's what I think," she said at length. "I

474

think having someone willing to talk this through with me instead of trying to nudge it aside to protect me helps me nudge it aside. And I think having someone who believes I'm going to be able to put this behind me helps me believe it."

Then she shrugged. "And, hell, women have been getting the blame since Eve. I wonder if they knew their mother started this ball rolling."

"If they did, it wasn't suicide."

She jerked back. "What?"

"Sorry, too far."

"No, wait. God." She sat back, found her bearings. "That makes horrible sense. She — the mother, the woman — betrayed the father. If we stick with not blaming him for cheating, but the women he cheated with. She betrayed him. If she'd just kept looking away, they'd have the father, the life, everything would be just fine. And how easy would it be to slip pills to someone already addicted to them? Just give her more, and more, until she's gone."

"She goes to sleep, forever. A quieter death. No violence because she's still the mother. She's blood."

"It starts with a blood tie, and ends with one. With me. It doesn't change anything, but it's oddly helpful to see how it might have all started, all formed."

"I could be completely off base."

"Right now, it gives me something solid to stand on. When someone wants to kill you, you want to know why. I'm going to talk to Rachael about all this. Tomorrow. Right now, it's a lot to ask, but let's put it away."

"It's away until you want to open it again. You can't raise kids, own a business, and find a space for life without compartmentalizing. So how about I tell you about a beach house on Buck Island, North Carolina?"

It took her another minute to switch gears. "You actually found something this late in the season?"

"Connections. Do you remember my friend Spencer?"

"Sort of."

"I'm going to lie and tell him you remember him well and fondly. Anyway, he lives in Connecticut, with his wife. They have a very slick vacation home on Buck Island, and generally spend the bulk of the summer there, but it happens Mrs. Spencer is expecting their first kid in July. They're down there now, and plan to come back in a couple weeks. Hope to go back, if all's well, maybe in August, rotate some of the family in and out. But we can have it for two weeks starting July fifth. Dog friendly, by the way, as they have two pugs. Game?"

"Two weeks?" She hadn't believed he could pull it off. And two weeks . . . "What do I do about all that?"

He looked out at the gardens, as she did.

"I'd say we both know enough people who'd take care of it, especially if they can haul off tomatoes or whatever."

"I haven't been away for two weeks straight . . . ever. Not in one place, not when it wasn't work-oriented."

"You can work there, so can I, when we need to. It's got a gym."

"Now you're toying with me."

"Its own pool, oceanfront. It's a quiet area, so you go for the beach, the views. You want more jazz, you head down to Nags Head or down to Myrtle Beach."

"I don't need the jazz. It sounds amazing."

"Potential downside. It's a drive, a substantial one. With two kids, two dogs."

"I like kids and dogs."

"I've noticed."

"Are your kids going to be all right with this?"

"They like you. Plus, beach."

"I'd love it."

Two weeks of beach and . . . nothing. She couldn't imagine it.

"If they're all right with it — really all right with it — I'm in. If they're not, you need to take them anyway. It's too good to miss."

"I'll talk to them. I know my kids. They'll be fine with it."

"Okay then. I'm going to check those potatoes."

"I'll deal with the salad. And how do you like your steak?"

"If I'm going to eat a hunk of meat, I want it rare."

"Now we're talking."

They cooked their first meal together, ate on the porch while the sun eased toward the western mountains. They talked about his kids, the youth center, his work, hers. She found it just wonderful to talk about things that mattered in the every day.

"You're always in charge of the potatoes." Replete, Raylan sat back with his wine.

"I'm impressed with your salad and grilling skills. And as a Rizzo, I don't say that lightly."

"Wait till you taste my mac and cheese. Only from a box in a pinch," he added when she narrowed her eyes. "It's my mother's recipe."

"Jan makes exceptional mac and cheese as I recall."

"See? I'll put it on our beach menu." Watching her, he poured out the last of the wine. "I like your face."

Amused, she propped her chin on her hand. "Is that so?"

"Faces and body types are an interest of mine for obvious reasons. I drew yours once, your face, when we were kids."

"You did?"

"Practicing. I drew Maya's a lot. Usually gave her demon horns or a forked tongue.

478

Your grandparents, such good faces. Sometimes I'd sit in Rizzo's after school when Mom was on shift and try to draw faces of people who came in. It was easier to draw characters with masks or cowls, so I wanted to practice. I wonder if I had a little thing going even back then?"

"For art? Absolutely."

"No, for you. Maybe a little thing. Seems to me I drew Cassie — remember Cassie? — as a snake girl, because she was sneaky. Not that I held that against her — I admired it. But I just drew your face. So might have had a thing. I sure as hell have one now."

She reached out for his hand. "That's a relief, because I have a thing going, too."

"I like thinking about you when you're not there. What's she doing now? Maybe I'll look out the window and she'll be going to see Teesha next door. Or maybe I'll drive to get groceries and see her out running. I didn't know I could feel this way again. That I'd want to."

Her heart just stumbled in her chest. She rose, gave his hand a tug so he stood as well. "I think we should take the dishes in, stack them up to deal with later."

"Later works for me."

"And we can give our very good dogs a chew bone while we go upstairs."

"They deserve it."

"And . . ." She moved into him, tipped her

479

face to his. "Then later than that, we can deal with the dishes before we have some cappuccino on the front porch, look down on the lights of Traveler's Creek, listen to the quiet awhile before we go upstairs again."

"All of that," he murmured before he kissed her. "I've got a bag in the car."

She smiled. "You can get that later, too. Dogs and dishes, then I want to be with you. Just you, Raylan."

CHAPTER TWENTY-THREE

When Adrian woke in the morning curled up against Raylan in the middle of the bed, rain pattered lazily outside. Its steady murmur sounded like music. The light, a soft, quiet gray, seemed to drift, a gauzy curtain shimmering in the breeze whispering through the open windows.

Another day, she might have found it gloomy, just damp and gloomy. But now it struck her as romantic as Camelot.

So she pressed against him, body to body, skin to skin, trailing her lips over his face, the scruff of morning stubble. And felt him harden against her even as his eyes, sleepy and green, opened.

"Good morning," she murmured.

"It already has possibilities."

"Probabilities," she corrected, and fisted her hands in his hair to bring his mouth to hers.

She wanted the heat, so she gave it, letting it spread, live embers smoldering to a spark.

481

A spark igniting a low, slow flame.

She rolled onto him to take the lead, to take control; pleasing herself as she knew she pleased him.

Strong hands roaming over her thickened her pulse, a drumbeat with the music of the rain. Lips seeking lips to slide, slide, slide into the deep quickened her heartbeat, an echo to his. She wanted the taste of him — the side of his throat, his jaw, the hard line of his shoulder.

Then, again, his mouth, a wonder of sensations with tongues gliding, teeth grazing. A quick nip to tease; a breathy moan in response. And those tastes of him filled her until every sense coalesced into pleasure.

Her eyes locked with his, no words spoken as she shifted.

When she straddled him, she took him in slowly, slowly, deeply, deeply, to spin out that pleasure. And watched it conquer him even as it swamped her.

She'd taken him from a dream into a dream with everything soft and heated and druggingly beautiful. Lost in her, completely lost in her, he surrendered to her, to the moment, to what they made together.

In the hazy light, her long, agile body rose over his, rocked to her own languid rhythm while the sound of the rain closed them in, creating a world for them away from everything, everyone, but each other.

Her eyes looked into him, through him, gold and green and heavy. He saw pleasure in them, and power, and knowledge, and everything that made a woman compelling, dangerous, irresistible.

When she broke, casting herself over that rising wave, her head fell back, her body arched, her arms lifted so her hands scooped and turned through the wild beauty of her hair.

She moaned, sighed, a woman embracing her own power, taking her own triumph. And never stopped moving, never stopped her slow, steady beat.

He had to grip her hips, hold on to her to stop himself from snatching that control and taking his release when she shook her hair back and smiled down at him.

No words, still no words.

Watching him, her breath coming on quick little sighs, she ran her hands up her body, gliding them over her breasts until he could taste them, he swore he could taste them, then down again. Then onto his.

She shifted, bowed down to take his mouth with hers. He felt her shudder, heard her quick gasp as she rolled over the next wave.

The sound, just that small sound snapped his restraint.

"I can't. I need —"

He whipped her onto her back, hiked up her hips. Undone, simply undone, he drove himself into her, half-mad when those long legs wrapped around him.

This time, the force of the tide swept them both under.

She lay limp, mildly concerned her heart might beat itself right out of her chest.

"Let's just stay here a minute," she suggested. "Or an hour. Maybe a day, until our vital signs level off again."

"What? Did you say something? I can't hear with the blood still pounding in my ears."

"That's not where it was pounding a minute ago."

He laughed, snickered, laughed again. Then lifted his head and grinned down at her. "You wrecked me."

"That was the plan. I'm not usually a fan of a rainy Saturday, but this one started off really well."

"Good thing for me because I'm going to be spending the rest of it dealing with two kids and a dog on a rainy Saturday." He lowered his head again to nuzzle her neck. "This should give me the strength to get through it."

"And you'll bring them to dinner tomorrow?"

"They're looking forward to it. Mo's picked out an outfit. Of course, she picks out an outfit to eat a sandwich."

"I like her style."

"She's got plenty of it. Lorilee used to say

she studied and critiqued the pages of *Vogue* in utero."

He caught himself, wondered if lying naked with Adrian was the best time to mention his dead wife.

"Anyway . . . Okay if I grab a shower?"

"Sure. I'll go down, let the dogs out, and I need to put a little breakfast together."

"You need to?"

"Yes, I do. After that workout, I'm starving."

While he showered, he wondered what he should do about what was happening to him. If he should do anything. How he should do it, if anything.

He'd meant what he'd told her the night before. He hadn't known he could feel this way again. But he did.

Holding up his hand, he studied his wedding ring. He'd worn it so long it felt like part of him. But was it fair, was it right, to wear it when he was sleeping with another woman?

When he was clearly in love with another woman?

It wasn't just sex. Maybe he'd half convinced himself it could be, would be, but he knew himself better than that.

What had she said that day — the day she'd brought the damn free weights? Love wasn't always about sex, sex wasn't always about love.

True, absolutely. But when it hit both, it was miraculous. He knew it because he'd had two miracles in his life.

But . . . he didn't know how she felt. Cared about him, sure, liked him a lot, sure. Added to it, he came with a package deal.

Two kids and a dog, he thought again.

A lot of people didn't want to take on a package.

He could ask her how she felt, what she felt. Generally, he preferred the direct way. But — one more but — was it fair or right to push there when she had real and serious problems?

Some crazy stalker was threatening her.

She didn't need pressure from him when she already had more pressure than anyone should deal with.

One thing at a time, he told himself as he toweled off.

He'd help her get through the problem, as much as he could. Spend time with her when he could. Have his kids spend time with her as much as she was willing.

Then he'd see what came next.

When he went down, she had the dogs eating kibble from side-by-side bowls.

"Perfect timing. Do you know how to use the coffee machine? I'll just put these together."

"First, what are 'these'?"

"You're having a poached egg on a whole

wheat bagel with tomato and spinach, and a side of Greek yogurt with berries and granola. It has it all."

"Okay. That actually sounds not scary. I can make you coffee, but I'd rather one of the Cokes I saw in your fridge. That's my usual morning caffeine."

"Really?" She stopped what she was doing to stare at him. She'd automatically made him coffee on Saturday mornings because she'd assumed he'd want it. "That's my favorite thing. A cold Coke in the morning. I let myself have it maybe once a week."

"Why once a week?"

"For many reasons, but I'll have what you're having."

She plated the food.

"I'd make this for my grandfather — if I beat him to the kitchen first. He usually went with cold cereal during the week, but weekends, he'd get down here, and it would be pancakes, French toast, bacon, and more bacon."

"Bacon is the god of all foods."

He sat with her, took a bite of the healthy alternative. "But this is great. I wouldn't have put the combo together. I can try this on the kids — with scrambled eggs."

"You can't poach an egg?"

"No clue, but an eight-year-old boy eating one with his little sister? It would be: *Hey, look, Mo, it's an eyeball!* Then he'd stab, stab.

Ooooh, gak, gak, it bleeds yellow. And she would never eat an egg again."

"I can see you know this because you have a sister, and did similar disgusting things."

"It was my job, and Wells men take their jobs seriously."

"And to think I used to wish for a sibling. Which, come to think of it . . ."

He put a hand on her arm. "Don't. Don't think about it."

"Don't worry. I have enough to do today to keep my brain otherwise occupied. Work out, followed by doing my weekend domestic chores, followed by taking another look at Hector's rough cut of the high school video. Then I have to start working on the content of my next solo."

He knew how to keep her brain otherwise occupied now. "How do you figure it? The content?"

"You've got to mix it up. People get bored doing the same routines. They may go back to an old favorite, but they want something a little different to try. I've got to keep up with what's current, what's safe, what's good for beginners, what works for the more experienced. And you've got to add some fun in there. Some challenge, too. It's like a healthy breakfast. It gets boring if it's all granola and quinoa."

She smiled as he ate the last bite. "Want another?"

"No, thanks. But that was a surprise. You should do a cookbook."

She jabbed his shoulder with a finger. "That's what I told my mother. I'm just starting to play with the idea."

"You'd be good at it." He kissed her cheek. "I'll get the dishes. I expect to ward off some of the rainy Saturday sorrows by telling the kids about the beach. There will be cheers and celebrations," he said as he started loading the dishes into the dishwasher. "Then Mariah will announce she needs new beach clothes."

"Well, wouldn't she?"

He aimed a hard stare over his shoulder. "She doesn't need your encouragement. And I'll face what fathers across the land dread and fear: a shopping trip."

"I could take her."

He turned completely around. "What?"

"I'm also going to need new beach clothes. I'll take her. Girl shopping, girl lunch, girl talk. We'll have fun."

"You have no idea what you'd be in for. I'm serious."

She sipped her Coke. "Challenge accepted. We'll talk about it over dinner, Mariah and I, and pick a day after school's out."

"I need you to swear something, right here and now."

"For God's sake, Raylan, I won't let her run in traffic or play with matches."

489

"Not that. I want your solemn oath that after this experience, you'll still have sex with me. No matter what happens."

She swiped her finger across her heart. "So sworn."

"I'm going before you come to your senses. Then I'm locking you in because when she brings up shopping, and she will, I'm telling her you're taking her."

"Fine with me." She rose, wrapped her arms around his waist. "Men. You're such wussies about a little shopping."

"Yes, and not ashamed of it. Don't work too hard, okay?"

"Just hard enough."

He kissed her, held on a minute. "We'll see you tomorrow. Kiss your sweetheart goodbye, Jasper. We gotta go."

When he got to his mother's, he saw Nana Magic had his kids working on — peacefully — a jigsaw puzzle on the dining room table. And his mother stood on a stepladder cleaning the high shelves in her kitchen.

"Get down from there. What are you doing standing on a ladder?"

"Since I don't have the ability to levitate, it helps me reach these shelves."

"Get down," he repeated. "I'll do it. You can't be standing on ladders."

She peered down at him, Orange Glo in one hand, rag in the other. "Are you saying I'm an old lady?"

490

"No, I'm saying you're my mom."

"Good answer. I'm done anyway."

As she came down — with him spotting her — he saw the various dust catchers she kept on the shelves. Cookbooks on the bottom, easy-to-reach one, he remembered.

"You just hold on," he ordered. "I'll put the stuff back — you can hand it to me. But hold on."

Now she slapped her hands on her hips. "I have to wipe it all down or wash it anyway. And just when did you start thinking you're the boss of me?"

"Since I saw you standing on a ladder. Just wait, and I'll do it." He walked into the dining room, put a hand on each kid's head, studied the puzzle.

"Candy store, very cool. You're almost done."

"It's raining, Daddy." Mariah tried a big, colorful piece in nearly every available spot before she found its place. "Nana said she has another one we can take home to do if the rain, rain, won't go away."

"You can help with that one, but not this one." Bradley, tongue caught in his teeth, found the center piece to a giant bag of M&M's.

"Then I will merely observe."

As he did, as they neared the finish, he saw Bradley slide two pieces under his hand while he reached for another.

When it came down to the last pieces, he started to give his son a poke, but his mother — in the kitchen, facing away — just turned her head.

Raylan hadn't considered, ever, the eyes-in-the-back-of-the-head mythos. He'd dubbed it, long, long ago, the Mom Mind Meld.

And she sent Bradley The Look.

Bradley wilted under it, as all humans, mammals, fish or fowl, or otherworldly creatures would.

"No more pieces! Where are the pieces!"

As his sister hunted, even looked under the table, Bradley slid one piece over.

"Here they are. Last two. Like Nana said, okay?"

Flushed with excitement — and thankfully oblivious to the attempted coup — Mariah snagged her piece. "We count down! Three, two, one!"

And they set the last pieces in unison.

"Yay! Look, Daddy, we did it all by ourselves. Yum, yum, candy!"

"Nana said if we finished it without fighting, we could have a Hershey Bar." Bradley looked up at Raylan. "Can we?"

"Nana rules. But go upstairs, get all your stuff together first. I'm going to help Nana finish this, then we've gotta go."

They raced off with Jasper on their heels.

Raylan picked up a dishcloth to start drying.

"They brighten my world," she said.

"You brighten theirs. I want to say, while the bright is out of earshot, I've concluded that, with your superpowers, you know Adrian and I are doing jigsaw puzzles together."

She smiled, handed him the old Delft teapot that had been his grandmother's. "I've also concluded doing jigsaw puzzles is making both of you happy."

"It is. We are. You know the crap she's dealing with."

"Enough to worry me, yes. Maya told me she — or Lina — hired a detective."

"And the detective's making progress. But in the meantime, and in the spirit of giving her a break, of seeing what comes next, I got Spencer's beach house for two weeks in July. I asked her to come with me and the kids."

"Then it's more than jigsaw puzzles for you. Up you go. Top shelf first. Don't question your feelings," she told him as she handed him the teapot. "Just feel them. You have a good, strong heart, and so much room in it."

"I have to talk to the kids about it. They have to be okay with it."

"Of course. You're raising good, strong hearts with lots of room in them." She handed him a Depression-glass biscuit jar. "Careful with that." Then she put a hand on his leg. "I loved their mother like my own child. She brightened my life, too."

"I know."

"Love isn't finite, Raylan. It always makes more room."

He thought of that as he drove home with the kids bombarding him with what they'd done at Nana's.

Built a fort out of bed linens, made s'mores, played the Game of Life and Yahtzee and Old Maid.

In the jigsaw mode, they wanted to start the new one as soon as they walked in the door. So he set them up, sat down to work it with them while the rain splattered and Jasper decided it was as good a time as any for a nap.

"How many more days until school's over, Bradley?"

"Thirteen! Only thirteen more school days to freedom!"

"Right. I've been working on a list of summer chores."

"Dad!" Bradley slumped, dramatically, in his chair while Mariah systematically looked for end pieces.

"Oh yeah, and the first one is to put up a basketball hoop. Been meaning to get to that. And there's porch sweeping, plant watering, room cleaning. I've got a long list."

"Summer's for fun."

"I'm working that in. Basketball hoop, the summer reading contest, bike riding, hanging out with pals, going to the park, a couple weeks at the beach, family cookouts —"

"The beach!" Mariah squealed it. "We're going to the beach! Can we get the same house like last time?"

"Well, no," he began as Bradley leaped up to do wild celebratory dances. "Because we're going to a different beach."

"How come?" Bradley demanded. "That was a good beach."

"Yeah, but so's this. You get to go to a whole other state. North Carolina. I'll show you on the map. My friend Spencer's letting us use his beach house, right on the ocean. And it has a swimming pool."

"A pool!" Bradley began to dance again, but Mariah reserved judgment.

"Is it a nice house like the other?"

"It's a very nice house."

"Will I still get to have my own room and not have to share with a stinky boy?"

"Yes." Raylan decided to ignore Bradley's mouth-farting spree. "It's a big house, lots of rooms. So I invited Adrian to come with us, if you're okay with it."

The mouth farts stopped as Bradley eyed him.

"Two girls, two boys." Mariah nodded. "She's nice. She helped me with my cartwheel once."

"I didn't know that."

"She came to see Teesha when I was at Phin's and helped me do a cartwheel right.

495

She can do bunches of them, and she smells good. I like her clothes. Phin said he saw you kiss her on the mouth. Is she your girlfriend?"

Well shit, Raylan thought. So much for easing into it. "She's a girl, and my friend, and we like each other." He looked at Bradley now. "You like her, don't you?"

"She can walk on her hands. That's cool. And she talks regular, not all: *Ooooh, aren't you getting big,*" he said in a rather excellent falsetto singsong before he rolled his eyes. "She knows stuff like why the Joker is Batman's nemesis."

"Essential things."

"I like her."

"Then it's okay if she and Sadie come with us to the beach?"

"Jasper loves Sadie. Sadie's Jasper's girlfriend for sure." Mariah hopped up. "I need beach clothes, Daddy. I need new clothes for the beach. Can we go shopping?"

"Funny you should ask. Adrian said she needed new beach clothes if she went with us, and said maybe the two of you could go together."

Mariah's mouth dropped open; her eyes went to saucers. "I can shop with a girl? Just a girl?"

"If you want. We're going to her house for dinner tomorrow so you could talk about it."

"I want to go shopping with Adrian. I have to go up to my room right now and see what

I need. I need sandals and flip-flops and three new bathing suits."

"Slow down. Three?"

"You can't wear the same one every day." A female eye roll this time. "You have to wash out the salt from the ocean and the stuff from the pool, and you need three. I'm going up right now. I can make a list!"

On the wings of a proposed shopping spree, his fashionista ran from the room.

Bradley sat back down. "I need to talk to you. Private."

"Okay."

"Are you going to make sex with Adrian?"

Inside his head, Raylan's brain exploded. He had to run a hand over his hair to make sure the flames were metaphorical. "Wow. Did not see that coming."

"You kissed her on the mouth."

"I did. One doesn't always follow the other." But when Bradley just watched him, he figured he had to shoot straight. "Sex is complicated and private. And it should be. But under the circumstances . . . I have feelings for Adrian, and we're both grown-ups. So . . . yes."

"You kissed Mom on the mouth. A lot. And you made sex with her because you have to make sex to have babies."

"I did, we did. We wanted you and Mo. Ah, you don't always make sex to have babies, so you . . ."

Eight years old, Raylan thought. Closing in on nine, sure, but still. How much was too much?

"I loved your mom, so much."

"But you don't love her anymore?"

Now Raylan's heart twisted. "Oh, Bradley, I do."

Reassurance, Raylan realized. The kid wanted reassurance, not a biology lesson.

"I'll always love her." He pulled the boy out of the chair, onto his lap. "And all I have to do is look at you, at Mo, and see her. She's in you, and I love seeing her in you."

"Mo doesn't remember as much, because she was just a baby practically. But I do. I still talk to her in my head sometimes."

"Me, too."

Bradley looked up. "You really do?"

"Yeah. I'm always going to miss her, but all I have to do is look at you and Mo, and she's there. I love her. I love that we made you and Mariah together."

His mother's words came back to him, as if she'd said them for just this moment.

"Love makes room, Brad. There's always more room for love."

After a long, rainy day, the afternoon play-date, a movie marathon he approved for his own sanity, Raylan checked on his kids one last time.

They slept as they always did, Mariah

cuddled with her stuffed animal of the week, Bradley sprawled out in a bed littered with action figures.

He went into his bedroom, sat on the side of the bed, and studied his wedding ring.

When she sat beside him, he just sighed out her name. "Lorilee."

"I'd be sad if you didn't keep a place for me in your heart."

"You're always there."

"I know, and you know. Our kids know. I bet Adrian knows. I really like her. You know that, too."

"I didn't think this would happen. That I'd feel this way about anyone else. Ever."

"But you do. I'm glad you do."

He looked at her, so lovely, so real to him. "Are you?"

"Why would you think I'd want you to be alone? I couldn't love you and want that. It's time to take it off, honey. It's time. It's not forgetting me to take it off. You're building a new life, for yourself, for the kids. This is a good house, Raylan, it's a happy one. You knew it was time for that. You know it's time for this."

"Yeah, I know."

"Put it in the keepsake box in your drawer, the one where we put the locks of our kids' hair, their sonogram pictures, all those sweet little memories. Keep it there."

He nodded, got up to open the drawer, take

out the box.

He started to take off the ring, turned back to her. "I'm not going to see you anymore, not after this, am I?"

"Not like this. But you said it yourself. You only have to look at the kids."

"Lorilee. You changed my world."

"We changed each other's."

"I remember the first time I saw you, when you walked into the fine arts class. You took my breath away. I remember the last time I saw you when . . . when you drove away. And so many moments between, Lorilee. But now I can remember so many of them and smile, or feel good, feel blessed, I had them with you."

She tapped a hand to her heart. "Keep that place for me there. I don't mind the company, honey. I'm glad for it."

He looked down at the ring, closed his eyes a moment. Then drew it off.

"You can see where it was, where the sun couldn't get through."

"That'll fade in time. You're letting in the light."

He put the ring in the keepsake box. And she was gone.

CHAPTER TWENTY-FOUR

On a sun-kissed June afternoon, Adrian sat
in Teesha's home office holding the baby
while her business manager went over financial reports, budgetary issues, and marketing
plans for Rizzo's and the youth center.

Chubby with mother's milk, Thaddeus
waved his teether while Phineas sat on the
floor apparently building a futuristic city with
Legos.

All the while the notes of Monroe's piano
drifted from upstairs in what Adrian thought
must be a ballad about heartbreak.

"Finally," Teesha concluded, "Jan's made a
very strong and well-thought-out pitch for a
raise and promotion for Barry. Since Bob-
Ray, the de facto assistant manager for the
last year or so, is retiring, she'd like you to
consider making Barry her official assistant
manager, with a raise and benefits com-
mensurate with that position. I have her letter of recommendation. I second it."

"And I'll read it, but I'm going to approve

because I know Barry, I know his work, his loyalty, and his love for Rizzo's. Isn't that right?" she asked Thaddeus as she gave him a bounce.

"Great. I'll let Jan know. Meanwhile, when you and Kayla start shopping again, stick to the budget."

"Yes, ma'am. We didn't go that much over on lighting and plumbing fixtures."

"You go a little over here, a little over there, and before you know it, you're a lot over everywhere. And you went one-point-six percent over on the lighting, and a full two percent over on the plumbing."

Adrian bounced the baby again. "Your mom is so strict."

"Daddy isn't." Carefully Phineas chose another block. "He says sometimes you just gotta have a wrestle even if it's bedtime."

"Somebody has to be the referee around here, little man of mine. What are you building this time?"

"I'm making Phinville. When I grow up, I'll make my own town and be the boss of everybody."

"How are you going to be an astronaut and boss of Phinville?"

He gave his mother the most patient of looks. "I'm gonna build Phinville in space."

"Of course. What was I thinking?"

"I don't have preschool all summer, but I start kindergarten after. I'll ride the bus with

Bradley and Mariah, and save a seat for Collin because the bus gets us first."

"How do you know it gets you first?" Adrian wondered.

"Because it picks up Mo's friend Cissy after Mo, and Cissy lives across the street from Collin, so I'll save him a seat because we're best friends. We won't need school buses in Phinville. Everyone will teleport."

Adrian looked at him with his gorgeous dark curls, his big beautiful brown eyes and fell in love with him all over again. "Very efficient, and speedy."

"Buses use gas, and it's not good for the air. And we have to make the air in Phinville because it's in space. Hey, Daddy! I'm building Phinville."

Monroe sauntered in, crouched down, and gave the emerging city a serious study. "You're going to live there." He tapped a tower. "Because it's the tallest. You can look out and make sure the city's at peace."

He gave Sadie, sprawled by Adrian's feet, a good rub. "Shift change. Sorry, I didn't hear you come in or I'd've gotten the kids sooner."

"I got to hold the baby and watch the erecting of Phinville. I loved what you were playing a bit ago. Do you have lyrics?"

"Working on them. The music came first this time. Let's take Thad for a stroll, Phin. Get us all some fresh. Mama won't mind if you leave your city for now, will you, Mama?"

"No, you go ahead. Thad might need a change."

"Got it covered, don't we, Phin?"

Monroe hauled the now-bouncing-on-his-own baby into his arms. And Adrian held hers out for Phineas. "Hey, handsome. I need one."

He gave her a hug, rocking side to side the way she found so endearing. "You can live in Phinville, too."

"I'm counting on it."

As he walked out with his father, Phineas's whisper carried back. "Are we going for ice cream, Daddy?"

"Boy, you're going to get me in trouble. Your mama's got fine ears on her."

Adrian shook her head. "You're not too strict for ice cream on a June afternoon."

"They like to play the game. I like to play it, too. We still have to go over some numbers for New Gen, but since other ears are now out of the room, I'm switching to personal. First the tough stuff. Any word from your investigator?"

"Actually, yes. She located fourteen more women — all alive and well. She's spoken to all but one of them, and is heading to Richmond — is probably there by now — to speak to the last in person."

"Okay." Teesha nodded slowly. "That's good, that's solid. That's a little better than forty-one percent alive and well."

"I can tell you it's brought me some serious relief."

"And it should. On the flip side, with those she found who aren't alive and well added on to fourteen, she's got the same percentage to locate. She will. She's thorough."

"She is. Nikki Bennett isn't back in DC yet. She detoured to another client, apparently. No luck locating the brother, not yet anyway. She did speak with some neighbors. Nobody's seen him in years."

"Maybe the sister killed him and buried him in the basement."

"Now that's uplifting."

"Just spitballing. Anyway, I feel better knowing neither of them are around, and your PI's digging. I want this shit over. You've dealt with it long enough. Case closed." She slapped her hands together. "Then you can go to the beach with my sexy neighbor and just enjoy."

"You're sure about taking care of the garden?"

"It's two weeks, Adrian, not two years. We can handle it. Now for the fun stuff. How's it going with you and said sexy?"

"It's . . . We had a really good dinner with the kids. Mariah's already got an agenda started for the shopping trip. You know, I thought: Hell, sure, I can take a kid shopping, no big. But I never have. Maybe you should —"

"Uh-uh-uh." Teesha ticked her finger back and forth. "First, you know I only shop when cornered, and second, she's revved about going with you. It's a bonding op. Take it. She's a good kid. They both are. When you live next door, you know."

"But do I just let her go wild, or do I rein her in, or what?"

"You're talking to the referee, remember? So I'm staying neutral on it. Go with your gut. And stop looking for obstacles."

"I'm not. Exactly. It's just . . . He took off his wedding ring."

"Oh." Puffing out her cheeks, Teesha sat back. "That's a big."

"Yes. I don't know, exactly, what it means. I don't know if I should tell him I noticed, or just not. I wasn't expecting, when we started what we started, anything like this."

"For you or for him?"

"Either. Both. You've known me forever, Teesh. I've never had a serious relationship."

"Because you avoided them."

"Maybe. No, not maybe," she admitted at Teesha's steady look. "Yes, I avoided them. And this one just happened. How do we . . . We've both got our own businesses, demanding careers. Add two kids to his plate. Add Rizzo's, and now the center, to mine. How do you possibly juggle all that? I don't know how you and Monroe juggle all you have to do."

"It's all in the rhythm, and the teamwork. Are you looking for an out?"

"I'm not, and that worries me. I'm not a worrier, not really. You just figure out what you need or want to do, then you do it."

She always had. She'd believed she always would.

"I don't know what I need or want, exactly, when it comes to this. I've never had to figure that out. And I'm probably overreacting, which I don't think I do a lot either."

Teesha angled her head, stared up at the ceiling. "I remember you laughing at me when I came home, insisting I had to move to South America the first time Monroe asked me to marry him."

"You were only going to move to the West Coast the first time he said he loved you."

"True. Both illustrate even sensible people worry and overreact a lot of times when they fall in love."

"God. I wasn't looking for that, or expecting that. You can't organize that into a program, you can't schedule it or decide what should come next and push to it."

"Hard for you to let things evolve. You've driven your own train a long time, Adrian. But," she added, holding up a finger, "you also know how to change tracks when needed. You changed tracks when I met you, and changed your life. And mine. You did it again when you moved back here. Maybe, for now, you could try sharing the controls with somebody else and enjoy the scenery for a while."

"I really wasn't nervous about any of this before."

"Because he wore that ring, and his wife was a kind of buffer."

"Jesus, Teesha, I don't want to think of her that way."

"I imagine he did, too, at least some. He just realized before you did that time was over. Relax into it, Rizz, and take in the scenery."

"I guess I have to try, because I can't come over here and not take Sadie over to visit her boyfriend. Bore me with numbers," she told Teesha. "Shut my brain down with them."

"Numbers are life and light and truth."

An hour later, her brain frazzled by those numbers, Adrian walked next door. Just play it casual, confident, easy, she told herself. It's just a quick stop so Sadie and Jasper could have a visit. And he, very likely, had his head in his work.

But even before she knocked, she heard the pounding music, saw lights flashing against the windows. She'd never known him to work with that kind of noise, but maybe he was trying out a scene.

She'd have knocked, but Jasper sent out a howl, and Sadie answered with a quick triple bark.

When Raylan opened the door, the music poured out in a flood and the colored lights spun around his living room where his kids, whom she'd assumed were in school, danced like maniacs.

Raylan wore sunglasses with rainbow shades, a backward ball cap, and a purple spangled vest over his T-shirt.

"Well," she managed, "this is unexpected."

Sporting a pair of fairy wings, a tutu, and a plastic tiara, Mariah raced over. "It's a dance party! Come dance."

"A dance party?"

"A School's Out for Summer Dance Party," Raylan told her. "Bradley, turn the music down a minute."

"Oh, you don't have to do that."

But Bradley, in a green wig, a Batman shirt, and a cat-eye mask, turned it down to a mutter. "Dad set it all up! We got off the bus and he had it all set up. It's Club Vacation."

He'd shoved all the furniture back to clear what was, obviously, the dance floor, and some sort of light machine shot colors onto the walls. Streamers and balloons spilled from the ceiling.

All her earlier worries simply dissolved in delight.

"Can't have a dance party without dressing for it," Raylan added.

"You can dance." Mariah tugged her hand. "You can."

"I'm afraid I didn't dress for a party."

"We got stuff!" She raced to a chest, flung it open, then raced back with another tiara and a pink boa.

"Wow. Who doesn't love a tiara? I don't want to push into your family party," she began.

"Club Vacation is open to all," Raylan told her as Bradley eyed her.

She started to make another excuse, but the boy stepped up to her. "You can walk on your hands. Can you dance on them?"

"Can I dance on my hands?"

"Can you do the splits?" Mariah demanded.

"Oh, I see." Nodding, she fit on the tiara, wrapped the boa around her neck. "It's an audition. Well then, Bradley, hit it."

"Hit what?"

"She means turn the music back up."

When he did, Adrian, grateful she'd worn leggings, toed off her shoes.

She did a couple of hip wiggles, a shoulder bump, then — flowed down, set her hands, flowed her legs up. She matched the beat, walking forward and back, side to side. Split her legs as she walked in a circle, then flowed down into a bridge, gauged her ground for a spring, and dropped into the splits. Threw out her arms for the flourish.

While the kids applauded, she tossed the loose end of the boa over her shoulder.

"Did I pass the audition?"

"That was super cool," Bradley said.

"Highest praise." Raylan held out a hand. "Looks like we're dancing."

While Adrian danced, Rachael sat in the tidy living room of Tracie Potter's sleek townhome in downtown Richmond.

She'd done a background check, and knew Tracie had been a year behind Lina at Georgetown, earned degrees in journalism and communication. She'd worked her way up to an anchor slot on the local NBC affiliate where she currently led the six and eleven o'clock broadcasts.

A local celebrity, she married in her late twenties, had two kids, divorced in her mid-thirties. And remarried at forty to a real estate developer.

She had three grandchildren, one from her eldest daughter, and two from her stepson.

She and her husband belonged to the country club, enjoyed golf, and owned a second home in San Simeon.

Even up close Rachael judged the woman could pass for forty, which meant some very excellent work even if she had superior genes going for her. Her hair, a thick and expertly highlighted medium blond, waved around a face of creamy skin with sharp blue eyes and a perfectly tinted mouth of deep rose.

She crossed her legs in snug white jeans

and sat back with her Wedgwood cup of coffee.

"I can give you about thirty minutes," she began. "I wanted to have this discussion here rather than at my office. It's old news, but I'd rather not fuel the gossip tank."

"I appreciate you meeting with me."

"Curiosity. What does my long-ago, ill-advised, and brief affair with Jon Bennett have to do with anything today?"

"You're aware Professor Bennett was killed during his attack on Lina Rizzo, her minor child, and her female friend in Georgetown a couple decades ago."

"It was all over the news at the time. I'm a reporter. Even if I hadn't slept with him nearly a decade before that, I'd have been aware. I'm also aware the child was his biological daughter. I'm aware he physically assaulted both women and the child. Did I mention ill-advised affair?"

"You did. Can I ask if you considered it ill-advised prior to that incident?"

"I considered it ill-advised when I saw Jon physically assaulting Lina Rizzo — though I didn't know at that moment who she was — in his office. I was meeting him there for a quickie."

She sipped more coffee.

"It shocked me — shouldn't have, I admit, to see him with a hand around her throat, her back to the wall. Just for an instant, but I saw that rage and violence on his face. I chose not to risk it being turned on me, and ended the relationship. Which wasn't a relationship."

She paused; Rachael waited.

"I was nineteen, and foolish, but not that foolish. Foolish enough to have sex with a married man — in the middle, he claimed, of a complicated divorce, though that was a lie — but not foolish enough to risk getting knocked around for some exciting, illicit sex.

"Why did Lina Rizzo give you my name after all this time?"

"She didn't. I'd assume she didn't know yours, or didn't remember it. You're on a list, Ms. Potter."

"What kind of list?"

"Of women, like you, who slept with Jonathan Bennett. There are thirty-four names on it. Four of them are dead — victims or near victims of murder. Four I've located and confirmed."

Tracie lowered her cup. Rachael gave her credit. She didn't jolt, didn't gasp. She stared, hard and long.

"I want to verify that. Off the record. You've just indicated I'm on some sort of kill list."

"I'll give you what information I can. Have you had any threats?"

"No. Oh, you get a few who take potshots over the Internet if they don't like your reporting. But nothing like this, no. When did this happen?"

"The deaths? Over the course of the last thirteen years."

"Thirteen years? Are you serious? You were a cop — I did my research before this meeting. People die, are murdered. Four people over that amount of time —"

"On the same list. And I still have more to locate."

"I assume Lina Rizzo's on that list. I assume she's your client."

"She's on the list. Did you ever meet or have contact with Jonathan Bennett's wife or his children?"

"No, why would I? I had a fling with him, Ms. McNee, a matter of weeks. Looking back, and I have, I should have reported him. So should've Lina Rizzo."

"Why didn't you?"

"It scared me, that one moment I saw him, really saw him. And that was a hell of a long time before Me Too. Who do you think would have taken the heat, if any heat came? The tenured professor — and others on the faculty had to know what he was — or the young undergrad who slept with him? Willingly."

"Understood. I know this is upsetting. I feel not only an obligation to my client, but to anyone I'm able to contact on that list so they're able to take precautions."

"He's been dead a very long time. Where did the list come from? Give me a break,"

Tracie snapped out. "How do I take precautions when I don't know what I'm up against?"

"His wife compiled the list. She knew."

"So," Tracie added, "not as oblivious as he assumed. You think his wife is, after all this time, killing women he slept with?"

"His wife died, an overdose of sleeping pills. About thirteen years ago."

"Ah." Now she put the cup aside. "Had she remarried? Have family — a brother, sister?"

"No."

"Someone, obviously, connected to his wife given the timing. They had kids? How old were they? If I ever knew, I can't recall."

"Old enough. Ms. Potter, I'm sure you have substantial resources considering your profession, but I'm, again, going to caution you. I intend to speak with both Professor Bennett's daughter and his son as soon as possible. Then I intend to turn my findings over to the FBI, and the applicable police departments."

"Is your name on the list?"

"It is not."

"Then it's a job for you. It's a little more than that for me."

"If you contact these individuals, or alert them to my line of inquiry, they could bolt. You'd only be worse off. I hope to meet with the daughter, at least, in a matter of days. I'm going to do everything I can to protect my client, and by doing so you, and every other woman on that list."

"I'm sure you will. You have an excellent reputation. I appreciate you warning me, and I will absolutely take precautions. Now I have to change and get to the studio."

No help for it, Rachael thought as she got back into her car for the drive home. The woman would poke around. The nature of the beast.

She could only hope the poking around didn't set off any alarms.

Summer, for a single dad, opened another world and required a sharp revision of schedule. No getting the kids up, dressed, fed, and out to the bus — to return to quiet and solitary work for a solid chunk of hours.

No setting his internal clock for their return so he could at least try to wrap things up and prepare for snack time, talk time, homework time.

Long summer days meant hoping the kids played together without bloodshed — because that occasionally happened. Or arranging for them to play at friends' houses. Which meant — by parental law — he had to reciprocate.

It meant making sure they had a decent lunch, didn't end up spending the bulk of the day staring at some sort of screen.

His mother, of course, loved taking them for a few hours if she had the morning or the afternoon off. Once a week, at her insistence, she took them to work with her for a couple hours.

Showing them the ropes, she called it.

And once a week Maya had them over.

Sometimes his backyard filled with kids, and that was fine because sometimes his kids filled other backyards.

And sometimes he blew off an hour playing basketball with them using the hoop he'd lowered to kid height.

Hoping he wasn't making a major mistake, he pitched a tent in the backyard for Bradley and his two best friends.

Three almost-nine-year-olds, he thought, backyard camping. What could go wrong?

A lot.

But as his mother had done for him, he set up a tent, and he'd stock snacks, drinks, flashlights.

Mariah, who'd turned her nose way up at even the idea of sleeping in a tent, was on her much-anticipated shopping spree.

What could go wrong there?

He didn't like to think about it.

"Phin's bringing over his telescope for a while so we can look at the moon and stuff." Tongue caught in his teeth, Bradley tried hammering in a peg. Which made Raylan question, again, the sentimentality of using his old tent instead of buying a new, basically pop-it-open deal.

"If we had a fire pit, we could cook hot dogs and marshmallows."

"We don't have one, and you're not building a fire."

"If we could use Ollie's dad's camp stove —"

"And again, no. Maybe double digits. Maybe when you're ten. You want dogs, I'll make them inside."

"Not the same. We'll eat the pizza, like we said."

"Good."

"We can get hot dogs when we go to the ball game Saturday night."

Something else that took him back. A warm summer night, baseball, sitting so close to the minor league players you almost felt like you stood on the diamond.

He stopped, ruffled his son's hair. "Hot dogs galore."

"And nachos. And fries."

"You're making me hungry. I think we've got it, kid. Let's get the air mattress inside."

"Cowboys slept on the ground."

"You want to sleep on the ground?"

"No. I'm not a cowboy." Bradley did a belly slide inside the tent, onto the mattress. "But we can stay up all night if we want. You said."

"That's right. But you don't leave the yard."

"I know, I know."

So had he, Raylan thought, and still he and Spencer and Mick and Nate had snuck off

518

for a midnight hike through the woods. Scared themselves stupid, he recalled. And Spencer had tripped, scraped up his shin, which bled like a son of a bitch for a while.

Good times.

"Tenting tonight." Monroe sang over the fence.

"Ancient tent. They get rowdy, open a window and throw something at them."

In the way of friends and neighbors they'd become, Monroe hopped the fence, then reached down to pop Phineas over.

They all stood, studying the tent.

"Bats come out at night," Phineas said helpfully. "But they won't bother you. They want bugs."

"Bats?" Bradley repeated.

"You like Batman. You could look for bats. Can I shoot the basketball?"

"Sure." Raylan watched the boy walk over, retrieve the ball, step back, shoot.

Swish.

"Every time." He could only shake his head.

"Boy's got skills. You got your ghost stories lined up?" Monroe asked Bradley.

"I got a real good one."

"Ghosts are — maybe — people who get caught for a minute in the time and space contin— What is it?"

"Continuum," Monroe supplied.

"Continuum," Phineas said.

Swish.

519

"Like *Star Trek*?"

"I like *Star Trek*." Phineas glanced back at Bradley before he swished again. "They boldly go where no one has gone before. That's what I'm going to do. I like Spock best."

"Shocker." Raylan had to laugh.

And Sadie let out a woof.

"Girls must be back." Raylan checked the time. "Want a beer?"

"I could get behind that."

"Ginger ale, Phin?"

"I like ginger ale, thank you. Ale's like beer, but ginger ale isn't."

Swish.

Raylan just shook his head again. "We're getting pizza later if you want in on that."

"Pizza's never wrong. I'll check with the boss, but it sounds good to me. So happens we've got the makings for ice cream sundaes."

"With whipped cream?" Bradley demanded.

Monroe let out a snort. "It ain't no sundae without whipped cream, son, it's just naked ice cream."

"Hold that thought." Raylan went in to get the drinks and see how the ladies had fared.

Once inside, he saw Adrian and Mariah hauling in a load of shopping bags.

"Wow. Looks like success." And, he noted, Adrian didn't appear to be pale, shaken, or glassy-eyed.

"See my new sandals, Daddy!" Mariah balanced on one foot to show off bright purple sandals with a strap of pink-and-white flowers. "And I got a white pair, and flip-flops — blue ones with a butterfly and purple ones with flowers — and slides and I got to pick out sneakers from what Adrian makes and she's going to give them to me."

"Another wow. By my math that's six pairs of shoes."

Adrian set down the two bags she carried. "And your point?"

"And I got shorts and dresses and tops and skorts —"

As his daughter rattled off more, he contemplated the fact that he was an adult man who knew what skorts were.

"I tried everything on, and everything is perfect! And we had lunch in a bistro, and I had bubble water in a wineglass. Then we got mani-pedis. I got purple on my toes to match my new sandals and pink on my fingers."

"I see. Nice."

"I'm going to take all my new shoes up and put them away." She turned to wrap around Adrian. "I loved shopping with you. I had the best time ever."

"Me, too."

Mariah bolted up the stairs, two shopping bags banging.

"Two more bags in the car. I'll get them, since I know which is which."

"Wait. Two more? She's this big. How many this-big clothes fit in six bags?"

"Be grateful I bought you some time on getting her ears pierced."

"What? Huh? What!"

"You owe me," she said and went back out. He followed her. "She's six."

"She'll be seven in just a few months, as she pointed out, firmly, when we ran into one of her friends in the salon who'd just gotten hers done." Adrian retrieved the two bags, passed them to Raylan. "You've got a battle coming."

He didn't want to think about it. He did, however, study the number of shopping bags still in the car. "Those are yours."

"All but this." She plucked out one more. "Which is, at your daughter's insistence — and sweetly — new bathing suits, rash guards, and slides for you and for Bradley. Some of that was altruistic," she continued. "And some, the lion's share, was so you won't embarrass us girls at the beach."

Adrian shut the car door. "I've been warned you and Bradley wear clothes that don't match, even to the point of wearing red trunks with a purple rash guard. It was difficult for us to enjoy our lunch after that, but we put it aside out of pity for you."

"You enjoyed all this."

"I have to use a cattle prod to get Teesha to shop for anything but absolute essentials.

Maya likes to shop. But Mo? She's a shopping goddess. I stand in awe."

"While you're standing in all that awe, want some wine?"

"I should follow the teachings of the goddess and go put my things away. But I could have a glass of wine first."

"Have more." He shifted the bags to one hand so he could take hers. "Bradley's having a couple friends over to sleep in the tent in the backyard."

"In a tent in the yard? Why?"

"Girls." With a shake of his head, he led her back toward the house. "Teesha, Monroe, and the kids are going to come over for dinner. We're having pizza delivered. And there's a rumor of ice cream sundaes. Stay."

"Wine, pizza, and ice cream, or the Thai noodle salad I was planning to make for myself. You win."

"Pizza always wins." He paused at the door, her hand still in his. "Then stay. Stay the night."

He could see, clearly, she hadn't expected him to ask. He hadn't expected to either. But it felt natural; it felt right.

"I'm not sure, with the kids . . ."

"We're going to the beach together soon," he pointed out. "And they already know I kiss you on the mouth. Phineas, who sees, hears, and knows all, tattled. And they're all right with it. So stay."

"Maybe you just want backup with the backyard campers."

He smiled, drew her in. "That would be a factor. Not the biggest one, but definitely a factor."

"I guess I can help you out, since I'm getting pizza and ice cream."

Knowing they were taking a big step, the next step, Raylan kissed her on the mouth.

CHAPTER TWENTY-FIVE

In the yard outside her studio, Adrian worked on a yoga routine using light weights. She aimed for fifteen minutes, so had a timer set. She had the concept for a new program, all yoga (maybe edging a little into her mother's territory), all fifteen minutes with four different focuses.

A good addition, she felt, to her streaming programs. And fun if she could do it all outside, she thought, holding a tree pose while doing shoulder presses.

She had the glass doors open so Sadie could roam in and out as she pleased.

When her timer beeped, she was on her mat, in bridge, doing chest presses.

"Okay, crap, too long."

Rising, she set down the weights to study the outline on her tablet, made adjustments.

Setting another fifteen, she started again.

This time when the timer sounded, she sat cross-legged on the mat, hands out to the sides, palms up. She brought them together in prayer, bowed.

"Nailed it. That'll work."

Because she could, she stretched back out, watched a puff of white cloud ease its way across the summer-blue sky.

Sadie came over, stretched out beside her.

She listened to the birds singing, the breeze sighing. She smelled grass, rosemary, the heliotrope from the nearby patio pot.

If only everything could stay just like this, she thought. Pretty and quiet and warm and bright. Or like the evening she'd spent at Raylan's — all noise and excitement, kids running, friends talking, Monroe plucking on a banjo, and all's right with the world.

But it wouldn't stay, and it wasn't all right with the world.

She knew Rachael had located four more women. Three alive, one murdered in the hospital parking lot where she worked.

And that changed the percentages again, she knew. She wasn't going to attempt the math.

And she knew Rachael planned to interview Nikki Bennett the next day. With the woman finally due back at her office, Rachael would go there, lay it out, push for answers.

If there were any.

There had to be answers. There had to be a time it would be all right in her world again.

Because she wanted to be able to stretch out in the grass with her dog under a blue sky and not think about the fact that someone she'd never met wanted to hurt her.

And why.

"Add to it?" she said as she stroked Sadie. "Mom's coming next week. I'm fine with that, I really am. It's just one more thing — so I need to get this routine set before she gets here and suggests changes."

Then she sighed. "Because they'd probably be really good suggestions. And I'm brooding because Raylan's going to New York tomorrow. Just overnight, and I'm brooding. Have you ever known me to brood over a man? No, you have not."

She shifted, snuggled with the dog. "So I'm going to stop, and I'm going to figure out the ab portion."

She got up to put the weights away before she consulted her tablet for a refresher. But when she started to set the timer, Sadie let out a woof — a friendly one — and headed around the side of the house.

Following suit, Adrian saw Teesha and Maya each get out of their cars.

"Well, this is a surprise."

Maya spread her arms. "We are kid free!"

"So I see."

"Mom's got Collin and Phineas — prearranged. Then she insisted on keeping her granddaughter. I have pumped, and I have dumped the baby."

"I'd already done that for Thad — Monroe's shift — so I texted him to say he was doing a double."

"And we came to make you blow off your workday and hang with us," Maya finished as they reached the back.

"I can do that. I've gotten most of it done anyway."

"Roll up that mat, girl," Teesha told her. "Let's pour something cold."

"I wish it was margaritas." Maya closed her eyes and sighed. "I wish we could spend the afternoon day drinking frothy, frozen margaritas in birdbath glasses rimmed with lime and salt. Do you remember drinking margaritas, Teesha?"

"I do. Fondly. Next summer our boobs will be ours again, and we'll day drink frothy, frozen margaritas."

"I made lemonade this morning," Adrian said consideringly. "Now I want to put tequila in mine."

"Don't taunt us. Lemonade. Got any cookies?" Teesha wondered.

"No, sorry. I've got —"

"Don't say hummus." Maya held up a finger. "Don't say raw veggies. We don't want to hurt you."

"I'll find something else. Front porch or back?"

"Out here's just fine. We'll go on up to the porch." Maya hooked arms with Teesha. "So you don't have to bring not-hummus refreshments far."

She put everything away, opened the kitchen door to the porch.

Teesha got glasses, Maya the pitcher while Adrian gathered snacks that would meet the current standards. She had guacamole, chips, herb crackers, and a very nice Gouda. Chilled grapes and berries.

"Nice." Maya sat, tossed back her sunshine-blond ponytail. And let out an *Mmmm.* "I haven't had a girl afternoon, just you guys, in so long. We have to figure out how to do this. Once a month. No kids, no guys, just us."

"A Girl Club instead of a book club." Teesha scooped up guacamole. "I love my kids, so much, but —"

"Right there with you, sister." Maya tapped her glass to Teesha's. "A few hours with no one calling me, needing wiping, changing, feeding. And you and me aren't doing it alone like my mother did. God, how Raylan is."

Maya smiled at Adrian. "And I heard you took the fashion queen shopping. How'd that go?"

"She talked me into buying — for myself — twice what I'd planned for or needed. I kept thinking, But I'm in workout gear or sweats ninety percent of my life. I don't need those adorable capris. And she'd say something about when clothes make you look good, they make you feel good. When you feel good, you're nicer to people. So I'd buy

529

the capris for humanity."

"As her doting aunt I'm glad she's got someone on her team who can appreciate her innate skills. Now . . . How are things going with you and Raylan?"

Adrian took her time selecting the perfect plump blackberry. "Things are going fine."

"Very vague." Maya nodded toward Teesha. "Don't you find that response very vague?"

"A sad and selfish lack of details, when we sit here, women with sex lives squeezed in between active kids, breastfeedings, floor walking, businesses running, diaper changings."

"Question answering, toy repairing, tear drying," Maya continued. "When's the last time you had the energy or opportunity for uninterrupted sex, foreplay included, with an encore?"

"An encore? Oh my, my." Leaning back, Teesha cast her eyes to the sky. "I believe that was back when the grandmas took Phineas for a long weekend to Hersheypark. And that's how we got Thaddeus. Pretty sure it was the encore."

"Mom kept both kids overnight a couple weeks back, even though our girl still wants the breast or bottle about two in the morning. Joe and I managed round one, then we both slept like the dead for ten hours. We have to give that another shot."

Now she smiled at Adrian. "Your turn."

Then she pointed when Adrian shook her head. "Not fair. When Joe and I started dating, you got flooded with details."

"Same with me and Monroe."

"Neither one of them is my brother," Adrian pointed out, and ate a grape. "Talking about having sex with my friend's brother to my friend shoots beyond awkward and straight into weird."

"He's not my brother." Teesha gestured with her glass with one hand, sliced some cheese with the other. "Maya can take a walk, you tell me, then I'll tell her later."

"How about if I say, as Raylan has two children older than yours, there's hope for both of you in this intimate area."

"Still vague," Maya mused, "but uplifting."

"So far, he's got no problem uplifting."

Teesha let out a hoot. "Now we're talking." She stretched out her legs. "God, this feels good. You get major points for thinking of this, Maya. I was going home and straight back to work."

"I was heading into the shop to finish updating the website. I love the shop. I love working with the craftsmen, the artists, working the counter, talking with people every day. But you sure can get in a routine that dips toward a rut so you forget who you are outside of work, wife, and mom."

She held up her glass. "Here's to remembering to be a girlfriend."

531

"You're both the best I ever had." Adrian tapped her glass. "Both of you, right there, are two big turning points in my life. That first summer here, you making room in your group for me, Maya. I really needed a friend."

"I'm going to tell you what I never did. When my mom found out what happened, and that you were staying here for the summer, she sat me down. She explained, and she said a lot of kids might push questions on you. Some might even make fun of you or just say something mean. And she asked how I'd feel if kids did that to me. I said it would make me feel bad, and embarrassed. She just said I was right, and knew I wouldn't do that. How she bet you could use a friend."

"I love your mom," Teesha murmured.

"Best there is. Of course, I said what if she's mean or stupid or I just don't like her? She said I should find out. So I did. And here we are."

"You asked if I wanted to come over to your house and see your Barbies, and changed what I thought would be a summer of sad and alone. And here we are. And you."

She shifted to Teesha. "I was so angry with my mother, sticking me in that school where I didn't know anyone, didn't want to be. Time to show her what I could do, time to grab my own. I walked over to that table in the cafeteria looking for a video crew. I got a whole lot more."

"You shocked the crap out of us. The new girl, the one who should've marched over to the popular kids — the jocks or the snobs for sure — walks right over to us and sits down. It was brave. You've always been brave."

"Pissed and determined. And here we are."

Because it seemed right, she set down her glass, took her friends' hands. "Next time I'll have cookies."

Rachael walked into the Ardaro Consultants offices in Northwest DC with a plan in mind, one she could adjust in several ways if necessary.

A couple days before, she'd called the office with the claim she was on the alumni reunion committee of Nikki Bennett's high school. She'd put on the chatty and perky, and though Nikki's assistant had been too professional to give her exact whereabouts, she had suggested Rachael call again in two days when Nikki would be back in the office.

Today, she intended to corner Nikki in her office as a frazzled owner of an independent bookstore in Bethesda, Maryland, who needed help restructuring her business.

At least until she got into the office, got that face-to-face.

She'd dressed for it — gray pants with her best black heels, a matching scoop-neck top, and a pale blue blazer. She'd borrowed her sister's diamond studs, draped on a few sparkly chains, replaced her own simple wedding ring with a flashy cubic zirconia she believed would pass.

A woman of means. A woman who could afford to hire a good expert and experienced consultant from a good firm to turn her sweet business around.

She stepped into the tastefully appointed lobby, fixed on a pleasant but slightly arrogant look, and walked to the receptionist.

"Good morning. Can I help you?"

"I certainly hope so. I'd like to speak with . . ." She held up a finger, took her phone out of her — also borrowed — Max Mara handbag. "Yes, it's Nikki Bennett."

"Do you have an appointment?"

Rachael peered over. "She came highly recommended. I was in the building on another appointment. I'd like five minutes of her time. Please tell her Mrs. Salina Mathias is waiting. You've perhaps heard of my brother. Senator Charles Mathias."

"I'm very sorry, Ms. Mathias."

"Mrs."

"Mrs. Mathias, Ms. Bennett is currently out of the office consulting with another client. I'd be more than happy to direct you to one of our other consultants, or have Ms. Bennett's assistant schedule an appointment."

"Well, when is she due back in the office?"

"Tomorrow. After her consult, she's scheduled to work from home."

"Working from home?" Rachael let out a short, derisive laugh. "I can see I've wasted my time."

She sailed out.

And wondered what it said about her that she'd enjoyed putting on the entitled snob the receptionist would bitch about to a coworker on her break.

Back in her car, she changed the heels for sneakers, then drove out of the parking garage to head to Georgetown.

She stopped for snacks, to empty her bladder, then parked a half block up and across the street from the Bennetts' dignified home.

She'd sit on the house — not nearly as much fun as pretending to be an asshole — until Nikki got back.

Pretty neighborhood, she thought, quiet, settled. Wealthy.

If somebody decided to report a strange car, she'd chat it up with the cops who came to have a look. She'd been one of them, after all.

She typed up her movements of the morning, the time involved, then put on earbuds, cued up her current audiobook.

She spent the next hour in the Scottish Highlands and nibbling on Fritos — a big weakness.

When the rugged chieftain and the fiery woman he loved finished their adventure, she checked in with her husband, with her office, then started to scroll through more audio choices.

The sedate black Mercedes pulled up to the dignified house.

Nikki Bennett, her short brown hair fluttering a bit in the breeze, got out. She wore a summer suit of pale gray, darker gray pumps with short, stubby heels. She swung a black briefcase on her shoulder before reaching in the back for a cloth market tote.

Rachael waited until she reached the door before she left her car, hit the locks, then crossed the street.

She rang the bell.

Moments later, Nikki opened it, studied Rachael with tired, suspicious eyes. "Yes?"

"Ms. Bennett, I'm Rachael McNee." She held up her identification. "I'd like to speak with you for a few minutes. May I come in?"

"No. What's this about? I've been out of town. I haven't heard anything about any trouble in the neighborhood."

"None that I know of. Your name's come up in a matter I'm investigating."

"What matter?"

"Poetry."

Nikki stared straight through her. "I don't know what you're talking about. I have work."

Before she could shut the door, Rachael moved in enough to block it. "Ms. Bennett," she began, and recited several names from the list, ending with the five murdered women.

"I don't know any of those people. If they're clients of mine or my firm, make an appointment with my office. This is my home."

"Adrian Rizzo."

That got a reaction, just a quick flicker in the tired eyes. "If you're a reporter looking to dredge all that up, I'm not —"

"I'm not a reporter." Again, Rachael held up her identification. "I'm investigating a series of threats, and a series of deaths, all of which connect to your father."

"My father's been dead for over twenty years. Now, if you don't leave, I'm calling the police."

"That's fine. If you don't speak with me, that's where I'm going. To the authorities. I can come in, you can answer some questions. We'll clear this up. Or you'll talk to the cops."

"You're not coming into my house." But Nikki stepped out, crossed her arms in front of the open door. "I was a child when my father died. My brother and I were children."

"So was Adrian Rizzo. Younger, in fact, than either of you."

"None of that had or has anything to do with me. But we paid for it anyway. We lost our father. We lived with the scandal, the press, the questions. We paid. My mother finally broke and killed herself over it. We paid, and it's done."

"Someone doesn't think so. Five of the names I gave you, five of those women, are dead, through violence. Murdered. All of the names I listed, and more, had affairs with your father."

Nikki's eyes shifted now, right, left, back. Nerves lived in them.

"It has nothing to do with me."

"You don't find that curious?"

"People die. My father did. My mother did."

"Murdered, Nikki, those names on a list your mother compiled."

"You're a liar." Heat rose now. "My mother knew nothing about it. She didn't know about the other women. She didn't have any list."

"She took that list to the reporter who broke the story the day before your father attacked Lina and Adrian Rizzo and Mimi Krentz."

"That's a lie." But the flicker came back.

"I have no reason to lie. You travel a great deal."

"So what? It's none of your business." Her voice pitched up. "It's my job. I've built a career, I've built a life. I'm not going to have you come around here and try to ruin it over something my father did when I was a child."

"Do you write poetry, Nikki?"

"I've had enough of this, and you."

538

"For the past thirteen years, right after your mother died, Adrian Rizzo has received an anonymous, threatening poem. The postmarks vary, as they would with someone who travels. Your father taught poetry, among other things."

"I don't write poetry. I don't send anonymous threats." But her breathing began to quicken, thicken. "My father's dead because he thought he could cheat on my mother with impunity. He's dead because he got drunk and violent. He's dead because he got one of his whores pregnant and fathered a bastard and wouldn't own up to it like a man."

"And that hurt you. It hurt you, and when your mother killed herself, it hurt all over again. More. All those women caused your mother pain, so much pain. And that child he fathered, a living reminder of the pain. You paid, you said. Do you think they need to pay?"

"They can all rot in hell as far as I'm concerned. I don't give them a thought. They're nothing to me."

"The last poem came from Omaha. Did you swing through Omaha on your recent trip, Nikki?"

"No. But it's none of your business. Get off my property or I'll have you charged with trespassing and harassment."

"Where's your brother, Nikki?"

"I don't know. I don't care. Go to hell!"

She stepped back inside, slammed the door.

Rachael took one of the cards out of her case, slid it under the door. You just never knew.

One thing she did know, she corrected as she walked back to her car.

Nikki Bennett was a liar, and not a very good one.

On the other side of the door, Nikki began to shake. Primarily from anger. She wouldn't, she would not let any part of her life upend again because of people she didn't care about, because of what her drunken cheat of a father had done when she'd been a teenager, for God's sake.

And she didn't believe for one minute her mother had known about all those sluts her father screwed around with.

Except she did. Except she did, she admitted, and covered her face with her hands.

All those years, just more lies.

Lies and betrayals and booze and pills. Her whole life, built on lies.

No, no, no, not her life. She'd built her own damn life. The hell with the rest of them.

When she dropped her hands, her eyes widened with shock as her brother strolled down the elegant curve of the steps.

"Hi, Sis. You got a sad?"

"JJ." She barely recognized him with the unkempt beard, the hair halfway to his shoulders. In the scarred cowboy boots and

540

gun belt he looked like a blur of redneck and apostle with the shadow of their father underneath. "What are you doing here? How did you get in?"

"Well, I'll tell you," he said. And plowed a fist into her face.

Rachael stopped at a Sheetz to top off her tank, grab a cold drink, and once again empty her bladder. She sat in her car to contact Adrian.

"Rachael here. I wanted to let you know I've just spoken with Nikki Bennett."

"What did she say?"

"She claims she doesn't know what I'm talking about, doesn't know any of the women from the list I mentioned. Lots of denial, lots of outrage. And some lies sprinkled through. Whether or not she's directly responsible for the threats to you, for the murders, she knows something."

"What's next?"

"What I'd like is to get my hands on her travel data over the past few years. See if I can put her anywhere near the murders. That adds a lot of weight to the pile."

"Can you do that?"

"I'm private so I can't tap-dance my way to a warrant there. I'm not confident I could get one if I was still on the job." She checked the time. "I have to get home now. I've got a family thing in a couple of hours, but with your permission, I'd like to lay out what I have for my uncle. He is still on the job."

"Whatever you think can help. Whatever."

"Then I'll pick his brain on it. I still have friends and contacts on the force. My uncle has plenty. I'll tell you my instincts say she's connected, and she's shaken. I'll write all this up for you, give you my observations and my impressions."

"I looked her up on her company's website. I wasn't going to, but I just needed to see her. She looks so . . ."

"Ordinary?" Rachael supplied.

"Yes. Just a pleasant-looking professional woman. I couldn't find any photos of her brother, except a few from rehashes of the Georgetown story, and those were when he was a kid. He just looked like a kid dressed up for picture day at school."

"He's not a kid anymore. Neither of them is. If either or both of them are behind this, I'm going to find out."

Because something about her put me off, Rachael thought. Something about her pinged on the radar.

"I'm glad you're on my side."

"You can count on that. Let me brainstorm some with my uncle. I'll get back to you."

Something was going to break, Rachael told herself as she pulled out of the lot. She'd seen, and she felt, waves of anger, fear, guilt

542

from Nikki.
And those waves were going to break.

CHAPTER TWENTY-SIX

Everything hurt. She couldn't think through the pain, and her body shook from the shock.

Terrible dream, Nikki thought. Wake up. Wake up.

As she pushed through the ragged, tearing layers, she tasted blood in her mouth.

Could you taste anything in a dream?

But it was copper, and nasty, made her want to cough and spit. But her face, oh God, her face throbbed and banged. Her head pounded, inside and out, as she struggled to open her eyes and come awake.

She found herself on the floor, lying on the cold tile, and the light too bright. It made her eyes ache and tear.

She tried to sit up, to push herself up, but her right arm was stuck. With her vision still blurry, doubling, she stared at the cuff around her wrist.

Frightened, she saw the chain welded to the cuff, the chain welded to a thick bolt scarring the tile wall.

544

The powder room under the stairs, her pretty powder room where she kept pretty guest towels for guests who never came.

In a panic, she tried to yank her arm free, but the cuff only cut into her wrist and gave her more pain.

So she screamed, despite the explosion it caused in her head, she screamed.

She heard the footsteps, tried to cower back. Because she remembered now. Dear God, she remembered.

JJ walked to the door. He carried one of her file boxes, which he set on the floor.

He crouched, grinned at her. "Woo, might've broken that snooty nose of yours, Nik. You're sure going to have a pair of shiners."

"You hit me. You hit me."

"Not as hard as I could've. You should thank me."

"What are you doing? What are you doing?"

He smiled at her, just the way she remembered. Lips spread wide, eyes cold as winter.

"Not killing you. You can thank me later. If you'd let that nosy bitch in here, I would've done you both. But you stood up, Nik, so we'll do it this way."

"What have you done, JJ?"

He wagged a finger in the air. "You know. If you didn't before, you know now. Just like you know you can scream till your lungs bleed and nobody's going to hear you. Inside room, Sis. Nice thick plaster walls, no window. So."

He rooted in the box, took out a bottle of Advil, a bottle of water. He shoved them both toward her. "I'd take four if I were you."

"You killed those women. The ones the detective talked about."

"They deserved it. They all do, and I'll get to them all. I've been taking my time there, but I see I have to move things along. Damn lucky break I was here when that bitch came by to grill you. I was just going to hit you up for some more money, a nice hot shower, a couple good meals. Got a big bonus out of it."

"Why? Why? Why?" Her swollen eyes began to leak again. "He cheated, he —"

"You shut the fuck up about him! They spread their legs for him, didn't they?" He pounded a fist on the little vanity. "How many times do I have to tell you they're to blame for it? A man takes what's offered, it's his nature. They're the reason he's dead, why we grew up shamed. They've got no place on this earth, and you should know that! Especially that whelp her whore of a mother didn't kill in the womb. She murdered our father. She's the reason."

She'd heard it all before, countless times, and knew there would be no reasoning with him. Especially since a part of her, a terrible part that shamed her, agreed with him.

With trembling hands she opened the bottle of water, the bottle of pills. She had to ease the pain and think.

"You've been sending her poems? The Rizzo girl?"

"I always had a knack for them, didn't I? Dad always said so. Mom, too, but Dad knew that shit. He was proud of me. More of me than you."

He sat on the floor in the doorway, looked over her head. "He loved me. Mom, she ragged on me more than half the time, but he loved me. 'Get off his back,' he'd tell her. 'The boy's got spunk. Boys will be boys,' he'd say."

He would, Nikki thought, he'd say those things even when they found out JJ stole something from a store, or started a fight, or snuck out at night.

"She was just trying to keep you out of trouble."

"She was weak. 'Pop another pill, Catherine.' He'd say that, too, when she started up the nagging. And she didn't give him what he needed or he wouldn't have gotten it from the whores and sluts, would he?"

"I know she was weak," Nikki said carefully. "She took pills. And I took care of you, JJ. I tried to take care of you, you know that. I made sure you had something to eat after nobody'd work for us anymore. I helped you with your homework, and washed your

547

clothes."

"Expected me to toe the line. Expected me to scrub floors and wash dishes."

"I couldn't do it all by myself." She tried to smile at him, but God, it hurt. "I needed your help."

"Went off to college, didn't you? Left me."

"I lived at home, but I had to get a degree. I had to get a good job."

"Liar. We had plenty of money."

"We had the family money." Again, she thought, go over it all again, stay calm. "But Mom wasn't stable, JJ. You know she wasn't, and she had control of the money."

You weren't stable either, she thought. I knew it. I always knew.

I did my best! It's not my fault.

She had to draw careful breaths as the words pushed up, wanted to spill out.

"I lived at home right through college. I lived at home when I got a job. I wanted you to go to college, JJ. To get away, start your life, but —"

"School's for suckers. You went off traveling around in your business suits."

"I took you with me whenever I could. Especially after Mom died."

"Before, plenty of times you left me with her, left me to clean up her messes, to hide the pills, to listen to her bitching. You weren't here to listen to her bitching, to hear her going off on Dad when she had one of her raves.

548

You weren't here when she laughed and laughed and said how she was glad he was dead. How she was glad she helped tell the world what a cheating bastard he was. How she'd laugh and laugh, and cry and cry."

She hadn't dated, Nikki thought. Hadn't gone to clubs, to the movies. It had been school and home, then work and home.

The traveling? She often thought the travel demands of her job had saved her sanity.

But she had to keep him calm, had to convince him to let her go.

"I'm sorry, JJ. I'm sorry I wasn't here all the time, but —"

"You weren't here when she told me she knew all along, she had a whole list of women he'd fucked around with. How I could stop worshipping at his dead feet if I wanted to be a real man. She kept that list, too. And she dug it out and tossed it at me. Said if he'd loved me so much, he'd have kept his vows. She said terrible things, kept saying them. I could've strangled her then and there.

"But I didn't."

She felt the cold, deep in her belly. More than fear now. "What did you do?"

"Gave her what she wanted. Pills. And more pills. Helped her upstairs and into bed, and gave her more pills. Then I watched her die, and went out and had myself a couple beers."

"She was our mother."

"She was a pill-popping bitch who killed

549

our father. Killed him just as much as the rest of them. And you came home, found her, called nine-one-one, called me while I was having those beers. Crying for her, crying like she hadn't been a chain around our necks for years."

He smiled again. "And we got the money, didn't we?"

He reached into the box, took out a package of Frosted Mini-Wheats, and began to snack. "I went traveling with you because I wanted to see some of the country, see if I saw a place that looked like mine. And you nagging me brainless about college or trade school or getting a good job. I was good with my hands, you'd say, and you had that much right. I used them to get myself in and out of houses, take what I wanted if I wanted. But I kept thinking about that list."

He popped cereal into his mouth. "Sure, stealing was fun, but it didn't have real purpose. A man's got to have real purpose in his life. I thought about killing those who killed my father. And what do I see one day on the TV when I'm bored shitless and you're off trying to make people do what you want them to do? I see that little bitch on some fucking talk show talking herself up. Talking about a new generation. And that bullshit.

"So I sat down and wrote her a poem. *Fuck you, you should be dead. And I'm going to kill you one day.* But poetically." That struck him

550

as funny, so he laughed and laughed.

Too much like their mother, Nikki thought.

"I wanted to kill her right off, but I knew something that sweet needs to wait. Not just a dish best served cold, but one you can heat up again when it's going to be the most tasty. So I killed one of the others. Felt so good. That held me awhile. And I liked writing the poems. One a year at first. I figure she'll get to know it's coming and that'll keep her scared."

"JJ, please listen to me."

He wasn't listening, he wasn't hearing her. He only heard his own thoughts.

"But she just kept on making those goddamn DVDs, kept doing whatever she pleased. Anyway." He closed the cereal box again. "Not for much longer."

"JJ, you need to let me go."

He gave her that smile again, the one that curdled her blood.

"After I went to the trouble of putting that bolt in the wall? And I was going to use this on her when I was ready. Figured we'd have a nice, long conversation before I beat her to death. That's how I want to end her."

"JJ, you know I won't tell anyone any of this. I've always looked out for you."

"Looked out for me when it suited you."

"That's not true, now, you know it's not. I'm afraid for you. You have to stop or you'll get caught. It's not your fault, but you have to stop. They don't know where you are, so you can go back, just say enough. I'd never tell them how to find you. You're the only family I've got left."

"Family, my ass." He sneered at the word, and his eyes went bright.

Too bright.

"Then again, if you weren't family, I'd've just killed you. Instead I've got you in here. You got a toilet, a sink so you can get water. I got food in this box."

He tapped it, then shoved it across to her.

"And don't worry about the office. I texted them from your phone. Said you had a family emergency out of town, and you'd need to take your two-week vacation. Oh yeah, texted your cleaning service. They won't come in for the next few weeks."

Her breath started coming too fast, short and fast.

"Please, please, please, don't leave me chained up like this. My vision's blurry, JJ, and I'm queasy. I could have a concussion."

"You'll live." He pushed up. "I'm going to get that nice hot shower now. I've been on the road awhile. Then I'm taking what I want, as what's in this house is as much mine as yours. Since I left the truck I stole in Kansas in a dicey neighborhood, I imagine it's stripped clean by now. So I'll be using your car."

"Don't do this. Don't. I'm your sister."

552

"You can reach the sink, the toilet. I'll be back when I'm finished in this part of the world."

"JJ, please. Don't leave me like this."

He just closed the door behind him.

She had to slap a hand over her mouth to hold back the scream. He might come back, hit her again. Or worse.

And he would do worse eventually, she knew that now. Because she'd seen, she'd accepted what she'd always known.

Neither of their parents had been stable.

And her brother was insane.

For a while she wept, and tried to chase away the voices in her head telling her she'd known, she'd always known her brother wasn't right.

She hadn't known he'd killed their mother — she hadn't. But she'd wondered. His voice on the phone when she'd called to tell him, so cool and easy. And his eyes when he came home, pretending to care, so empty.

But she hadn't known. And it wasn't her fault.

If her mother had ranted and raved to her sometimes, about how faithless men were, how never to trust one, she hadn't known for certain. If her mother had thrown out a number, had even spewed out names, she hadn't known her mother had talked to a reporter. She hadn't known. So it wasn't her fault.

She shouldn't have to pay. She shouldn't be hurt. She shouldn't have to be afraid.

She'd done her best. She'd worked hard to solve other people's problems.

She'd covered for JJ countless times, and this is what he did to her.

She wept and wept, bitter, self-pitying tears, until the sobbing, the ringing in her ears had her heaving in the toilet.

Exhausted, she dozed, then shot awake again when she heard the front door slam.

Giving in to hysteria, she dragged at the chain until her wrist bled. She screamed until she had no voice.

No one heard. No one came.

Routinely, when JJ killed, he spent weeks, sometimes months, learning about his prey, observing her, recording her habits, analyzing her weak points.

It was, for him, a highlight of the process.

He considered himself an intellectual. After all, look at his father. A professor in one of the nation's most prestigious universities. He himself hadn't wanted or needed all those years in classrooms.

Boring!

All those rules, all that structure would have stifled his innate intellect rather than enhanced it.

Hadn't he learned, almost entirely on his own, how to pick locks, subvert alarm systems, steal cars? And most important of all, how to disappear in plain sight.

He knew how to blend, how to become part of the landscape.

Which meant, he considered as he drove — at precisely three miles an hour over the speed limit — he needed a shave, a haircut.

He'd lived the life of a solitary prepper in the wilds of Wyoming for the past couple years. Keeping to himself, making no waves. Just a hard-bitten, flag-waving (when appropriate) survivalist who lived alone on his scrub of land, whose visits to the bumfuck town for supplies were few and far between and unremarkable.

He made no friends, made no enemies.

Whenever he took one of his extended trips for what he considered his mission in life, nobody noticed or cared.

He blended wherever he needed to be. A hipster here, a businessman there, maybe just a traveling man wandering on the road of life.

He knew how to look harmless. A white man of average height and weight with no distinguishing marks.

He had two sets of fraudulent identification at all times. After paying the exorbitant fee for them when he'd first gone off the grid, he learned to make them himself.

He kept them, and his cash, in a fireproof steel case under the floorboards of his cabin.

Along with them he kept the photographs

of each woman he'd killed. Those taken during the stalking phase — using a long lens — those he'd printed out from any social media or media articles.

After he'd killed the wrong woman in Foggy Bottom, he'd taken a photograph after death to make sure never to make that mistake again.

You lived and you learned.

He'd often considered going back to rectify that mistake, but the mistake itself rubbed him wrong.

He had his identification for this trip, the driver's licenses, a Visa card, a voter registration, his gun permits. He didn't expect to get stopped, but accidents happened because people were idiots. His problem here, of course, was driving his sister's car. Or it would've been a problem if he hadn't spent the time and effort to make a fake registration that should pass any casual cop stop.

Bases covered, he thought, adjustments made.

He'd intended to head north and west from DC, spend a little time camping near Traveler's Creek.

Since he'd spent years observing Adrian Rizzo, he'd calculated a week, tops, before he ended her.

The bitch had challenged him. She'd done that stupid, arrogant, bullshit video to mock him, and that couldn't stand.

He'd planned to wait until August, those lazy dog days, to take her out, but he'd moved up the timeline.

A good thing, and luck was obviously in his pocket. If he hadn't come early, if he hadn't been right in the house when his idiot sister opened the door to that asshole cunt, he wouldn't have known anyone had started piecing things together. He wouldn't have known anyone might be looking for him.

He couldn't figure out how they had, and that troubled him.

He'd been smart; he'd been careful.

Had to have come from the reporter, but why go there after all these years? He'd have to ask the son of a bitch before he killed him. But right now, he needed a boost.

The detective — probably a dyke — had said the names on the list. And one was a reporter, not so far away, so she'd stand in for the asshole in Pittsburgh for now.

He hadn't done more than basic research on Tracie Potter, but he knew enough, and would find out more.

So he headed down to Richmond. He'd get himself a cheap motel room for a day or two. Three, tops. One if that luck in his pocket held.

But one day or three, she'd be dead before he left Richmond.

And since the dyke had left her fucking calling card, he'd pay her a call, too, on his way

557

to Traveler's Creek.

He'd take his time with Adrian. Oh yeah, he'd waited years to take his time with the bitch who'd killed his father, ruined his life.

And when he'd finished beating her to death — the only just method — he'd head back to DC. By then, he figured he'd have decided on what to do with Nikki.

Let her go or shoot her in the head.

He figured the second option had more weight because God knew you couldn't trust a woman.

When the idea sank in that he'd kill four women — including the slut who'd started it — inside a couple weeks, he felt happier than he had in months.

New record! High score!

If he tracked down Browne in Pittsburgh, he'd cap the streak off there — five for five! — before he headed back to Wyoming.

And decided what, or who, came next.

Adrian sat on her porch on a perfect summer evening going over Kayla's links for furniture and decor choices on her tablet. She had a glass of wine, a bowl of tart green grapes, and her dog snoozing at her feet.

Close to perfect in her estimation, she thought a moment before Sadie's head lifted with a woof.

Then she saw Raylan's car coming up the hill, and decided: Perfection reached.

Apparently Sadie agreed, as her tail began to thump.

She watched Raylan get out, Jasper leap out.

"Where are the rest of you?"

"Bradley's getting a guitar lesson. Mariah's having a birthday party sleepover with her second best friend. Her first best among six others are also attending. I pray to the gods of sanity for the parents."

He came up on the porch while Sadie and Jasper licked faces.

"Jasper wanted to see his girl. I wanted to see mine. And give her this."

He put the graphic novel on the table. "Hot, so to speak, off the press."

"Oh God, it's the real deal. It's gorgeous!" She grabbed it up, trailing a finger over the cover image of Cobalt Flame, spear in hand, riding her dragon. "I love, love it." She flipped through. "Oh, the art, Raylan, it's fantastic. I'm going to devour every page all over again."

She lifted her head, pulled his down for a kiss.

"We're pretty damn proud of it, and preorders are zooming."

"Let me get you a glass of wine and we'll toast."

"Make it a Coke, and I'll get it. I've only got about a half hour. Bradley and I are having a guys' night in later. I'm picking up pizza. Then there's popcorn and an *X-Men*

559

movie marathon."

"I'm so glad you came by first. I'll be spending my girls' night in reading Cobalt Flame's debut novel."

"You want me to top off your wine while I'm in there?"

"No, I'm good."

Even as he went in, she opened to the first page, read the credits.

When he came back out, she stared at him. "You put my name in the credits. 'Adrian Rizzo, the inspiration.' You didn't tell me you were doing that. It wasn't in the mock-up. I'm so . . . honored. I mean really honored."

"It wouldn't be if it wasn't for you." He sat, stretched out his legs. "I think it's some of our best work, I really do, and it spring-boarded the *Front Guard*."

"How's that going?"

"Some bumps, a couple turns, and solid progress. And how are you?"

"All good. I was going over more options for the youth center. It's looking so good, Raylan. They're working on the grounds now, the court, the playground. And I've got my concept well in hand for the new streaming program for fall. So, all good."

He put a hand over hers. "All?"

She blew out air. "Well, Rachael finally had that face-to-face with Nikki Bennett, and doesn't think she was altogether truthful. She wants to talk to her uncle, he's a cop, get his take on what to do next. If there's enough, I don't know, to officially question her or search the house, or whatever the hell they'd do."

She hesitated a moment. "It — all this part? It feels like it's not connected to me somehow. I know better, but that's how it feels. I don't know her. I don't know her brother. And I was sitting out here on this really nice evening after a really productive day, and it doesn't feel connected to me."

"It shouldn't be."

"But it is. I know."

"You were sitting here where anybody could drive up that hill."

"I can't stay locked in the house. Don't push on that. I've got my mother pushing for me to go to New York and lock myself up in her apartment. I won't, so she's coming here. I've got Teesha or Maya or Monroe or Jan dropping by pretty much every day. Add you."

"We love you. I love you."

"Raylan."

He tightened his grip on her hand. "I never thought I could or would fall in love again. But I did."

"You took off your wedding ring," she told him.

"Yeah, I did. If it was just sex, I'd still be wearing it. But you know that."

"The thing is . . ." She didn't know quite how to say what she felt, or meant. "I haven't

561

had — I've deliberately and carefully avoided having a serious relationship. So I haven't had any."

"You're having one now. You know that, too."

"I don't know if I'm any good at it."

"You're doing fine so far."

"It's early days yet, isn't it?" she pointed out. "And you aren't seeing my flaws."

"I see them."

Now she shook back her hair and eyed him. "Oh really?"

"Sure. You're impulsive, especially when you're pissed or upset. So, the in-your-face video you did, on angry impulse, directed at your asshole poet. You're scarily goal-oriented. You're pushy under the guise of *Let me help you out*. Like, *Hey, here's a little workout guide just for you, and I'm tossing in this equipment.* And you're stubborn about handling things yourself. I figure that comes from your mom overregulating you, and you breaking that hold — impulsive snap — the minute you could. Can't blame you."

Coolly, she sipped her wine. "Some people might view those as positive traits."

"Some might." He shrugged that off. "Like some people might view my obsessive scheduling as, you know, obsessive. Or my tendency to still run late after obsessive scheduling as careless. Some people might think that talk-

562

ing to my dead wife about taking off my wedding ring equals crazy."

Adrian let out a sigh. "As an obsessive scheduler, I don't find that a flaw. And I've never known you to be careless. It's absolutely not crazy for you to talk to Lorilee. Still . . .

"I don't know if I'm good at maintaining a real relationship. If I'm good at doing the work, and I know it takes work."

"Teamwork. Individual work on both sides," he added. "And a lot of teamwork."

He had those eyes, she thought, and that heart.

"I know I've never felt about anyone the way I feel about you. Just like I know I have a deep, unshakable need to be really good at what I do, and refuse to see that as a flaw. And I know you had someone who was really, really good at what we're talking about here. Probably perfect. That's intimidating."

"She was really good at what we're talking about here. But cliché time: Nobody's perfect."

He took a moment, drank some Coke. "It's hard for me to tell you this about her."

Sincerely appalled, Adrian threw up both hands. "No, don't. Raylan, I'm not asking you to compare, to somehow smooth out my self-doubts."

"I think you need to hear it. It'll help you understand there are things, however harsh, you learn to deal with in a relationship, you learn to tolerate, even come to understand, in someone you love. Lorilee —"

He broke off, shook his head. "I'm just going to say it, get it done. In all the years we were together, no matter how many times we talked about it, she still — God, she still got *Star Wars* and *Star Trek* confused."

For a second, Adrian could only stare. She felt the laugh bubble up into her throat. Swallowed it down again. "My God, Raylan, that's . . . I don't know how you lived with that."

"I loved her. She tried to make up for it in countless ways, but . . . She actually called Spock 'Dr. Spock.' Every single time. I think it got to be deliberate, just to torture me."

"No!" Holding up a hand, Adrian turned her head away. "I don't know if I can hear any more."

"Once, I brought home a toy lightsaber for Brad, and she thought it was so cute I'd gotten him something from *Star Trek.* Or, say a group of us were having a discussion on the history and capabilities of the *Millennium Falcon,* and she'd ask if that was Captain Kirk's spaceship. It was humiliating."

"Don't say any more. You've said enough."

"I could go on, but I won't. My point is, love outweighs flaws. I loved her. I love you. I figure that makes me a lucky guy."

"This isn't a conversation I expected to have sitting on the porch tonight."

"I'll have to drop over between guitar lessons and pizza more often." He glanced at his watch, popped right up. "Shit, shit, shit, I'm going to be late getting home. See, I knew exactly how much time I had, worked it out, and I'm still going to be late getting Bradley from Monroe."

He leaned down, kissed her, and she snagged his hand.

"If I tell you I love you back, are you going to be even later?"

He paused, took her face in his hands. "I've got to go, but tell me anyway."

"I love you back."

Eyes open and on hers, he kissed her again. "I knew that, but it's really good hearing you say it."

"There's another flaw. Your smartass flaw."

"Still gotta go. Jasper! We're going. Damn it, why didn't I order the pizza while we were sitting here? Now, Jasper!"

"What do you want?" she called out as he jogged to the car. "I'll call it in for you."

"Large, pepperoni and Italian sausage. No judgment cracks on the meat. We're men. In the car, Jasper." He had to give the reluctant dog a boost in.

He paused again. "I promised the kids I'd take them to the carnival at the fairgrounds day after tomorrow. Come with us."

"I like carnivals."

"We're going to eat funnel cake and peanut

oil fries and sliders, so deal with it."

She sat back as he got in the car. She would, she thought as she picked up her phone to call in his order — with the addition of a summer salad for two. She'd deal with it, because that's what you did when you loved.

CHAPTER TWENTY-SEVEN

After her conversation with her uncle, Rachael decided to take what she had to the DC police. Not enough for a warrant, not quite enough even to pressure Nikki to come in for questioning, she knew, but she appealed to a detective she knew to go to the house.

A police badge carried more weight than a PI license.

The detective, one she'd worked with years before, took her file, agreed something smelled off.

It wouldn't be top priority, and she had to accept that, but he and his partner would get to it.

Especially since she pressed on the fact that she had another conversation scheduled with the FBI agent heading Adrian's case.

Nothing like a little competition with the feds to get the ball rolling.

So Nikki could expect, over the next day or two, visits from the local LEOs and the FBI.

Shake the tree, she thought. And something would fall out.

After her meetings, she drove back — through horrendous traffic — to her office to write up her report. She dashed through pounding rain to the building that held her offices, the offices of a small legal firm (which often kicked work her way), and a photography studio.

She took the stairs to the second floor, walked through the frosted glass door into her reception area. Three chairs with padded leather seats and backs sat against both side walls, a narrow alcove provided a space for hanging coats. A snake plant as tall as she was speared out of a bright blue pot by the double window. Her receptionist kept it thriving.

Her business subscribed to a handful of magazines, including *Forbes* and *Vanity Fair*. Rachael had personally selected the trio of pencil sketches by a local artist framed on the café au lait–colored walls.

A high-class reception area, her marketing genius husband told her, brought in high-class clients.

In the years since she'd opened the doors to McNee Investigations, he'd proved mostly right.

"Traffic." Rachael rolled her eyes as she hung her umbrella in the alcove. "Unspeakable. It's pouring out there."

"Moving south, they say, but slow. Rush hour's going to be horrible."

"Great. Something to look forward to."

On the way to her office, she had short update conversations with her two colleagues, hit the tiny break area for coffee. After another longer conversation — with wedding plans sprinkled in — with her office manager, she sat down in her office.

Then sat back, sipped coffee, closed her eyes to let the tension of battling DC traffic in a summer deluge wash away.

The rain also meant her husband's softball game would be canceled, so she — or he — would have to think about dinner. Order in, she decided. They'd both be fine with that, especially since they'd both deal with the traffic to get home.

And if neither of them had to bring work home, they could open a nice bottle of wine, have a leisurely family meal neither had to cook. Maybe even work in some sex before they conked out.

Which meant, if she wanted all that to happen, she'd better finish up work.

She wrote the report, attached it in an email to Lina, as that's how her paying client preferred it.

She sent her office manager her hours for billing said paying client.

Before she reached for the phone to contact Adrian for an update — as both of them

569

preferred — the phone rang.

"McNee Investigations, Rachael McNee."

"Ms. McNee, it's Tracie Potter."

"What can I do for you?"

"It may be what I can do for you. I've been doing a little research — and yes, you suggested I shouldn't do so, but it's what I do. In any case, in doing so, it jogged some memories. One being I remembered overhearing a phone conversation Jon had with his wife. And yes, I was eavesdropping."

"So would I under the circumstances." Or any, Rachael admitted. Nosy was in the DNA of an investigator.

"I recall him being very dismissive of her. Something about the kids, or one of them. How no, he couldn't drop everything and come home. He had work to finish. How she should just handle it. Then I remember him snapping at her. 'If you can't deal with it, just take another pill. I'll be home when I'm home.' Or something of the sort."

"All right."

"I admit, I was amused. I stood in the bedroom doorway of the little apartment he kept for his trysts. Said something like, 'Trouble at home,' or 'Trouble in paradise?' I remember his response, as it was fully my intention at the time: 'Never get married, and if you do, don't have any goddamn kids.'"

Tracie let out a little laugh. "That's nineteen for you. In any case, he went on a short rant, which surprised me because he never talked about his family. I never talked about them. But we'd both had a couple of drinks."

"Do you remember what he said?"

"I remember the gist. He said his wife had wanted the brats in the first place, and he should've made her get rid of them before they were born. And now, even though she had someone come in to clean, to cook, she couldn't handle them."

Tracie paused a moment. "I wasn't interested in his family issues, but I remember wondering how he could afford all that household help on his salary. I didn't know it was her money at the time, and it struck me. Mostly the conversation bored me, so I said something like, 'Why don't you come to bed and handle me?' And that was that."

"Interesting."

"I think so. It occurs to me Lina Rizzo might not have been the only bed partner he got pregnant, as he resisted suiting up."

She'd already thought of that possibility herself, and had pursued that area of inquiry before.

"I assume this wouldn't apply to you."

"No. Then again, our affair was brief. I was on birth control, and I insisted he use a condom. He didn't want to, complained and resisted, but that was a deal breaker for me. Maybe my impression's colored some, but it struck me he had nothing but contempt for

571

his wife, and considered his children a burden. And that leads me to a second, somewhat vague memory."

"Go ahead."

"I honestly didn't recognize any names on the list you showed me, but college was a long time ago. But this memory made me think of this girl in the Shakespeare Club — Jon ran that. I stayed in it because, whatever else he was, Jon was an exceptional teacher, and his insights on Shakespeare were brilliant. I couldn't remember her name even when I thought of her. I do know she was new — a freshman — and I think I was a junior or senior at that point."

"You think she and Jon had an affair."

"Jon had a type, I think. He liked them young, bright, attractive, and with good bodies. She had all that. On the shy side, but she bloomed in that club. And since I'd once had a fling with him, I recognized the signs."

"What about her stands out to you now?"

"She stopped coming abruptly and, as I said, she bloomed there. I figured the affair had gone south, and she was heartbroken or embarrassed. I said something to a friend who happened to live in the same dorm. Catty, I admit. That's when I heard the story.

"The girl — and I refreshed with my old college friend who remembered her first name. Jessica. Jessica came home to the dorm one night, beaten up. Now this is thirdhand, as while in the same dorm, my friend wasn't even on the same floor. But she heard Jessica staggered into the dorm with bruises all over her face, an eye swollen shut, and more, with her pants soaked with blood. A miscarriage."

Rachael circled the name Jessica on the notes she took, underlined *miscarriage.* "Police report? Medical records?"

"The word was she claimed she'd been mugged, couldn't identify the attacker. Wouldn't, anyway. She refused to let her dorm mates call an ambulance or the police, which of course they should've done anyway. She dropped out, according to my friend."

"I'd like your friend's name and contact information."

"I asked, and she'd rather I didn't give that out — unless it becomes clearly relevant."

"It's part of the whole, Ms. Potter."

"I agree, but a source is a source. I'll press her on it, but for now, I can't give you that information. And I can't tell you where this Jessica lived back then or even her last name. However, I want to say I'm sure, but in fact can only say I'm about seventy percent sure, that this was the same time Jon came into class with his right hand bandaged. He made a joke about English professors never attempting home repairs. We all laughed, and that was that."

"This is very helpful."

"Is there a Jessica on the list?"

"Two, in fact. A fairly common name. Do you remember what she looked like?"

"Ah . . . A brunette, and my image is of young, fresh, pretty. Slim but curvy. But that's it. I wouldn't recognize her if I saw her, I'm sorry. We interacted in the club, but that was once a week for a few months."

"Do you remember when this happened?"

"I'm nearly sure it was in my junior year, and after the winter break. I know it was cold, and I'd moved into a group house off campus. Wait, yes, now that I'm pinning it, I'm positive it was early January. The first or possibly the second club meeting after the winter break. I think the first."

Nodding to herself, Rachael wrote down the probable year, circled that. "Okay."

"I'd like to know if and when you locate her. I could've warned her, but I didn't. She may not have listened, but I could've told her what he was.

"I have to get into makeup. I have some promos to do before *News at Five.*"

"If you remember anything else, I'd like to hear it. Thanks for passing on this information."

Rachael sat back, considered.

She'd managed to track down both Jessicas on the list. One, who predated Lina with her relationship with Bennett, lived in London. Born and raised in England, and Tracie would certainly have remembered an accent.

Plus, an earlier liaison.

But the second Jessica hit the right age. She'd vehemently denied having any sexual relationship with Bennett, which even in the brief phone conversation came off as an angry lie.

Rachael pulled up her notes. Yes, Jessica Kingsley, née Peters, married to Robert Kingsley — pastor of the Church of the Savior — for twenty-four years, mother of four, who lived in her hometown of Eldora, Iowa.

First time away from home, Rachael mused, shy and excited. Falls for charming professor. Goes home for winter break and finds out she's pregnant. Tells Bennett, who reacts as he did with Lina Rizzo, but this one can't defend herself. Shamed and shocked, she manages to get back to her dorm as she miscarries. Makes up a story, goes home.

Probably blames herself, hides the incident, buries it.

Does she tell her future husband before the wedding, or tell him ever? Unlikely. She'd fear she wouldn't be forgiven. Instead, she made her life in her little town and kept it buried.

"I could've warned her," Tracie'd said. And though Rachael had, or had tried, she knew she had to try again.

She got a bottle of water from her mini-fridge, walked around her office chugging it as she considered her approach.

If she didn't try, and something happened to Jessica Kingsley, she'd have to live with it. She didn't want to live with it.

She closed her office door — a signal not to disturb — then sat and pulled the phone number from her file.

The woman answered, obviously distracted. "Hang on a minute. I'm getting a pie out of the oven."

Rachael heard rattling, humming, footsteps. "Sorry. Hello."

"Ms. Kingsley, this is Rachael McNee. We spoke a few weeks ago."

"I told you this doesn't involve me, and not to call me again."

"Please don't hang up. You don't have to say anything. I'm just asking you to listen for a minute. Whatever happened or didn't at Georgetown, your name is on a list. What I didn't know when we spoke before, but have confirmed now, is five women on that same list are dead. Were murdered. I need you to be aware of that, aware there may be more I haven't yet found. The police and the FBI are investigating, and you may be contacted. I couldn't, in good conscience, withhold this information from you, and am only advising you to take precautions."

"Why should I believe you?"

"Why would I lie?"

"For all I know you're some reporter, trying to spread fake news like all the rest of them."

Rachael just closed her eyes. "You can google my name, the name of my agency. I simply want you to be aware someone is killing women who went to Georgetown University, whose names are on a list. As yours is."

"Fine. You've told me. Now leave me alone."

Rachael only shook her head when the phone slammed in her ear. Apparently Jessica hadn't just buried the incident, she'd put it in a concrete bunker, filled it with denial, then sunk it in the ocean's depths.

"Did my best," she mused.

She had an hour before she had to fight her way home because maybe the rain would move south, but it didn't seem to be in any hurry. She'd spend it working on finding one more name on the list.

Just one more tonight.

It took nearly two hours, which meant her fight home would be a brutal battle, but she found two.

One alive — a professor herself at Boston College who not only admitted to the affair, but took Rachael seriously.

And one dead, a lawyer who'd been stabbed repeatedly in the parking lot of a supermarket a few miles from her home in Oregon.

Since her purse, her watch weren't found, and her car located more than a week later in

Northern California, the motive was ascribed to carjacking and theft.

"He took the car, so how did he get to the parking lot? He had to have followed her in another vehicle. Stolen, too? I say absolutely. But let's find out."

She glanced at her watch, cursed.

"Later." She gathered her things, shut down her computer.

And, she noted, once again left the office after everyone else.

She really had to stop that.

She grabbed her umbrella, locked up the office behind her. And called her husband to let him know she was on her way.

And to order pizza. And open a bottle of wine.

She ate with her family, drank wine, even managed to sneak in a quick — quiet — romp with her husband.

But she knew she wouldn't sleep.

She slid out of bed, shrugged into sweats, then went into her office. She could hear the TV blasting from the family room, so she shut the door.

It might have been after eleven in DC but it was barely eight in Oregon. She could get lucky and find somebody who'd care enough to check on stolen cars recovered from the parking lot where Alice McGuire — née Wendell — was killed five years before.

578

■ ■ ■

About the time Rachael used her persuasive powers on a detective with Portland PD, Tracie Potter sat in her tiny dressing room cleaning off her TV makeup, which by the end of her eleven o'clock broadcast felt like it weighed fifty pounds.

And when she slathered on moisturizer, she swore she heard her grateful skin make slurping sounds as it drank it in.

With the rain pounding, she wanted to change out of her TV-friendly suit, switch her heels for the rain boots she kept on hand for nights just like this.

She cursed herself for parking at the far end of the lot, which she did whenever she was shy of her ten thousand steps a day.

Which was, she admitted, most of the time.

Her husband would be dead asleep when she got home — and who could blame him? But she thought she might unwind with a snifter of brandy before joining him.

Her crew long gone, she called a good night to the stragglers who remained. She took the back door, let it slam securely behind her as she opened her umbrella.

Even with the security lights she could barely see two feet ahead as the rain whooshed down in sheets blown by the wind.

She blessed the boots, told herself how

smart she'd been to take the time to change into jeans as the rain splashed up on her legs.

She had the key in her hand, hit the button on the fob to unlock the doors.

The lights blinked. She didn't hear the usual thump of the locks, but the rain pounded. She half jogged the rest of the way then, closing her umbrella, all but dived into the car.

"Jesus Christ," she muttered, and reached to press the starter button.

She didn't have time to scream. The hard yank on her hair pulled her head back. The knife sliced deep across her throat.

She gurgled, eyes wheeling, arms flapping.

"Like a fish on a line." JJ snorted with laughter. He shoved her toward the passenger seat. In his disposable painter's gear — including bonnet, gloves, booties — he jumped out of the back.

He gave her — no longer gurgling — a harder shove as he took the driver's seat.

"You made a real mess of things," he told her as he started the car. "But that's okay. We're not going far."

He congratulated himself on knowing, just knowing, tonight was the night. The rain, the perfect sign, the perfect cover. He'd dump her car in the strip mall lot a few blocks away where he'd left his sister's.

Bag up the protective gear, and get rid of that somewhere along his drive to DC. A handy rest stop would do.

He glanced over at Tracie and thought: One bitch down, three to go!

Adrian often used either Maya or Teesha as guinea pigs. Today, she used Teesha to fine-tune a cardio dance segment for a project.

"Come on, Teesh, this one's supposed to be fun."

"Teething baby. Broken sleep. Nursing boobs."

"Cardio like this gives you a nice energy boost. Triple step now. Right, left, right. Use your hips! That works the core. Where's your rhythm? You're a Black girl."

"Don't you stereotype me!" But she laughed. "And my rhythm is desperate for a nap."

"Chassé, back step, right, left, right. Now the turn. Remember those happy hips."

"My ass!"

"It's definitely good for that, too."

She whipped, cajoled, snarked Teesha through it.

"This is going to work."

"I never want to see the recording."

"For my review only. I think I need to funk it up more. It may be a little too easy."

"Again, my ass."

When Teesha dropped down in a chair in the studio, Adrian got her an energy drink.

"Perk it up. I need to work on the strength yoga."

"I am not doing that."

"I have to nail it down first anyway. I want the whole program solid before my mother gets here. I've got most of a week. A short one today though. I'm going to the carnival with Raylan and his kids later."

"Carnival, with kids. You're in deep, Adrian."

"I am. He dropped over for about a half hour two days ago, and one thing led to another —"

Teesha leaned forward. "Tell all."

"Not that another. Jeez, it's sex, sex, sex with you."

"I wish. Monroe and I are down to one-point-six bangs a week."

"Point-six?"

"Coitus interruptus. We average one-point-six right now. We've vowed to increase our average to a solid two, and work up from there when Phin — thank you, Jesus — starts kindergarten at the end of August. We can grab a nap-time quickie once a week."

"Well, that's a plan."

"Spontaneous sex is overrated . . . I seem to recall. Anyway. What thing led to another thing?"

"He told me he loved me. It scared the crap out of me. I knew it was coming — I'm not stupid — but it still scared the crap out of me."

"Awww."

The *Awww* had Adrian throwing up both hands. "And I'm babbling around making excuses or reasons or putting up roadblocks, and he's so patiently determined. Determinedly patient? Both, and also quietly, firmly sure of himself. And me. And us. He pointed out my flaws."

"Well, that's romantic."

"It actually was. Because he sees them, knows them, and he's fine with them. He listed some of his own, and all I could think is, I'm fine with them. And I . . . I told him I loved him. Because I do."

"The L word was exchanged, the biggest four-letter word there is. Yay! And about time."

"About time? Teesh, we've only been together for a few months. Barely."

Teesha just waved that aside. "You've known each other forever. And you've always had a thing for him."

"No, I haven't."

Now she flipped a decisive index finger into a point. "Have, too — and don't make me sound like Phin. Way back when you told me about Maya, you talked about her older brother. And there was this spark."

"No."

"Yes. That was more than ten years ago.

583

You had a lot to say about him."

"I did?"

"His art, his green eyes."

"Oh God." She sat down, laughed at herself. "You're right. I did. I think, now that I can think about it, I fell for him the day I saw the drawings on the walls of his room. And then the way he looked at me — those eyes — when I said I really liked them.

"What was I? Seven? God." With equal surprise and amusement, she slapped her hand on either side of her face and shook her head. "Then he shut the door in my face, as any respectable boy of ten would. I guess I never let it surface, especially after Lorilee."

"Because in the endless stream of the space-time continuum, this was the time and the place."

"Sure, that explains it."

"Yes, it actually does. You're good together, Adrian, so that's number one, because a lot of people who fall for each other aren't. And I've got to go." She pushed up. "You know, Raylan's kids are going to tell Phineas about the carnival. I'm going to end up getting my ass dragged there."

"Yes! Let's meet there. It'll be fun. I'll text Maya, see if she and Joe and the kids want in."

"Are you making a crowd to hide your love?"

"No. We all deserve some fun. And hey, it's a carnival."

Long before the summer sun set, music blasted, rides whirled and twirled, kids — and plenty of adults — squealed. The air, filled with scents of fried sugar, grilled meat, bubbling grease, radiated heat and humidity.

Midway games drew hopefuls who'd shell out twenty bucks for a chance to win a two-dollar toy. Bells clanged, wheels spun, air guns popped.

The minute they parked in the field with dozens of cars, Bradley grabbed Raylan's hand. "Let's go, Dad! I'm starving. I want two hot dogs and fries and funnel cake and ice cream and —"

"If you eat half of that before you get on the rides, you'll puke."

"Nuh-uh!"

"Yuh-huh. Pick some rides first, then chow, then we'll do some games before any more rides."

"I want the Matterhorn and the Tilt-A-Whirl and the Ferris wheel." In her delight, Mariah executed a very nice cartwheel.

"You up for this?" Raylan asked Adrian.

"Absolutely."

At the admissions booth he bought four full-access passes. Then scanned the wild maze of booths and rides. "Looks like Matterhorn's first up."

"I can ride it this year." Mariah reached up for Adrian's hand. "I wasn't tall enough last year, but I grew. We measured and everything. I only have to do baby rides if I want."

"How about you ride with me, Mo?"

"I can ride with Adrian, Daddy. We're the girls."

"We're good," Adrian assured him.

And they were, tucked together in the bobsled car, swinging out and in, faster and faster until the world was a blur. Beside her, Mariah let out screams, wild laughs, screams.

When they slowed, she beamed up at Adrian. "This was the most fun in my whole life!"

"There's more where that came from."

The minute they hit the ground again, Mariah leaped up into Raylan's arms. "Can we do it again? Can we?"

"My fearless femme." He rubbed his cheek to hers. "Sure. But why don't we hit something else first?"

"Text from Teesha. They're parking, and Maya and Joe pulled in right behind them."

"Why don't you tell her we'll meet them at the Tilt-A-Whirl?"

"Can I get cotton candy when we eat?"

As they walked, Raylan looked down at Mariah, then over at Adrian. "You might have to put on blinders."

"Do the ring toss, Dad. Can I have a penknife when you win?"

"When you're thirteen," Raylan told Bradley.

"That's forever away!"

"How come you claimed you were almost a teenager the other day?"

Bradley executed the one-eighty flawlessly. "I almost am, so I should have a penknife."

"Does not compute." But Raylan paused by the ring-toss game, bought tickets. He spotted a fancy pink penknife, flipped the ring. Ringed the bottle with it.

"How did you do that?" Adrian demanded.

"It's just hand-eye coordination and some basic physics." He handed her the prize. "You're old enough to have this. Be responsible."

He won a gaudy necklace for Mariah, a pen with multicolored ink for Bradley.

"That shouldn't have been possible," Adrian commented as they continued to the next ride.

"Yeah, that's what the guy running the game usually says."

When they met up with the rest, Phineas studied the whirling ride with sorrow. "I'm not tall enough."

"You will be next year," Mariah told him. "I just got tall enough."

"It's all right, my man. I'm tall enough, but I don't go on those puke machines." Monroe already had the baby kicking his feet in his stroller. "You, me, and Thad are going to hit

587

the other rides. Why don't you give me your short stuff there, Maya, and I'll take her with us."

"Three to one?" Patting Quinn's bottom in the front pack she wore, Maya shook her head. "I'll stick with you this round."

"I'll rotate with you." Joe leaned over to kiss Maya. Then rubbed his hands together. "I love me some puke machines. Ready for your first whirl, Collin? You just hit tall enough."

He bit his lip. "I guess."

"You don't have to. You can come with us," Maya told him.

"No, I can do it."

He did it, but unlike Mariah, came off with eyes wide and shocked. He managed two more rides with eyes like blue glass moons.

"Let's give Mom a chance, okay with you? We'll help Monroe with the little guys."

"Okay. We gotta be fair." Wobbling a little, Collin took Joe's hand as they walked toward the kiddie rides. "I didn't puke."

"Guts of steel."

After the first round, they ate what Adrian judged to be a ridiculous amount of meat, sugar, and fat, then walked off what they could on the midway as dusk settled in and the lights began to beam.

Like magic, she thought.

And like magic, Raylan popped balloons with darts to win Mariah a huge stuffed unicorn. At the shooting range, he consistently pinged wolves, roosters, bears, coyotes as they rotated, taking away a robot for Bradley.

"No, seriously," Adrian demanded. "How do you do that?"

He just shrugged. "It's my superpower. Ball toss over there." He pointed. "See anything you like?"

Adrian laughed. "Have some pity on the carnies, Midway Man."

"I like the octopus," Phineas told him. "Octo means eight, and they have eight tentacles."

"Let me see what I can do."

He bagged the octopus for Phineas, a stuffed snake for Collin.

"I got this." Joe pointed toward the high striker. "Swing a hammer plenty. I'm gonna ring that bell." He handed Maya the light-up sword he'd won, rolled his shoulders.

He swung the hammer up, slammed it down. When it stopped just short, he claimed practice round, passed off more tickets.

The second swing, the bell rang, lights flashed.

"My strong man." Maya fluttered her lashes, and took the stuffed, big-eyed cow.

"Don't look at me." Laughing, Monroe waved his hands in the air. "I already won these magic crystals by pure luck. I'm a music man, not Thor."

Before Raylan could step up, Adrian raised a hand. "I'll try it."

The operator smiled at her. "Good luck there, missy."

The hammer had more weight than she'd anticipated, but she planted her feet, hefted it, brought it down.

The weight stopped a full ten inches short of the bell.

"That was a nice try, little lady." The operator handed her a hair band with light-up, bouncy flowers.

She put it on, rolled her shoulders back, rolled them forward. "One more time."

Raylan peeled off the tickets.

She gripped the hammer, took her stance, tipped her head side to side. Breathed in. Breathed out. Breathed in, and swung on the exhale.

The weight flew up, banged the bell, set the lights flashing.

"Little ladies don't have these." She flexed her biceps.

The carnie laughed. "Guess they don't."

CHAPTER TWENTY-EIGHT

About the time Adrian rang the bell, Rachael found two more dead women, making her total eight.

More than twenty percent, she thought.

No one could ignore that. No one.

She wrote it up, sent copies to the DC investigator assigned, to the FBI agent.

She left voice mails for both, pushing action on interviewing Nikki Bennett.

And the hell with it, she thought. She was giving that another shot herself.

She texted her husband.

Sorry. Sorry. And one more sorry. I know I'm already really late, but I have one more thing to deal with. Maybe another hour to hour and a half.

As she shut down the empty offices, he texted back.

Working too hard, Rach. All's good here. Maggie's hanging out at Kiki's tonight. Sam trounced me twice in Fortnight so I'm taking my solace in a book. If you've got time, pick up some Butter Crunch ice cream. I may need more solace.

It made her smile as she locked the door behind her.

I'll make time, and solace with you. Luv.

When her cell phone rang, she noted Caller Blocked on the display. In her line of work, she couldn't just ignore.

"Rachael McNee."

"Ms. McNee, this is Detective Robert Morestead with the Richmond PD, Major Crimes Unit."

"Richmond," she repeated as her blood chilled.

"Your name and number were found in the address book of Tracie Potter."

Rachael leaned back against the locked door. "If I could have your badge number so I can check your bona fides?"

As he gave her the information, including the name of his lieutenant, she unlocked the door again and put on the lights.

"Just hang on a minute, please."

Back at her desk, she used the landline to verify. Then sat back a minute, closed her eyes.

"Detective Morestead, I contacted Tracie

Potter, and have spoken to her twice in connection with an investigation I'm conducting. What happened to her? Detective, I was on the job in DC for a decade. You can check on that. I'm currently working with Detectives Bower and Wochowski, MPD, and Special Agent Marlene Krebs of the FBI."

She got up for a fresh bottle of water as she spoke. "You're Major Crimes so I have to assume' Tracie Potter is injured or dead."

"Ms. Potter's murder has been all over the news down here."

"I'm in DC, not Richmond." Goddamn it, she thought. Goddamn it, that's nine.

"Potter makes the ninth homicide victim, female, on a list I have of thirty-four females. You make those calls, Detective, and give me a contact number where I can send you the data and evidence I have to this point. And when you make those calls, get those law enforcement officers off their asses. I've given them my prime suspect, and they have yet to interview her."

"Where'd you get this list?"

"I'm going to send you copies of my files and reports. They're very detailed." She turned on her computer, waited for it to boot up. "These murders cover a number of years, a number of methods, and a number of jurisdictions across the country."

"And the connection?"

"Retribution. I'll answer any questions you

593

have after you read the files, make the calls."

"I'll make the calls. I'll give you a contact to send the files. And I'm going to ask questions. We're already in the field and can be to you in under two hours."

Nearly nine-thirty already, she thought. Well, fine. Just fucking fine.

"All right. I'm still at my office, but I need to get home shortly. You can talk to me there." She rattled off her address. "I have one question myself, Detective. I'd like to know how she was killed. Whatever you've released to the media is enough."

"The victim was killed between twenty-three and zero-one hundred hours last night. Her body was discovered in the parking lot of a strip mall a few blocks from her studio at approximately oh-eight hundred this morning. It appears to be a carjacking gone south."

"It's not. Contact?"

When he gave it, she began sending files.

"On your way here, run these individuals. Jonathan Bennett Junior, Nikki Bennett. Siblings. I'll see you in a couple of hours."

She hung up, sick, furious. No solace tonight, she thought. And no visit to pressure Nikki Bennett herself again. She needed to get home, calm herself down, prepare to talk to Richmond.

Before she did, she wrote up the phone conversation, the name of the Richmond detective, the times and dates. Then did a quick search on Detective Morestead.

Twenty-two years on the job, and the last nine in Major Crimes.

Good and solid.

She pulled up the Richmond papers and, holding the line on personal guilt, read the details of the crime.

"Carjacking, my ass," she muttered. And figured Morestead knew it.

But he didn't know her, she mused. In his place she'd hold back, too.

Got in the car, lay in wait in the car — like with Jayne Arlo in Erie. Killed her right off — why take chances? But drove the car from the studio lot to the strip mall. It would take longer to find her that way, Rachael concluded. More time to get some distance.

Left her in the car, so the killer had a car, probably in the same lot.

Get in, get gone.

She made copies of the news reports for her files before she shut down again, locked up again.

Nine now, she thought. At least nine women dead. But by Christ, they were going to end this. They were going to shut this murderous revenge spree down.

She considered calling her uncle, decided to wait until she got home, settled some.

After ten now, she noted, but he'd be up.

And she'd stop for the damn ice cream. The

least she could do since she'd probably be up half the night on this — and bring cops into the house.

Struggling against guilt and anger, she stepped outside and started toward her car.

She saw the flash, felt the sharp bee-sting pain in her arm.

She whirled, grabbed for her keys and the panic button on them.

Pain speared into her chest, her shoulder. As she tumbled back, she struck her head on the door of her car, felt herself start to drift away.

He moved in. He'd used a .22 semiauto to try to keep the noise down. But he knew he should've gotten closer first — the .22 didn't pack a lot of punch!

He was, he had to admit, better with a knife than a gun.

But he liked the way a gun barked in his hand, the way bullets just punched into people.

She was bleeding pretty good, but he'd just give her one in the ear for good measure.

As he closed in, he heard a burst of wild laughter, raised voices.

Let her bleed to death, he thought as he got down, duckwalked back. Let her lie there and bleed out on the ground like the nosy bitch she was. "Two bitches down," he mumbled.

He eased back, back, then used the dark to

circle wide around the building before he strolled onto a sidewalk and whistled away.

Stay awake, she ordered herself. Don't fade off. Oh Jesus, oh God. Ethan, our kids. No, no, no, she wasn't going to do this to them. She wasn't going to die like this and leave them.

She tried to call for help, but her voice barely made a croak.

Shaking, she shifted enough — oh God, it hurt! — to draw her phone out of her pocket. It slipped out of her fingers — sweat, blood, shock, shakes — but she gripped it again. Pressed nine-one-one.

"Nine-One-One. What's your emergency?"

"Shots fired. Shots fired. Officer down. No, no, not officer anymore. I'm shot. I'm shot. Parking lot." She gave the address while her teeth began to chatter.

"I'm dispatching the police and an ambulance to your location. Stay with me. Stay with me. What's your name?"

"I'm Rachael McNee. Hit, three times. Maybe four. Maybe four, I think. Hit my head. Head shot? Dunno. Chest is the worst. Losing blood. Suspect is . . ."

"Stay with me, Rachael. Help's coming."

"Cau— Caucasian male. I saw him, I saw him. Middle thirties. Five-ten, a hundred fifty. Blond, got a beard, little beard, and . . . can't remember. I'm going out."

"Stay with me, Rachael. I can hear the

sirens from your phone. Just stay with me."

"Can't . . ."

And she faded.

She came around again briefly while the world whirled. Light, too bright in her eyes. Voices, too loud. She couldn't think over them.

Shut up, she thought. Shut up so I can think.

She flailed out with a hand, and someone — a stranger — leaned down. "We've got you. Hold on now."

"Bennett." The word slurred. She couldn't feel her tongue. "Junior. Shot me."

"Okay. It's okay. Hold on."

But she'd already faded again.

In the bathroom, Nikki huddled. Sometimes she was so cold her body shook. Sometimes she was so hot sweat poured.

She stank. She'd tried to wash herself, but she stank anyway.

She couldn't reach the light switch.

Sometimes she prayed for the bulbs to burn out so she'd have some dark. Then she shuddered at the idea of being left in the dark.

Her right wrist, bruised and bloody, ached. Her face, where he'd struck her, pounded. She took the pills JJ left her, and it helped. In her head she visualized how some animals chewed off their own paw to free themselves

598

from a trap.

Could she do it? Should she try?

Then the idea of that had her vomiting again.

She didn't know how much time had passed. A day? A week?

She ate dry cereal, crackers. An apple. A banana. And started to fear she'd run out of food, then slowly starve to death.

She feared he wouldn't come back.

She feared he would.

She'd known.

Whenever she fell into weeping, she admitted she'd known what he was. Not right, not ever really right. Prone to meanness and violence, and covering all that up with adoring smiles for their father.

He'd always hated her; she'd known that, too.

Because, he'd told her once, she'd come first in birth order. Because she took parts of their father's love and attention that were rightfully his.

And still, she'd protected him, hadn't she?

Covered for him when he snuck out at night. Washed blood out of his clothes before anyone else could see. Distracted her mother — oh, so easy to do — whenever she started to rage at him.

He'd killed their mother.

Had she known that? No, no, she didn't think she'd known. Maybe suspected. A little.

But she hadn't known.

She'd sent him money when he needed it. Never asked questions.

Didn't want to know the answers. Relieved that he mostly stayed away. She had her own life, didn't she? Didn't she? Didn't she?

She huddled, weeping, laughing, aching, throbbing, hearing the gibbering of her own voice as she talked to no one.

She feared she'd lose her mind for wanting to have a life.

She hadn't known about the poems. She hadn't known about the killings — the women he'd killed.

But she'd known it for the truth when that detective had come. She'd known, and she'd covered for her brother.

Her father had told her, again and again and again, that was her job. She just wanted to do her job.

She didn't want to die for doing her job.

Detective Morestead read Rachael's files while his partner drove. Morestead, a spit-and-polish sort, had his tie carefully knotted, his shoes perfectly shined. He'd been on the job for twenty-two years, and attached to Major Crimes for nearly a decade. He kept his hair trimmed, his square-jawed face closely shaved.

He had been, always would be, a detail man.

In Rachael's report he found a lot of details.

600

His partner — five years and counting — Lola Deeks, had a more casual appearance. She kept her hair in a close-cut cap, but he knew — as she'd told him — that was to give her more time for important things.

Like sleep.

She wore suit jackets or blazers, but went for flashy colors. Generally she had a T-shirt under them rather than a button-down. She always, except dead of winter with snow, wore sneakers.

By his guess she owned at least a dozen at any given time.

If he was detail, she was over-all picture.

He read her snippets as they pushed up 95.

They discussed and debated.

"There's one here that reads like our case, except for the murder weapon. Twenty-two caliber, back of the head for that. But in the car, from the back."

"Already in the car, like we reconstructed on Potter. She had eight out of thirty-four before we added Potter? That ain't just bad luck, Bobby. She — if the PI's right on this Nikki Bennett — travels for work. Pick a target, hit the target, leave town."

"Statistically —"

"Yeah, yeah." She spared him a glance. "Not typical female weapons or methods. Female serial killers are rare birds. Sometimes you catch yourself a rare bird, Bobby."

"Sometimes you do. She's requested the

locals get a warrant for Bennett's travel schedule. We'll add our weight there." He pulled on his ear. "The motive's thin."

"Not thin so much as nuts. Straight revenge goes after the Rizzos — mother, daughter, and the nanny. Nuts decides all the women who banged the drum with daddy are complicit, so they all have to pay."

"It's a lot of years, Lola. A lot of patience. No mention of poems or threats, except the Rizzo girl."

"She's about thirty, Bobbie. That's past 'girl,' my friend. She's the one who matters most, so she gets the poems."

"Shared blood," he agreed.

"Make the connection, torment her some. Stupid, but it's ego, too. We'll be getting off this god-cursed road shortly."

"I'm going to reach out to the lead investigator in DC. Maybe we have a conversation there, too, while we're up here."

He located the number in the file. It surprised him when the DC cop picked up on the first ring.

"Detective Bower."

"Detective Bower, this is Detective Morestead, Richmond PD. We're investigating a homicide, and believe we've made a connection to a case you're working on. We're on our way now to speak with a PI in Georgetown. Rachael McNee."

Lola glanced over when her partner's

shoulders inched back. She knew his body language. Something's up. And nothing good.

"When?" He started scribbling on the pad in his lap he'd used to make personal notes on the files. "Where is she now? We'll meet you there." He glanced at the GPS, recalculated. "Fifteen minutes."

"There's another one?" Lola asked when he ended the call.

"The PI took four bullets right outside her office. Maybe a half hour after I talked to her."

"She dead?"

"Not yet. I'm going to program in the hospital. She's in surgery."

JJ made a stop at Reagan National Airport to dump the car in long-term parking, and steal another. He stuffed his tied Hefty bag of bloody gear in a trash can.

Though he hated giving up his smooth ride, the fucking cops had his sister's name, so they had the car.

Time for a change.

He got lucky with an aging, basic van with no alarm system. He broke in, transferred his bags, his weapons, his tools. Since hot-wiring the piece of shit was child's play, he headed out again inside ten minutes.

He'd need to gas up, he noted. And he'd find a safer spot to switch out the tags. Better safe than sorry!

Maybe he'd pull off at a truck stop, or a rest stop, grab some snacks, catch a few z's. He still had a couple of his handy pills to give him a boost, but he had time, so maybe the z's.

No real hurry, and he wanted to savor his moments. Cops, as he'd proven time and time again, were too stupid to put the slice and dice of a reporter — news reader, that's all she'd been — down in Virginia together with the bang-bang of a PI in DC.

They'd chase their tails on both while he drove up to bumfuck and had some quality time with his father's bastard.

His father's killer.

He used his phone to locate a truck stop along the way. He had a fondness for truck stops, for the long-haul truckers. More than once he'd asked one to mail a letter to his sweetheart at their next stop. Just a little game they played, he'd tell them, and pay for their coffee.

He didn't have a poem to mail this time. But maybe he'd write one. One final poem, and leave it with her bloody, broken body.

Yeah, he would. That's just what he'd do! And that poem would be published in newspapers, on the Internet. Bitches like the one he'd just killed would recite it solemnly into the TV screens.

He'd be famous. Make his father proud!

So he should sign it this time. Not his

name, of course. A title.

The Bard, he thought. His father had loved Shakespeare like a brother, so that was like honoring his old man.

He'd get himself some steak and eggs, some hash browns, some good, strong truck-stop coffee, and write his finest poem yet.

He'd read it to the bitch before he finished her.

When he'd finished, when he'd taken some good pictures of her dead body, her bitch face, he'd make a quick trip back to the old homestead to deal with sister number one.

No poem for her, he thought. Just a bullet in the brain. Quick and easy.

A shame, he mused, he wouldn't have that well to tap for more money down the road, but she knew too much. And women couldn't keep their bitch mouths from flapping.

Besides, plenty of valuables in the house to take with him.

Then, like a long-haul trucker, he'd head back to Wyoming. He'd pick off the rest of the bitches on his list at his leisure.

Spread them out, like always.

A man didn't rush his life's work.

While JJ tucked into his steak and eggs, Morestead and Deeks got off the hospital elevator. They both recognized cop in the man pacing a few feet away.

Morestead reached for his badge. "Detective Bower?"

"No." The man, burly in a T-shirt and mom jeans, gave them the hard eye. "Sergeant Mooney. It's my niece, my sister's girl, up in surgery. Bower and Wochowski stepped out."

"We're sorry about your niece, Sergeant," Deeks began and told him their names. "Do you know her status?"

"Don't know a damn fucking thing except she took four bullets. They got 'em out, and they're in Evidence. Two in the chest." He tapped a fist on his own. "Called it in herself, that's what she did. That's what she's made of."

"Is there a suspect?"

The hard eye shifted, hot now, to Morestead. "Don't stand there asking stupid questions. You're coming up to talk to her 'cause you connected the dots. Or she connected them for you. You Homicide boys don't get a damn warrant for Bennett, I'm heading out myself, waking up a judge, and I will goddamn get one myself."

"Sergeant." Deeks spoke softly — one of her skills. "We caught this case less than eighteen hours ago. It looks like my partner was the last person to speak with your niece before this happened. She did connect those dots for us, and we read her files, which she sent to us, on the way here. If Bower and Wochowski are unable to secure a warrant to bring Nikki Bennett in for questioning, for a

606

search of her home, her office, her vehicles, we will do so."

Mooney held up a hand, breathed out. "I jumped on you. I had to step out of the waiting room. Rachael's husband, her two kids, my sister, my brother-in-law, my wife, Rachael's brother, her sister, hell, most of the family, and there are a lot of us, are packed in there, or outside trying to walk this off."

"My brother was shot. He attended Virginia Tech — 2007. I was just a kid. I've never been so scared in my life as I was sitting in that waiting room. It's why I became a cop."

"Did he make it?" Mooney asked her.

"Yeah. He was the first of my family to graduate from college."

"I'm glad to hear it." He pushed a hand over his grizzled hair. "Let's get you some coffee."

The elevator doors opened again.

"Bower, Wochowski — Morestead and Deeks."

Mooney waited for everyone to shake hands. "You get it?"

"In the works, Sarge," Bower told him. "It's in the works. They're getting a judge out of bed." He rubbed the back of his neck. "Wochowski talked to the LT while I talked to the prosecutor — and I got her out of bed."

"We're going to put a team together," Wochowski told the others. "A takedown team, a search team. Bowers and I will get her into interview. You all are welcome to observe. She's got money," he added, "so she can afford a good lawyer. We need some hard evidence. Physical evidence."

"If this woman shot Rachael," Bower continued, "we're going to nail her for it. That's a goddamn promise, Sarge. We need that search team to find us something that ties her to Rachael, to any of the others Rachael believes this woman killed."

"Still in surgery?" Wochowski asked, and Mooney just nodded. "When she comes out of it, when she comes around, she'll help us nail it down."

"We were moving on it." Bower lightly pounded his fist on his thigh. "We were going over to talk to Bennett today. We couldn't get to it before. Then we got slammed with that double."

Mooney waved it away. "I didn't see it as hot either. I should've. I didn't."

He broke off, strode away when he saw one of the doctors in scrubs. His heart pounded in his throat, in his ears. "You were operating on Rachael McNee. I'm her uncle. I'm —"

"I remember." The quiet-voiced, weary-eyed woman nodded. "Dr. Stringer. Your niece is stable. She's strong, and she's stable. She's in serious condition, and we'll watch her closely for the next twelve hours. She came through the surgery well."

"Can you tell the family? They're going to

want to see her. I know that horde can't all go see her, but her husband, her kids, her mom. They need to see her."

"She'll be sedated through the night, but yes, we'll arrange for that."

"They ain't going anywhere till she wakes up."

"Cafeteria's twenty-four-seven. I can arrange to have a cot brought in for her husband once she's out of recovery. The shoulder and arm wounds were minor. The chest wounds more serious, as we already discussed. She also lacerated the back of her head, in the fall, I believe. I want to say it's a wonder she stayed conscious and able to contact nine-one-one."

"You don't know Rachael."

The doctor smiled. "I do now. I hope you find who did this to her."

"Count on it. Family's all in there. Or most of them."

He turned to the other cops. "Give me five minutes with the family, then I'm in on this takedown."

"Sarge —"

"Don't fuck with me on this. I've been a cop damn near as long as you've been alive, Bower. I'm not going to do anything to jeopardize the case against the individual who put my niece in the hospital. And I'm going to be there when you take her in."

"Five minutes. We need to get back to the

house, suit up, brief the team."

"We'll be on that." Morestead waited for the frustrated looks. "To observe and assist only. It's your takedown, Detectives. But we will need to interview the suspect regarding our victim."

"Fair enough. Take your five, Mooney. Sarge? I'm really glad Rachael's coming through."

Deeks looked toward the waiting room as she heard the weeping. "Relief tears," she said. "They sound different from grief. It's good to hear them."

CHAPTER TWENTY-NINE

Since the pain wouldn't die, Nikki took more pills. She dozed off and on, then took more. Her ears rang, and though it seemed impossible, her head ached more. Like jackhammers digging into her brain. Because of the length of the chain, she could only stand in a crouch, but when she tried, her head spun, and she'd have to sit again.

Or vomit again.

So she took more pills.

Sometimes she heard voices, but when she held her breath to scream for help, she realized the voices were her own. No one but JJ could get in the house, and he wouldn't come to help.

She surfaced again, sick and shaking, eyes tearing, ears ringing.

A pounding. Her head, God yes, her head, but something else.

Was someone pounding on the door? They couldn't get in, no, they couldn't get in, but maybe, if she could scream, they'd hear. If she could stand up, or nearly stand, fill her lungs and scream.

Maybe.

She tried, sobbing as she struggled to pull up on her trembling, buzzing legs. As she sucked in air, as she managed a rusty croak, the dizziness swept over her in a wave. She fell forward, struck the toilet lid face-first.

Fresh blood exploded from her broken nose. Both front teeth drove hard into her lip before they shattered. The pain, wild and feral, lasted only an instant before she slipped limply to the floor.

Outside the house, Bower used his fist to pound again.

"No lights on inside." Deeks jogged up. "No car in the driveway. She's got a Mercedes sedan, new, registered in her name."

"Could be on the run." Bower stepped back. He nodded to the uniform behind him. "Take it down."

The battering ram struck, once, twice, and on the third took down the heavy mahogany door.

"This is the police!" Bower called out as officers went through. "We are duly authorized to enter the premises. Come out with your hands up."

Deeks hit the lights. "Shit, looks like we got some blood here." She crouched down. "Dried blood on the floor. Maybe she's not on the run."

"Let's clear it."

"Old houses like this are a maze of rooms," Mooney pointed out as Bower directed a team to take the second and third floors.

Weapon ready, Deeks pulled open a coat closet as Morestead moved toward the back of the house, still announcing police presence.

Wochowski cleared the front room, the side parlor, and Mooney moved to the door under the stairs.

Another closet, he thought, maybe a powder room.

He smelled it as he reached for the door handle.

Blood, puke.

"I got something here," he called out, then yanked the door open. "Well, fuck me. We need a bus!" Holstering his weapon, he stepped in, crouched down. He put his fingers on Nikki's throat. "She's alive. She's out. Christ, she's been in here awhile."

It was Deeks who stepped up, looked over Mooney's shoulder. "Some of that blood's fresh. We need bolt cutters in here!"

"Lost a couple teeth. That's fresh, too." Mooney turned her on her side so she wouldn't choke on her own blood. "Bashed her head on the john's what she did. Look at the spatter. Went down hard, but she's got older bruises, and I'm betting her nose was already busted before she face-planted."

"Food in this box. Cereal, crackers, got some nasty-looking apple cores, banana peels. A nearly empty bottle of Advil. Whoever chained her to the wall didn't want to kill her."

"She's got a brother."

Bower walked up. "Christ, she's a mess. Bus is on the way. We put out an APB on the car."

"Might want to put a BOLO out on the brother," Mooney said.

Bower took in the unconscious woman, the chain, the box of supplies. And nodded.

She came around, a little, in the ambulance. Her eyes rolled open, shiny as glass, rolled up, rolled side to side.

"You're all right now, Nikki." Bower leaned toward her as the EMT checked her vitals. "You're safe now. I'm the police, and you're on your way to the hospital."

"Why?" She lisped it, then moaned. "Oh, my face. I can't feel my face."

"We gave you a little something to help with the pain," the EMT told her. "She's in shock, Detective."

"I can see that. Almost there, Nikki, and they're going to take care of you. Can you tell me what happened? Can you tell me who did this to you?"

She felt floaty, and a little sick, and numb, and too cold.

But she did her job. She couldn't seem to help herself.

"Don't know. Man at the door. Pushed me. Hit me. Then I was in the bathroom. The chain."

She let herself weep.

"Did you recognize him? Did you know him?"

"No. Hit me. Why?" She closed her eyes, tried to think. "Experiment?" she tried out the word. "Did he say? Can't remember. Laughed. Hurt. Everything hurt."

"What did he look like? Can you remember?"

She remembered the boy she'd wanted in college, the one who'd smirked at her when she'd tried to attract him. The one who'd made her feel ugly and stupid.

And described him.

"Tall. Young. Brown hair, wavy hair. Blue eyes. Very blue. I remember. Pretty face. Dimples when he smiled. Accent. Southern, soft, southern. Hurt me. Tired now."

She closed her eyes, and though she stayed awake, let herself drift.

JJ couldn't hurt her here, she thought. She would go back to her life now. Soon. She didn't care if he hurt somebody else. She'd paid enough. It wasn't her fault.

At the hospital, Bower huddled with his partner, with Mooney, and with the two Richmond detectives.

"She said she didn't know the guy who locked her up. She was in pretty bad shape,

615

and doped up, but she gave a halfway decent description. Nothing like the last photo we have of the brother. She went out before she could give me more detail, but brown and blue — wavy hair — young, tall. Dimples and southern accent."

"Some strange guy hits her house, punches her, locks her up, steals her car — but leaves her food and pain pills? And two days before my niece gets popped?" Mooney just scowled. "That's some major bullshit."

"We'll go at her again, get more details. And if it's bullshit, we'll push her right into it. But she came right up with that description. Said something about an experiment. Like a question, like she wasn't sure."

"We've got a BOLO out on the brother, and we're looking for the car," Wochowski pointed out. "And maybe I lean with Mooney on the bullshit, but you have to ask: Why would she lie? If your brother punched you out, chained you up, why would you lie about it?"

"Maybe the whole family's crazy." Morestead shrugged. "Sure, her record doesn't show anything out of line. The fact is, it shows bupkes. You can ask yourself, too, was she part of the whole thing? The two of them working together, and so they had a falling-out?"

"I follow that." Deeks nodded. "And I like that angle. But then you have to wonder why she wouldn't flip on him straight off. Claim, *Oh my God, my brother. What's he done? He said this, that, he's lost his mind. I had no idea!* And who's not going to be sympathetic to a woman whose brother punches her in the face, chains her up, and then leaves her with boxes of cereal for what had to be at least two or three days from the looks of it."

"We'll take another run at her when they get her patched up."

He checked the time. "Shit. Look, I'm going to check on her status. The way I see it, we should try to catch a couple hours down, come at this fresh. You sticking, Richmond?"

"We'll stick until we talk to her." Morestead looked at Deeks, got a nod.

"There's a crib at the station, but I wouldn't recommend it if you've got room on your expense account for a motel."

"I'm going in to sit with Rachael. I'll wait for the status, and I want to be in the room if you talk to her, but then I'm going to be with the family. Same hospital, and ain't that a kick in the fucking head?"

Mooney looked back at the ER doors. "One thing we know. She didn't shoot my niece. But that doesn't mean she wasn't part of the whole."

"Search team's on the house. If there's anything that ties her, they'll find it. I'll go check on her."

Bower listened to what he thought of as the

usual medical spiel. Patient needed rest and quiet. Added to it, he got confirmation that she had facial injuries more than forty-eight hours old, and the lacerations, abrasions on her wrist went back the same amount of time.

Which put her out of the running for the Richmond murder.

In addition to the broken nose, the chipped cheekbone, the severe wounds to her mouth and her right wrist, she'd suffered a concussion.

And would likely have confusion and memory gaps.

After he pressed — hard — he got clearance for five minutes with her — which he planned to stretch. Then the doctor insisted on eight hours of rest.

In the interest of fairness, he took Mooney and Deeks — hoping for a female perspective there.

He put on his Officer Friendly face as he stepped up beside Nikki's bed.

"How are you doing, Nikki?"

"I don't know. I'm so tired. I'm in the hospital."

"And you're safe. Nobody's going to hurt you. I rode with you in the ambulance and we talked a little. I'm Detective Bower."

"Ambulance? I can't remember."

"That's all right. You told me about the person who hurt you. I need to ask you a few questions, then we're going to let you rest.

You said he was young. Can you tell us what you meant?"

"Who are they?" Her swollen eyes landed on Mooney and Deeks. "I don't know them!"

"They're police, like me. We're here to help you, to keep you safe. How old would you say the person was who hurt you?"

"The man." She closed her eyes again. She nearly said twenty, because he had been. But worried that would seem too young. "I'm not sure. Late twenties. Maybe thirties. I'm sorry."

"That's fine. Just fine. A white male?"

"Yes."

"What was he wearing?"

"I'm not . . . a uniform? No, I don't think . . . maybe. No, I can't remember. I'm sorry."

"Could you describe him again, as best you can?"

"I . . . tall."

"How tall?"

"I think, taller than you, I think. A little. Strong. I think he was strong. Wavy brown hair and beautiful blue eyes. So pretty, so charming. The dimples, the accent. Like a movie star."

"When you're feeling a little better, would you work with a police artist?"

"I can try. I'm so tired now."

"You said experiment. Did he say that to you?"

619

"Experiment? Did he say that? I cried. I was crying, and he laughed. I had the toilet, didn't I? I could get water, couldn't I? Here's some food. Take these pills. I'll come back."

"He said he'd come back?"

"I think . . . yes. I was afraid he wouldn't. I was afraid he would. I was afraid."

"Did he come back?"

"I don't think . . . I don't know. Sometimes I thought I heard voices. But I don't know."

"Where do you keep your keys? To your house, to your car?"

"The dish on the table by the door. If you put them there, you always know where they are. I want to sleep now. Just sleep."

Mooney stepped slightly closer. "Was the man in the house when Rachael McNee came to see you?"

She actually felt fear shoot down her spine. "Who?"

"Rachael McNee. She came to see you. She's a private investigator."

"Yes, yes. No. I remember someone came. I just got home? I think I just got home. Had groceries. Why did she come? What did she want? My father." Nikki closed her eyes. "I don't want to talk about my father. None of it was my fault. I was a child. I wanted her to go away. She upset me. I didn't let her inside, did I? And she went away. Was the man with her? I think he came right after. Soon after. I thought there's that woman again, and I want

620

her to go away. I was angry. I opened the door, but it wasn't her. And he smiled, and he hit me."

"He hit you in the doorway?" Deeks pressed. "When you opened the door?"

"I . . ." What had she said before? How was she supposed to remember? "I'm not sure. It's blurry. He looked so nice. I don't know why he was so mean to me. I want to sleep. I have to sleep."

"Okay, Nikki." Bower patted her hand. "You get some rest."

With some reluctance, Mooney stepped out. "It's pretty damn convenient how she remembers some things real clear, and others are all blurry."

"I'm not disagreeing with you, but trauma can do that. One way or the other, the trauma's real."

"Trauma doesn't mean she's not lying," Deeks pointed out. "And I think she is."

"So do I. Why do you?"

"There's something almost dreamy about how she describes the guy. Like she's got a crush going. And if she doesn't know him, if he's never been in the house before, how'd he pick a room with no window, an inside room? How'd he know just how long to make the chain so she could reach the sink to get water, but not reach the door? I'm seconding Mooney's bullshit call. He was so mean to her? You call bashing her face and chaining

621

her to a wall 'mean'? Something's off."

"Not disagreeing with you either. Maybe she had a lover, and things went south, this went down. But we're not getting any more out of her tonight. Soon as it's light, we'll have some cops canvass the neighborhood, knock on doors. We'll see if anyone saw this guy. She started to say *uniform,* but changed her mind. But maybe he passed as a delivery guy, a repair guy, a cop to blend in.

"And we'll go over it with her again tomorrow. Maybe we'll get lucky on the car tonight yet. But I've been on shift for damn near twenty-four now. I need a few hours down. So does everyone else. We can meet back at the station at eight, and we'll interview her again as soon as we can. If something breaks before, we're up and on it. Meanwhile we keep a guard on her door. Nobody gets in who shouldn't, and she doesn't get out."

"I'm going up to check on Rachael."

"If she wakes up before eight, and she remembers anything, you let me know. We got it, Sarge."

JJ pulled the van onto an old logging trail about a quarter mile from Traveler's Creek. The van didn't much care for it, but he wouldn't need it much longer. He needed a little sleep, and didn't want any idiot cops or good Samaritans checking on a van pulled to the shoulder of the road.

He'd considered breaking into Adrian's house while she slept, but he knew — because of her stupid blog — she had a dog. A big one. And he suspected she'd have an alarm system.

He figured he could handle the alarm system, but dogs barked.

And they bit.

He'd do better to wait, deal with the dog outside.

Since he'd worked out a plan, he could catch some sleep, set his phone alarm for, say, thirty minutes before sunrise. Then he'd hitch on his backpack holding his tools and hike to the woods — he'd studied the lay of the land since she just fucking loved doing her fitness shit out there. He'd find a good spot to watch her house.

Once he'd dealt with the dog, he and his baby sister bitch would have a nice long get-together.

Years in the making, he thought as he settled down to sleep.

And he'd deliver her final poem in person.

She didn't sleep well. Too much in her head, Adrian admitted as she gave it up and rolled out of bed at dawn.

She'd fallen in love and didn't know how to handle it. And, she knew very well, when she didn't know how to handle something, she picked at it until she found some fix, some work-around.

But this wasn't a program or a recipe or a hairstyle.

Love was a singular condition.

And her mother was coming. She'd have to deal with the new complexion of their relationship, those cautious steps. And there might be a conversation in there about that singular condition.

She'd never talked to her mother about something like this, never considered that kind of sharing. So how to handle that?

Using her phone, she switched off the alarm so she could open the porch doors. She stepped out, studied the fire of the waking sun in the eastern woods, laid a hand on Sadie's head as her dog joined her.

"Pretty morning, Sadie, so that's something."

She had a dozen decisions, big and small, to make on the youth center. It had to be right, had to be just what her grandparents had wanted.

Would they care if she chose the checkerboard pattern instead of a solid color for the safety tiles for the playground area? Probably not, but she'd pondered that at four in the morning.

Pondered it, and the choice of foundation plantings, the style of the juice bar. Worried over that and more to keep herself from thinking about the fact she had two half siblings who might want to kill her.

Out of her control, she thought, and she hated having anything out of her control. She had to depend on Rachael for this, and hoped she'd hear from her before the end of the day.

"She'll tell us when she knows something, right?" She leaned down to give Sadie a rub. "So we just wait. Let's go salute the sun, what do you say? Get out of our own heads."

She changed into yoga pants and a tank, pulled her hair back in a band. And in bare feet, went down to the kitchen with her mat. Restless night or not, she loved early mornings, the quiet of them, the air, the sense everything but her and Sadie and the birds still slept.

She freshened Sadie's water bowl, filled a bottle for herself, and left the porch doors open to the air as they went down to the patio. Taking the unrolling of the mat as her signal, Sadie wandered off into the yard.

Adrian stood a moment, facing the light, pink and gold now just above the tree line. Somewhere a woodpecker drummed busily for its breakfast, and a hawk circling overhead hunted his.

Tomatoes ripened on vines she'd planted, and the lush sweep of hydrangeas her grandparents had planted years before thrived with heads that would soon turn madly blue.

A pretty morning, she thought again. And

another fresh start.

Hands in prayer, she breathed in, then lifted her arms high.

From his perch in the woods, he watched her. It thrilled.

There she was! Not on a screen, not in a crowd as she'd been when, years before, he'd traveled to New York after he'd learned she'd appear on the *Today* show.

But in person, and alone.

What a way to start the day!

He hadn't expected her to come out so early. And she'd left the door open. He'd almost shouted with joy when she'd stepped out on the second-floor porch, just stood there, looked right over where he hid.

Maybe the dog was bigger than he'd thought, but he'd take care of that. Sadie, he remembered from the blog. Bitch dog for a bitch.

He liked dogs. Couldn't stand cats, and had plugged his share of strays in his time, but he liked dogs. Maybe he'd get himself a dog one of these days, he considered as he loaded the rifle.

Not a bitch though, and he'd be damned if he'd have his dog's balls cut off. A man had to be a man, didn't he?

As the dog wandered closer to the woods, JJ shouldered the rifle. A little closer, big girl, he thought.

But when her head came up, when she sniffed the air — maybe scenting him — he fired.

The sound, no more than a muffled pop, didn't reach Adrian on her mat as she lowered into Chaturanga. JJ watched the dog take a stumbling step, and one more, then go down.

Night night, he thought.

Mind clear, breath steady, Adrian continued her flow. Her muscles warmed; her mood mellowed. She held in Warrior I, let the stretch work its magic, then slid fluidly into Warrior II.

Deep, so her body sighed with it. And with her gaze focused along her right outstretched hand, she saw the man come out of the woods.

Everything froze, and in that frozen moment, she hurtled back, years back, to Georgetown. Not possible, not possible because she'd seen him wheel over the railing, she'd seen him fall.

She'd seen him die.

But he walked toward her now, smiling a terrible smile.

Run! she heard the voice scream inside her head. But when she started to swing around and charge the steps, he leveled a gun at her.

"Take a step, I'll shoot you. I won't kill you, but I'll take you down."

Beyond him, just to the left, she saw Sadie

sprawled on the ground. Warning or not, the terror and grief spiked.

"Sadie!"

When she started to run for the dog, he stepped in front of her. "One more step, I shoot you in the knee. It'll hurt like hell, and you won't run again. She's just sleeping."

He beamed that smile again out of the face of a dead man.

And for a horrible instant she was seven again, and helpless.

"I don't kill dogs. What do you take me for? Tranquilizer gun. Picked it up back in Wyoming, just for her, just for today. Now you're going to walk on up there into the house so we can have some privacy."

He smiled that smile again. "We've got a lot of catching up to do. Sis."

Not The Man, she realized. His son. Almost a mirror image, but she could see some differences now. The son had a slighter build, and no silver glinting at his temples. The hair itself, choppily cut, not styled.

But the eyes, oh, the eyes were the same. Despite the smile, rage and madness lived there.

And she wasn't seven anymore. She wasn't helpless.

"You're Jonathan Bennett."

"Just call me JJ."

"You've been sending me poems. For a long time."

628

"Got another for you, but that'll wait. We'll talk inside."

If she could keep him out here, she might still find room to run. Or Sadie — if he told the truth — might wake up.

"We were just children. You, your sister, me. We didn't do anything."

"The child makes the man, or the whore-bitch, depending."

"Is your sister here, too? Does she want to talk to me?"

"It's just you and me. Nikki? She likes to put up walls, tune out. She's like our mother that way, without the pills and booze. Well, she's inside four of them now, and there she'll stay."

She heard pleasure in his voice. Not rage, not fury, but an almost dreamy pleasure. Maybe she could reason with him.

"I don't know anything about you, or her. I just —"

"You'll find out plenty. Up the stairs, nice and slow. You try to bolt, I blow out your knee. Move!"

And that rage, that fury flashed to burning in his eyes.

"Or I'll put you down and drag you in bleeding."

He would, she could see he would. She turned for the stairs, tried to think, just think, through the screaming fear.

She knew the house, every inch. He didn't.

629

A moment's distraction, that's all she needed.

Dozens of places to hide, dozens of ways to fight back.

But she needed a distraction. And couldn't risk it with a gun at her back.

Get to her phone. In the bedroom on the charger. Get to her phone, call for help.

She stepped into the kitchen, scanned over to the knife block. Maybe, maybe, if an opportunity came.

"Close the doors, and lock them."

She obeyed, but she was thinking now.

If he'd wanted to kill her outright, she'd be dead. He wanted to talk first. He wanted to tell his story, or rage at her, or both.

He wanted to hurt her before he killed her.

That gave her time, and with time came opportunities and distractions.

"Some place," he commented. "Big-ass house. I grew up in a big house, but I've been making do with a nice little cabin for a while now. Upstairs."

"Upstairs?"

"You left doors open up there, too. You thought you were all safe here, didn't you, in your big-ass house."

Upstairs, she thought. Her phone on the charger.

She walked, considering places she could hide, or areas where she could fight, weapons she could use. A lamp, a heavy vase, a paperweight, a letter opener.

630

"Why poems? Why did you send poems?"

"Because I'm good at them. Even as a kid. My dad was proud of my poems."

"It was hard for you, losing him."

"I didn't lose him. You killed him." He jammed the gun into the small of her back. "If you hadn't been born, he'd be alive."

Training kicked in so she calmed herself with breath. "I didn't know about him until that day. My mother never told me. She never told anybody."

"I don't give a gold-plated fuck about who she told, who she didn't. He's dead because you're alive."

She glanced at the bronze statue on a table in the upstairs hall.

Heavy, she thought.

She walked past it, and into the bedroom.

"Close and lock."

Phone on the charger, just a few feet away. Distraction.

She turned toward him, let all the fear shake into her voice. "I don't know why you're doing this. I don't understand why —"

He backhanded her with his left, hard enough to knock her to the floor and send pain rocketing through her face.

"Close and lock. Do what I say when I say it, or I'll knock some teeth out next time."

She pushed herself up, closed the doors, turned the lock. And when he sidestepped, picked up her phone, her hopes dropped.

He tossed it to the floor, stomped on it. Grinned.

Said, "Oops!"

He gestured with the gun toward the love seat, the reading chair. "Take a seat. Now! Unless you want another smack."

She'd be ready for it next time, and she knew how to counter.

He had a couple of inches on her at best — and she had longer limbs. Wiry muscles, yeah, but she'd pit hers against his.

She'd have to.

But he still held the gun.

She sat in the corner of the love seat nearest the door.

He shrugged off the backpack, set it down, took the chair.

"Now we're all cozy."

CHAPTER THIRTY

In the yard, under the strengthening sun, Sadie's legs began to twitch. Her eyes rolled open.

When she tried to stand, they wouldn't hold her, so she lay panting, confused.

She vomited up the sick in her stomach, lay whining. She wanted Adrian, and cool water.

When she managed to get up, she stumbled forward a few steps. Sicked up again. Slowly, drunkenly, she walked toward the house. She wanted to sleep again, but she wanted Adrian and the water more.

She stopped at the yoga mat, sniffed at it, felt some comfort when she smelled Adrian. But there was another scent, one she'd smelled before something hurt, before she got sick.

Human, but not familiar. She didn't like it. It made her growl.

She walked to the patio doors, but they were closed, and she didn't see Adrian inside. It was hard to walk up the steps. It took a long time, but there was water, and she drank and drank.

The food bowl was empty, but she didn't want to eat.

Adrian didn't come to let her in, so she waited as she'd been taught. She whined again, hoping. Then looked up the stairs.

She didn't want to go up; she wanted to go in. But she walked toward them, and with a canine sigh, started up.

In the bedroom, JJ held the gun steady. "Damn big house for one skinny woman."

"It's my family home."

"The grandparents croaked, didn't they? Grandmother all smashed up in a car, and the grandfather just died of old. Fucking pizza, right? Maybe I'll grab some when we're done here. You think you're special. You think you're important, with all your DVDs and the streaming and the blog, telling people how to live, what to eat, getting them to jump around and buy your overpriced bullshit."

"My father was important. Dr. Jonathan Bennett. My father. You got that?"

"Yes. He was a teacher. That's very important."

"He was smart, smarter than you. Smarter than anyone. He only stayed with our pill-popping mother because of me. He loved me."

"I know he did."

"He protected me."

"Of course. You're his son."

"And he's dead because of you. Because your whore of a mother got herself pregnant and tried to trick him. I don't see any of him in you, never have, so that was probably a lie. Doesn't change what happened. She came on to him like all the others. A man who doesn't take what's offered is a fool, and my father wasn't a fool."

Let him tell his story, she thought as she sat with her hands quietly in her lap. And considered the weapons in the room.

Her grandmother's candlestands — heavy, easy to grab and swing. The copper bowl she'd bought at Maya's shop. Decent weight, throwable. The letter opener on her writing desk, the scissors in the middle drawer. Sharp.

Keep him talking.

"None of the others had a child from that, or . . . pretended to. Why have you killed them?"

"That nosy bitch you hired got to that asshole reporter, didn't she? He'll be sorry about that. She already is."

Cold washed over her, brought popping chills to her skin. A terrible twist inside her belly. "What do you mean?"

"She thought she was smart, too, but not as smart as me. I'm my father's son. I killed her last night, left her bleeding in the street."

"Oh God." Adrian gripped her elbows, rocked.

"Got what she asked for, coming around to my house, trying to get my sister to blab on me. Well, Nikki won't be blabbing."

He smiled, so wide.

"You — you killed your sister?"

"Not yet." He snickered and grinned again. "But when I do, that's on you, too. You hired the nosy, you brought Nikki into it. So, you killed them both, just like you killed my father. You ruined my fucking life, you whore, you took away the only person in this world who loved me. You should never have drawn a breath."

"None of this will bring your father back."

"I know that!" He pounded his fist against the arm of the chair. "Do you think I don't fucking know that? Do you think I'm stupid?"

Her heart beat in her throat now, wild as the rage in his eyes. "No, but I don't understand what you're trying to do by killing. I'm trying to understand."

"I'm avenging him, you idiot. That's what a son, a true son, does when his father's been murdered."

No, no reasoning with him, she realized. But she could stall.

"Do you think he'd want you to do this? To spend your life doing this? You said he protected you. He wanted the best for you. You could have been a teacher, like him. Or a

636

poet. Your poems are so compelling."

"He taught me to stand up for myself." He jerked his left thumb at his own chest. "I'm standing up for myself, and for him. My poems are an homage to him. And I saved the best for last."

With his left hand, he unzipped the top compartment of the backpack, drew out a carefully folded sheet of paper. "How about I read it to you?"

She said nothing, but she braced. She'd charge him, she decided. If he was going to shoot her, it wouldn't be while she sat like a helpless weakling.

JJ cleared his throat.

"At last, long last when you and I meet, true justice, my justice will be complete. And when you breathe your last gasping breath, I will smile upon you in death. For when your blood drips from my hands, I'll sing and shout to beat the band."

He let out a hoot of laughter as he set the paper aside. "Beat the band! I added a couple more lines to this one because I wanted to end with a little levity. It's a happy day for me, a goddamn red-letter day! And I wanted some irony, because I'm going to beat you to fucking death."

He got to his feet; Adrian drew in a breath as she prepared to rush him.

And with an explosion of barks, snarls, Sadie charged the glass doors.

Distraction, she thought. Terrified as much for the dog as herself, Adrian kicked his gun hand. She managed one punch, connecting with his shoulder instead of his face, as the gun clattered across the room.

Then she ran. "Run," she shouted at Sadie. "Run, Sadie. Go run!"

She hoped to make it to the stairs, but she could already hear him coming. Instead, she ducked into one of the bedrooms.

Places to hide, she reminded herself. Ways to fight back.

"Going to hurt you worse now. It's just going to be worse now."

She grabbed an antique letter opener from the desk in the guest room, slipped into the Jack and Jill bath and silently into the next.

They'd see about that.

Since he woke early, Raylan decided he'd try to get some work in before his kids got up and scattered his day like dandelion fluff.

Mariah wanted the training wheels off her bike, which scared the crap out of him. But her brother rode a two-wheeler, and now she was determined to do the same.

So he'd promised he'd teach her.

Since he'd work, he pulled on jeans and a shirt before heading to the kitchen where he considered: coffee or Coke.

Coke usually won, and today was no exception.

He let Jasper out, stood enjoying that first hit of caffeine, enjoying the quiet of the house. Following well-established routine, he got Jasper's breakfast, toasted a bagel, let Jasper back in so they could both eat in peace.

He'd managed one bite of bagel when Jasper's head shot up out of his bowl. And he howled.

"Quiet, Jesus, you'll wake the kids. I need an hour!" He rushed to the door. "They must've gone for an early run. Okay, okay."

Jasper howled, and outside Sadie barked like a maniac. He opened the door to let Jasper bullet out. "We both get a morning girlfriend fix. But shut the hell up, both of you."

He went around to the gate, where Sadie, who rarely let out more than a woof, stood on her hind legs, rattling off barks.

"Hey, hey, take it down, girl." He reached for the gate with one hand, laid the other on Sadie's head to stroke.

"You're shaking. Where's Adrian?"

Now with both dogs howling, he saw Sadie didn't have her leash. Adrian never took her for runs without her leash.

"Christ, oh Christ." Struck with terror, he ran into the house for his phone, his keys. And running still, hit the memory key for Monroe and Teesha.

"Yo!" Teesha said cheerfully. "Yes, I hear the dogs, Phineas."

"He's got her. I think he's got Adrian. Call the cops, watch my kids. I'm going."

"What? What? Monroe, Raylan says that bastard has Adrian. He's going. I'm calling, Raylan. I've got the kids. Go. Crap, Monroe's coming. I'm calling nine-one-one."

Both dogs jumped in the car before Raylan could. Monroe burst out of his front door wearing a T-shirt, gym shorts. His feet were bare, and he held a baseball bat.

"What the fuck?" Monroe said as he all but dived into the car.

"Sadie — she's shaking, no Adrian, no leash. That's all I've got." He reversed out of the driveway, turned on a dime. "And a sick feeling."

"Sadie wouldn't run off for nothing." Monroe looked back to where Sadie panted and growled and shook as he called Adrian. "She's not answering, and now I've got the same sick feeling. Floor it."

In her hospital bed, Rachael made a sound somewhere between a groan and a sigh. Her eyes fluttered. At her bedside, her husband squeezed her hand.

"Come on, baby, come on back."

Her eyes opened, looked through him for a long moment, then focused. "Ethan?"

"Yeah, there you are." He pressed her hands to his lips, struggled not to weep. "There she is. You're okay, baby. Everything's going to be okay now."

"Can't keep a Mooney down." Her uncle stepped to the other side of the bed, bent to brush his lips over her forehead. "I'll get the nurse."

"Wait. Wait." She fumbled for his hand. "Shot. Shot me. Jonathan Bennett. Looks like his father. I saw him before he fired. I saw him."

"We're already looking for him. Don't worry."

"Wait. Richmond cops called. Gonna get ice cream, but Richmond called. Can't remember the names. Killed Tracie Potter down there. Came here for me."

"Richmond's here, in a hotel a couple blocks away. I'm going to let them know you're awake."

"He said something. Something." She had to dig down. Things were waking up, and awakened hurt like a bitch. "He said something, going to finish me, don't know why he didn't. Thought he did? He said . . . Two down. Two bitches down." Her eyes shot open again. "Potter, me. He's going after Adrian Rizzo. Traveler's Creek. You've got to notify —"

"I'm on it," her uncle replied, and stepped out of the room.

Once the door closed, Rachael turned her head toward Ethan.

"The kids?"

641

"They were here, everybody was here. They're okay, and they're going to be a lot better when I tell them you're awake."

"I could sure use some good drugs right about now." She managed a smile. "Never got that ice cream. Sorry, babe."

Pressing her hand to his face, he let the tears come.

He couldn't shut up. Adrian knew where he was, the direction he took because he couldn't shut up. He cursed her, taunted her, while she, in bare feet, her breathing carefully controlled, moved silently. She knew he'd gone back for the gun because she'd doubled back to do the same, but he'd beaten her there.

She hadn't found a way to get to the stairs and down without exposing herself. But she calculated how long to get to the doors leading to the porch. Unlock the doors, pull them open — which wouldn't be completely silent. How long to get outside and outrun a bullet?

The thought of it coated her skin with fear sweat. She was fast, but nobody was that fast.

Still, she'd try it, have to try it if she had no choice. But she had another idea.

Still gripping the letter opener, she grabbed a small bowl and tossed it into the room across the hall.

When she heard him pounding down toward the sound, she melted into another

642

room. She began her careful, silent backtracking, and this time she stayed ahead of him. With sweat stress sliding down her back, she had to wait, breathe, listen as he made his way from room to room.

Being more careful now, she judged, more thorough now.

Time to go. Time to move. She braced, then dashed out of cover, exposing herself for the few seconds it took her to sprint back into her bedroom.

She turned the locks on the doors to the porch, dragged them open.

The creak of the hinges sounded like a scream.

Seconds later, it felt like seconds later, he rushed into the room, eyes wild, gun sweeping. When he charged to the doors, onto the porch to look for her, she sprang from behind.

She drove the point of the letter opener between his shoulder blades. When he shouted in pain, swung around, she blocked most of the blow. But what landed struck the cheekbone already throbbing.

She used the pain to fight. Gripping his gun hand, shoving it up, she dug her nails hard into his flesh. She learned he was stronger than he looked, but nearly swept his legs out from under him as they grappled. He tried to punch out with his left, but only glanced off her shoulder. She brought her knee up, a violent piston. Though she caught more quad than balls, she saw the fresh pain ripple over his face.

And with their faces close, she got her hand on the grip of the gun.

It fired twice into the ceiling.

Raylan leaped out of the car before it came to a full stop. He rammed himself against the front door. Then just whirled to the window.

He used his elbow, shattering the glass, and ignoring the tear of shards, reached through for the lock, shoving it up, vaulting through.

He didn't have to shout for her. He could hear thuds, crashes upstairs. As he flew up them, the shots rang out.

It wasn't terror he felt, not then, but a blind, blazing rage.

Adrian risked taking one hand off the gun, used it for a short-armed punch to JJ's throat. He choked, gagged, but before she could follow through with a second, he shot his elbow up. It caught her under the chin and knocked her head up.

She saw stars, a thousand stars. And he managed to fling her, as his father had so many years before, so she hit the deck of the porch.

With instinct, muscle memory, she drove her hands down, pumped up her legs. He tried to dance back, tried to aim the gun.

And Raylan was on him.

She heard that ugly sound of knuckles against bone, saw them grappling for control of the gun as she shook her head to clear it. She saw blood, Raylan's blood, and levered herself up, balled her fists as she prepared to wade in.

"Run."

She bared her teeth. "Like hell." She snarled it, and picked up the bloodied letter opener that had dislodged from JJ's back.

The gun went off again, the bullet smashing through the wood of the railing. As the sound rang in her ears, the dogs leaped through the door together in one snarling, snapping mass.

JJ screamed as teeth sank into his calf, his hamstring, his shoulder. Raylan wrenched the gun away as JJ wheeled back.

He struck the railing. The crack of wood snapped like another gunshot as the force sent him, like his father, over.

Monroe, holding the bat like a man prepared to swing for the fences, dropped it, pulled Adrian back.

"Cops are coming. I hear them. We'll get an ambulance. Don't look, honey."

"I'm okay. I'm okay."

"You bet you are." He hugged her tight, then turned her into Raylan. "Unlock the door next time, bro."

"Sorry." Wrapping around Adrian, he pressed his face into her hair.

"No worries. I'm going down to check on him, and call Teesha. She'll be plenty worried."

Because the dogs still snarled, still growled as they looked over the porch, Adrian called to them. "Quiet down. Good dogs. Sit. Stay. Stay." She looked up at Raylan. "Stay."

"Count on it."

"He's got a pulse," Monroe called up. "Smashed himself up real good, but he's breathing. I'll bring the cops around."

"Thank God." She dropped her head on Raylan's shoulder. "I don't want him dead. I don't want him dead like this, and in this house. Not in this house. How did you know to come? How did you know I needed you?"

"Sadie told me."

"Sadie." That broke her, broke the chain of control so the tears flowed.

Raylan picked her up, kissed her hair when she laid her head on his shoulder, and carried her downstairs.

In under twenty-four hours, Adrian had a houseful again. Her mother, Mimi, Harry, Hector, and Loren all came to join what she thought of as the Traveler's Creek brigade.

The youth center crew sent flowers, as did the staff of Rizzo's. Others called or came by to see her. The dogs received many gifts of chew bones, balls, and boxes of biscuits.

Friends, and family, she thought. Friends

646

who were family.

She felt lucky; she felt blessed. She felt finally and completely safe.

She had a long phone conversation with Rachael, and cried more than a little.

Jonathan Bennett Junior would recover from his injuries. The stab wound between his shoulder blades, the black eye, bruised throat she'd inflicted. The broken nose delivered by Raylan, the multiple dog bites. And the concussion, broken leg, shattered elbow, and internal injuries sustained in the fall.

She'd been assured he'd live to spend the rest of that life in prison.

His sister broke under questioning, and provided a long, detailed statement from her hospital bed, including his confession to her that he'd killed their mother.

Considering the circumstances, no charges would be brought against Nikki Bennett.

And considering the circumstances, Adrian thought herself lucky and blessed to have survived the encounter with only some bruises, some bumps and scrapes.

She'd talked and talked and talked some more with the police, with the FBI, and for now, at least, refused any reach-outs from the media.

All she wanted was to set everything aside and just live.

She sat on the opposite side of the house

from where the crew rebuilt the railing on the top porch and replaced bloodstained boards on the lower. More gratitude, she thought, as they'd simply come, unasked, as soon as the police cleared it.

So now she sat with her two oldest girl-friends, drinking lemonade. Jan and Mimi lorded over the kitchen making who knew what for what Monroe decreed would be the world's fiercest cookout.

Monroe, she thought, her sweet friend she'd never heard raise his voice except in song, had literally run over broken glass to help her.

She looked out over the slope of the lawn, over to the mountains, down to the rooftops, the covered bridges of Traveler's Creek.

"I think this must be the most beautiful spot in the world."

"It ranks," Teesha agreed. "And I want to say, again, that Hector and Loren can bunk at my place, give you some space and quiet tonight."

"I like having them here. I love how they just showed up, knew they could. That they just needed to see me for themselves." She glanced at Maya, shook her head. "And I can't believe Joe talked them into going fish-ing."

"It shocked him to the core of his being when he heard neither of them had ever sunk a line before. He swears we'll be grilling up some fresh trout tonight."

"And bless his heart for taking Phin, Collin, and Bradley along with them," Teesha added.

"He'd have taken Mo, too, but she just said" — Maya put on her best incredulous face — " 'Why would I want to do that, Joe? Worms are slimy.' God, I love that girl."

"Me, too." Adrian sighed. "And I love our world." She glanced over to where Sadie and Jasper lay snuggled together snoozing. "Every bit of it."

Lina stepped out, a glass of ice in her hand. She came to the table, poured from the pitcher. "I've been evicted from the kitchen," she said as she sat. "Deemed woefully inept and inadequate. Mariah's accepted, and helping make cookies shaped like hearts. I'm rejected."

"Good thing you don't like to cook."

Lina nodded at Adrian. "Good thing. Your Monroe's also accepted and, after some serious discussion, is in charge of deviled eggs."

"He makes the best deviled eggs in the history of deviled eggs."

"He and Jan and Mimi debated the various ways to boil them to ensure easy peeling." Now Lina laughed. "I'm so glad they kicked me out."

Maya and Teesha exchanged a look.

"Better check on the babies," Maya said as they rose together, and Teesha picked up the baby monitor.

Lina looked after them as they went inside. "They're good friends. I know what it's like to have good friends. I've had Mimi most of my life. Harry and Marshall, too, but Mimi? Lifetime girlfriend."

She looked at Adrian then, touched a hand to her bruised cheek. "I'm not going to bring it all up again. I know you've had to go over and over it — like we did after Georgetown. I need to say I'm so grateful for your strength, your courage, your smarts."

"A lot came from you."

"You made your own. That day in Georgetown, I thought: This isn't going to define her. Or me. But not her — I won't allow it. It didn't, but it never really went away. I hope it can now."

"Can and will."

"All those women, Adrian, all those others, and nearly you. I've asked myself again and again, what could I have done differently to stop any of it from happening?"

"Nothing. Mom." She laid a hand over Lina's. "Nothing. He doesn't just look like his father. He has that same lack, that same twist inside him. I saw it, in both of them. It was the fact I existed that enraged them. He said something to me, JJ. He said he didn't see any of his father in me. Neither do I. I'm Rizzo, through and through."

"Yes, you are."

Sadie's head came up, and Jasper's an

650

instant later.

"That's Raylan's car. He said he had a couple of things to do. I guess he's done them."

When the car crested the hill, Lina rose, walked out across the lawn. She went to Raylan, put her arms around him. She kissed both his cheeks, then walked away.

Raylan stood a moment, touched and bemused, before he continued up to the porch.

"She's not a hugger, so that was a moment," Adrian told him.

"It felt like one." Gently, he took her chin in his hand, studied her face.

"Cobalt Flame, you took a hit."

"You, too, Midway Man."

"But we kicked the bad guy's ass. With a little help from our friends. So this is for them." He sat and took two dog collars out of the bag he carried, one bold red, one bold blue. He handed them to Adrian.

She read the engraving. "Ms. Sadie Wells. Mr. Jasper Rizzo."

"I thought we'd make it official, a sharing of the last names."

"I think it's the sweetest thing ever. Here you go, Sadie, let's put on your new bling."

"Now you and me," Raylan continued as Adrian started switching collars. "I think we need to make it official."

"What?" She glanced up with a smile, then

651

blinked when he just looked in her eyes. "What?" she repeated.

"I planned to give you more time. Plenty of it. But, can't. Moments matter, and moments change things. I don't want to waste any more of them. I love you. I love everything about you. I want everything about you. I need everything about you. So marry me. Let me marry you. Let's be a family."

"Oh, Raylan, we're just getting used to . . ."

"You never get used to being in love. Not really. I'm a family man, Adrian. I'm good at being married."

"You are, yes, you are. Were. Are. I don't know if I'd be."

"You're a quick learner. I know I come as a package, just like I know the package is crazy about you. We can add to the package, if that's something you want."

"More children?"

"If it's something you want. We're both good with kids, but you have to want them."

"I just need to . . ." She rose, walked to the rail, looked out.

A houseful, she thought. A house built for family, for children, given to her. Her legacy.

"I've always wanted children," she murmured.

"Share mine. Have more with me. Be Ms. Adrian Wells, and I'll be Mr. Raylan Rizzo."

"Trust you to make me laugh at such a moment." She closed her eyes. "When Sadie

652

couldn't get to me, she knew where to go. To you and Jasper. She needed help, and knew where to get it. I know where to go when I need."

She turned to him. "It's always going to be you."

Rising, he stepped to her, took her hands. "We can get married tomorrow or a year from tomorrow. You can plan whatever kind of wedding you want."

He reached in his pocket, took out a box, flipped it open. And took out a ring.

Not flashy, she thought. He knew she wouldn't want flashy. A simple channel-set diamond in a white-gold band.

"But I'm really hoping for a yes now. The rest is details. We're both good at those, too."

"You have to go and pick out the perfect ring for someone like me. Someone who does what I do, who is what I am."

"I know who you are. I love who you are. Say yes."

"I love who you are, too." She looked at those wonderful green eyes, laid a hand on his cheek, bruised like hers. "You told me you hadn't believed you could feel this way again. I didn't believe I could ever feel this way."

"Is that a yes?"

"I have a question first."

"Ask it."

"How soon can you and the kids and Jasper move in?"

Smiling, he framed her face. "How about tomorrow?"

"You need to ask them first."

"I already did, while you were working out this morning." He pressed his lips to her forehead, pressed them to her hands. "They love you. I love you. Say yes, Adrian. Just yes."

So simple really, she realized. So right.

Because it would always be him. Maybe it always had been him.

"I love them. I love you. Yes, Raylan. Just yes."

When he kissed her, slow and strong, when he put the ring on her finger, she felt her life click into place.

When she wrapped around him, she thought again:

This is the most beautiful spot in the world.

And now it's ours.

ABOUT THE AUTHOR

Nora Roberts is the #1 *New York Times* bestselling author of more than 200 novels, including *Hideaway*, The Chronicles of the One trilogy, *Under Currents, Shelter in Place, Come Sundown,* and many more. She is also the author of the bestselling In Death series written under the pen name J.D. Robb. There are more than 500 million copies of her books in print.

The employees of Thorndike Press hope you have enjoyed this Large Print book. All our Thorndike, Wheeler, and Kennebec Large Print titles are designed for easy reading, and all our books are made to last. Other Thorndike Press Large Print books are available at your library, through selected bookstores, or directly from us.

For information about titles, please call:
(800) 223-1244

or visit our website at:
gale.com/thorndike

To share your comments, please write:
Publisher
Thorndike Press
10 Water St., Suite 310
Waterville, ME 04901